Doctor **Frigo**

Books by Eric Ambler

DOCTOR FRIGO   1974

THE LEVANTER   1972

THE INTERCOM CONSPIRACY   1969

DIRTY STORY   1967

A KIND OF ANGER   1964

THE LIGHT OF DAY   1963

PASSAGE OF ARMS   1960

STATE OF SIEGE   1956

THE SCHIRMER INHERITANCE   1953

JUDGMENT ON DELTCHEV   1951

JOURNEY INTO FEAR   1940

A COFFIN FOR DIMITRIOS   1939

CAUSE FOR ALARM   1939

EPITAPH FOR A SPY   1938

BACKGROUND TO DANGER   1937

(EDITOR) TO CATCH A SPY:
AN ANTHOLOGY OF FAVORITE SPY STORIES   1965

Doctor Frigo

Eric Ambler

New York Atheneum

1974

Copyright © 1974 by Eric Ambler
All rights reserved
Library of Congress catalog card number 74-77836
ISBN 0-689-10609-2
Manufactured in the United States of America by H. Wolff, New York
Designed by Harry Ford
First Edition

"*My position, as will easily be understood,
was one of the greatest difficulty, owing
not only to the overwhelming responsibility
of the case itself, but to what I may call
its external complications.*"

SIR MORELL MACKENZIE
The Fatal Illness of Frederick The Noble

"*Nothing works against the success of a conspiracy so much as the wish to make it wholly
secure and certain to succeed. Such an
attempt requires many men, much time and
very favourable conditions. And all these
in turn heighten the risk of being discovered.
You see, therefore, how dangerous conspiracies
are!*"

FRANCESCO GUICCIARDINI
Ricordi (1528–1530)

"*You refused to believe it would ever come
to this. You see you were wrong.*"

THE EMPEROR MAXIMILIAN OF MEXICO
*Words said before his execution by firing
squad at Queretaro in 1867. They were
addressed to his Hungarian cook.*

Contents

PART ONE   *The Patient*   3

PART TWO   *Symptoms, Signs and Diagnosis*   77

PART THREE   *The Treatment*   177

Part **One**

The Patient

Thursday 15 May

The new night Sister from Guadeloupe appears to be intelligent and to know her job.

A relief.

There is one thing to be said for a tour of night duty at the hospital. The food one is expected to eat may be disgusting and the bed on which one is supposed to rest may be too near the main air-conditioning compressor; but, unless there is an unusually messy traffic accident or the night Sister in charge is inadequate, there is privacy and time for thought.

The duty man also has a desk and a supply of hospital stationery. So I shall make what use I can of these two nights to do something I should have done before: that is, put my side of this Villegas business down on paper so that in case of need I can later produce it, signed and dated, as evidence of my good intentions—if not of my good sense.

Naturally, I hope that the need will not arise. However, during the past twenty-four hours, I have had reason to suspect that there is more going on than I at present understand. So, I shall take no chances.

I will begin by recalling the circumstances of my father's assassination.

Already needlessly interrupted by new Sister with request I authorize pheno-barb for cardiac patient in

3

Ward B. On checking found she had not consulted
night staff instructions which clearly authorize her use
own discretion and prescribe drug to be administered
this case. So much for appearances of efficiency! Chal-
lenged, she declared procedure in Pointe-à-Pitre dif-
ferent.

An absurd lie, and any of the French doctors here,
white or black, créole or from metropolitan France,
would have told her so bluntly. I could only be ex-
cessively polite. She countered by speaking in patois.
When she realized that I understood perfectly what
she was saying, and could answer her too, she flounced
out. Her nurses have doubtless warned her that young
Dr. Castillo is a béké-espagnol *with an unpleasant dis-*
position. Now she has seen for herself. Good. Perhaps
she will think twice before she again comes asking
questions.

About the assassination of my father, Clemente Castillo
Borja.

As those obliged to interest themselves in the political
and economic affairs of Central America will know, an
aura of mystery still surrounds some aspects of the case.
From time to time journalists claiming special knowledge
of the country and inside information have written articles
purporting to reveal all; but none of them has ever produced any new facts, and the "alls" revealed have been no
more enlightening than the guesswork and speculation of
which everyone else has long since grown tired.

The two gunmen who actually did the killing that night
on the steps of the Hotel Nuevo Mundo were, of course,
identified immediately. The scene was flood-lit and there
were dozens of witnesses. What has never been established
beyond doubt, however, is the identity of those who hired
and paid the killers. All we know is that they had the fore-
thought to booby-trap the getaway car in advance of the

operation. It was expertly done. The gunmen were blown to pieces long before there was even a chance of their being caught and questioned. Police records had both men down as, "Wanted for armed robbery. No known political connections."

The most widely held, you could almost say the "official," view has always been that the assassination was ordered by the military junta immediately after their October coup, and carried out under the direction of a Special Security Forces action squad.

That could be the truth.

There are those, on the other hand, who still insist that, although the junta had every reason to want my father dead and were quite capable of organizing his destruction, the last thing they would want was to risk making a martyr of him. These more devious thinkers contend that both the assassination and the booby-trap murders were engineered by a left-wing, and violently anticlerical, faction within my father's own Democratic Socialist Party. So, the thing was done partly to discredit the junta before it could stabilize the post-coup situation, and partly because this left-wing faction knew that my father had secretly committed the Party to a coalition in the Assembly with the Christian Democrats.

That could also be true—just.

Until her own death in Florida last year, my mother thought that it was; though for no clear reasons that I could ever discover. A highly emotional, deeply feminine woman —the self-willed kind who is nevertheless at sea without a husband to dominate her—she became the center of a woolly-minded, self dramatizing bunch of compatriot exiles. As doyenne of such a group she doubtless preferred the more exotic theory, with its byzantine trappings of conspiracy and betrayal, to the mundane alternative. At all events, she never ceased urging me to seek out the traitors and to exact an only son's proper revenge—blood for blood.

In that, as in other ways, I was a disappointment to her. My only defense—and in this I was sometimes backed by my sisters and their husbands—was to insist that I found the betrayal theory totally incredible. This annoyed her, of course, because these unknown traitors she postulated were the only objects of my filial vengeance who could conceivably be accessible to it. Not even my mother could expect me to mount a one-man punitive expedition against the junta and the SSF on their own ground. After the '68 upheaval the vengeance situation became even more confused. Under the Oligarchy, backed by its so-called "patriotic militia," the casualty rate among former members of the junta was high, and by the following year those senior officers who weren't serving time in subordinate diplomatic posts abroad, were either ailing or dead.

What then did I really believe about the Castillo assassination plot?

A few days ago I would have answered that I had long ceased to care much who was the mastermind, if indeed there was one, or which cabal was responsible.

If that sounds callous or unfilial, let it. Twelve years have elapsed since my father's death, and when he was killed I was an insecure nineteen-year-old just entering a French medical school an ocean away from home. What I remember most vividly now about that time is not the grief and confusion, not even the funeral in the pouring rain with armed troops crowding the mourners and police taking names at the graveside. What I remember are the blinding flashlights of the press photographers at Orly Airport as I left to fly home, and the reporters bawling inane questions at me. There was a man there from our Paris Embassy who was supposed to be helping me through, but he could do nothing. The newsmen elbowed him aside and one thrust his face right up to mine. He was sweating and out of breath and sprayed saliva over me as he shouted in Spanish above the din. "What were your feelings," he demanded,

"when you heard that your father had been assassinated?
You must have known how much he was hated. Were you
surprised?"

I drew back my fist to hit him, but the Embassy man
clutched my arm. Then the airport police moved in surrounding me and I was hustled away.

Today I am wiser; I know now that my feelings about
my father were mixed and that even then I had begun to
understand the kind of man he was. Now I can accept with
equanimity propositions that once would have been unacceptable: the self-evident truth, for example, that even had
he lived and come to power, Clemente Castillo would have
served the people of my native land no better than the
inept junta or the civilian Oligarchy which now manipu-
lates a figure-head president. A Castillo administration
might have presented a better appearance, a more liberal
image, to the outside world, but that would have been the
whole extent of its accomplishment. My country's difficulties, like those of other coffee republics which were once
colonies of Spain, are rooted in history and they will not
be solved by images of government, however glossy; nor
by lightweight opportunists with simplistic programs of
reform.

I am aware that most of my colleagues in this hospital
dislike me. In supermarket French the word *frigo* is used
to mean not only refrigerator or freezer but also, a shade
contemptuously, frozen meat. "Dr. Frigo" is the nickname
by which I am usually known here. Of course I am always
careful to treat it as a joke; but on re-reading the above
paragraph I can see why, in a parochial little society such
as ours, it has gained currency.

Lightweight opportunist? Is that the best the loyal son
can say of the murdered father? Why then, if he were so
negligible a person, was he assassinated? Other politicians
have made enemies and lived. And why, if the pompous
young Dr. Frigo has really ceased to care about the cir-

cumstances of his father's death, does he now start scratch-
ing at those well-healed wounds?

Fair questions. I must try to answer at least some of them.

As a young boy I both loved and respected my father;
no doubt about that; ours was a happy family. But as I
grew up, though I still loved him, my respect became qualified.

He was a lawyer before he became a political leader and
it is as a lawyer that I remember him best. When he practiced in the courts it was his habit over the evening meal
and after, to regale us with an account of his day's work.
It was generally a tale of triumph, of course, of dangerous
opponents outmaneuvered and of the discomfiture of fools
—all most enjoyable. And even when a defeat or set-back
had to be reported, the reasons for it were presented with
so much wry humor and apparent moderation that the vil-
lain of the piece would seem more worthy of our com-
miseration than of hatred or contempt. While my father
clearly enjoyed the sun of our uncritical admiration he was
at the same time exercising and developing the rhetorical
skills to be deployed later before larger audiences.

Most of his practice was concerned with defending persons accused of petty criminal offenses and of cases involving debt. Over the years we children acquired, just through
hearing so often about such things, some knowledge of
court-room tactics, of the seamier aspects of pre-trial investigation and of the rules of evidence. Though I doubt if
my sisters retained much of it—for them my father's tales of
legal derring-do were only entertainments—I did and still
do. Indeed it was that smattering of knowledge so gained
that fostered my prejudice (doubtless ill-founded) against
the law as a profession and encouraged me to hold the belief (no less erroneous, as I have since found, but shared
then by my high-school biology teacher) that medicine is
an exact science.

My father accepted my declaration of intent philosophically, and when later he agreed to pay for my studies in Paris he became his usual businesslike self. "I'm glad you didn't press to go to the United States," he said; "that would have been even more expensive. Anyway, I have no doubt that you will work hard and make the most of your opportunities." And then he added thoughtfully: "Some medical doctors have done quite well in politics. They seem—God knows why—to be trusted."

But if those lessons, learned, so to speak, at my father's knee, did not predispose me to the law as a career, they did instill in me an awareness of some of the accepted ways of avoiding legal pitfalls.

The subject of written evidence was one of which he never tired.

"Beware the policeman with his dog-eared notebook," he would say. "The man may be, indeed probably is, unable to write more than his own name and only just able to read. But when he gets into court, what is down in that notebook, no matter when or by whom it was put there, will be treated as if it were Holy Writ."

And he would wag his finger at us. "So remember, children," he would say after some horrendous account of justice mocked or perverted, "and remember carefully. If ever you should commit a crime, which God forbid, or if ever you have reason to suppose that you may be falsely accused of some misdemeanor or indiscretion, keep a written record of all your actions and thoughts at the relevant time. Keep it in your own handwriting, date it and never make subsequent alterations in it which can be seen unless you have a creditable and convincing explanation for them."

This is one of his injunctions that I have not forgotten. From time to time I have kept written records of the kind suggested and often found them useful later. Not, I may add, that I have been, or have expected to be, accused of a crime, but because, while most foreign nationals obliged to have dealings with French bureaucracy must expect to suffer minor inconvenience, a foreign doctor so placed, even if he has qualified in France itself, is at a more serious disadvantage. When he is Dr. Frigo working in the state-subsidized medical service of an overseas department of France, he is peculiarly vulnerable.

Again interrupted, though this time not without cause. Terminal uremia in Ward C extremely restless and demanding that he go home to die. Sister had taken care check instructions. Paraldehyde 5 c.c. given as prescribed but without desired effect.

Saw patient with her. Cane-cutter in fifties. Listened and humored as best I could, but explaining need for continuing treatment to dying man was, as it always is, depressing. Authorized chloral hydrate 0.5 gm. Sister raised eyebrows—slightly—but made no verbal comment.

Revised my opinion of her. Very good with patient —sensible, kind, firm. Really rather handsome woman. Almost black, but with delicate features of chabine. *Good complexion spoiled by apparent thread wart on neck below left ear. Electrodessication could easily remove. Why has no one suggested this to her?*

At the moment it seems to me that the extent of my vulnerability has been suddenly and considerably increased.

Hence this written record. I should have begun it three days ago.

Now, while my actions and thoughts at what may prove to be the relevant periods are still fresh in my mind, I must make up for lost time.

Monday 12 May Morning

Only three days ago? It seems longer.

I was in the hospital mortuary assisting Dr. Brissac at an autopsy when the summons came from the Préfecture.

The male cadaver on which we were working was that of a middle-aged Belgian who had been with a package tour party staying at the Hotel Ajoupa. He had collapsed while listening to the steel band there and had been dead on arrival at the hospital. The apparent cause of death was an aortic aneurysm, but the man's widow had made a strong statement to the police. She had said that he had died of food poisoning and accused the hotel. Although no one else in the group had suffered anything worse than the indigestion and ill temper which are the normal after-effects of an Ajoupa barbecue—charred island beef is virtually inedible —the examining magistrate had ordered a full autopsy and we were following strictly the prescribed procedures.

Dr. Brissac is our Medical Superintendent as well as senior surgeon of the hospital, and if it should be thought surprising that he had not delegated so menial a task, I can only say that nowadays Dr. Brissac always insists on doing the autopsies himself. Why? I can only guess. Some of my colleagues consider that as a surgeon he is inclined to undue timidity, that many interesting surgical cases which could and should have been dealt with here have been cravenly flown to Fort de France. They say that he ought to make way for a younger man. If those judgments are valid it may well be that Dr. Brissac, inhibited by memories of occasional mistakes with live patients, now prefers to exercise his skills on the dead. I must say that he does display a certain gusto at the mortuary table. His work there is invariably swift, sure and a pleasure to watch.

He had just made the abdominal incision. I was pulling on the ascending colon so that he could snip away the peritoneal reflections, when the mortuary attendant came in to say that I was wanted on the telephone.

I told him to take a message. He said that it was someone from the Préfecture on behalf of a Commissaire Gillon and that the matter was urgent.

Dr. Brissac stopped cutting and waved his scissors impatiently. "Tell the Préfecture from me that Doctor Castillo is too busy to speak," he said. "Tell them that he has a man's entrails in his hands and that he will call back."

The attendant went away grinning and we worked on. Dr. Brissac grunts a good deal as he works but does not usually talk much. However, when he got to the transverse colon he glanced up at me.

"Do you know Commissaire Gillon?"

"Very slightly, Doctor. A week or two ago his youngest boy gashed a leg swimming by a reef. The Commissaire brought him in to have the wound attended to. I happened to be on duty."

Dr. Brissac pursed his lips. "He did not tell me about that." After a bit he went on. "He was at my house for bridge the other evening and was making inquiries about you. Not about your professional qualifications—he would have all that information in your dossier—but about your personal interests, your character."

"Oh."

"What did you do with your spare time apart from bedding your girl friend and that amateur photography of yours? When you were in charge of the mobile clinic last year what had been my impressions of your work? Were you self-reliant or are you the type who always has to have his hand held?"

"Interesting questions." I tried to sound as if I didn't care much how he had answered them.

He didn't tell me anyway; he was cutting his way into the splenic flexure. When he spoke again he said: "I take it you don't know who Commissaire Gillon is or what precisely he does here?"

"I assumed that he was a policeman. I didn't know that police worked in the Préfecture."

"He is a policeman, but not an ordinary one. He commands the DST antenna in this department. At least 'antenna' is what he calls it. Officially the unit is a brigade, I believe, but perhaps he thinks that antenna sounds more mysterious and important. These political types. . . ." He broke off as if aware suddenly that he had been straying on to dangerous ground. "It's as well to be polite to them," he added.

I got no more out of him. It was clear that he knew more about the telephone call and the reason for it than he was prepared to tell me.

When we had finished with the cadaver, I typed out the preliminary report for his signature and had the various specimens we had taken sent to the laboratory for examination. By then it was ten o'clock. I was due in the out-patients department, but there was little privacy there and I did not want to be overheard talking to the Préfecture about personal matters. In spite of Dr. Brissac's hints about Gillon's interest in my character, the only reason that I could think of for my having attracted the attention of the DST was that I was an alien in government service and therefore in some way suspect.

I was put through to a secretary. She was brusque. Dr. Brissac's little joke about entrails had evidently not gone down well. Commissaire Gillon wished to see me in his office at eleven-thirty. Not at twelve, nor at a quarter to twelve, but at eleven-thirty please. Yes, it was understood that I had my duties at the hospital, but no doubt I could arrange with a colleague for those to be attended to in my absence if necessary. Eleven-thirty in Commissaire Gillon's office then, on the second floor of the annex. Thank you, Doctor.

In the out-patients', as it happened, there were only a few persons for me to see that day; but one of them was an old fisherman with diabetes whose case I had come across when I had been out covering the smaller islands with the mobile clinic. The local dispensary now took care of his insulin requirements, but every three months he came in for me to look him over. His wife always came with him. She could never quite understand the nature of the disease—or remember what I had told her about it last time—and, as I had difficulty translating my oversimplified explanations into patois, patience on both sides was necessary. It was eleven-fifteen before I could get away. Then I had trouble starting my moto and had to pedal up to the main road. That made me hot as well as nervous, so the fast ride down the hill into the town was not as refreshing as usual.

The island of St. Paul-les-Alizés was first sighted by Columbus on his second voyage to the Indies and named San Pablo de la Montañas. The "mountains" then visible were twin peaks of the volcano now called Mont Velu, the two craters of which became joined during the eruptions of 1785. San Pablo was never colonized by Spain. The indigenous Caribs were a ferocious lot and three Dominican missions sent to convert them to the Faith were all in the end massacred. It was not until a French trading company took possession a century and a half later that the Caribs of St. Paul were, by better-armed savages from Europe, themselves massacred. Aside from a temporary occupation by the British during the Napoleonic wars, St. Paul has been French territory ever since.

Although, like Martinique, Guadeloupe and other islands of the French Antilles, it is fast being "developed," few of St. Paul's recent acquisitions—the Plan Five light industry complex and commercial center, the municipal low-cost housing estate, the new elementary school, the Alizés supermarket and the Hotel Ajoupa—have yet impinged on the old port of Fort Louis and the streets above it. Within the amphitheater bounded by the Vaubanesque ramparts on the headland, the Môle du Bassin and the foothills of the Grand Mamelon, the place still looks much as it did in the 19th century. True, there are now microwave dishes mounted on the roof of the citadel beside the flagstaff, jumbo jets from the lengthened airport runway now thunder overhead, and out across the bay the concrete pylons of the new Club Nautique can be seen sprouting like toadstools on the green slopes of La Pointe de Christophe; but the town of Fort Louis itself is little changed. It is still ugly, overcrowded, ramshackle, noisy and, for the most part, squalid.

The Préfecture occupies one side of the Place Lamartine half way up the hill.

The claim, made in the guidebook put out by the Bureau de Tourisme, that the old quarter of the town is "a picturesque evocation of the colonial past," though not completely false is certainly misleading. A few years back the balconied façades of a street of early limestone and maçonne-du-bon-dieu houses near the old church were restored. That is all; and, for those of us who actually live in the houses, it was not enough. Nothing was done about our plumbing. This continues to evoke the colonial past in ways which can sometimes surprise even the hard-faced men of the Service Sanitaire. The money that should have been spent on it was used instead to install an air-conditioning system in the Préfecture. The bureaucratic tricks employed to legalize that bare-faced swindle are still resented.

Built in 1920 to replace a wooden predecessor destroyed by fire, the Préfecture looks like a mairie of the period transported from some industrial town in northeast France and then whitewashed. It stares brazenly across the Place at the statue of Lamartine, the poet who as a statesman sought to make men free and who was so little corrupt that he became penniless.

The black policeman under the drooping tricolore eyed me curiously when I asked for Commissaire Gillon's office and then directed me to the annex.

I know the main building and its creaking parquet well enough—the Bureau des Étrangers is on the entresol—but I had never before penetrated as far as the annex. This was put up after the "assimilation" of 1946 and occupies most of what was once the Préfet's garden. It is approached, I found, by a narrow bridge-of-sighs leading from the second floor. A signboard with a pointing hand told me that it housed among other things the divisional offices of the Ministère de l'Intérieur and the Direction de la Surveillance du Territoire.

The DST is sometimes described by North American news magazines as the French FBI, but although this may be a convenient shorthand explanation it is not strictly valid. The FBI exists to combat a number of federal crimes within the United States, one of which happens to be espionage by foreign powers. The DST deals only with counter-intelligence and related matters on French territory, and, although it is a branch of the Sûreté Nationale, it more or less confines itself to crimes against internal security. There are other differences. Films and television programs depicting "G men" as heroes may not be popular any more but at least they exist. If even one film depicting a DST agent in a sympathetic light exists I should be very surprised. Certainly I have never seen it. While an ordinary citizen of the United States invited to talk to FBI representatives could conceivably feel flattered, most Frenchmen, who distrust all policemen anyway, would accept a similar invitation from the DST with extreme reluctance and the deepest misgivings. I may not be a Frenchman born but France is my adopted country. Going to keep my appointment with

Commissaire Gillon I was very much on the defensive. My reception in his outer office did nothing to reassure me. The secretary, an imperious brown woman with a lot of gold inlays on her teeth, tapped the face of her watch accusingly to remind me that I was late and then motioned me to a wooden bench saying that I would now have to wait. To underline her displeasure she slapped some dossiers about on her desk and then lit a cigarette. A telex machine chattered quietly in one corner of the office. There was a young white man operating it and every now and then he would groan aloud, though whether in boredom or disgust it was hard to tell. Some sort of argument seemed to be going on through the machine. The white man's groans began to intrigue the secretary. A carefully thought out joke was on her lips when the intercom buzzed on her desk. With an impatient wave she told me to go in.

The Commissaire Gillon I had seen at the hospital had been a concerned, sweating father in a beach shirt with an injured and querulous small boy. The Gillon I now faced was a composed senior official in an air-conditioned office. He is stocky and well-muscled, in his forties. That day he was wearing a grey suit. He has steel-framed half-glasses, a pale healthy tan, short fair hair and good teeth. A handsome man with a retroussé nose and heavily-lidded but lively eyes. He speaks Parisian French. He contrived to shake my hand and steer me into the chair facing him with a single economical arm movement.

"Good of you to come at such short notice, Doctor," He was leaning back in his own desk chair by now. "Doctor Brissac made no difficulties?"

"None. I hope your son's leg healed all right."

"Perfectly. Dr. Massot changed the dressing for us. He's our family doctor, you understand. I didn't want to trouble you people again unnecessarily. You know Massot?"

He was talking about the private practitioner who looks after most of the white establishment in Fort Louis and is the owner of the expensive Clinique Massot.

"Slightly. He sometimes makes use of the hospital services."

Gillon's faint smile suggested that my reply, though guarded, had insufficiently disguised my true feelings on the subject of Dr. M. Through a gross error of judgment on the part of the hospital administration, Dr. M. had been appointed an honorary orthopedic consultant. The fact that the post was unpaid had been taken by Dr. M. to mean that when he wanted to make use of our X-ray and Institut Pasteur facilities for any purpose in connection with his private patients or clinic he was always entitled to claim priority. He is often a nuisance.

The next question, though, was a little puzzling. "Has Massot ever spoken to you in any language other than French?"

"Once or twice, yes." Dr. M. has smatterings of several languages and likes to air them. He is said to make a good thing out of the Hotel Ajoupa where he is on call during the tourist season.

"How is his Spanish?"

No professional etiquette required me to be guarded about that. "I found his German easier to understand, Commissaire. But then I don't speak German myself."

He grinned, picked up a green dossier from his desk and showed me the front cover with my name on it:

CASTILLO Reye, Ernesto.

The idle chit-chat—or what I had taken to be idle chit-chat—was over. Now I would find out why I was there.

His expression had become formal. "You understand, Doctor, that in our business the status and activities of foreigners in our midst must always be of interest and concern, even when they are valued medical men."

"Yes."

"But, of course, we can never be omniscient. We may observe what the subject does, how he behaves or misbehaves, who his friends and associates are, et cetera, et cetera. And from such information we can deduce much. But, unless we are dealing with those whom experience enables us easily to classify—crooks, prostitutes, petty adventurers—we cannot always know how a subject thinks, what he truly believes. In certain areas such knowledge may become important. Doctors, I imagine, sometimes have the same problem when it comes to diagnosis. Symptoms do not always tell you the truth."

"Neither do patients."

He looked surprised. "They actually lie to you?"

"Sometimes, though not often consciously. Mostly they lie to themselves. The doctor is merely invited to join the conspiracy. What was it you wanted to know about me, Commissaire?"

He gave me a wry look. "Quite right, Doctor. Laymen should not attempt to use medical analogies. A few questions then. Two years ago you became eligible for French citizenship and could have begun the process of naturalization. This you evidently knew because you consulted a lawyer, Maître Bussy, about procedure. Indeed you went further. You prepared and supplied him with the necessary curriculum vitae. Then, only a month later, you informed him that you did not wish to proceed with the application. Why?"

"My mother objected."

"Your *mother!* On what grounds?"

"Perhaps objected is not the right word. She appealed to me as a good son not to abandon the country for which my father had died a martyr's death."

"And you accepted that . . . that view?"

"No. But she was in failing health and beginning to suffer physical pain. I had no wish to add emotional stress to the rest of her troubles."

"But your three sisters had already changed their national status." He was referring to the dossier. "Two are American by marriage, the third Mexican, also by marriage. Did your mother not appeal to them in the same terms?"

"With women of my mother's generation and upbringing it was always the sons who were counted upon. And in the case of an only son . . ."

"But counted upon to do what? Return one day to his native land and avenge his father's martydom?"

I thought for a moment before I answered that. On some subjects it is inadvisable to speak plainly, even to an intelligent and apparently unsentimental man like Gillon.

The truth is that, except to my mother and perhaps a few of his more starry-eyed associates, my father was never, in any real sense of the term, a martyr. He was no Martin Luther King, no Kennedy, not even a Lumumba. Oh yes, he could stir a crowd with his eloquence, he could even move some of them to tears; but there was nothing romantic, no underlying love in their regard for him. They might believe that he could better their lot, that he was committed to them and wholly their friend; they might applaud him and shout their encouragement; but when he went in among them they would never press forward to touch him. In a crowd he was the one for whom both men and women would respectfully make way. He lacked the true demagogue's essential quality, the ability to forget, and in doing so make others forget, that he was at heart a politician. The assassination of such a man may be a sensational event; but it is rarely the inauguration of a martyrdom.

However, I know that good sons are not supposed to speak in that way of dead fathers. Gillon might be a DST chef de brigade, but he was also, as I had reason to know, a devoted father and family man. There was no sense in antagonizing him needlessly, so I evaded his question.

"My mother drew comfort over the years from the belief that my father's death could, should and eventually would be avenged. It was never a belief that I shared."

"Did you ever tell her that?"

"Whenever possible I avoided the subject. You might say I cheated. When I agreed two years ago not to renounce my patrial citizenship I'm sure she assumed that, in bowing to her wishes then, I was also accepting her vision of the political future. And I have no doubt that she was encouraged by those in her immediate circle to make that assumption."

"By her 'immediate circle' you mean, I take it, those members of your father's party, the Democratic Socialists, living in exile?"

"I mean those members of it—cranks, crooks and former place-seekers mostly—who had managed to hole up in southern Florida."

"Do you now have any contact with them?"

"As little as possible, virtually none."

"No correspondence?"

"From time to time they have sent me a rubbishy news letter they publish. I also have occasional requests for money. Those, too, I ignore."

"Your mother supported members of the circle with substantial sums."

"She did indeed. As you may know, the junta found it politically expedient to deal generously with my father's estate. Exchange controls were relaxed in my mother's favor when she settled in Florida. The exiles there battened on her for years. When her medical expenses became heavy, though, my brothers-in-law and I had to pay the bills. Her money had all been frittered away or just stolen. After she died the treasurer of a Cuban Committee there was kind enough to do a free audit. He advised us to take the result to the police and prosecute in certain cases."

"But you didn't."

"No, we only threatened. Unfortunately, we couldn't afford to add legal expenses to the medical ones already incurred."

"The American FBI and ourselves exchange information on an unofficial basis. Would it surprise you to learn that, according to a report received recently, you are the person designated by the Florida group as heir to the Party leadership and potential head of a provisional government?"

"My sister Isabella wrote telling me of that, Commissaire. In fact the news coincided with a number of those requests for money that I mentioned. No, it didn't surprise me. No nonsense put out by the Florida branch of the Party could do that. It saddened me, however, because I had to assume that my mother had given permission for the use of the Castillo name. But by that time she was dying and our name was all that she had left to give."

"You personally then have no belief in the future of your father's Democratic Socialist Party, Doctor? You see no prospect of the present government's eventual overthrow?"

"Not if it's left to that Florida gang. Whether they are in any way characteristic of the whole opposition in exile is another matter."

"What is your opinion?"

"Commissaire, I don't know enough to have an opinion. I read the same news items about the other factions as everyone else. The one based in Cuba seems to be more or less what one would expect, that is Marxist. As for the Villegas group. . . ."

I hesitated and he prompted me. "Well, what do you think of the Villegas group?"

"They're based in Mexico as you know. According to my sister Isabella, and I have no other source of information there I can assure you, the Villegas group has strong ties with the urban guerilla movement in the capital, the young militants who have been giving the Oligarchy so much trouble. That's pure hearsay of course. The Florida lot doesn't like the Mexico lot because in Mexico they don't seem to be short of money. There was some talk of Villegas being subsidized by the CIA. Again only talk. But that's more or less standard, isn't it? In Central America any political action group that isn't begging its bread must be subsidized by the CIA. As far as the political spectrum is concerned, I gather, again from my sister, that the Villegas lot is left of center."

"Not too far from where your father would have been in fact."

"I suppose not. Though I can't see my father leading a band of devoted followers in exile from any position in the spectrum."

"You can't, Doctor? He was after all a politician."

"My father liked political power, yes. But he also liked money. Accused of being a political opportunist he laughed and took it as a kind of compliment. If he had been driven into exile instead of murdered he would have gone back to practicing law, or, if that had not been possible, into some profitable business. He had no stomach for long-drawn-out battles even when the banners waved for social justice. The ends he would fight for had always to be foreseeably attainable."

He looked at me oddly for a moment, as if he couldn't quite believe his ears; then he shrugged. "I have been told that you had a great affection for your father, Doctor. What you are saying now doesn't sound very affectionate."

Having now fallen into the trap I had successfully avoided earlier, I did my best to talk my way out.

"My mother once used the very same words, Commissaire, when she was urging me yet again to avenge his murder."

The ploy succeeded. His face stiffened. He did not like being identified, however remotely, with my mother.

"From what I know of your countrymen," he remarked,

"few of them would need urging in such a matter. Isn't there something called *machismo*, a pride in manhood?"

"Not only in my country, Commissaire. All over Latin America. But I agree. A lot of senseless murders are committed by men who believe that killing someone who has offended you somehow proves virility. I happen to believe that it doesn't. The demoralizing effect of a French education perhaps."

"Perhaps." He paused, apparently considering that heresy. "Or is it," he went on, "that you have never succeeded in finding the guilty man, or men? The ones who planned the assassination I mean."

"Would I sink still further in your estimation, Commissaire, if I told you that I have never really tried to find them?"

"Lack of curiosity, Doctor?"

"No. Whatever you may have been told, I am not that cold a fish. But I happen to have a respect for evidence. None that has ever come to light has been worth a sou. I think you must know that. Perhaps I should have looked harder for the truth, but I am not a trained policeman, nor am I an amateur detective with time on his hands."

"Do you think that real evidence still exists?"

"It is possible that somewhere in the Defense Ministry, within sight of the very steps on which my father was killed, there are documents still preserved which positively identify those responsible. Especially if they were members of my father's own party, of course. And even if they were Special Security Forces men acting on the junta's orders there could still be documents to prove it. Bureaucrats are cautious men, reluctant to destroy records even when ordered to do so. No one can ever quite be sure that they will not one day prove valuable."

"I understand. The documents may exist but nobody is going to produce them out of the blue for you to see. And even if you knew where they were you would still have to know which bureaucrat had charge of them and what sort of bribe would be required. Am I right?"

"There is also a yearly ritual, Commissaire, designed to shield me from any revival of the temptation to satisfy my curiosity. When I visit the consul at Fort de France to have my passport renewed, I am always reminded firmly that its use is limited. It is valid for travel everywhere except to my own country."

"Well, your mother has been dead for six months now. Do you intend to go on respecting her sentimental wishes about your national status forever?"

"With her people the customary mourning period was at least one year. I shall respect that. I have no doubt, though, that if I were ever to produce a French passport at the Fort de France consulate and ask for a visa, my request would be refused. The regrets would be differently phrased, that is all."

"Yes, I see. Well, one final question, Doctor. The present régime—the Oligarchy as it is called—is known to be far from stable. If a revolutionary coup backed by the armed forces were to result in the establishment of a government headed by Democratic Socialists or by a coalition disposed to remove these restrictions you speak of, would you then wish to return there from exile?"

"For a brief visit perhaps. Not permanently. My work is here and I enjoy doing it."

"As the son of your father you might even be offered a post in the new government—as Minister of Health perhaps." He said it with a smile, but he was far from joking.

"I would certainly refuse it. My childhood immunized me against political ambition, Commissaire. I am a doctor and the only advancement I look for is in my profession."

Apropos my profession, it is now 02:00 hrs. Sister brought me a glass of freshly made tea. Clearly a peace offering. Emboldened, I decided to broach delicately

*the subject of her wart. A crass error on my part from
all points of view. It is not a wart but a pigmented
nevus. She deeply offended. My apologies profuse.
Her acceptance of them theoretical only, as pressed
lips and inward look made clear. In future must mind
own business. After rounds should try sleep, but feel
must finish Gillon account first. To hell with pigmented nevi. To hell with Gillon.*

He had said that it was his final question and I assumed
that with my answer to it the interview would be at an
end. My failure to proceed with the application for French
papers had been explained; the suspicion that I might have
been dabbling in émigré politics had been, I presumed, satisfactorily allayed. So, to save him the trouble of dismissing
me I got up to leave.

He responded irritably. "I am afraid we haven't finished,
Doctor. Sit down please."

I obeyed. "You said that you had questions. I've answered them."

"And now you will kindly listen to my reasons for asking them."

I said nothing and probably looked arrogant. I am told
that this is Dr. Frigo's usual reaction when he is in any way
put out.

Gillon's response was to lean forward with narrowed
eyes. "In the matter of your eventual application for papers,
Doctor, you may as well know that all such applications by
foreigners are normally referred to us for approval and
comment." He pointed a finger at me. "We can say yes or
no. You may like to think about that before refusing your
cooperation."

"I haven't refused anything."

"Good. Then we can proceed." On his desk there was a
second dossier, one with a yellow cover. With a forefinger

he turned it around so that I could read the name lettered on the front.

VILLEGAS Lopez, Manuel.

"How much do you know about him?" he asked.

"Apart from the fact that he leads the Mexico group, not a great deal. For the past ten years he has worked as a lecturer in the Ciudad Universitaria. He must be about fifty now, I suppose. As a student he went to the United States. I'm not sure which university there, but it was for training in architecture I believe."

"Civil engineering, and that is what he has been teaching in Mexico City. He has been an Associate Professor at the university."

"When he was elected to the central committee of the Party he was working with a firm of architectural consultants I know. It could have been as an engineer, I suppose. I was studying for my baccalauréat at the time. That would be sixteen or seventeen years ago. I remember my father saying that Villegas was the sort of new blood the committee needed—young but not too young and trained in a profession, a socialist who had been able to shed most of the doctrinaire cant without compromising his convictions."

"You sound as if you're quoting. Were those the exact words your father used to describe Villegas?"

"Yes, but I mustn't mislead you, Commissaire. It's not because of Villegas that I remember them. Those were the words my father always used to describe an up-and-coming Party member who had earned his approval. They meant that the man in question had become enough of a pragmatist to see eye-to-eye with him, or that my father thought he had. He wasn't always right of course. When he was wrong the man who didn't see eye-to-eye after all was said to have gone wild again."

"Did Villegas ever go wild again?"

"I don't know."

"What else did your father say about him?"

"Nothing that I recall. I wasn't very interested anyway. Villegas was just a new boy on the committee. The leaders there were all of my father's generation, men like Calman, Acosta and Hermanos."

"What about Segura Rojas?"

"Uncle Paco you mean?"

"*Uncle* Paco?"

"That's what we called him as children. Segura used to come to our house a lot at one time. Because he often brought us expensive presents he became an honorary uncle."

"Villegas now refers to him as his Minister of Foreign Affairs. They're very close it seems. You didn't know that?"

"I knew that Segura was in Mexico. The last I heard of him was that he had bought a house in Cuernavaca. Uncle Paco was always one of the rich socialists. He had family money from land holdings in Venezuela. He must be very old now."

"Sixty-eight, if you call that old. I suppose that at your age you do. But you still think of him as Uncle Paco, eh?"

"I hadn't thought of him for years until you mentioned his name just now, Commissaire."

"Well, you will probably be seeing him soon. You referred, Doctor, to Villegas as being based in Mexico. That is no longer true. For the last two months he has been based here. Segura is with him."

I stared at him in disbelief, but he was suddenly busy tidying his desk, stacking Villegas' dossier with several others in a neat pile.

"Here, Commissaire! In heaven's name why?"

Commissaire Gillon finished with the dossiers, folded his arms across his chest and then looked up.

"He applied for permission to reside here temporarily for the purposes of vacation and on health grounds, and permission was granted. The decision to grant permission was made in Paris. Why it was made is none of my business and certainly none of yours. I would strongly advise you not to speculate about or discuss it. My task is to see that the stay here of Monsieur Villegas, his family and his entourage, of which your Uncle Paco is a member, remains uneventful, protected and, as far as possible, unpublicized. It is also my responsibility to see that he remains in good health. That responsibilty, Doctor, I am now delegating to you. You will become Monsieur Villegas' regular medical attendant, and I can tell you now before you ask that Doctor Brissac has been consulted and given his consent to the arrangement."

I said the first thing that came into my head. "And what about Monsieur Villegas? Has he given *his* consent?"

"When he was given permission to reside here it was made clear that all arrangements for his security and welfare would be in the hands of this office."

"But where a doctor is concerned he is surely entitled to some freedom of choice."

"Certainly, and he has already exercised it by dismissing Doctor Massot."

"On what grounds?"

"Lack of communication. You said yourself that Massot's Spanish left something to be desired. So does Villegas' French. A certain amount of ill-feeling was generated between them, I gather."

"You say that Villegas came here, at any rate partly, on health grounds. Is there anything in particular the matter with him?"

"According to Doctor Massot, the man is a hypochondriac and perhaps also a secret drinker. I have the Massot report here if you would like to see it." He reached for the Villegas dossier.

"I don't think that would help. Has Villegas been told about me?"

"Of course. Son of his old leader, qualified in Paris, a valued member of the local hospital staff with immediate access to modern diagnostic facilities and consultative advice, plus complete fluency in Spanish—we gave him all the facts needed on which to base a judgment."

"And he agreed to accept me?"

"Unhesitatingly and with expressions of the warmest approval. He already knew, by the way, of your views on the subject of your mother's Florida associates. I dare say he will question you, as I have, on your other political leanings. From what you have told me I don't anticipate any difficulties there. He may try to convert or indoctrinate you, of course, and enlist you as a supporter, if only because of your name. But I imagine—" he smiled sweetly— "that you will be as evasive or equivocal with him as you have been with me."

I did not respond to the provocation. "It sounds, Commissaire, as if you are expecting me to be making regular calls on this patient. Do you know of any medical reason why I should do so?"

"I know of no specific illness. However, I would like you to see him not less than twice a week, Doctor, to become in effect a friend of the family." He paused briefly to let that sink in. "You will be entitled, I should add, to an honorarium of five hundred francs a month from DST funds for this service. That is the sum Doctor Massot was being paid. It should compensate you adequately, I believe, for the extra time and work involved both in visiting Les Muettes—that is the villa in which Villegas is living—and in making your reports to this office. . . ."

"Reports?"

He held up his hands defensively. "Please allow me to finish. You doctors! I had the same initial reaction from Massot. I am not asking you to violate your oath, your professional code of ethics. That, I am well aware, enjoins secrecy on you—at least, secrecy in matters which ought not, in the doctor's judgment, to be spoken of. Naturally, I would not presume to ask you to report to me on the state of your patient's liver or kidneys. On his general state of mind, however, and of that of his entourage, on the effect on his disposition, say, of any particular visitor he may receive—those are matters, I feel, of a non-professional nature on which you could properly give your impressions for our guidance. I would also hope that, should you be approached —and you may well be approached once it is known outside that you are the man's doctor—by any person or persons seeking information about the occupants of Les Muettes, that too would be known here at once. So, regular reports. As I told you, our task is to protect our guest. And not only from diseases of the flesh, but from all other threats, actual or potential, to his wellbeing. You see?"

"I see." Despite its thick coating of sugar the taste of the pill inside was unmistakably nasty. But there seemed no point at that moment in prolonging the interview by telling him that I had no intention whatever of acting as a DST spy.

He nodded approval. "Good. In anticipation of your understanding and cooperation we have made an appointment for you to see Villegas at his villa tomorrow morning at eleven. I hope that will not be too inconvenient for you, but I am sure that Doctor Brissac will be helpful."

"Very well, Commissaire."

"Reports may be made verbally by telephone but must be confirmed weekly in writing."

I got up to go but he raised his hand. "I have referred to Les Muettes as the patient's villa. I should perhaps mention that for security reasons of his own—perhaps he hoped to deceive the press—Villegas did not lease the villa himself. That was done on his behalf by Segura, your Uncle Paco. So that it is his name that you will see on the postbox at the outer gate. You will also find one of my security boys on duty there. He will have his instructions. Just identify yourself to him."

"All right."

I again made to leave. This time he let me get as far as the door.

"One more thing, Doctor. A small piece of information, but it may serve, when you are thinking over what has been said in this room today, to set your mind at rest in a sensitive area." He paused then went on slowly. "Colleagues of ours in another department made a secret but very full investigation into the circumstances of the plot against your father. And they made it immediately after the tragic outcome. A précis of their report was recently made available to us by the Quai d'Orsay." He picked up a sheet of paper and read from it. *"No conclusive evidence was found by our investigators which implicated any particular member of the Democratic Socialist Party in the Castillo assassination plot. This information may be communicated to Doctor Castillo at your discretion."*

"Thank you, Commissaire. No *conclusive* evidence?"

"That's right."

"Does that imply that there was *in*conclusive evidence?"

"I haven't the slightest idea, Doctor. I was merely giving you the information I was told I might give just as I received it."

I thanked him again.

When I went through the outer office on my way out, the telex machine was silent; but the operator, now sifting through the long tearsheets on the table beside it, was still groaning as he worked.

It is now 04:00 hrs. Must get at least some sleep. Accounts of information obtained from Elizabeth evening 12 May and first interviews at Les Muettes 13 May much too important record when tired. Liable skimp,

*forget salient points. Can only hope quiet night here
tomorrow.*

Evening

Late that afternoon, after I had seen Gillon, I met with
Dr. Brissac in his office. Naturally, he wanted a detailed
account of my interview at the Préfecture; but as I was
sure that he would chatter about it to Gillon the next time
they played bridge I was careful to be discreet. However,
I told him about the honorarium, and, although I doubted
very much whether he had anything to do with obtaining
it for me, thanked him for doing so. He waved my thanks
away graciously and offered to lend me one of the hospital's
portable electrocardiograph machines if I thought I needed
it. I would have to borrow a car in which to transport it
though. He disapproved of my motocyclette which he considered an insufficiently dignified mode of transport for a
doctor. He reminded me that, with an extra five hundred
francs a month coming in, I would be able to afford the
down payment on a car.

When I left the hospital for the day I went to see Elizabeth.

She, too, lives in one of the restored houses, though hers,
unlike mine which is split up into apartments, is undi-
vided. She has her studio there and a full-time housekeeper.
She also owns a gallery in the shopping arcade of the Hotel Ajoupa. Through the gallery she sells the work of other
local painters, as well as her own, and that of a talented

créole sculptor who earns his living as foreman of a rum distillery.

St. Paul is full of artists. The majority of them are pretty bad. The ones Elizabeth sells most of are a woman flower-painter with a hibiscus fixation and a garage mechanic who does oil-on-board daubs of island beauty spots. He uses a contraption made up in the garage to spray sand on his paint while it is still wet. The process serves both to conceal, at least partially, his banal incompetence and to impart the illusion of an original technique. His work is much in demand during the tourist season (an American airline magazine called him "the Grandma Moses of St. Paul") and Elizabeth takes a malicious pleasure in charging high prices for it. The talented sculptor, on the other hand, is hard to sell. However, one or two American galleries, including the Museum of Modern Art in New York, now have examples of his work and Elizabeth is trying to get him a one-man show in Paris.

Her own work is of two kinds: trompe-l'œil, which sell quite well, and her "vowel paintings" which don't.

It was I who coined the term "vowel paintings." She calls them "commemorations." They are large, violent canvases depicting, as if they were human participants in medieval torture sessions, massacres or dances of death, the letters A E I O U.

To understand them, or at any rate to understand why she goes on producing them, you have first to look at her passport.

The name she normally uses is Elizabeth Martens. The name in her passport, however, is: Maria Valeria Modena Elizabeth von Hapsburg-Lorraine Martens Duplessis. Martens is her nom-de-jeune-fille. Her father, Jean Baptiste Martens, a Belgian national, owns textile factories near Lille. Duplessis is the name of the French husband from whom she is separated. The rest of that imposing list derives from her mother who is—and Elizabeth has genealogical tables to substantiate the oddity—a great-great-great-granddaughter of the Empress Maria Theresa of Austria.

Hence, Elizabeth is, through a Spanish branch of the family, a Hapsburg; and A E I O U is an acronym. It was invented by, or for, a 15th century Hapsburg, the Emperor Friedrich III; and the invention was intended to support his belief, justifiably waning at the time, in the ability of his line to endure. A E I O U stands for *Austriae Est Imperare Orbi Universo*.

Elizabeth sees nothing absurd in her obsession with it; and there seems to be no ordinary snobbery in her inability to ignore or forget that part of her genetic heritage and the long, bloody chapters of history it represents. Indeed, her feelings towards this monstrous dynasty which haunts her are decidedly ambivalent. Though in the vowel paintings she is always ridiculing or reviling it—there is a sickening "commemoration" of an imperial funeral at the Kapuziner Crypt—she is also capable of springing to its defense. She has been known to point out fiercely that it was not the British Empire upon which "the sun never set" but the Hapsburg Empire of Charles the Fifth, who ruled "from the Carpathians to Peru". Once, when she had drunk rather too much rum, she startled an inoffensive Boston art dealer and his wife, with a sudden, passionate appeal for their understanding of the pitiable plight of Charles the Sixth—gout, stomach trouble and disastrous pregnancies. It transpired, but only after some moments of utter confusion, that the pregnancies were those of his Empress and that what Elizabeth was justifying was the Pragmatic Sanction of 1713.

If all this makes her sound somewhat eccentric I should explain that for most of the time she is reasonably level-headed. The locals' word for her is *toquée*, but on St. Paul this is not necessarily a derogatory term. A measure of dottiness is allowable, and if the possessor of it looks like Elizabeth it may even be regarded as an asset. There is

nothing Hapsburgian about her lower lip and her jaw is
anything but prognathous. She has a print of a Stieler por-
trait of the Archduchess Sophie which looks like a picture
of her in fancy dress. If she herself seldom wears anything
fancier or more voluminous than slacks and a shirt, only
the wives of certain French officials have expressed disapproval. *Mal elevée* is their verdict.

I suppose it could be argued that few Hapsburgs have
ever been anything but badly brought up, though not perhaps in the sense that the officials' ladies are using the
phrase. Elizabeth, well-informed by her maternal grandmother who as a young girl knew the court of Franz Josef,
can be eloquent on the subject. The King of Hungary who
sneered that, while wars were fought by strong nations,
"happy Austria" could usually get what it wanted by marriage, was not far wrong. When one hears about those
wretched little archdukes and archduchesses with their pet
names—the Franzis, the Maxls, the Bubis, the Sisis, the Lisls
—all being taught deportment and court etiquette almost
as soon as they could walk, and having their marriage contracts negotiated long before they reached puberty, it is
hardly surprising that as adults most of them were more
than a trifle neurotic. What *is* surprising is that over the
centuries so few were manifestly insane.

Hearing Elizabeth speak of such things it is easy to assume that she shares one's own abhorrence of them. To do
so, however, is to misunderstand her. If she does not live
in her family's past to the extent of approving its grosser
stupidities, she never wholly disapproves. For her the lovers
of Mayerling were a disgraceful pair of fools who caused
the poor old Emperor intolerable pain and inconvenience.
The notion that they might be deserving of some pity is unacceptable. True, mistakes were made with Rudolph's education. There was that fool of a tutor who locked the boy
in a zoo with wild animals to teach him courage. Clearly
not the way to teach a boy of six anything. But Rudolph

was the Crown Prince, the Throne Heir. His sense of responsibility should have been innate. "Oh yes, I know you think I'm talking nonsense, but still . . ."

Elizabeth's own formal education may have been of the kind appropriate to the daughter of a prosperous Belgian manufacturer, but her thinking in certain areas remains that of the maternal grandmother who curtsied to Franz Josef.

Her attitude towards her parents' divorce is characteristic. It goes like this: since her father was a Protestant and always intended to remain one, the marriage was doomed from the start and ought never to have been sanctioned. It would have been better if she had been born a bastard.

Her parents' reception of this pronouncement has been mixed. Martens père, who has two other children by his second marriage, now accepts it with a resigned, kindly sort of amusement. On the other hand, her mother, who now lives with her second husband in Paraguay, resents it deeply. On her last visit to St. Paul there was a bitter quarrel, with both sides hurling what appeared to be deadly insults at one another. I say "appeared to be" because both charges and countercharges involved historical allusions which were to me largely incomprehensible. It was for this reason that my attempts at mediation met in the end with some success. My abject ignorance became so evident that ultimately both disputants were driven to laughter.

On the subject of her own marriage Elizabeth is no less dogmatic. She has been legally separated from her husband for five years now. There are no children of the marriage. She neither needs him nor even uses his name. Yet—though to my certain knowledge she never goes near a church or a priest—she still considers herself irrevocably married to the man. She will not even consider divorce, and if he were ever to bring, as he could, a civil action for annulment of the marriage, she would contest it by every means available to her. Once, looking through one of the books she inherited from her grandmother, I found a passage about

Anna of Tyrol who married the Emperor Matthias. It said
that she kept a silver-tipped thong with which to lash herself for her sins. When I asked Elizabeth if, in clinging to
her marriage, she wasn't doing the same thing, she lost her
temper and threw a palette knife at me. There was paint on
it and I had to send the slacks I was wearing to the cleaners.

It was just after that incident that she gave me, as a gesture of conciliation, one of her vowel paintings. The subject of it was The Defenestration of Prague. In my opinion
Elizabeth is still fighting the Thirty Years War.

I didn't tell her immediately about what had happened to
me with the DST that day. There was work to be done
first, and in any case I hadn't then made up my mind how
much of it I was going to tell. The extra five hundred francs
a month would have her approval, I knew; but unless I
played down the Gillon interview I was sure that she would
start pursuing the obvious lines of inquiry and speculation
which I myself, at that moment, was trying to ignore.
Better, I thought, to appear to be taking none of it very
seriously. Better perhaps to concentrate my concern on
Dr. M.'s diagnosis of Villegas as a hypochondriac and deplore the prospective waste of professional time.

When it came to the point, though, I told all.

It was working with her that did it. Having to concentrate on something other than the troubles of the day, I
became relaxed and started telling her what had happened
almost without thinking.

What Dr. Brissac calls my "amateur photography" is
simply a chore I do for Elizabeth. When she was studying
in Paris she worked part-time in a gallery on the Right
Bank. The dealer who owned it taught her a lot about the
business, and when later she started her own gallery in St.
Paul, she adopted his trading practices. One of these had
been to photograph every work, good, bad or indifferent,
that passed through his hands. Some of these photographs

would be used to send to prospective buyers abroad, but most were for record purposes; prints or transparencies of every work handled were kept on file and cross-referenced to the account books.

For a while Elizabeth used the Fort Louis commercial photographer who usually covers local sporting and social events; but for what she wanted he was pretty useless. Photographing paintings in color is easy if it doesn't matter how faithful the results are to the original; but if fidelity does matter the job is anything but easy. Indeed, in many big cities there are professional photographers who specialize in the work. The man in Fort Louis couldn't really be bothered; he has a shop selling cheap cameras and hi-fi sets that takes up much of his time. So, two years ago when I was in Florida seeing my mother, I bought some books on the subject and a secondhand five-by-seven "view" camera that was going cheap. With the help of one of the technicians in the X-ray department and after some experimenting I managed eventually to get acceptable results. With practice and the discovery of a reliable color-printing laboratory in Caracas the results became fairly consistent.

For these photographic sessions we set up the camera and lights in a corner of the studio and do a whole batch of pictures, as many as we can, in one go. This way I can always use freshly-opened film packs and seal the whole lot in damp-proof airmail bags immediately after exposure. That evening we had ten canvases and a piece of sculpture to do. With color negatives as well as transparencies to shoot, that meant a long session. At intervals Elizabeth's femme-de-ménage brought us cold white wine and little sea-food concoctions. It was during one of these pauses for refreshment that I again brought up the subject of our getting a new camera.

"We've been into all that before," Elizabeth said. "This old thing works quite well for flat paintings, but this new module type would be more flexible when we are photographing three-dimensional objects. We would have more perspective control. Yes?"

"Exactly."

She waved a piece of bread at me. "I know what it is with you, Ernesto dear. You've been bitten."

"Nonsense. I merely wish . . ."

"It isn't nonsense. All this talk about perspective control may be true enough, but what you really want is to make beautiful pictures that will be reproduced in some New York gallery catalogue or shiny paper magazine with your name there as photographer. I know. You have developed artistic ambitions."

As there may have been a particle of truth in the allegation I was careful to dismiss it with no more than a shrug. "It's you who wants to push Molinet's work, not I." Molinet is the talented rum distillery foreman. "Personally," I went on, "I don't think this shot we're doing now is going to do the piece justice."

"The inferior workman blames his tools. You can light it differently, bring out the texture."

"It will still look like a block of limestone with holes in it."

"Not to the educated eye. Besides, you told me yourself. This new camera would cost fifteen hundred dollars for the basic carcass alone, without even a lens. What it will have cost by the time you are ready to produce your masterpieces, God alone knows. Three thousand dollars? Four? My darling, the gallery is not actually losing money, even though those hotel pigs have increased the rent, but we cannot afford these American boxes of tricks."

I was sponging some food I had spilled off my shirt, so my reply was less forceful than it might have been. "I'm not talking about American boxes of tricks," I said plaintively, "but about a widely-used German camera system of proved design. Nor am I asking the gallery to indulge my soaring ambitions as a photographer. Today Doctor Brissac suggested that I should get rid of my moto—which, incidentally, again refused to start outside the hospital—and buy a car. I may decide instead to have the moto properly serviced for once and spend the money on a camera."

"What money?"

So then I told her.

She listened carefully but made only one comment at the time. If Dr. M. had been getting five hundred a month, I should have asked for a thousand. It was latish before we had finished taking photographs and put everything away.

As Elizabeth's bedroom is practically part of the studio it always smells faintly of turpentine. This is a smell I find pleasant and when it is mingled with the scent she uses the effect is curiously exotic. On getting back to my own bed I often find that some parts of my body, particularly the arms and shoulders, have brought the mixture with them. This reminder of Elizabeth is always an agreeable prelude to sleep.

But that night it was different. We were lying there quietly in bed and I was thinking drowsily that soon I would have to get up, dress and walk back to my apartment, when all of a sudden she announced that she wanted to go for a swim.

I wasn't utterly flabbergasted, but I was a bit surprised—and puzzled. Swimming at night is for Elizabeth a kind of instant psychotherapy, a means of ridding herself of excess adrenalin, reducing tensions and restoring equanimity. But when she had resorted to it before I had always known about and understood her immediate reasons for doing so —we had had a heated argument, she had received a letter from her mother or was worked up over the tax man's cheating her—and the decision had always been made when we were both dressed. There had never before been talk of swimming *after* we had gone to bed. So, I was puzzled. It seemed to me—and I don't think I am unduly vain or in-

clined to delude myself in these matters—that any tensions
she may have been experiencing had already been thoroughly and satisfactorily relaxed some twenty minutes
earlier.

And then a thought occurred to me. There had been one
thing left unresolved. "About that camera," I said. "I wasn't
really being serious you know. You're right. It would be
an extravagance."

"You don't have to decide now." She got out of bed.
"We're going for a swim."

"We? You know, I have to be. . . ."

"At the hospital early, of course. You also have an appointment to examine the great Villegas, your country's
man of destiny. You need sound sleep. A good swim will
ensure that you get it."

It had rained heavily that evening. I pointed out that the
hotel pool would probably be unusable.

"Would you prefer to swim in the sea?"

The question was rhetorical. In these parts swimming in
the sea at night is a recognized way of committing suicide.
I reached for my clothes.

We drove to the hotel in her Peugeot station wagon.

Ajoupa is the old Carib word for a palmetto or plaited
bamboo hut. The Hotel Ajoupa (*"200 air-conditioned
rooms on a white sand beach"*) is neither. It has a stylized
representation of an ajoupa on its writing paper and some
beetle-infested cabanas of similar design down by the
Beach Bar, but the connection ends there. The Ajoupa is
owned by a Franco-Swiss hotel corporation and is, according to Elizabeth, one of what the North American package-
tour operators now call "five-star automats."

The term is not an architectural criticism—though many
of these vast concrete slabs with their serried rows of windows do indeed look like outsize automatic food dispensers
—but a description, far from critical, of their role in a
profitable confidence trick. Once the customer, bemused

by the promises of sun, sea, sand and palm trees in the brochure, has put his money in the slot he has to take what comes out. It will, of course, be precisely what the brochure said it would be, because people might be able to get their money back if it weren't. Only the flavor of the dish may be a little unexpected. The brochure never claims that what is promised will always be palatable.

The Ajoupa swimming pool, for instance, looks splendid in the hotel's brochure because the photograph was taken in the dry season. What is not explained is that the landscape architect, more familiar with the French Riviera than the French Antilles, sited the pool at the foot of a slope artifically created by bulldozers. So, every time it rains heavily a torrent of mud pours down over or around the retaining wall into the pool area. The cost of providing adequate drainage for the site without rebuilding the pool is currently estimated at a million francs. Management has responded to the challenge so far by removing the warning signs about the dangers of sea bathing and giving out-of-season visitors free rum-punch vouchers redeemable only at the Beach Bar. Casualties to date have been light and caused mainly by sea-urchin spines and jelly fish.

That night the rain had had its usual way with the pool. The water was dark brown with a thick coating of muck on it. The skimmer outlets were choked with leaves and twigs. But for the smell of chlorine we might have been swimming in a mangrove swamp.

I did two lengths, then got out and stood under the freshwater shower to clean myself off. I was still wondering why we were there. Obviously Elizabeth had had a delayed reaction to something said earlier in the evening. If the new camera was out, that left Villegas.

And then I thought I saw light. She had referred to him slightingly as "the great Villegas, your country's man of destiny." No doubt she had heard something to his discredit and hadn't been able to make up her mind whether or not to tell me about it. That would certainly bother her. Elizabeth has quaint ideas about the doctor-patient relationship. She is not alone in this, of course; lots of people have them. The main fallacy is that between doctor and patient there must always be mutual liking and respect, that it is not enough merely for the patient to trust the doctor: a doctor who secretly dislikes or disapproves of a patient cannot effectively treat that person's ills.

In the past I have told her that she is thinking of witch-doctors; but that evening she was obviously in no mood for levity. While she swam to and fro I recalled the standard professional arguments on the subject.

None of them was needed. When she had showered she sat down beside me in the darkness, still drying her hair, and began to cross-examine me about my interview with Gillon.

"What role did he adopt?"

"Role?"

She snapped her fingers impatiently. "What was his manner, his approach? Surely you understand what I am asking. I don't suppose he bullied you. You may be a foreigner but you are also, after all, a doctor and a respected member of the community. But these types have ways of saying things. The words they use may read harmlessly enough when they are transcribed from a tape recording, but the tones of voice in which they have been said, the manner and gestures which accompanied them, can sometimes mean more than the actual words."

"Was he unpleasant, do you mean? No. At times he was quite amiable in fact. Of course, he mentioned at one point that if and when I apply for naturalization his office will have to pass on the application."

"Ah."

"I imagine that's normal when they want you to do something for them that they know you won't like."

"The spying you mean."

"He didn't call it that, but it was plain what he meant.

He was firm but, as I say, not unpleasant. Anyway, what difference does it make?"

But she wasn't yet prepared to explain. "Did he in fact tape the conversation do you know?"

"If he did, I didn't see the microphone or the recorder. I would be inclined to think not. He was quite chatty and informal at times. He even admitted at one point to having used a false analogy."

"Did he tell you why Villegas has moved his base here?"

"He said that Villegas had applied for permission to stay here temporarily—vacation and health reasons. I told you."

"But surely you didn't believe it. Didn't you ask him for the real reason?"

"He didn't give me a chance. The decision to let Villegas come here was made in Paris, he said. He also said that *why* the permission was granted was none of his business and none of mine. He also, by the way, advised me not to speculate about or discuss it—not in fact to do what we are now doing."

She waved the objection away. "In other words all this stuff about vacation and health is just the formula he's been told to use by Paris."

"Probably. If Villegas had a health problem which could be helped by a change of climate of this sort he could have moved somewhere else in Mexico. They have climates of all sorts there."

"Then Paris wants him here for some other reason?"

"It looks like it."

She put her towel down. "Aren't you going to ask?"

"Ask?"

"What possible use could Villegas be here—or anywhere else for that matter—to Paris?"

"As you obviously think you have an answer, all right I'll ask. But what do you mean by Paris? The Quai d'Orsay, the Minister for Overseas Departments and Territories, the Prime Minister, the President?"

"Being facetious never suits you, Ernesto, but, since you ask, more likely the Minister of Finance and Economic Affairs—eventually. But from the way Gillon spoke to you, and from some of the things he said, I would think that, at the moment, S-dec is handling this one."

I sighed.

"S-dec—SDECE. Service de Documentation Extérieure." She made a slightly obscene island gesture normally used for warding off the evil eye. "Secret service."

"Oh, those."

"Yes, those. They need a success. You must remember the Ben Barka scandal—I showed you that piece about it in *Paris Match.*"

"I remember."

"Of course you do. And so does everybody else. Poor S-dec! They long ago got rid of those brutal Corsicans, or so they say. They have been reformed and reorganized and taken over by the army. They no longer kidnap people and torture and kill. They are pure in heart. But still nobody loves them, because nobody quite believes. They need a brilliant coup to help them with their new image. Once that is established it won't matter whether they are loved or not. They will still be feared, but they will look like a responsible and efficient secret service again, steadfastly upholding the glory of France."

I sighed again, rather more loudly. "Elizabeth, I haven't the slightest idea what you are talking about."

"You mean what has S-dec to do with Villegas? Surely, it is obvious. Ultimately they hope to control him. But they can't do so yet. The DST hates S-dec—always has and always will—that is well known. But while Villegas is on French soil it is DST which has the control. Why do you think Gillon wants these reports from you? Against whom do you think he is warning you when he refers to persons who might approach you seeking information about the occupants of Les Muettes? The press, the CIA? Well perhaps those also. But mainly he is warning you against S-dec."

"Why on earth should S-dec be interested in Villegas? You know you still haven't told me why you think he's really here."

"No, I haven't, have I."

I was beginning to get annoyed. "I've just thought of one very good reason for myself," I said. "In fact I'm pretty sure it's the right one. Climate may have nothing to do with it, but it could be his health. He's suffering from dyspepsia. He just can't take any more Mexican food."

She had the grace to smile and then kissed my cheek. "Very good, darling. I wish it were true, but I don't think it is. I think that there is a game being played and that in it Villegas has suddenly become a card worth having, one that might make the difference between winning and losing a wonderful fortune."

I got to my feet and yawned.

"Yes, Ernesto, I know. You're tired and you have to get some sleep. We'll drive back now and I'll tell you about it on the way."

And in the car, at last, she told me.

"Three months ago," she said, "a group of men, four traveling together, spent two nights in the hotel. They were all booked on the Friday Air France flight to Paris, but they broke their journey here, instead of going on through to Fort de France, because one of them had been sick and still had a touch of dysentery. Two of them were French, the sick man was Norwegian. The fourth was a Dutchman and it was him I got to know. He came into the gallery just to look, and ended by buying a Molinet. Naturally we talked."

I nodded. Anyone who buys a Molinet is always of special interest to Elizabeth. There would have been quite a lot of talk.

After a moment she went on.

"This Dutchman happened to mention where they had been, where it was that the dysentery had been picked up. They'd all four of them had it in turn, he said, and considered themselves lucky to have picked up nothing worse. They had been in the Coraza Islands. You know them, Ernesto?"

"I saw them once."

The very name was an evocation of childhood.

The Corazas are a group of off-shore islands about a hundred kilometers south of the capital and just visible from the mainland at Careya Point. I had been a small boy when I had seen them. It was just after my father had bought his first car, and we had gone down there, the whole family, on a picnic. From the headland where we stopped you could just see two of the islands. They looked like small blue-black clouds on the horizon. I remember asking my father if we couldn't one day get a boat and go out to them.

It seemed that there were many reasons why we couldn't do that.

I can still remember what my father said.

"Well yes, we could go there, Ernesto, but first we would have to obtain permission from the Minister of the Interior, the Minister of Marine and the Minister of Fisheries. And even if we were fortunate enough to be granted all those permissions, it still might not be a good thing to do."

"Why not, Papa?"

"Ernesto, the people who live on those islands are very poor—Arawak Indians from the old days before the Conquest who cannot even now speak our language and who have no schools. There are not very many of them because there is spring water on only one of the islands—the bigger of the two we can see— and not much food any more. Once upon a time the

big turtles used to come and breed there, but some-
thing bad happened to spoil the sea shore and the
turtles stopped coming."

"Then why do the Indians stay?"

"Because the islands have always been their home
and because they have kept their old gods, their idols.
This is supposed to be a secret, but the Church knows,
of course, and has tried to help them in its own way.
A mission was started there and for a time the brothers
sent copra to the mainland to earn money for the
islands. Then the plague came. It was a type of yellow
fever but more virulent than any we knew. Our vac-
cine did not give protection. So a lot of Christians died.
There were other diseases too. At the same time our
diseases from the mainland killed a lot of the Coraza
Indians. So, since neither the Indians nor their islands
were a source of profit to our feudal masters, the
Corazas were designated a primitive reservation. Quar-
antine regulations were also made to make sure that the
Indians kept their diseases to themselves. Now they are
allowed to starve to death in private. Soon, perhaps,
there will be no more of them to trouble us."

My father spoke bitterly; in those days his social conscience was much in evidence and embraced many causes.
Five years later, when he was writing his Party's manifesto
for national progress and social justice, the plight of the
Coraza islanders wasn't even mentioned.

"So they're doing something at last," I said to Elizabeth.
"I've always thought the Corazas might be interesting,
though I can't see what they've got to do with Villegas
being in St. Paul."

Elizabeth was negotiating the fish market—always tricky
at night because drunks there tend to ignore the traffic.
"Interesting in what way?" she asked.

"Socially and archeologically I imagine. Medically, too.

This Dutchman of yours, what was he? An anthropologist or a biologist?"

"Neither. He was a geologist."

"But there are no minerals in the Corazas. The government would have soon been at them if there had been. There's not much of anything except guano, and even that's not in commercial quantities."

"The Molinet this man bought was too heavy to go with him on the plane. I had to ship it home to him via Le Havre. That meant documents, so I had a good look at his passport. His occupation was given as petroleum geologist."

I was silent.

She went on. "Talking to him I found out about the others in the party. One of the Frenchmen was a hydrographer. The other two were engineers. He didn't say what kind. Uncultured types though, not interested in anything but stress calculations, whatever they are. Still they were all experts together, a consultant team."

"Did he say what the team had been doing?"

"Working on a survey vessel. He said that the technicians on board had been British, the crew Jamaicans and the food terrible."

"Off-shore oil? Is that what they were looking for?"

"Oh they already knew that the oil was there. Their business was to decide how best to get at it." She gave me an apologetic glance. "I'm sorry, Ernesto. I must admit that at the time I didn't listen very carefully. All I was worried about was that he might change his mind about the Molinet when he found out that it was so heavy. So, though I was relieved when he went on talking about his job, I didn't pay much attention. That's why I needed a swim, to try to remember more of what he said."

"But he did say that they already knew the oil was there?"

"Oh yes. Apparently this situation is cropping up all the time nowadays. Knowing about the existence of oil is nothing, you see. Knowing how to get at it and whether it's worth the cost of doing so are the things that count. If the price of a barrel of crude is three dollars and it will cost five to get it you don't bother. But then the price of a barrel goes up to twelve dollars or more and you think again. Still, it's the engineers and scientists who have to solve these equations. He said that teams like his were the new wealth-makers."

"But why a European team?" I asked. "If the Oligarchy gave anyone an oil-drilling concession for the Coraza area it would surely be to some American company. Those people have teams of their own."

"Ah, but this one specializes in deep-sea work. Over three hundred meters! He was very proud of that. It's not the same as ordinary off-shore drilling. The rigs have to be different. Lots of things are different. Anyway, these men didn't sound particularly European in spite of their passports, and among themselves they spoke American English, even the Frenchmen. What's more they weren't working for a company but an international consortium. I do remember that. The Consortium, he called it, as if it were God."

"How many companies in it? Did he say?"

"Five, I think. Naturally, I didn't know then about Villegas coming here or I might have asked him who the companies are."

"And if there's a French company what percentage of the consortium it has?"

"That too." She parked in the Place Carbet.

I listened for a moment to the crickets chirping. A lot of people find the noise soothing. I don't.

"You still haven't explained why Villegas is suddenly so important," I said. "You called him a card worth having. You didn't say in what sort of game."

She was combing her hair. "If you were an oil consortium, Ernesto, and about to invest billions of dollars in a

coffee republic, wouldn't you look twice at its government
before you finally committed yourself?"

"I suppose so."

"And if what you saw was a group of feudal landowners
running the country with petty gangsters disguised as a
militia and an eighty percent per annum rate of inflation,
what would you do?"

"Ask the CIA to change the government, I expect."

I smiled as I said it.

She frowned. "Oh the CIA wouldn't do that, not any
more, and certainly not in Latin America. They're trying
to become respectable again."

"I was being facetious again."

She ignored that. "What they *might* do, though, is to
get someone else, some other agency with an interest in the
area, and the consortium, to do the dirty work for them.
And, naturally, put up with the embarrassment if things
went wrong. They've done deals with the British and the
West Germans on that basis."

"You seem to know a lot about it," I remarked; "or are
you just making this up?"

"I know a lot about it." She shook out her towel. "I
wouldn't be at all surprised if now they've made a deal
with S-dec and the French."

I made no comment on that and she didn't seem to expect
one.

"What I don't understand," she went on thoughtfully,
"is why they make you his doctor. Of course Franz Josef
was always a little jealous of Maximilian's popular following, especially in Lombardy, and sometimes afraid of it too.
This Uncle Paco of yours, what's his name?"

"Segura."

"Yes, this Segura may be the Count Grünne of the court
whose confidential advice plays on those fears."

A Hapsburg parable was the last thing I was prepared to
take at that moment. "Oh for God's sake Elizabeth!" I

snapped. "They've appointed me as his doctor because he asked for one who could speak Spanish. I happen to qualify. It's as simple as that."

She was good enough to allow me to go on thinking so.

Later though, as I was trying to go to sleep, I kept recalling things she had said and things I had remembered.

That bad thing that had once happened to the shores of the Corazas, the thing that had stopped the turtles coming back to breed—had it been a massive undersea seepage of oil?

And what really happened when a coffee republic struck it rich?

Perhaps, I thought, Uncle Paco would tell me.

Sister coolly formal, much on dignity. Clearly still angry with me. My gaffe about wart doubtless regrettable but possible beneficial side-effects. Believe will not be disturbed now except case dire necessity.

Tuesday 13 May Morning

Kept appointment 11:00 hrs. made for me by Commissaire Gillon see new patient Señor Manuel VILLEGAS Lopez at Villa Les Muettes.

Gillon had said that there would be one of his "security boys" on duty at the outer gate. There was. He sat in a 2 cv. parked under a tree to shade it from the sun and so placed that it could, if necessary, be driven across the entrance to block the opening of the iron gates. When I stopped he got out and slid back a locking bar which looked as if it had been recently installed.

To my surprise I recognized him. He was a middle-aged black with a goatee beard whom I had seen once or twice entering and leaving the Préfecture. Because he always wore a tie and white shirt I had assumed that he worked as a clerk. Now he was also wearing a holstered pistol.

He nodded amiably as he took a paper from his shirt pocket and glanced at it.

"Doctor Castillo?"

I produced my identity card which he examined carefully before handing it back.

"My name's Albert, Doctor," he said. "Seems we'll be seeing quite a lot of one another. You always going to be visiting the subject at this time?"

"Not always. When I'm on night duty at the hospital I sometimes sleep late in the mornings. We get emergencies too. Does the time make any difference to you, Monsieur Albert?"

"No, but there are three of us on this job, you see, eight hour shifts. I'm senior so I'm taking the morning shift. The others'll have to get to recognize you too if you come at other times. Just thought you might save yourself two more lots of quizzing. Very important subject inside there, Doctor." He grinned and then glanced at the leather case strapped behind me on the moto. "Medical bag?"

"Yes. Do you want to look inside?"

"Any guns or grenades?"

"No."

"Well—" he grinned again—"maybe I will look anyway. That way I'll know what a medical bag ought to have in it as well as a stethoscope. Besides," he added as I undid the straps, "I can mention your bag was opened and inspected in the report. Thoroughness. The Commissaire likes that."

He was good about it though. He just looked and didn't attempt to touch anything. Of the drugs there he said dryly, "You wouldn't need a gun to kill an enemy, would you Doctor?"

But his question about weapons and the fact that he had taken the trouble to check the case interested me. In spite of his joking reference to his report he struck me as too intelligent a man to embellish reports unnecessarily. Obviously he was obeying orders which envisaged the possibility of someone trying to get to my patient with the intention of killing him. At first I had assumed that the "threats to his well-being" mentioned by Gillon would be represented chiefly by importunate newspaper men.

I did not trouble to strap the case back on the carrier and soon wished that I had. The track up to the house was quite long and wound through a jungle of wild bananas. In places the rains had scoured deep transverse ruts across the surface which made it difficult to ride with only one free hand for steering. In the end I dismounted and walked the rest of the way.

Les Muettes, or at least the original version of it, was built in the mid-19th century by a planter who spent so much money on it that his heirs soon went bankrupt. By the end of World War II it had been derelict for years. However, it had been built of stone on good foundations, and in the fifties a Parisian banker bought it together with two hectares of land giving access to a beach. An architect was brought in to restore the house, adding bathrooms and other modern amenities, and a landscape gardener set to work on the surroundings. When they had finished the place was a luxury winter villa. The banker and his family now spend January and February there. For the rest of the year, when tenants able to pay an exorbitant rent can be found, the villa is leased. The only all-year-round occupants are the servants.

I had been there once before, by ambulance on an emergency case. All I remembered from that occasion was a magnificent view from the terrace and a kidney-shaped swimming pool. It was the latter which had caused the emergency. A gardener, trying to scrub the tiling when the

pool was almost empty, had fallen in and broken a leg. We
had had a job getting him out.

The track became an asphalt drive which descended into
a paved courtyard. There was a portico over the entrance
and two big shade trees so that visitors were protected from
both sun and rain. A three-car garage to one side housed a
Citroën DS (the banker's?) swathed in a protective cocoon
of plastic, a small Renault and a speedboat on a trailer. I
left the moto beside them.

A black butler in a wasp-striped waistcoat opened one of
the mahogany double-doors and held out a silver tray for
my card. When I told him that I had no card and gave my
name, he bowed and led me across marble flooring to a sort
of alcove separated by jalousies from the main drawing
room and the terrace beyond.

"You wait please," the butler said. "I tell madame."

To one side there was a wrought-iron table with a glass
top, neat rows of bottles and a grouping of ice-bucket, mar-
tini mixer and drinking glasses of various sizes. On shelving
built along the inner wall was an array of hi-fi equipment
and a record library. Since there was nothing there on
which to sit down I looked at the records. Arranged carefully in alphabetical order were Bach, Bartok, Beethoven,
Brahms, Chopin, Debussy, Mozart, Scarlatti, Schumann,
Stravinsky and Wagner. On top of the small pile by the
turntable was *An Evening with Cole Porter*. I was about
to take a look at the next record on the pile when I heard
approaching footsteps on the marble.

I had seen photographs of Villegas' wife, Doña Julia, and
heard that she was a handsome woman, but, allowing for
the usual flattery of studio portraits, had not expected her
to look so handsome in the flesh. For one of my country-
women she was of above average height and although she
was in her late forties and had borne three children her
figure was surprisingly youthful. Her pale, aquiline features
were somewhat lined about the eyes—though the lightly

tinted glasses she wore almost concealed this—but her sleeveless blouse revealed smooth, firm arms. Her sleek black hair looked untouched by age.

The Uncle Paco who introduced us I scarcely recognized.

He had always, since I had known him anyway, had narrow shoulders, a big belly and pigeon toes; but in the old days those defects had been relatively unobtrusive. With the belly restrained by a corset and the shoulders modified by suits from expensive tailors he had achieved an appearance which, though chubby, had been somehow dapper. Now, he was an ovoid hulk of a man, bald with tufts of white hair sprouting from his ears and large crimson dewlaps which quivered with every movement he made. The patterned Mexican shirt he wore, creased horizontally from sternum to crotch, did not help. Only the odd blue eyes, peeping out from their puffy surroundings through black-rimmed glasses, were the same—amused, wary and ever ready to twinkle with malice.

They twinkled now as he watched Doña Julia uttering conventional politenesses and trying to size me up as she did so.

"I am of course aware, Doctor," she continued smoothly, "that etiquette prevents your listening sympathetically to any criticism of a professional colleague, but perhaps I am allowed to say that it is a relief to encounter again a doctor with whom one shares a common language."

"It is kind of you to say so, Doña Julia."

"In Mexico, you know, we had access to the American British Hospital. The lingua franca there was English of course. However, there are, I understand, basic differences other than language between medical teaching practices in France and North America."

"Hardly basic."

"No? Doctor Massot's readings of my husband's blood pressure caused some confusion I can tell you."

"Is your husband specially interested in his blood pressure?"

"Isn't every man of his age?"

"Some I know prefer completely to ignore it."

"That's true enough," said Uncle Paco. "Personally, my blood pressure is the last thing I want to hear about."

"Dear Paco. Nobody can be expected to want to hear bad news." She patted his arm affectionately, but I thought that the fond smile with which she accompanied the gesture had a leavening of dislike in it. "I was merely warning Doctor Castillo of Don Manuel's appetite for fact."

Uncle Paco's grin revealed extensive bridgework. "I've no doubt he'll find out about that soon enough, my dear. That is, if we ever give him a chance to do so."

"Of course, I was forgetting." Her smile switched to me. "Doctor Castillo has his responsibilities at the hospital as well as his duty to the police." There was dry ice in the smile now. "Will you show your young friend up and introduce him, Paco dear?"

With a curt nod to me she left.

As the heels of her sandals clacked away over the marble Uncle Paco took a cigar case from his shirt pocket.

"A stupid woman," he remarked. "Arrogant. When he gets to power she'll make enemies for him. Not of old friends perhaps, but among the doubtful, the undecided." He drew a cigar out and slid the case shut. "In which category will you be, Ernesto? You don't object, I hope, to my presuming on our earlier acquaintance by addressing you familiarly?"

"No, Don Paco. As for your other question, I shall be in the category of the totally uninterested."

"That is what your Commissaire Gillon told me." He turned and waddled out onto the terrace.

I followed, thinking that I was being taken to see the patient, but after a few paces he stopped and eased himself down onto the leg end of a chaise longue.

"Sit down for a moment, Ernesto." He waved me to a chair facing him. "There's nothing wrong with Don Manuel that won't keep. Would you like a drink?"

"No thank you."

"Quite right. Much too early."

I sat and waited while he lit his cigar. Finally he looked up.

"Are you very angry with me, Ernesto?"

"Angry, Don Paco?"

He tossed the spent match into an ashtray.

"For getting you mixed up with us here."

"Should I be?"

"You might. It took a lot of maneuvering I can tell you. Paris wanted us in Guadeloupe. Tight security very easy there, they said. I suggested St. Martin. I knew they wouldn't fall for that. Easy access to the Dutch is the last thing they want for us at the moment. So we compromised on St. Paul. They made a big concession of it, of course. They knew I wanted you in the picture, though they pretended not to. Giving us that idiot Massot when I asked for a Spanish-speaking doctor must have seemed a pretty little joke. But the joke turned sour on them. It seems they took Massot's own word for it that he could speak Spanish. Didn't check. Once I had that fiasco to dangle under their noses they couldn't refuse me. Though they tried. Talked about how essential your work was to the hospital. Even had the impertinence to suggest that it might be politically unwise to bring you in. Provincial half-wits!"

I was by now quite angry but did my best not to show it.

"Is Don Manuel aware of this maneuvering of yours, Uncle Paco?"

He smirked. "That's better. I was waiting for you to call me that. Had to annoy you first though."

"I asked if Don Manuel knows that . . ."

"Of course he doesn't know." He spoke sharply. "Foreign affairs—and in our case that means relations with the governments that kindly tolerate our presence on their territory—are my business. And a very squalid business it can be. You know that even though you've tried to keep out of it. But someone has to take the kicks and see that the leader keeps his dignity. It's too easy for conspirators in exile to become ridiculous. That, too, you must know." He paused. "I was sorry to hear about your mother."

"Thank you."

"Though I think you were wise not to relieve your feelings legally on those thieves who swindled her."

"You know about that then?"

"That, and a great deal more, Ernesto. More perhaps than you realize. I made it my business to keep tabs on Florida. And on you of course."

"Avuncular interest, Don Paco?"

"Certainly not. Your name's Castillo. Do you think it's forgotten at home?"

"Sentimentally remembered by a few perhaps. For political purposes, I would think, quite forgotten."

He shook his head. "Even those Florida fools know better than that. They designated you heir to the Party leadership. There was even talk of making you president in exile. Oh, I don't blame you for keeping your distance from that kind of foolishness, but that's not to say that there was no element *at all* of sense in it."

"There's gold in every liter of seawater I'm told. That doesn't make it worthwhile to keep bottles of the stuff."

He grinned. "So that's the way you see it. I am both glad and relieved. But I should warn you, Ernesto. Don Manuel thinks differently. His view is that those Florida idiots always mishandled you—" he leaned forward slightly —"that you have never been *effectively tempted.*" The moment he had said the words, he flung up his hands defensively as if I had been about to strike him. "You must make allowances, Ernesto, please. Many things have changed with us recently, things I cannot yet discuss even with you. Don

Manuel has been subjected to unusual, sometimes terrible, pressures. We all have."

"So I would imagine. One oil company would be bad enough. A consortium of five, plus—" I hesitated elaborately—"plus other interested parties must be quite oppressive."

I hadn't really expected much of a reaction; all I had meant to do was try out Elizabeth's theory on someone to whom, even if there were only a grain of truth in it, it might mean something. The result was surprising. Uncle Paco's dewlaps suddenly became still.

"I suppose Gillon has been talking," he said finally. "Or was it Delvert?"

"It wasn't Gillon and I don't know anyone named Delvert." I stood up. "My appointment here was for eleven o'clock. It is now ten past. My patient is leader of the Democratic Socialist Party and entitled to respect as well as courtesy. I don't think I should keep him waiting any longer."

The smile returned but very faintly. After a moment he nodded towards the terrace door.

"There's a bell there," he said. "Ring it. The man, Antoine, will show you up."

I found the button and pressed it, but as the sound of the distant bell reached the terrace he spoke again.

"Don Manuel will try to change your mind."

I looked back. He was pointing his cigar at me and moving the end in small circles as if he expected it to cast some sort of spell on me.

"About what, Uncle Paco?" I asked. "Oil consortia?"

He giggled. "No, Ernesto. About the amount of gold in seawater."

By then the butler was approaching. It was to the butler he spoke as I turned away.

"I'll be here when the Doctor comes down, Antoine. Make sure that he doesn't leave without seeing me. Monsieur Villegas will receive him now."

Villegas has a vast bedroom-cum-study with three tall windows looking out over the Grand Mamelon to the sea. The air-conditioning is formidably efficient.

He rose from his desk to greet me and for a moment I thought it was my father standing there. Then I remembered something long forgotten. My father's political protégés, the up-and-coming Party men he favored, had always been of the same physical type, youthful projections of himself. It must have been a disappointment to him that I took after my mother's side of the family.

Villegas, anyway, is remarkably like him. Is it possible that the similarity has been cultivated?

He is tall with only a small paunch, and, for a man of his age, apparently well-preserved. The complexion is pale, smooth and clear, the thick grey hair carefully tended. There is a patrician air about him, which makes it easy to forget that *his* father was a customs inspector; just as the candid brown eyes, staring through one into the middle distance as if in a search for truth, make it easy to forget that he is a politician. He has glasses which, while I was there, he held mostly in his left hand, raising them to his eyes now and then as if they were a lorgnette. It is the sort of mannerism that could have been acquired through his work as a university lecturer. He wore a pale blue shirt with a dark blue cardigan, white slacks and espadrilles. On the desk I noticed a box of cellulose tissues. As he came forward he stuffed a used one into his shirt pocket.

He shook my hand warmly. "Delighted to see you, Doctor Castillo. Truly a pleasure." He smelled faintly of cigar smoke and an eau-de-toilette.

As I made the appropriate responses he patted my shoulder and held up his glasses to look me over.

"I can recognize you, I think," he went on, "but only just."

"From old photographs, Don Manuel?"

"Not at all. We have in fact met before, though I would be most surprised if you had remembered." He led me to a sofa and we sat down sideways so as to face one another.

"It was at the Mass for your father," he said.

"Oh."

"Yes. You behaved with great dignity and calm. I have a son who is now just about your age then. He is reasonably serious, I think—indeed he has hopes of being accepted as a student by the Massachusetts Institute of Technology—but he has never had to face that kind of situation."

"We all hope that he never has to, Don Manuel."

I was also hoping fervently that he would now drop the subject, but he seemed determined to pursue it.

"Naturally in your case the Mass was only one of a series of ordeals. There had been the fracas at the airport and then the funeral, to say nothing of the student demonstrations and the street fighting. The Mass was in the nature of a culmination. That is why I would have been surprised if you had remembered our meeting, even though poor Hermanos introduced us. I had the impression, admirably calm and dignified though you were, that you were beyond feeling very much that day, that your senses were by then completely numb."

"Not entirely, Don Manuel, though I was certainly pre-occupied. There had been talk by the army commander of forbidding a public Mass for my father. My mother was deeply disturbed by the threat. The Mass was permitted only after she and I had agreed that we, the whole family, would quietly leave the country immediately afterwards. The agreement was negotiated on our behalf by a man my mother trusted, a man we believed to have been my father's friend."

"Ah yes. The trusted, the ever-faithful Acosta!" The sneer in his voice was more weary than bitter. "*Just for a few weeks, Doña Concepcion, until passions have cooled. I can almost hear him saying it.* Naturally your mother be-

lieved him. I've no doubt you believed him too. And who
could blame you? How could she, how could you, have
known that tricking the Castillo family into exile was just
part of a larger plan of repression and that the total pro-
scription of our Party had already been decided upon? Let
me tell you, Doctor, I was deceived myself at first."

His tone and raised eyebrows invited me to question the
statement.

"You were, Don Manuel?"

"At first, yes. For a few hours anyway. You were not
alone believe me. The loss of our Party leader at that junc-
ture was a demoralizing blow. But it should not have deprived all of us of our senses. If the Party Committee had
acted promptly and cohesively, if instead of merely threat-
ening a general strike, the Committee had called one instantly and held to its resolve during those three decisive
days, things would have been very different. But instead
of acting they debated, instead of attacking they listened
to what they deluded themselves into believing were the
voices of reason."

He shook his head sorrowfully and leaned back on the
sofa arm as if better to support the weight of his memories.
After a moment he cleared his throat.

"I at least had some excuse," he said. "When the major
crime was committed, at the moment of the assassination, I
was in New York. I will never forget it. There was a television news flash. The announcer didn't get your father's
name quite right and I called the Washington embassy hoping to find that it was all a mistake. But no. So, for most
of those critical three days I was in airport lounges waiting
for flights delayed by the weather, or in piston-engined
planes missing connecting flights which had taken off on
time. When at last I arrived back in the capital the damage
was already done. Not that my presence, my lone voice,
would have made much difference. We of the true left were
already thought of as intransigent doctrinaires. But even

one small voice can inject doubt if nothing more. As it was, attending the Memorial Mass with the rest of the Committee was my last official act as a member of that august body. Forty-eight hours later most of us were fugitives. The rest, including the faithful Acosta, were busy making their peace with reaction."

He tried unsuccessfully to repress a sneeze. It seemed a good moment to remind him that I was there in my professional capacity.

"Well," I said briskly, "most of them are dead now, and from natural causes."

"Including the faithful Acosta, yes. What did he die of, Doctor? Do you know?"

"I've no idea. Except in accident cases the newspapers here don't usually give medical details when they report a death."

"You weren't curious enough to inquire?"

"No, Don Manuel. My medical curiosity is mostly confined to living patients. You, for example. I can hear that you have some sort of sinus congestion. Is that what you consulted Doctor Massot about?"

The name did the trick. He sat up instantly. "Don't talk to me about that fool. He came, authorized by that policeman of yours, to make a general examination. In passing I told him I'd had a stuffed-up head ever since I came here."

"You've had it for two months?"

"Well, for the past few weeks anyway. I thought at first that it might be the change of altitude after Mexico City, or perhaps the different pollens in the air."

"Do you suffer from hay fever?"

"Not seriously and never before at this time of the year."

"Have you taken your temperature?"

"Of course. Every day. Normal. I told Massot all this. I thought he might give me an antihistamine to clear it up. He did give me some pills."

"They didn't do any good?"

"I had violent diarrhea for two days, if you call that good. They did nothing for my sinuses."

"You told Doctor Massot?"

"Of course. He told me to increase the dose. Naturally I didn't. I threw the things away. Obviously the man was incompetent. We told Gillon so."

"I see."

And I did see. Spanish-speaking persons suffering from sinus congestion or head colds commonly describe themselves as being *constipado*. With French- and English-speaking physicians who don't happen to know that the usual Spanish word for constipated is *estrenido* this has often led to misunderstandings. But as there seemed no point in trying to salvage Dr. Massot's reputation in that household I didn't bother to explain.

"Do you sleep here with the air-conditioning turned up like this?" I asked.

"Of course."

"How about Doña Julia? Doesn't she find it a little extreme?"

"Oh she sleeps in her own room. Anyway she doesn't like air-conditioning."

"The windows are well screened against insects here. Have you tried sleeping with the windows open and the air-conditioning turned off?"

"Why should I? What is the use of air-conditioning if you turn it off? Then you get the humidity."

"Your sinuses might prefer it. If they didn't you could always turn the air-conditioning on again."

"Very well. I will try doing as you suggest. You don't think an antihistamine would help?"

"I'll know better later when I've had a chance to examine you. Have you any other troubles?"

"Yes, here." He put a hand on the left lower quadrant of the abdomen. "Pain and cramps, except that I don't seem to have them at the moment. It is always the way when one sees doctors. Pains disappear."

"Any nausea, vomiting?"

"When I had the cramps, yes. This was two weeks ago. It went away. Some sort of food poisoning I suppose. I had a little temperature, but then I often have temperatures. For no reason that I know of."

When I had extracted as much of his medical history as I could from him I put my notebook aside.

"Well I'd better have a look at you, Don Manuel. Would you take off your clothes?"

"All of them?"

"Please. And, if you agree, it might be wise if we turned down the air-conditioning a bit."

The examination was as thorough as I could make it under the circumstances. He was completely cooperative and took a keen interest in everything I did; almost too keen. The check-up procedures employed by the American British Hospital in Mexico City were highly familiar to him and he amused himself by comparing them with mine. Examining a patient for the first time calls for a good deal of concentration. It was disturbing to have to answer his questions as I worked, even the easy ones.

Why, for instance, did American and British doctors measure blood pressure in one way while doctors with European training measured it in another?

Answer: they don't measure it differently, they merely use different units of measurement to express the result. The Americans and the British use millimeters, the Europeans centimeters. For example, his blood pressure was 190/100 in millimeters and 19/10 in centimeters. Yes, it should be lower; but I would take it again in a little while and perhaps it would be different. Sit up please and take deep breaths through the mouth.

Not all the questions were irrelevant. As I was taking a blood specimen from him he asked if a serum thyroxine check would be done. I told him that it would.

"You will find the figure a little high, as much as sixteen."

"Yes, that is on the high side."

"The hospital has its own laboratory facilities?"

"We have an Institut Pasteur attached to us."

"Do you do radioactive iodine uptake tests?"

"Not here. We get those done in Fort de France."

"Don't trouble about it in my case. I had the test done six months ago. Everything okay."

"I'm glad to hear it." Later I said: "I must ask you to come into the hospital for X-rays, Don Manuel. Just for an hour or two."

"The lower bowel?"

"It's probably nothing to worry about, but we'd better be sure. We can do some other tests at the same time."

"Well you don't have to worry about kidney function. I had a serum creatinine done at the same time as the iodine uptake. Point nine milligrams percent. Nothing wrong there."

"It doesn't sound as if there is, no."

He watched me closely, sitting on the bed in his underpants, as I packed away the various specimens I had taken.

"These X-rays you want. Are they absolutely necessary?"

"I'm afraid so. You see, these abdominal pains you complain of—you didn't have them when you were in Mexico, did you?"

"I had good health in Mexico. When will you know about the tests you're doing?"

"I will have some results tomorrow, the rest the day after. If I may telephone when I have them all we can perhaps arrange another appointment for me to give you my report."

"What about the X-rays?"

"We can arrange for those by telephone also."

"Very well." He went to the nearest windows and flung

them open. "Hot and sticky," he commented as the air from outside came in. "I hope it pleases you, Doctor."

"I hope you sleep well tonight, Don Manuel."

He got the tissue box from his desk. When I left he was blowing his nose vigorously.

Uncle Paco called to me from the terrace as I reached the bottom of the stairs.

I went in and sat down facing him. An iced rum drink stood in the arm recess of his chaise longue. He pointed to it.

"Do you want one of these, Ernesto?"

"No thank you. I have to go back to the hospital."

"Well?"

"As I have told Don Manuel it will be a day or two before I have the test results. I shall also want him to come to the hospital for X-rays."

"What's the matter with him?"

"With his nasal passages, excessive air-conditioning. I told him to try sleeping with the windows open. That may or may not be good advice. I'll know in a couple of days."

"And what else?"

"I don't know, Uncle Paco. I hope to find out. If there is anything to find out, that is. Meanwhile, there is one question I didn't ask him. I thought I'd ask you instead."

"Well?"

"How much alcohol does he drink?"

"Your colleague Massot asked me the same question. I don't think he believed the answer he got from Don Manuel himself. The answer is none at all."

"No wine, no beer? Nothing?"

"No alcohol. By that I mean rum, whisky, vodka, gin, brandy, tequila—alcohol. He drinks wine in moderation, beer occasionally. It's the slight slurring in his speech that you're talking about, isn't it?"

"Yes."

"His thoughts sometimes race ahead of his capacity to

translate them into words. It is an old failing of his. Or a
strength some might call it, an asset. With some men whose
minds work like lightning, ahead of their speech, the result
is a stammer, or even incoherence. With Don Manuel it is
elision of some consonants. Delivering a prepared speech,
when he knows in advance what he is going to say, his dic-
tion is impeccable. But try to explain such a thing to Doctor Massot!"

"I see what you mean."

Uncle Paco beamed. "I'm so glad, Ernesto."

"You said that it's an old failing of his. How old?"

"Ever since I've known him. Now tell me, Ernesto. Be
frank. You liked him? It's important you know. He wants
you on his side. Oh, I don't mean just politically, but for
the sake of the past." He heaved himself forward on the
chaise and took a swallow of his drink. "I will tell you
something in confidence. When he knew that you were to
be his doctor he confessed to being ashamed."

"Of what?"

"Of what indeed! You may well ask, as I did. Do you
know what he answered?"

"I can't imagine."

"He was ashamed because when your father was murdered by those hoodlums, he, Don Manuel, was being
wined and dined far away in New York. He even went to
bed and slept. It wasn't until he saw the morning newspapers hours later that he knew. He still remembers, you
see. He is a sensitive man. He has a heart, Ernesto."

"I'm sure he has. So he had to read about it in a newspaper."

"In New York how else would he find out?"

"You're behind the times Uncle Paco. Even twelve years
ago most New York hotel rooms had television sets. According to Don Manuel there was a news flash, after which
he called the embassy in Washington for confirmation. Not
that it matters how he heard the news. The important thing

is, I gather, that he was far away in New York at the time
and in no way involved with what was happening at home.
Is that right?"

We stared at one another for what seemed a long time,
then I went to the bell and rang it.

When Antoine came Uncle Paco told him to show me
out. That was all. We didn't say another word.

The following is the report I wrote up from my notes
when I got back to the hospital. It was written as a preface
to the hospital case history and for inclusion in the medical
dossier normally kept on every patient treated here.

VILLEGAS LOPEZ, MANUEL. *Age 51. Civil
engineer, politician.*

FAMILY HISTORY. *Father died age 48, probably of
peritonitis. Mother still living and well, aged 73. Has
one sister living and well. Married: two sons, one
daughter.*

PERSONAL HISTORY. *Appendix removed age 25.
Patient had urinary tract study carried out in Mexico
City (A. B. Hospital?) 6 years ago. Intravenous pyelo-
grams were made. Study appeared normal. Doctor told
him he had probably passed gravel two weeks earlier.*

*Cardio-respiratory history negative. Has a little ar-
thritis, occasionally helped by physiotherapy.*

*Complains of pain left lower quadrant, nausea, ab-
dominal distention and cramps, malaise. Also unex-
plained fevers. Symptoms not now present having
"gone away" two weeks ago.*

*No dysuria, no hematuria. No history venereal dis-
ease. Former tests (also Mexico City) negative.*

ON EXAMINATION. *Extra-ocular movements were
normal. Pupils are round, regular, reacted to light and
accommodation actively. Ears negative. Patient has
some sinus congestion. Pharynx clear however. Teeth
in fair condition. Gums not inflamed. Thyroid not en-*

larged. *No adenopathy. Thorax full and rounded. Breasts normal. Lungs clear to percussion and ausculta- tion. Pulse 96. Temperature 37.4. Respiratory rate 22. The blood pressure was taken several times. Range was from 19/10 to 16/9.5. Cardiac rythm was regular. Ap- pendix scar. Liver and spleen not enlarged. There was tenderness over McBurney's point. No hernia but right inguinal ring appeared to be widely patent. Rectal tone was normal. Extremities well-formed, symmetrical. Back straight. Feet normal. Knee kicks and biceps were equal and active. Babinski and Romberg negative. Kid- neys normal to palpation. No costovertebral tender- ness. Bladder negative. Penis and testes normal. Pros- tate soft, benign.*

Blood and urine specimens taken.

Patient said radioactive iodine uptake test made Mexico. No abnormality found. Serum creatinine test (also Mexico) also stated to be satisfactory.

Informed patient necessity X-ray examinations.

PRELIMINARY FINDINGS. *Diverticulosis. Possible diverticulitis. Hypertension probably connected pa- tient's political activities and related emotional factors. Mild thiazide therapy should be considered.*

OTHER OBSERVATIONS. *Patient has slight speech im- pediment involving slurring of consonants. Patient seems conscious of difficulty and endeavors correct it. Not always able to do so. Said to be very light drinker. Saw no reason to doubt this.*

N.B. *According to P. Segura, friend of patient, impediment is of long standing and due inability speech faculty to keep pace with mental processes. Patient's awareness impediment and partial ability to control or correct seems contradict Segura's view.*

SIGNED: CASTILLO

That was written on Tuesday afternoon.

Later I spoke to Dr. Brissac who in turn spoke to the technician in charge of the X-ray department. As a result (the X-ray dept. is always overworked and understaffed) I was able as a favor to obtain a choice of appointments for Villegas—10:00 hrs. on either Thursday, Friday or Saturday.

Then telephoned Les Muettes and asked to speak to Don Paco. Instead I was given Doña Julia.

She promised to let me know by the following morning which appointment would be acceptable, and did so. That was on Wednesday 14. The appointment chosen was for Friday morning. On her husband's behalf she asked if the results of the tests taken were then known. I said that I would go through the results with him when I saw him at the hospital on Friday.

On the morning of Thursday 15 the manservant Antoine telephoned to say that Villegas would not be keeping the Friday appointment. No reason given. I asked if Villegas was ill and was told that he was not. I also asked if he wished to make a later appointment. Antoine did not know.

I informed Commissaire Gillon by telephone of the situation. He informed me, in turn, that he had just received by hand a letter from Paco Segura.

The letter informed him that neither my services nor those of any other doctor were at present required by Señor Villegas or his family. Their health was excellent. In case of need, or in an emergency, Commissaire Gillon would be at once informed. Meanwhile he could be assured of Señor Segura's distinguished sentiments.

Gillon was understandably annoyed.

"Well, Doctor," he asked curtly, "what's gone wrong?"

"I don't know."

"What about these stomach X-rays that you had arranged for? Are they important? Urgent?"

"Important, obviously, or I would not have ordered them.

Urgent, not particularly. They are needed to confirm, or dispose of, a tentative diagnosis I had made."

"Of what? Some dread disease? You didn't frighten the man out of his wits in order to impress him by any chance?"

"Certainly not. There was no discussion of a dread disease as you call it, and I didn't hint darkly at any such possibility. I don't see how I could possibly have scared him. In fact he was interested in knowing the results of his blood and urine tests. Obviously he wasn't enthusiastic about having a lower tract X-ray. It's not painful, but as it involves a barium enema it's not something that anyone would look forward to. But a frightening prospect? No. Does the letter ask for the results of the tests?"

"No. In effect, it requests nothing but your future absence from Les Muettes. The request can be denied of course."

"You don't expect me to force my way in there?"

"Not quite. Your instructions are, for the moment, to do nothing."

"Do I inform Doctor Brissac?"

"No. I said you do nothing. Nothing more, that is, until you hear from me."

"When is that likely to be, Commissaire? I shall be on night duty here tonight and tomorrow."

"I'll bear that in mind. However, I don't think that I shall have to disturb your sleep. This development means that I must consult with Paris. It will be at least two days, I suspect, before the situation can be clarified. Just keep yourself available, Doctor."

"Very well, Commissaire."

Night Sister came bearing coffee and a somewhat peculiar kind of olive branch. Concerning her pigmented nevus, what would be my advice? Should she have it surgically removed?

I was obviously being tested. Replied that unless nevus changing texture or was causing irritation best left alone. Possibility scar unless highly skilled (and expensive) cosmetic surgery resorted to.

Rewarded approving smile. Specialist in Fort de France had given her exactly same advice. Dr. Frigo is forgiven.

I wasn't absolutely frank with Gillon when we spoke on Thursday morning and this troubles me.

Uncle Paco's letter was a surprise, of course, but it was not to me as totally inexplicable as I made out.

Clearly I had offended him, and the letter to Gillon had been his way of expressing his displeasure.

But had it been only that?

Could he have concluded belatedly that letting me into the magic circle had been a mistake, and that the possible value of having someone named Castillo around and involved was after all outweighed by the risk that this particular Castillo represented?

Twice in twenty-four hours, and in two different ways, I have been told that when my father was murdered Villegas was far away in New York. I have also been told that there is no *conclusive* evidence that any other member of the Party was involved.

Why?

When I had been offensive to Uncle Paco had I only wounded him a little, or had something been said to give him cause for a deeper anxiety?

Perhaps that is why my services are no longer required at Les Muettes. If I'm not there, I can't ask inconvenient questions.

But I can ask them of myself.

Must make a list—QUESTIONS FOR MYSELF: in particular, questions hitherto regarded as irrelevant because too hypothetical.

1. *If ever I were to find out for certain who was behind Papa's assassination, who it really was who made those efficient arrangements for killing him, what would I do? Assuming that there was one specially guilty man, i.e. a ringleader among the culpable, would I expose his guilt to the world, and, if so, how would I expose it?*

2. *Would I try to bring him to justice, and, if so, whose justice?*

3. *Would I try, if it were in any way possible for me to do so, to kill him myself?*

4. *Or would I try to forget the knowledge gained, pretend to myself that it was inconclusive and steadfastly look the other way?*

No answers.

Should try to think of some.

It will be interesting to see what Gillon's consultations bring forth.

I am already vulnerable. If it is decided that I am, after all, to continue as Villegas' medical adviser, then I shall be doubly so.

As Monsieur Albert so rightly said, a doctor doesn't need a gun if he wants to kill.

Part Two

Symptoms, Signs and Diagnosis

RUE RACINE 11
FORT LOUIS
ST. PAUL-LES-ALIZÉS

Friday 16 May Morning

The temptation to postpone until tomorrow what I should do tonight is strong; and if I were just now advising a patient in my condition I would tell him to yield to it.

"During the past two days," I would say brusquely, "you have had at most six hours sleep. You have also been subjected to psychological pressures greater than those usually associated with your work. You need proper rest. No arguments, please. Throw away that coffee. Take two of these tablets with a glass of water and go straight to bed. Now."

Instead, I shall drink the coffee.

So much has happened today; and if this record is to have any protective value at all as far as I am concerned it must be immediate as well as complete.

So, strong coffee and plenty of sugar. The sleeping tablets will have to wait.

At eight-thirty this morning I was telephoned by Commissaire Gillon. My initial incoherence must have made it plain that I had been asleep, for he was grudgingly apologetic.

"I am aware, Doctor, that after a period of night duty you normally have a free day. I am sorry."

"Well, what is it? Has Villegas changed his mind about the X-rays? If he wants them today after all, I'll have to check with. . . ."

"No, no. We have heard nothing more from Les Muettes. But I have heard from Paris. I must ask you to be in my office at five this afternoon. It is most important, essential."

"You wake me now to tell me that?"

"As I say it is important. I could not risk failing to contact you later. You might have been out."

"Even when I am off duty I am on call. The hospital always knows where to find me."

"I didn't know that. Nevertheless. . . ."

"Five o'clock. Couldn't you make it six?"

"No, Doctor. Five o'clock, please."

"If you're expecting me to bring a written report. . . ."

"No, that will not be necessary today."

"All right."

I tried to get back to sleep but only succeeded in dozing.

The femme-de-ménage arrives at eleven. Mine is the second apartment on her list and Friday is the day on which she assaults it with the electric floor polisher. This is one of her set routines, none of which can be varied unless one is prepared to engage in a major shouting match and ignore the subsequent sulks.

I was lunching with Elizabeth at the Hotel Ajoupa. Partly to kill time, but mostly to get away from the noise of the polisher, I took my moto to the garage for its long overdue servicing. The man there said that he would do what he could but again repeated an earlier diagnosis: a new plug might relieve some of the symptoms but the improvement would only be temporary. The scrapheap beckoned. Why postpone the inevitable? What I really needed was that nearly new Simca over there, a car which he had personally serviced and could personally guarantee. Just the thing for a busy doctor, and for me there would be a special discount. On the subject of my moto he and Dr. Brissac were obviously of the same mind.

Lunch at the Ajoupa can never be entirely enjoyable. At its best the food may be just palatable, but the restaurant service is always bad. All the competent waitresses work in the more profitable bar areas. Those in the restaurant are

either languid beauties who do nothing but admire themselves in the mirrors or boisterous village girls who shout a
lot at one another, bang their hips against the furniture and
drop things. They are largely unsupervised. The chefs de
rang supposedly in charge are hard-faced women who
patrol their tables looking not for inadequacies in the service, but for dissatisfied guests whom they can intimidate.
They carry heavy leather-bound menus which they slap
against their thighs menacingly or weigh in their hands like
police truncheons when receiving complaints.

Of course, Elizabeth is treated with more consideration
than a mere guest in the hotel, but not even she goes totally
unscathed. On one occasion she found her usual table en-
gulfed in an all-male luncheon organized by the St. Paul
chapter of Lions International; on another she was mistak-
enly charged with a Modified American Plan bill for a
party of forty Italian tourists. Still, though I had no ex-
pectation of eating well, I had been looking forward to our
lunch. During the past two days we had only spoken on the
telephone, and although my accounts of the visit to Les
Muettes and its sequel had been necessarily guarded, I had
told her enough to let her know the sort of predicament I
was in and how worried I was about it.

So, I had expected sympathy. Instead, I was subjected to
a hostile interrogation concerned with the very subjects
about which I was least willing to speak freely.

She began by demanding a word-for-word description of
everything that had been done and said at Les Muettes.
Then she began to cross-examine me, picking over what I
had told her as if it were all somehow suspect.

Not realizing immediately that I was under attack, I was
at first indiscreet. Then, becoming defensive, I foolishly
took refuge behind the fact that Villegas was, technically
speaking anyway, still my patient.

She pounced on that instantly. "Uncle Paco isn't your
patient. You weren't prodding *his* stomach, were you?

Couldn't you have asked him about these absurd alibis?"

"Alibis?"

"Well, that's obviously what they were." She pointed her fork at me. "And from what you told me before you started babbling about ethics, that's how they were presented, all gift-wrapped and ready for you when you arrived like—" words failed her for a moment—"like bottles of cheap scent."

"I made my feelings plain enough. The fact that they now want to get rid of me shows that."

"Who knows why they want to get rid of you? Perhaps Madame decided that she would like an older man after all. You didn't question the alibis."

"I was there as a doctor, not an examining magistrate. Besides, what was there to question? The fact that Villegas was in New York?"

"Of course not. What difference does it make where he was? When the Archduke Franz Ferdinand was assassinated at Sarajevo, Colonel Dimitrijevic, the great Apis of the Black Hand, was far away in Belgrade. Did that make him innocent of the crime?"

"The circumstances were entirely different, Elizabeth, and you know it."

"A bit different, I agree, but not entirely so. Those who incite or organize political assassinations are usually somewhere else when the event itself takes place. We are speaking of conspiracies, remember, not the unassisted acts of madmen. What use would alibis have been to Apis? None. There can only be three explanations of these alibis you have been given. The obvious one is that these people think you are stupid."

"Yes, that *had* occurred to me."

"But you didn't believe it. Neither would I have done so. What about the alternative explanations?"

"I've considered one. Aware of my past associations with those Florida idiots, Villegas and Uncle Paco may imagine that I believe, or half-believe, in that old nonsensical treason theory about Papa's murder."

"Well don't you?"

"No." I spoke firmly enough but with Elizabeth I am not good at dissembling. When she smiled I amended the denial. "All right, let's say then that I haven't thought of it as anything but discredited for a very long time."

"You mean until another set of persons you don't altogether trust start telling you that it is not only nonsensical but also inconceivable and impossible?"

"I suppose so."

"Then hadn't you better start considering the third explanation?"

"What third explanation?"

She pushed the remains of her food aside as if about to draw maps on the tablecloth.

"When there is guilt to be hidden," she said, "pointless but insistent protestations of innocence can make an effective smokescreen—not too thick to see through, but thick enough to make the eyes water and keep them peering in the wrong direction."

She squinted at me through narrowed eyes to show me what she meant.

"I'm not peering in any direction."

She showed signs of impatience.

"You've been told twice in one day what Villegas was doing and thinking twelve years ago at the time of the assassination, so you must be peering at him. Has anyone told you in the same elaborate detail what Uncle Paco was doing and thinking at the time?"

I snorted.

"Well *have* they?"

"I know what he was doing."

"But not what he was thinking. According to you, Uncle Paco has always been an intriguer. He is also rich. Do you think that assassination plots like the one against your father can be organized and carried out by amateurs? Of course not. It was a professional job. Even you have never disputed that. Professional criminals were employed by other professionals clever enough to cover their tracks. Who paid these professionals? The security forces of the junta? Perhaps. But why not Uncle Paco?"

"You're talking nonsense, Elizabeth. Uncle Paco! What possible motive could he have had?"

"Motive? The usual one for an intriguer. Perceiving, or so he thinks, that the time for decision has arrived, he resolves an uncertain situation by polarizing the forces involved through an act of violence. Always with the best of intentions naturally. What motive did Apis have when he ordered the assassination at Sarajevo? The starting of a World War? Absurd! Franz Ferdinand was killed not just because he was a Hapsburg but because he was the throne heir with plans for conciliating the Serbs. There was to be a South Slav state within the Empire. Apis well knew, and so did lots of others, that such a state would have at once deprived the northern Serbs of their grievances and the Serbian Nationalists of their legitimate complaints. That wasn't mindless terrorism, but an act of political calculation."

"Or *mis*calculation."

"Certainly. It failed. But it failed because events took a turn that a petty intriguer like Apis could not have foreseen."

"Very upsetting."

She ignored my feeble sarcasm. "According to Villegas, or so you tell me, that is what happened when your father was murdered. Events took an unforeseen turn. Instead of seizing their chance and exploiting the situation, the left lost its nerve and let the junta decide the outcome. Your father's Party needed a Cavour, or perhaps a Trotsky. All they had were Party hacks and young Señor Villegas far away in New York."

"All of which suggests that you're mistaken, Elizabeth. The man, or group of men, with the ability and resources to plan my father's assassination must also have been prepared to exploit it. The junta was so prepared. There's your answer."

"Answer? Nonsense! The junta? A lot of brass-braided geriatrics prepared for nothing but their pensions and the consolations of the Church. They took three days to act and only then because the landowners and their bullyboys were poking sharp sticks in their behinds."

Her voice had risen and we were beginning to attract attention. I said: "There's no need to shout."

"I'm not shouting. I am simply trying to point out that men able to plan assassinations can't necessarily plan at the same time for all the consequences of success. They are tacticians not strategists. By winning one battle, their privately conceived battle, they often lose the campaign. Next time you see Uncle Paco ask him what *he* was doing at the time of the assassination."

"I told you. I *know* what he was doing at the time. He was in the news photographs, standing on the steps of the hotel about four meters from my father when the shots were fired. He was carrying a large bouquet of flowers."

She pounced. "What for? To distinguish him clearly for the marksmen across the street? To make sure they didn't shoot by mistake the nice man who was paying them?"

"The occasion," I said patiently, "had been a reception inaugurating a new cut-flower export co-operative. Several of the men with my father had kept their presentation bouquets. Two of them were wounded."

"But not Uncle Paco. What color was his bouquet?"

"I don't know. The pictures were black-and-white."

But I did know. I once saw a color picture taken by the official Party photographer. All the bouquets except Uncle Paco's had been red, and mostly of arum lilies. His had been made out of orange strelitzia.

I went on quickly to smother the lie before she became suspicious. "Anyway, Commissaire Gillon isn't peering through smokescreens," I said. "According to a secret report made to the Quai d'Orsay at the time there was no conclusive evidence implicating any member of the Democratic Socialist Party in the plot. He told me this officially."

"Pooh! Who made this secret report? S-dec?"

"I didn't ask."

"Why not?"

"Because it was made clear that I wouldn't get an answer."

"You're too timid."

"Possibly. Frankly, the less I see of Commissaire Gillon the better I like it." I told her then about the five o'clock meeting to which I had been summoned. "It can't last long," I added. "I thought that I might reserve a table at Chez Lafcadio for dinner."

Unexpectedly she poured the rest of the wine into her glass and drank it.

"I'm sorry, Ernesto dear, but I can't see you tonight. I hadn't expected it but I'll have to be here."

"Business?"

"Of a sort. I have to dine with an emissary from my husband."

"A lawyer?"

"Not exactly."

I didn't pursue the matter. I could have suggested our meeting later in the evening and she might have agreed; but I know by now that Elizabeth depressed prefers to be, and is better, left alone. Later that evening, after a conversation about her marriage, she would certainly be depressed, and probably quarrelsome too.

I walked with her back to the gallery in the hotel shopping arcade.

There was a man there peering through the window and trying the locked door. When he saw Elizabeth he straightened up and said, "Ah, madame." Then he pointed at the door. "I wasn't trying to break in. It says here that you open again at two-thirty."

He spoke French easily but with an accent that I couldn't place; not Yanqui, I thought, though that was the nationality his height, clothes and general appearance suggested. He was about forty with plenty of straw-colored hair and looked as if he played tennis or swam a lot to keep fit. The face intelligent, a certain air of authority. An upper-echelon executive of some sort was my first impression.

Elizabeth answered him in English as she took out her keys. "In this place, Mr. Rosier, you can never believe notices like that. Most people take a siesta. Did you want to have another look around?"

"Well, since you're here, that was the idea. I thought I might browse a little if that's all right with you." He looked inquiringly at both of us.

"This is Doctor Castillo," she said, "a friend who works at the hospital. Yes, by all means browse. I only came back to write some letters."

"Doctor Castillo?" We shook hands. "I'm Bob Rosier. You may not know it, Doctor, but you have a reputation with the help here. If a man's just a *little* sick he takes aspirin or entero-vioform. If he needs help badly he takes a cab to the hospital and asks for Doctor Castillo."

That story could have come from only one source.

"You've been talking to an old porter named Louis, Mr. Rosier. As a young man he fell into the hold of a banana ship and suffered brain damage. He's quite harmless but a little peculiar sometimes."

"I'll bear that in mind. Lots of interesting work here, eh?" He looked vacantly about him.

"Yes." I turned to Elizabeth. "Shall we talk tomorrow morning?"

She had been sitting at her desk scribbling something on a pad. As I spoke she tore off the sheet on which she had been writing, folded it and thrust it into my hand. "That's the address you wanted," she said. "I'll call you at the hospital."

I started to look at the paper but she gripped my hand and smiled brightly up at me. "Thank you for lunch, Ernesto."

In fact she had signed for it on the gallery account; but as I opened my mouth to say so she rolled her eyes and I knew that I was being told to go.

Mr. Rosier was gazing thoughtfully at one of the hibiscus canvases. However, as I opened the door he glanced round.

"Nice meeting you, Doctor," he said. "Be seeing you around I hope."

"I hope so too."

Elizabeth waved casually as I left. I waited until I was outside the hotel before I looked at the paper she had given me.

On it she had scrawled: *This one is a spy. Certainly not S-dec. Possibly CIA. Be careful.*

Presumably she meant Rosier. There was a waste basket in the hotel driveway. I thought of discarding the paper in that, then decided that perhaps messages about spies were not the sort of things one casually threw away. Spy fever is infectious. Before getting rid of it I tore the note into small pieces.

Afternoon

At the garage I heard more about the Simca, promised to think it over and at once forgot about it. My moto was running much better on the new plug. By the time I had done some weekend shopping, picked up my laundry and collected a registered package of contact prints from the post office it was getting late. I changed my shirt and walked to the Préfecture.

This time there was no waiting. I was shown straight in to Gillon's office.

There was another man with him who rose as I entered. Gillon, I thought, seemed ill at ease as he introduced us.

"Doctor, this is Commandant Delvert." He cleared his throat before adding: "Commandant Delvert is from Paris."

"Though only just," said the Commandant cheerfully, "and somewhat overfed by Air France on the way. Enchanted to meet you, Doctor."

He did not look in the least overfed.

Commandant Delvert is a tall, lean man, very handsome in an old-fashioned military sort of way. In uniform he would be an imposing figure. The bone structure of the face is quite pronounced with the skin stretched tightly over it. In his forties, brown hair greying and with a small clipped moustache. Not a kilo of superfluous fat anywhere. He reminds me of a photograph, once seen in a book, of General Weygand as a World War I Chief of Staff. I doubt though if Weygand had a particularly pleasant smile. Delvert has. However, it does not reassure me. In my experience unusually pleasant smiles have often been cultivated to conceal highly unpleasant dispositions. Besides, the Commandant is undoubtedly a senior official of S-dec, a "case officer" or something of the sort I imagine, and if even a small fraction of what one has read and heard about that service is true—it appears that Elizabeth may well after all know what she is talking about—a pleasant disposition would not be among the qualifications normally required for the job.

There was an opened bottle of mineral water and a glass on Gillon's desk. Delvert filled the glass and took it with him when he returned to his chair.

Gillon cleared his throat again. "The Commandant is familiar with current developments in the Villegas matter," he said. "However, one or two questions have arisen which we would like you to answer as completely as you can, Doctor. This appointment you made for an X-ray examination which was later cancelled, was it in any sense a routine affair?"

"No, Commissaire. It had a specific purpose."

"What purpose?"

"From the patient's description of his symptoms, though not, I should add, from any direct indications present when I examined him, it is possible that he may suffer from diverticulosis which occasionally flares up into diverticulitis."

"And what, if you please, is that?"

I started to explain when Delvert interrupted.

"Forgive me, Doctor—" the smile came into play—"but I think that this may be one of those occasions when a lay explanation can save time." He turned to Gillon. "I expect your car has tubeless tires now, but when all tires had inner tubes one sometimes saw samples of diverticulitis on the road. Through age and decay or damage, the walls of an outer cover would sometimes split and then the inner tube would bulge through forming bubbles. The same sort of thing can also happen to the human bowel. Most unpleasant I'm told."

"You mean that it could blow out, burst?"

He sounded so horrified that I decided to take over again. "Not often, Commissaire. The Commandant's comparison is valid up to a point, but the pressures involved are rather different. What happens with the colon is that the cavities formed, those bubbles of inner tube he mentioned, sometimes become pockets of infection."

"Like a bad appendix."

"Something like, but . . ."

"Is it serious?"

"It used to be. At one time the length of intestine involved was often removed by surgery. Now the condition
is usually treated quite easily with antibiotics. The patient
is also given advice about diet."

"And Villegas has this condition?"

"I think he may have. It often shows up in persons of
his age. It's quite a common disorder, in fact. It used to be
diagnosed as a colic."

"All very interesting, Doctor—" this was Delvert again—
"but why do you say only that you *think* Villegas may
have it? Can't you tell without X-rays?"

"Usually one can be pretty sure, yes. There is tenderness
and resistance over the infected bowel and abdominal
spasm. It's almost unmistakable."

"But not with Villegas?"

"There were other factors to be considered." I told them
about Dr. Massot and *constipado*.

"Would a powerful laxative have relieved an attack of
this diverticulitis?" Gillon wanted to know.

"No. In fact it could well have made things worse. The
point was that the symptoms he described were exactly
those of diverticulitis."

"But your examination didn't confirm it."

"The diverticula did not seem to be infected at the time.
That wasn't to say they weren't there though. These attacks sometimes subside spontaneously. That's why I ordered the X-rays."

Delvert gave me the smile again. "Did it occur to you
that Villegas might be lying?"

"About his health, do you mean, or about other matters?"

They both gave me sharp looks.

Delvert said: "It's his health we're discussing at the moment."

"It crossed my mind later that he might not have been
entirely truthful about his experience with Doctor Massot."

"Why?"

"It seemed unlikely, when I thought about it, that a man who had been used to having check-ups at the American British Hospital in Mexico City would not long ago have found out that constipation isn't a cold in the head."

"Any conclusion?"

"That Doctor Massot's attempts to speak Spanish had exasperated him, and that he had used the *constipado* blunder as an excuse to get rid of him."

"And have you been appointed in Massot's place?"

"He couldn't have counted on my appointment even if he'd wanted it. Uncle Paco told me that he personally had engineered that. According to him there was strong official opposition to it. I took that to mean opposition from the SDT, the Commissaire here."

Delvert glanced at Gillon. "Would you like to tell him what really happened, Commissaire?"

Gillon looked bland. "There was no official opposition at all," he said. "We asked one simple question. We asked Paco Segura if, in view of your family's political connections, they would not prefer to receive you at Les Muettes as a friend rather than as our official representative. He said that they preferred to receive you in an official capacity. They did make one other request." He glanced questioningly at Delvert.

"Let's leave that for a moment." Delvert reached for a briefcase propped against the leg of his chair. "Let's dispose of the medical items first." From the briefcase he took a thin folder and held it up. "This is a photocopy of Villegas' medical history as it exists at the American British Hospital in Mexico City. I'll trouble you not to inquire how it was obtained. However, it may interest you to know, Doctor, that your diagnosis of diverticulitis was quite correct. It was suspected and confirmed there by X-ray examination three years ago."

I felt myself flushing.

"Your annoyance, Doctor, is understandable, but bear

with me for a moment. I would like to examine some possibilities. Doctor Massot considers Villegas a hypochondriac. Do you?"

"I think he's the kind of man inclined to worry about his
health. If you mean do I think him a *malade imaginaire*, no
I don't."

"Might he be one of those patients who can never wholly
believe what they are told? Could he have been looking to
you for a second opinion?"

"How did they treat the condition in Mexico?"

"They used an oral antibiotic and put him on something
called a low residual diet. That's what you would have
done, too, I gather." He flicked through the file. "Do you
want the name of the drug they gave him?"

"It was ampicillin I expect. Do they say if it worked?"

"Apparently yes. It had to be used, though, on three
separate occasions."

"Three attacks in three years. Not bad. The first would
be the worst—cramps, nausea, high temperature—but once
it had been diagnosed there would be only minor discom-
fort because the antibiotic would be administered promptly
in the early stages of an attack. As I said, this is a very common complaint. There's nothing mysterious about it, Commandant. If the antibiotic used has been found to work
well, with no side-effects, nobody in his senses would be
looking for second opinions."

"Could he have been testing you?"

"He did quite a lot of testing while I was there, referred
to specific blood analyses which, as he probably guessed,
we don't normally carry out here to see if I understood
their importance. He has a certain amount of superficial
expertise. We get this occasionally, especially with patients
who have been exposed to the American yearly check-up
system. They tend to keep scores on themselves. But as for
testing me with diverticulitis, I don't believe it. The symptoms he described would obviously call for X-rays. The

X-rays would show what the trouble was. There would be no test of my competence in that."

"Then we are left with the third explanation—that he wanted to establish a special relationship with you."

I laughed. "By permitting me to diagnose and treat a condition he already knew he had?"

"Why not? In that way he could express his gratitude to you, and you in turn could bask in his confidence. A charade perhaps, but an excellent foundation for mutual trust and esteem, wouldn't you say?"

"Excellent. Except that he changed his mind and dismissed me."

"We don't know that he did."

"The message sent was clear enough."

"But Villegas didn't send it. It came from your Uncle Paco. What did you say to frighten him off, Doctor? Or don't you know?"

I hesitated.

"I would welcome the utmost frankness," he said. "In fact, Doctor, I insist on it."

A long time seemed to elapse before I made up my mind. It can't have been much more than twenty seconds, but after ten of them Commissaire Gillon began to tap his desk with a ballpoint pen. Delvert silenced him with a glance.

Finally I said: "I'm not sure whether I know or not. I think I may have offended Uncle Paco, yes. He was patronizing, treated me like a half-wit, so I responded in kind."

"How?"

"I was a trifle impertinent, I suppose, and I reminded him that I wasn't there to see him but Villegas. One thing he didn't like at all was a reference I made to the Coraza Islands oil consortium. He assumed that I had been told about it by one of you two gentlemen. I don't think he believed me when I denied it."

"And who *did* tell you about it?" Gillon's reaction was quite violent.

Delvert intervened smoothly. "I expect the Doctor heard some gossip at the Hotel Ajoupa." The look he gave me was faintly amused. "Wasn't that it?"

"Yes."

"What were the other things he didn't like?"

"I objected to being told for the second time in one hour that Villegas was in New York when my father was assassinated."

"Just that?"

"I pointed out some inconsistencies between Villegas' account and his own. Minor details, but he was obviously affronted, or pretended to be. I left then."

"And that was all?"

"Yes, that was all." A spurt of exasperation with them made me go on. "Not much, was it? After all, Commandant, I could have pointed out that Villegas' movements at the time were quite irrelevant. That is, if they were being offered as evidence, a defense against his possible involvement in the conspiracy."

"Then why didn't you point it out?"

"It hadn't occurred to me then. You see, Villegas' own account had been more circumstantial. Besides, what he had emphasized had been the political consequences of his absence—the Party's failure to call a general strike. That made sense of a kind. Uncle Paco's protestations didn't." I paused and then decided to get it over with. "Any more than did Commissaire Gillon's solemn information on the same subject."

I expected another violent reaction. None came. He merely glanced with raised eyebrows at Delvert, who nodded.

"That information, Doctor," Gillon said heavily, "was given to you at Segura's express request."

"You said that it came from a secret French report, Commissaire. Was that just to make it palatable?"

"Not at all. Segura asked us to confirm to you that there was no evidence connecting any member of their Party with your father's death. We were able, by reference to our own records, to do so."

"No *conclusive* evidence," I reminded him, and then Elizabeth's Paco theory suddenly became more than just tenable; it was the only one that made sense. I opened my mouth to say something to that effect, but Delvert seemed to have read my mind.

"Paco Segura," he interposed firmly, "is an aging man who has always had more money than sense. In his unofficial capacity as Foreign Minister to the Provincial Government in exile of Manuel Villegas, he tends to act rather high-handedly. As sole paymaster of the group—at least until recently—he has become accustomed to getting his own way. I believe that, in the matter of your dismissal, Villegas was not even consulted. The Commissaire, I think, agrees with me."

Gillon nodded.

"So we can suppose," Delvert continued, "that at the moment there may be a certain amount of heart-searching going on at Les Muettes."

"We can do more than suppose," said Gillon. "According to a report I received an hour ago violent arguments broke out this morning and have continued at intervals for much of the day."

"You know this for certain?"

"My men are friendly with the villa staff. Antoine, the major-domo, is the informant. He can't speak Spanish, of course, so we have no details, but apparently Madame Villegas is supporting her husband against Segura. Even making allowance for the fact that to Antoine high words in Spanish might sound more violent than they really were, we can be sure, I think, that Segura's decision has been bitterly criticized."

"Good." Delvert smiled. "So now we must make it easy for Villegas to reverse the decision. With minimum loss of face to Segura of course. You agree, Commissaire?"

"I agree. I think the best way would be for Doctor Castillo to act as if he knew nothing of Segura's letter, to assume that all is well. Will you be at the hospital tomorrow, Doctor?"

"Yes."

"Then you will please make a further series of X-ray appointments for next week and send a note of them in writing to Villegas. You, or the X-ray department, can request acceptance and confirmation of one of the appointments by telephone. That is all. Just as if nothing untoward had happened."

"Even though the X-rays are not now necessary?"

Gillon glared at me. "How do you know they are not necessary?" he snapped. "Have you changed your diagnosis, Doctor? You have heard nothing here to cause you to do so. You know nothing about anything except that your patient found it necessary to cancel an appointment. Very well, you do your professional duty. You offer him a new one. Is that understood?"

"Yes, Commissaire."

Delvert glanced at his watch and picked up his briefcase. "Just to make sure of a speedy response," he said, "I think it might be advisable to put a little additional pressure on Segura. That is something we might discuss privately tomorrow, if you agree Commissaire."

"Of course."

"As it is—" Delvert got to his feet—"the Doctor and I have already taken up too much of your time."

"As always, a pleasure to cooperate, Commandant. I look forward to our further meetings. The hotel telephone operator will know how to reach me at any time convenient to you. Meanwhile, I imagine that you will not be sorry to rest after your journey."

He could not quite conceal his pleasure at the prospect of our departure.

Delvert and I walked in silence over the bridge-of-sighs. As we went down the stairway to the Place, however, I prepared to part company with him.

"I'm afraid I have no car," I said, "or I would gladly drive you to your hotel, Commandant. Still, at this time there should be a taxi by the café on the corner."

He nodded. "You yourself will be walking home, eh Doctor?"

"Yes."

"People are always complaining these days of what the Anglos call 'jet-lag.' Something to do with the body's metabolism I believe. Now I am one of those fortunate persons who have no trouble at all with long plane journeys. I may eat too much, but I always sleep soundly as well. Would you object if I walked with you?"

"Of course not." What else could I say?

He took off his jacket and slung it over the briefcase as we walked down into the old town.

"Pleasant houses, nicely restored," he remarked. "Are they very uncomfortable?"

"The plumbing is original."

"You have my sympathy."

When we reached the rue Racine he turned along it as if he already knew the way. "Your apartment is in number eleven, I think, Doctor."

"Yes."

"The Commissaire's mineral water was refreshing enough, but you wouldn't happen to have something more sustaining, would you? Rum for instance?"

"Certainly."

My lack of warmth at the prospect of entertaining him

must have been noticeable, but as he chose to ignore it I did the best I could. Inside the apartment I took his jacket and put it on a hanger. He seemed to want to keep the briefcase so I asked whether he would like lime juice with the rum.

He didn't answer for a moment. He was staring incredulously at Elizabeth's vowel painting. It does tend to dominate the living room.

"What in God's name is that?" he asked.

"The Defenestration of Prague."

"Ah. Yes, thank you, a little lime juice."

When I came back he was still staring at the picture. He took his drink absently.

"A E I O U. *Alles Erdreich Ist Österreich Untertan.* Is that right, Doctor? The whole world is subject to Austria."

"According to the painter it's *Austriae Est Imperare Orbi Universo.* The house of Austria is intended to rule the world."

"Well I dare say it depends on which history book you prefer to read. What a ridiculous way to start a major war though!"

"Ridiculous? Throwing Imperial Catholic envoys out of a window? That wasn't exactly a conciliatory gesture."

"Well none of the envoys was really hurt, was he? Humiliated, perhaps, but not hurt. I mean that blood spurting all over the place is what you might have expected—after all, the Protestants were throwing them into a stone moat from a castle window twenty meters high—but it didn't actually happen that way, did it?"

"No?"

"Well of course not. The moat was full of dung heaps. Smelly yes, but quite soft. Those poor gentlemen just bounced. The only one who was a little hurt was Baron Martinitz, but that was because his secretary landed on top of him. A young man called Fabricius. He apologized to the Baron and the apology was accepted, but the poor fellow never recovered from the shame of it. Breach of etiquette, you see. All that blood though—" he chuckled—"it just wasn't there."

"As the incident started the Thirty Years War I presume the blood is symbolic. Besides, it's only the letters which are bleeding."

"You're probably right. That's the way Madame Duplessis would see it anyway."

"The painter is E. Martens."

"Yes, I see that's how she signs her work, but I know her as Elizabeth Duplessis. Her husband, Raoul, works for me."

His tone was pleasant but he was watching me carefully. I said "Oh" with as little expression in my voice as possible. Then, to conceal my confusion, I turned away and started to mix myself the drink I hadn't intended to have until he had gone.

When Elizabeth had said that she knew about S-dec, I had assumed that she knew about it—as she knew about most other things except the Holy Roman Empire—through assiduous reading of the books and periodicals that came to her weekly from Paris. The discovery that neither her estimate of the situation in which I found myself nor the things she had said about my father's death could now be quite so easily dismissed as uninformed speculations was disturbing enough. The realization that this gap in my knowledge of her background had been due more to my own stupidity than to any reluctance on her part to close it came as an even more unpleasant shock. I could remember now a moment when she had started to tell me something about her husband's work. I had refused to listen. Jealousy preferred ignorance. All I had wanted to hear from her on the subject of Captain Duplessis had been an undertaking to divorce him.

Now I had the man's superior to cope with. I put more ice in my drink and turned to face him.

"Then you must be the emissary," I said.

He raised his eyebrows.

"Elizabeth told me that she was dining tonight with an emissary from her husband."

"Captain Duplessis is a friend as well as a brother-officer. It is natural, I think, that I should pay my respects to his wife while I am here. Do you object, Doctor?"

"Obviously I am in no position to object, even if I wished to do so."

"And you don't."

"Not in the least. I know, as you must, that Captain Duplessis wants his wife to divorce him. I too would like her to divorce him. But. . . ." I shrugged.

"But you don't believe that an emissary, particularly one from the service for which her husband works, is going to do much towards changing her mind."

"I wasn't aware that Captain Duplessis worked for S-dec. That is the service you mean, I suppose?"

"Our press critics use that term, so I'm sure Madame Duplessis does. Perhaps with a difference though. The affair Ben Barka is the stick usually used to beat our scrawny backsides. Madame Duplessis probably chooses to equate us with the Carbonari, and talks darkly of a second battle of Novara. Am I right?"

"Novara?"

"An Imperial Austrian army crushed a Carbonari-inspired Piedmontese revolt there in eighteen twenty-one. She has not mentioned it?"

"No."

"Nor the treachery of the third Napoleon who was a Carbonaro himself?"

"Not in that context."

"Then there is hope." He moistened his lips with rum and lime; he was a cautious sipper of drinks. "May we talk about Villegas for a moment?"

"I thought we *had* talked about him."

"Only in a general way." He put the drink down and

reached for his briefcase. "I wondered if it would interest you to read the Mexico City medical reports on your patient."

"It would."

He took them from the briefcase and handed them to me. I opened the file and then looked at him.

"They're in English."

"From the American British Hospital what did you expect? You read medical English don't you?"

"Not easily. May I keep this until tomorrow?"

"I'm afraid not. Those reports were unofficially obtained and are therefore classified."

I handed the file back to him.

"A pity." He thought for a moment. "Still, I have read them all quite thoroughly myself. Perhaps I can satisfy your medical curiosity."

"I doubt it."

"Guesswork, but let me try. You would like to know if there is any mention in the reports of slurring, of a speech impediment."

I managed to keep calm. "A good guess, Commandant. I take it that, with you people, obtaining unofficial photocopies of confidential medical reports is a normal routine."

He pretended to look wounded. "Since we are on SDT territory here, Doctor, copies of local hospital records would be a matter for Commissaire Gillon's office. Even so, I can sympathize with your annoyance. If you knew the lengths to which some of our foreign colleagues go in the medical field you would be truly appalled. There is one service—I won't mention the name—which keeps a team of thirty permanently employed on such work."

"Indeed."

"It is understandable surely? Think. Two great powers, let us say, are about to enter into critical negotiations in a highly sensitive area—phased reduction of conventional forces or some such thing. Both the leaders concerned and their most influential advisers are likely to be middle-aged or elderly men in whom the normal processes of physical decay have already begun. And where there is a loss of physical powers, psychological changes must also be taking place. The extent of them will vary with individuals, but change there will be. We all know about the role of the plague in the history of the Middle Ages, but have you ever thought about the part played by arterio-sclerosis in the history of the past fifty years?"

"Who hasn't?"

"Well then, you must see that to the old exhortation about knowing your enemy we have been obliged to add a new one—know your friend. Nor do we confine ourselves to the state of his arteries. We must consider the whole man." This time when he raised his glass he actually took a drink from it—at least two cubic centimeters. "So, Doctor, what about Villegas' slurred speech? What suspicions did it arouse? That he may have had a minor stroke?"

"I found no evidence to suggest it. Since you have read my report you know that there is some hypertension there which can and should be treated. When, if, he comes for his X-rays I intend to run some other routine checks, an electrocardiogram for instance. But I don't expect to find anything much out of the ordinary. For a man of his age the state of the cardiovascular system seems good."

"Then what *do* you suspect?"

"I'm not sure."

"No mysteries, I beg you."

"I'm not being mysterious. I've seen this man just once, as a patient I mean. I noticed a slight speech impediment, a slurring of consonants. You tell me that this wasn't observed at the Mexico City hospital. Did the examinations there seem to you to be thorough?"

"At least as thorough as yours, probably more so."

"When was the last?"

"Ten months ago."

"Then this is a relatively new development. There could be a large number of possible explanations."

"Did you ask him about it?"

"No. Lots of persons have speech impediments, including politicians. I took note of it, that's all. So, apparently, did Doctor Massot. He thought that Villegas might be a secret drinker."

"But you didn't."

"No. Though I asked Segura about alcohol."

"And what did he say?"

"That Villegas drank very little. Of course, he also told me that this speech difficulty was due to thoughts running ahead of the ability to express them. I guessed at the time that that was a lie. Segura probably suspects, as you did, that there's been a minor stroke and wants to hush it up. Bad for the image."

"But you believed him about the drinking."

"He confirmed the opinion I had already formed. Villegas isn't a drunk. I do think, though, that he is worried about himself and looking for reassurance."

"Though not in a hypochondriacal way?"

"As I said in my report, he seemed aware of the speech difficulty and tried to conceal it. At first, that is. Later he seemed almost to be drawing my attention to it."

"In what way?"

"Villegas is a talkative patient. As I told you, he asks questions—tests you, or tries to. Stroke interests him."

"He thinks he may have had one, as Segura does and I did. But you say we're wrong, so what's the answer?"

"When I have all the test results in I may know more. Villegas is aware of that too. You can understand why the decision to dismiss me came as a surprise."

"Well, we know now that that was Uncle Paco's decision, not your patient's. The discovery must have given you food for thought, Doctor."

"Yes."

He put his drink down again. "Then there's one question I'd better ask you now, I think." He saw my mouth opening and raised one hand defensively. "No, no more medical guesswork. It's simply this. Do you believe, or half-believe, or vaguely suspect that Villegas may, in spite of or because of all this insistence on his having been in New York, have had some part in the plot against your father?"

I stalled. "That's a lot of questions."

"Not really."

"About his having been in New York when my father was killed, it has been suggested that all that's an elaborate smokescreen."

"Suggested by whom?"

"Elizabeth."

"You've discussed it with Madame Duplessis?" He was displeased.

"Why not? There's nothing secret about it surely. She pointed out that the absence of Apis from Sarajevo when the Archduke Franz Ferdinand was assassinated didn't absolve him from complicity in the crime."

"I asked you what *you* thought, Doctor."

"Assuming—a very large and unlikely assumption indeed —that the planners were of my father's own Party?"

"Yes, Doctor. Let's pretend for a moment that we know that to have been the case."

I shrugged. "Well then, for what it's worth, I don't think that Manuel Villegas could himself have been one of these notional plotters. It's possible, I suppose—still playing your game of let's-pretend—that he could have known in advance of the existence of a plot. He could even have been invited to play some part in it."

"And refused?"

"And decided that an urgent business trip to New York would save him from having to make a commitment either way. He could have thought the plot would fail, that there would be incompetent planning or that someone would talk too much. In my country either or both would be reasonable expectations. When it succeeded he was caught off balance. He was too far away. When he told me that if he had been there at the time and could have made his voice heard the Party might have been able to seize the initiative, I certainly believed him. There's no let's-pretend about that."

"Then you don't subscribe to the smokescreen theory."

"On the contrary, I think that if you accept all this Party-plot stuff it's very sound. The theory is, you see, that the smokescreen was intended not to hide a guilty man but to distract attention from one."

He stared for a moment. "Uncle Paco?"

"According to you and the Commissaire, he's the one who seems to have decided that the smokescreen isn't working."

He picked up the drink again. "Well, we have ways of dealing with Paco. Anyway, he's not your patient. Villegas is. How do you feel about him now?"

"As a physician with a patient. How else should I feel?"

He gave me an unpleasant look. "I am aware that you have a local reputation to sustain, but don't play Doctor Frigo with me, please."

When I just stared at him sullenly he went on. "You could have reason to believe that Villegas, though not actually involved in the plot to murder your father, knew of its existence in advance. That would ascribe at least some guilt to him. I'm asking you how that belief would affect your attitude towards him as the leader of a Provisional Government in exile which—and I am in a position to know—could very shortly become the real Government of your country, *de facto* and *de jure*. Would you support and assist him or would you be looking for the first chance that came your way to destroy him?"

I stood up. "Oh for God's sake, Commandant. All this is too absurd."

"What's absurd about it? I know quite a number of your countrymen who, just on the basis of the vague suspicions you now have, would be seriously considering how best to put a bullet through Uncle Paco's head. Supposing other, more cogent suspicions were to grow and that they pointed in more critical directions, what then?"

I was getting really sick of him. "Suspicions, Commandant? Psychopathic fantasies, you mean. Until these people, members of my father's own Party, started explaining so vociferously why they could have had nothing to do with his murder, the only ones who ever entertained the idea were a few crackpots. I've always assumed, and so has everyone else with a grain of sense, that those responsible were the junta's men. To my way of thinking that explanation still makes the most sense."

"Please, Doctor Castillo." He produced a God-give-me-patience look. "Your capacity for self-deception may be large, but it's not that colossal."

I said as politely as I could: "I know you have a dinner engagement. More rum before you go?"

He stared up at me. "I'll go when I'm ready. Meanwhile, I asked you a question."

"Two answers then. First. If you're in the slightest doubt about my professional attitude towards this patient, get him another doctor. Second. Villegas, assisted and supported by you people, might as you suggest be able to move in and take over. God knows the present government is unstable enough, and if the CIA keeps to the hands-off-Latin-America policy they seem to have adopted lately, or at least advertised, there shouldn't be too much difficulty. A little bloodshed here and there perhaps, some firing-squad work and torture sessions in the militia barracks, nothing serious. But if you think that my support or assistance could make any conceivable difference to the outcome you are sadly misinformed. The same value can be placed on my ability to oppose or hinder—that is, nil."

He was looking at me curiously. "I think you really believe that."

"Why the surprise? Of course I believe it. If you'd had the education in political idiocy and ineptitude that I have, you'd believe it too."

"I dare say. But has it occurred to you that judgments based on the mindless behavior of your mother's Florida associates may not necessarily be valid elsewhere? All political movements, all systems of thought have their lunatic fringes. Would you condemn your own profession as a whole because some members of it still practice homeopathic medicine and orgone therapy?"

"Political fantasies are not always so innocuous."

"Agreed. That is why we must try to deal in the realities. For instance, there can be no doubt that you, Doctor, probably through ignorance, totally underrate the present importance in your country of your father's name and memory. He has become something of a folk hero. There is a Castillo legend."

"So they used to tell me in Florida," I replied acidly.

I might not have spoken. "In certain areas, Doctor, where the legend has the dimensions of a cult, the making of photographic memorials to the hero has become a backroom industry. Quite remarkable. I'm talking about the last few years by the way. This is entirely a post-junta phenomenon and it is growing."

"And I can guess the sort of areas in which this cult, as you call it, is practiced. Remote mountain places where they don't often see a priest, I would imagine."

"Do you call the slums of the capital remote mountain places? You see how it is, Doctor? You have to recognize that there is quite a lot you don't know about your country these days. You may say that you don't care, that you are not particularly interested anyway. That I will accept. But when you tell me that, in a revolutionary situation, the position taken by the son of Clemente Castillo would be irrelevant, I have to disagree. For an incoming régime your support, or lack of it, could be an important factor. Not one of critical importance necessarily, but certainly one to be taken into account." He stood up. "Think about it."

"I think I'll be better occupied thinking about my patient."

It was Doctor Frigo at his stuffiest and I knew it even before I saw the amusement in his eyes. I did my best to erase the impression quickly. "That's if Villegas still is my patient. And by the way, Commandant, there is something that you might be able to do to help."

"In what way?"

"If it is possible I would like to see specimens of his handwriting. Any handwriting, short notes, even signatures if there is nothing longer."

"For what purpose?"

"To test a vague hypothesis. I would like to compare his writing of a year ago with his writing now."

"You wouldn't like to explain a little further?"

"As I say, it's only a vague hypothesis."

"All right. I'll see what I can arrange."

"Photocopies would be acceptable."

"Thank you for the drink, Doctor."

I went down with him to show him out. I was regretting the remark about the photocopies. It had been unnecessarily bitchy. After all, he had been a guest of a kind. Feeling guilty and slightly stupid, I proceeded to become totally inane.

As I opened the outer door I said: "About my father. You know he could never be a folk hero. The idea's preposterous. He was a lawyer and a politician."

He shrugged. "Not many of those who heard the Gettysburg address thought much of it at the time. Look at that cloud."

He appeared to have lost interest in me and was pointing up at the sky.

There was a long streak of black cloud smeared at the edges with red and gold by the setting sun.

"Pretty," he remarked and walked away.

Evening

I went back upstairs. Delvert had left two thirds of his rum and lime. I threw it down the sink and added some rum to my own.

After a while, when I had calmed down a bit, I decided to have an early dinner at Chez Lafcadio. I knew that Elizabeth and Delvert would not be going there.

Although the 19th century writer Lafcadio Hearn is best known for his prettifying of the Japanese people and their culture, his most accomplished work is an earlier account of the Lesser Antilles. A first edition of *Two Years in the French West Indies* fetches a good price and the house in which he is said to have lived while in St. Paul is mentioned in the official guide. It contains a restaurant now, and although the framed mementoes of his brief visit which decorate the walls are probably bogus, the food is good. Bernard, the patron-chef, comes from Périgord.

At that time of the evening I had no trouble getting a table; there were only a few other early diners there. I ordered the Langouste Lafcadio and a bottle of the Hermitage blanc they like to serve with it, and was looking forward to an hour of peace when I saw the man Rosier, Elizabeth's "spy," approaching from the bar.

He beamed at me. "Doctor Castillo, I thought it was you I saw coming in through the garden. We met this afternoon at the Marten Gallery. Remember?"

He was speaking his peculiar French. I nodded, not very affably. "Monsieur Rosier, isn't it?"

"Bob Rosier, yes. This is a very pleasant surprise, Doctor." He looked at the single couvert on my table as we shook hands. "On your own I see. Mind if I sit down a moment?"

He was already easing a chair into position. The bar waiter was already there bearing a half-consumed Campari-soda. If my presence there had been a surprise to spy Rosier he was recovering from it with remarkable speed.

"Cocktail, Doctor?"

"No thank you. I'm drinking wine."

He dismissed the bar waiter with a flick of the wrist and a five-franc piece.

"A surprise, as I said, and a coincidence too." He shook his head wonderingly at the strange workings of fate. "As a matter of fact, Doctor, I tried to call you at your house earlier. Around five-thirty. No reply."

"I wasn't there. Stomach trouble, Mr. Rosier?"

He chuckled. "You've heard of the Mayo clinic? I guess everyone has. They once told me I had the digestive powers of a goat. No, Doctor—" he flipped a wallet from his hip pocket, slid out a card and placed it beside my plate—"just a little matter of business."

The card said that he was Robert L. Rosier, a Senior Assessor, Actuarial Division, with ATP-Globe Insurance Inc. of Montreal. Address: ATP-Globe Building. There was a cable address, too, and a spattering of telephone and telex numbers.

"You're Canadian, Monsieur Rosier?"

"My mother was."

That accounted for the accent. He hadn't said what his father's nationality had been or what his was now. An evasion? Possibly CIA had been Elizabeth's diagnosis. Oh well. . . . Try him in Spanish.

"What can I do for you?" I asked.

"You prefer to speak Spanish, Doctor?" His had evidently been learned in Mexico.

"My father was a lawyer. He told me never to discuss business in any language except my own. You said you had a matter of business to discuss."

"Yes."

At that moment my food arrived, steaming and delicious. "Smells good," he said.

"It is."

"Mind if I join you, Doctor?"

"All right."

As he was already sitting there, nothing short of an insulting "yes" plus an appeal to Bernard would have removed him. Besides, I was curious. If he were a spy—and although Elizabeth's judgments on friends and acquaintances are apt to be wild, she does with strangers have a certain flair—it might be interesting to discover what he wanted from me and to see how he would go about getting it.

In any case, he took my acquiescence for granted. Almost before I had given it he was ordering Langouste Lafcadio too, though with that wretched Languedoc instead of the Hermitage. I reflected that if, after all, he wasn't a spy, but a bona fide French-Canadian insurance man out to sell me an endowment policy "specially tailored for the up-and-coming young doctor"—I had had that before—I was in for a very boring hour.

"I'll bet," he said, "that you think I'm here to try to sell you insurance."

"Yes."

He shook his head sadly. "We've brought it on ourselves. Too many hard-sell artists with last year's record figures to beat. My card there says I'm an assessor. Naturally, you don't believe it. Having suffered already, you think that's just tactical, a kind of foot in the door to keep it from closing before I can make the sales pitch."

"Possibly."

"It's the same all over, Doctor, and not only in insurance. Salesmen give themselves fancy titles—area service adviser, complaints investigator, customer survey coordinator—because if they come out and say what they really are that'll be the end of the friendship. They'll be blown before they start."

If, I thought, he were indeed a spy masquerading as an insurance man he was certainly not without a sense of humor. For a moment I thought of challenging him, but only for a moment. Whatever he really was, all I would get by way of an answer would be a lot of injured innocence and a shower of ATP-Globe credentials. Both would spoil my dinner and I wasn't going to let him do that. So I just nodded and began to eat.

"Know anything about insurance, Doctor?" he asked. "About the actuarial side of it, I mean."

"Only what everyone knows. Insurance is gambling. Someone has to calculate the odds. On a race course, pari-mutuel or bookmakers do the work. In an insurance office there are actuaries and the stake money is called a premium."

"Well—" he grinned indulgently—"that's one way of putting it."

His wine came. When he had tasted it he returned to the attack. "All right, let's talk about it in terms of gambling and odds. Example—a man gives his wife a fur coat worth ten thousand dollars. The value's agreed. What are the odds against her losing it? That depends. Main risks are theft, destruction by fire and, say, accidental damage. But how serious are they? How many times has this couple's apartment been burglarized? Do they travel a lot? Abroad too? Does she take the coat along? Is it vault-stored during the summer? And so on. Okay, we have actuarial data on fur-coat risks. They're our guidelines. But they don't give a whole answer to our question. This particular man with this particular wife and life-style wants to bet that she won't lose this ten-thousand-dollar equity. How much should his bet be? A fellow like me looks at the deal and comes up with a figure. He hopes he's right."

He was still speaking Spanish but adulterating it now with snatches of North American business jargon.

"You must know a lot about fur coats," I said.

"Me, Doctor? Not a thing. That was just an example." He drank a little of his wine. "I'm an assessor. I assess. But the equity I'm concerned with is life."

"Then you must know a lot about life."

He gave me a coy look. "More about the other thing really."

His langouste arrived. He surveyed it for a moment or two, assessing it no doubt, then went to work with care as if it were a small-boned fish that should have been filleted. As he picked away, probing the sauce suspiciously before every mouthful, he told me about life.

"It's not like a fur coat," he explained. "You can put a precise market valuation on that, or rather a licensed appraiser can. But with life the sky's the limit. A husband buys insurance on himself for his wife's benefit, say. How much he buys will depend on his earnings, actual or potential, his tax situation, how many children or other dependents they have and maybe on how much or how little he likes the lady. Many variables there, but so long as our medical examiner gives him a clean bill and he's not an amateur free-fall parachutist, things like that, he can have more or less what he's prepared to pay for at reasonably low rates. Actuarial life-expectancy tables are fairly definitive. That sort of insurance is easy to write."

"They don't need you."

"Exactly." He looked faintly surprised that he had made himself clear so quickly. "It's when you get outside the family relationship, the domestic field, that my problems start. They say that in business nobody's indispensable.

Well that may be true. But take a big electronics corporation with a lot riding on an R-and-D program for some new type miniaturized circuitry. The man in charge of it will be pretty special. Ten to one they had to bribe him away from a competitor in the first place. One way or another they have a lot of shareholders' dough invested in him and the project. Okay, he's hit by a drunk driver running a red light and killed. The widow gets his personal insurance and maybe a slice of cake from the drunk's insurance carrier. What does the corporation get? A headache. Nobody's indispensable, but being compelled to dispense with a key man suddenly because of some stupid accident can cost plenty. So, if it has any sense, the corporation covers the risk. In some situations, sense or no sense, they're obliged to cover. Take a movie producer. He borrows money from a bank to make a three million dollar picture. To do that he's had to come up with a star who can carry it at the box-office. What happens if, half-way through production, the star falls off a rostrum and cracks his skull? Does the bank lose its dough? It does not, because part of the loan deal will have been that the star is covered by insurance. No cover, no loan."

"What about the actuarial tables? Don't they work just as well for the research and development man or the film star as they do for anyone else?"

"Not quite in the same way. In the first place you're nearly always dealing in big amounts, millions of dollars. Second, the person insured is not himself paying the premiums. Third, and most important, it's not his loved ones who are going to benefit if there's a claim, but a corporate third party."

"You mean there's room for dishonesty?"

"Well there's always plenty of room for that, isn't there? I mean that there's a greater disposition to it in some of these cases. A man who wouldn't dream of making a false statement on a proposal if it might invalidate his personal life policy and so deprive his family, could maybe shrug off the prospect of depriving a corporation when he won't be around to take the consequences anyway. Contrary to popular belief insurance companies like ATP-Globe don't enjoy disputing claims. It's bad for business as well as messy and expensive. So before we write this sort of cover we take care that we know what the score is. The *whole* score. Okay, the R-and-D man passes his physical, but what if he makes a habit of running red lights himself? He may figure that, since all the moving violation tickets he's got were acquired in another state, they don't count when he's answering the questions about his driving record here and now. As for that movie star, how do you know he isn't on pep pills? Except on the day of the medical, of course, because he's no fool. But how do you know? You check."

"It sounds more like private-eye work than assessing."

I had thought that the jibe might irritate him. It did; although, as he was now on the point of getting down to brass tacks, he managed to conceal his irritation within a further offering of rhetorical questions.

"Isn't all research private-eye work, Doctor? Isn't an inquiry into the possible relationship between virus infections and cancer a detective process?" He put down his fork. "Isn't every judgment made on a basis of information received in its essence a form of assessment?"

"I suppose so, Señor Rosier. Does it matter much what you call it?"

He swallowed his annoyance with the unchewed food still in his mouth and pushed his plate away. "Too much tarragon for me in this sauce," he said fretfully.

"But you didn't come to St. Paul to find out about sauces. Why did you come, Señor Rosier?"

He wiped his mouth, drank some wine and lit a cigarette. "Right now, Doctor, we have a proposal from a multi-national corporation for fifty million dollars worth of cover on the life of one Manuel Villegas or Manuel Villegas

Lopez." He gave me a sidelong glance. "Surprise you?"

It did. I don't quite know what I had been expecting, but it hadn't been that. I shrugged.

"It's certainly a lot of money. What will you be quoting them in the way of odds?"

"That depends on how we assess the risk. And, like I said, before we can do that we need information. That's where we think you can help us, Doctor."

"I?"

"Well you're his doctor, aren't you?"

"He happens to have been my patient for the last three or four days, yes. But I don't see how. . . ."

Word gets around."

"I dare say it does, but what I was about to say was that I don't see how I could possibly be of help to you."

"Oh come now, Doctor!"

I drank some wine before I answered. I was really quite angry myself now and Doctor Frigo was all to ready to mount his high horse; but I had a suspicion that indignation was what he was ready for and prepared to deal with. I tried mild sarcasm instead.

"If, as you say, your business is with life insurance you must have encountered this difficulty before, surely?"

He smirked. "What difficulty?"

"Doctors don't talk about their patients to outsiders."

"The idea is that you should be an insider, Doctor. No, let me finish. What I'm talking about is your appointment by ATP-Globe as one of their registered medical consultants. Everything communicated in total confidence and entirely ethical. Is there anything in French law or hospital regulations that would prohibit such an appointment? In case you're not sure, I can tell you—there isn't. The fee, by the way, would be five thousand dollars Canadian."

A new camera *and* the Simca.

"Very nice," I said. "There's just one other problem that seems to have escaped your notice. When a man is examined for life insurance by a company-appointed physician he knows in advance about the purpose of the examination and the special interest of the examiner."

"Where's the problem? I haven't suggested that you should conceal your interest, have I? Naturally, he'd have to know. In insurance we have our own code of ethics, believe it or not. You can't take out a life policy on a person without that person's knowledge. In a lot of countries it's actually illegal. Oh yes, I know about the man who took out airport accident coverage on his wife and then blew up the plane she was on, but that doesn't happen any more, believe me. Anyway, when it's a corporation insuring an individual who isn't even an employee, there isn't a chance of his not knowing."

He was getting me confused. "You seriously expect me to inform Señor Villegas that ATP-Globe proposes to pay me five thousand dollars for an opinion on the state of his health, so that some unnamed corporation can insure him for fifty million dollars?"

"Of course not. Clearly, we would inform him formally of the proposal and request his formal acceptance in due legal form. We're not crazy, Doctor. Neither is Señor Villegas, as far as we know. You may come up with a different opinion on that score, naturally. An involutional psychosis, say, would boost the premium quite a bit. But assuming that all is well in that department, I think you'll find Villegas one hundred percent cooperative. Why should he have to go to a strange doctor when we are prepared to accept the opinion of his own? It will be no surprise to him, I can assure you, that there are businessmen who place a high value on his continued wellbeing."

"No surprise at all?"

He laughed gently. "He will even tell you the name of the corporation in advance of his receiving our formal notice. You are involved here with intelligent, aware men, Doctor."

"Some corporate member of the Coraza Consortium, I take it."

"Who else? I'll bet you've even guessed which one, too. Well, that figures. The only son of Clemente Castillo would scarcely be left in the dark, especially as he also just happens, by a curious coincidence, to be the new liberator's personal physician. This must all be very heartening to you, Doctor."

I pretended to have my mouth too full to be able to speak. Raised eyebrows were sufficient to set him going again.

"After so many years of the men of Florida, I mean the Miami dreamers. These new techniques are really something."

"Techniques in what, Señor Rosier?"

"Coup-making, of course." He gave me a merry smile. "No, Doctor, there's no need to be careful. We know all about Plan Polymer. The new style coup, the rationalized accounting someone called it, I believe. The deal made in advance—token show of strength, minimal rough stuff, maximal courtesy, no victimization and the special plane to destination of choice—no surprises in any sector because surprises mean foul-ups. Right? Mind you, Polymer's not the best name for it in my opinion, but then I'm no whiz-kid. Those boys go for scientific analogues even when they're basically inappropriate."

As I had only the flimsiest idea of what he was talking about I chose my question carefully.

"What would you call it?"

"Operation Fait Accompli." He chuckled. "Crude, but to the point. Anyway, it isn't really new. Nothing is. You've read your coup history, I'm sure. Do you remember that telegram the generals sent Mussolini before the famous march on Rome? 'Come. The food is cooked. The dinner is served. You have only to sit down at the table'. That's the way to stage a coup d'état. Come and get it! All that

street-fighting the blackshirts got into later didn't mean
a thing."

"Except to the casualties, I imagine."

"Right. The more blood there is the more bad feeling.
A couple of palace guards who haven't been told the score
in advance, okay. The assistant chief of police whom nobody liked anyway, also okay. But that's it. Bloodless if
possible. Virtually bloodless will do. It'll be acceptable to
the media. Always supposing, of course, that the timing's
right."

"Ah yes. The timing."

"Your friends, the French," he began and then fell silent,
plainly revising, or seeming to revise, what he had been
about to say.

I noted the turn of phrase, however; I am becoming
familiar with it. "My Uncle Paco" and "my friends the
French" are just two items on the list of my acquaintances
now considered by others to be undesirable. Guilt by association is heavy in the air.

"I'm going to be perfectly frank with you, Doctor,"
Rosier went on after a long pause.

I waited patiently for the lies that so often follow that
particular declaration. They were delivered hesitantly, with
a lot of chin-pulling and cheek-smoothing, the reluctant ad-
missions of some inner man succumbing to threats of torture.

"You must realize," he said, "that our clients have peculiar problems with this deal. There's this Coraza oil field.
Okay . . . it's been known for quite a while that it was
there, but nobody was much interested. Too costly to bring
in. Then OPEC goes haywire and Coraza becomes economically viable. Still needs a big capital investment,
though, so a consortium is formed to spread the ante. Problem one. The government it's doing business with is, to put
it mildly, unstable. Okay, so you change the government
before you get a Chile-type situation or the Cuban trainees

move in. A Guatemala-type operation is obviously out."

"Why obviously?"

"Jesus, Doctor!" He was momentarily indignant. "What sort of a question is that? A Central American Watergate you want now?"

"I only asked."

"Well forget it. We're back to real self-determination. Deeds not simply words. Accepting the need for change we come to terms with those who can make it stick, and if that means coming to terms with something farther left of center than we like, so be it. We massage our goosepimples, smile and do some breathing exercises. *But*, there's problem two." He poured the rest of his wine. "The process of change is one thing. My clients' losing a hunk of their equity in the process is quite another. They don't want to do that."

"I suppose not."

"So we're dealing here with two risks. Both cover a ninety day period. The first begins any day now, as you know."

"No, I don't know, Señor Rosier."

"Oh come on, Doctor. Around the first of June your patient and our-good-friend Villegas steps into a plane and takes off. I've no doubt that you'll be in there with him checking his pulse and blood pressure. Right?"

"Wrong."

"Have it your own way. The point is that from the moment he starts, the risk starts. From then on it escalates. Granted the coup has been carefully and competently planned, granted that known sources of potential opposition have been neutralized, granted that his allies and advance men on the ground have done their jobs loyally and effectively—granted all that, the risk still escalates. Among the people showering flowers on the liberator there's one nut with a hand grenade. Where there are coups there can be counter-coups. The consolidation phase falters, there's a

wrong move or two and we have a one hundred percent
fiasco. That's number one risk. Let's say, though, that we
know enough to assess and cover it. All right?"

"If you say so."

"But what about risk number two? Also ninety days, we
figure, but starting later, during phase three. In fact, immediately after diplomatic recognition of the Democratic Socialist régime and announcement of the formation of the
new National Mineral Resources Agency. Revocation of
the existing Coraza concession follows and friendly talks
with the consortium begin. Object, of course, to negotiate
a new deal, to inaugurate a finer, friendlier, more equitable
relationship between people's government and foreign ex-
ploiters. That's when my clients are liable to get screwed."

"Is being screwed something that can be insured against?"

"Of course, Doctor. Everything can be insured against.
In these cases there's an established technique. It's called
'spreading the premium'."

"You mean hedging the bet?"

"No, that's not what I mean."

His tone had suddenly become casual, almost bored, and
his eyes had taken on a faraway look. Since I had, hitherto,
neither been offered a bribe myself nor been invited to act
as intermediary in the bribing of someone else, I failed to
recognize immediately the characteristic signs that one or
both of those possibilities is under discussion.

"Then you'll have to explain," I answered.

The casual tone went as suddenly as it had been assumed.
He slapped the table hard enough to make the cutlery rat-
tle. "Look, Doctor," he burst out angrily, then paused and
drew a deep breath as if to master an upsurge of exasperation in the face of stupidity.

Another characteristic sign, I imagine. Proposer shows
teeth and growls. Any hostile reaction from the subject is
forestalled by making him feel that he's in the wrong. Pre-
emptive anger I suppose you could call it.

He forced himself visibly to become reasonable. "Let's take it a step at a time," he said and flicked his wine glass with a finger nail. "Do you know El Lobo?"

"I know of him, of course."

El Lobo is the cover-name, at least for external propaganda purposes, of Edgardo Canales, the urban guerrilla leader whose organization has done so much recently to make the Oligarchy and its henchmen look incompetent as well as corrupt. Six kidnappings-for-ransom in as many weeks, with two of the victims, whose companies or families had refused to pay, killed and dumped contemptuously at the gates of the militia barracks, are crimes that even the controlled press and radio have been unable to conceal. The official contentions that they have been committed in the name of the Democratic Socialists and that El Lobo's clandestine group—avowedly Marxist-Leninist—is under the Party's orders have never been explicitly denied by Villegas. The Party, he has said solemnly, is one of peace, and if some younger members of it have been driven to acts of desperation the responsibility must lie with those who create despair.

"This El Lobo might interest you professionally, Doctor." Rosier snapped his fingers commandingly at the sommelier who, very properly, took no notice. "That's if you're interested in psychopaths," he added.

"I'm not."

"You may *have* to become interested in this one. Your patient Villegas certainly will, especially when he gets to be El Presidente Villegas."

"*If* he gets to be president."

"Oh he'll do that all right." He snapped his fingers again. This time the sommelier was too close to ignore him and took his order for brandies.

Rosier lit another cigarette and coughed. "Given the right conditions," he went on when the spasm had subsided, "just the right conditions—an economically backward popu-

lation with political power in the hands of a few big-heads,
no risk of superpower intervention, disaffected armed
forces, an apathetic bureaucracy and a few well-led militants to rough up the gentry—it's pretty easy to make a
coup. Agreed?"

"I suppose so."

"Yes. But what happens when the new incumbents, those
who take over, have been living outside the country for a
few years as exiles in foreign lands? I'll tell you what happens. When the first fine flush of enthusiasm for the liberators has worn off, the people who weren't in exile start
thinking and taking second looks. And those who do the
most thinking and looking are the militants, the subversives,
those who made, or think they made, the whole coup possible. In this case that's going to mean El Lobo and all those
bright kids, the *really* bright, hard ones, he recruited from
the university. What's going to be their reaction when they
start thinking about and looking at liberators like Paco
Segura? Okay, no need to answer."

"I wasn't going to."

"Right. We both know the answer. Militancy and sub-
version are habit-forming. So are kidnapping and political
murder. El Presidente's first problem is going to be his allies within. Take El Lobo. How does he reward him? Make
him police chief or head of intelligence? Won't work. The
army and air force brass who sat on their hands while you
moved in have got to be taken care of. Besides, a head of
intelligence with real ability is too dangerous. He could
soon be heading a counter-coup. So what's left. Patronage
of another sort. Give him a post in which he can make himself rich."

"If he'll accept it."

"El Lobo's not that much of an idealist, whatever he may
tell those adoring students. Fast cars, yachts, fancy boy
friends, and girls. You name it, he likes it."

I was curious. "What about the really dedicated Marxist-

Leninist supporters. You said they were bright. They can't all be corruptible."

"Not all in the same way, no. Some men would give their arms for the chair at the head of a committee table that meant power, or the illusion of it anyway."

"*Bright* young men?"

"And women too these days. Believe me there's a form of patronage to suit every kind. The trouble is they all cost money and that's going to be your patient's basic problem."

"I should have thought it was the least of them."

"Money that *he* can control I'm talking about. He personally. I don't see those people in Paris being very helpful in that area, do you? They'll be watching the sous and keeping a tight rein. What he's going to need are associates who understand that particular set of problems and are ready to help solve them. And when I say help I don't mean with sympathy. I mean with cash on the line."

"I'm his doctor, Señor, not his financial adviser."

"You're the son of his old friend and leader, aren't you? A friend yourself? What's wrong with a friend telling him that my clients happen to have a five-million-dollar floater already allocated to the private Villegas presidential patronage fund? I'd say he'd be glad to hear that particular piece of good news."

"And that's what is meant by 'spreading the premium'?"

"Right."

I should have become indignant, I suppose, but I didn't. As I say, I've never been involved in bribery before. One of my colleagues at the hospital was approached last year by Venezuelan pushers trying to get hold of narcotics. The police set traps, there were arrests and the island papers made a suitable fuss, but that was all. The colleague in question seemed to have enjoyed the experience. Had I been in his shoes perhaps I would have done so. As it was, sitting in Chez Lafcadio listening to Rosier casually offering, through me, to buy Villegas for five million dollars, my dominant feeling was one of embarrassment. To this was added a sudden, and obviously psychogenic, need to empty my bladder. I controlled it as firmly as I could and signaled for my bill.

He gave me a surprised look.

"Time I went," I said.

"But I just ordered brandy."

"You'll have to drink it yourself, I'm afraid."

He gave me a beady look. "Doctor, we have things to talk about; business. I've made you a serious proposal. Remember?"

"Medical consultant in St. Paul for ATP-Globe?"

"That would be additional, of course, the official first step."

"But not for me, Señor Rosier. However, I can strongly recommend Doctor Massot. He's in private practice here."

He started to protest. "Doctor, if I've said something to offend you. . . ."

"Nothing much. And Doctor Massot has an additional qualification from your point of view. He dislikes Señor Villegas. For assessment purposes that could be important, I think. You would get a strictly objective opinion from him."

My bill arrived. I already had the money ready. I put it down and stood up.

"He could also pass your other offer on to the patient. He would probably be more tactful about it than I would."

I had expected some further protest from him. However there was none. Disconcertingly, he was grinning.

"Doctor Frigo rides again," he said in English.

"I beg your pardon."

"Be seeing you, Doc." He was still grinning.

I left.

By the time I got back home I had decided to telephone Gillon.

Had he not ordered me to report all approaches by outsiders? He had. True, it was late and he would probably be at home with his family, but that couldn't be helped. His call to me this morning woke me from a very sound sleep. Quite unnecessarily. If I should happen to wake him from a sound sleep, too bad.

He was certainly not asleep.

He had told Delvert to get his private number from the Hotel Ajoupa operator, so that's what I did. It rang for a full minute before anyone answered. The answerer could have been a Frenchwoman, his wife presumably, though it was difficult to tell because she was shouting above the noise of a hi-fi playing an old Piaf record at full blast. I heard Gillon bellowing for the volume to be turned down long before he got to the phone himself. It was turned down, but not much. He went on shouting over the music.

"What is it, Doctor?"

I told him about Rosier. When I got to the insurance policy he began to snigger. By the time I reached the five thousand dollar fee as medical consultant he was laughing heartily.

"Magnificent! I hope you accepted, Doctor."

"What?"

"I said I hope you accepted."

I started to say that of course I hadn't, but he had started laughing again. Piaf moaned on in the background.

"What else did he want?"

I told him about the five million dollar bribe which I had been invited to offer Villegas.

More laughter.

"What a rich and splendid evening you have had, Doctor," he said when he could draw breath.

"I'm glad you think so, Commissaire."

"Anything else?"

"Isn't it enough? Who is this man Rosier in fact?"

"But I thought you said he told you. Insurance."

"That doesn't mean I believe him."

He started cackling again. "But you should, Doctor, you should."

"Should what?"

"Believe him. Insurance is a most exact description of the kind of work he does."

With a final laugh he rang off.

He seemed to me to have been drinking.

If, after that idiot display, he expects a written report from me he is much mistaken.

Saturday 17 May Morning

Have at last had a few hours sleep.

At the hospital I made a fresh series of appointments for Villegas and had the letter informing him of them typed up on X-ray department paper.

During the lunch break I went up to Les Muettes myself —the new plug is still working well—and handed the letter to Monsieur Albert at the gate. He promised to see that Antoine delivered it personally to Villegas.

He was eating his lunch from a basket in the 2 cv. and invited me to join him. I didn't accept, but as he was clearly bored with the assignment I stayed for a few minutes. We chatted.

"Have you heard about the visitors we're having next week, Doctor?"

"Visitors? Here?"

He nodded. "I expect the Commissaire will be warning you. Countrymen of yours, I understand. Three of them. Important."

I didn't get much more out of him on the subject. He

had warned me because from Monday next the guard on the villa is to be doubled. Extra men are being sent from Martinique. This means a revision of the duty roster and strange faces.

Afternoon

To my surprise Doña Julia telephoned me. The Monday X-ray appointment now proposed, she said, would be convenient for her husband. She wanted to know if I would be present. I said that I would be there and would see that he was put to a minimum of inconvenience. She thanked me politely.

I was surprised because, despite Gillon's confidence and Delvert's dark talk of putting pressure on Uncle Paco, I had not expected such a prompt reply to my letter. I telephoned Gillon to report Doña Julia's call. The assistant told me that he was in a meeting and could not be disturbed, so I left a message and got on with my work.

I had just finished for the day when there was a call from Delvert. Yes, he had heard about the X-ray appointment for Monday. He wished to speak to me on another matter. On my way home would I mind stopping by to see him at the Hotel Ajoupa, room 406?

Going to the hotel involved a twenty-minute detour and I had arranged to be at Elizabeth's by seven; but he gave me no chance to tell him so. The moment I started to speak he cut in to say that he would expect me shortly and then hung up.

Room 406 turned out to be the sitting-room of a suite. Expensive. Or does S-dec get special rates?

There was a uniformed army lieutenant already there when Delvert let me in, but he made no effort to introduce us. Instead he waved me towards a side table on which there was a bottle of whisky, glasses and an ice bucket.

"Please help yourself, Doctor. I won't be a moment."

It was an odd situation. In fact I know the lieutenant quite well. His name is Billoux and he is a technical officer in charge of the signals section at the Fort. He is also a fellow tennis member of the Club Savane which has two good clay courts and where we have occasionally played as partners in men's doubles.

This evening, however, he did not seem to want to meet my eyes, much less recognize me. He was carefully inserting a wad of papers into an official-looking satchel attached by a chain to his wrist and sweating slightly as if he were engaged in fusing a peculiarly sensitive bomb. Perhaps, in a way, he was. Obviously Commandant Delvert and S-dec prefer to use army channels of communication rather than those of Préfecture telex or the post office.

When military courtesies had been exchanged and Billoux had left, satchel under his arm but still without a flicker of recognition in my direction, Delvert visibly relaxed.

"My apologies for the delay, Doctor." He glanced at my drink, added a little more whisky to it and then poured one for himself.

"I think that you and that young man must know one another," he remarked.

"We've played tennis sometimes, yes."

"Oh, so that's it. I saw you trying to catch his eye. Why didn't you say 'hello' to him?"

"Because he obviously didn't want me to."

He sighed. "I thought the same. I'm afraid, Doctor, that you are now smeared at your tennis club with the tar-brush of S-dec. I should have introduced you and said that you were here to give me a typhoid injection or something like that. I'm sorry. You see now how it is with us. We are suspect and unloved."

"It takes a lot to make me weep, Commandant."

He smiled and took one small sip of his drink before unlocking the drawer in the table and taking out his brief-case.

"I know you have an appointment with Madame Duplessis," he said, "so I won't keep you long."

He took papers from the case. "Yesterday," he went on, "you asked for specimens of Villegas' handwriting. I have them, such as they are. Generally he dictates into a tape-recorder and his wife or a secretary types the stuff out. However, we've done our best. Here are two drafts. One is of some lecture notes, the other of an article for his party news sheet. Both have fairly extensive handwritten corrections." He handed them to me. "The dates on the top were added by us. The notes, as you see, are over a year old. The article was written three months ago. Will they do for what you want?"

I took the papers over to a chair by the window, sat down with them and made the comparison.

They were photocopies but very clear ones. "You're sure that this is his handwriting and not his wife's or the secretary's?" I asked.

"Quite sure." He had followed me over.

I handed them back to him.

"Well, Doctor? You look unhappy."

"It had crossed my mind that Villegas' speech impediment might be an early symptom of Parkinson's disease. Do you know what that is, Commandant?"

"Yes."

"The slightly fixed expression he has would also be characteristic. But it's difficult to spot in the early stages. You can sometimes get a clue from the handwriting. It gets much smaller and the lines tend to curve down. That can happen before there's any visible tremor. If you can catch

Parkinsonism in the early stages, treatment nowadays can do a lot to help the patient."

He compared the two samples himself. "The fact that the writing *hasn't* become smaller, is that in any way conclusive?"

"Only of the fact that one shouldn't make guesses based on insufficient data. I'm sorry I wasted S-dec's time."

"The relief in knowing that this particular patient does not suffer from Parkinsonism is ample compensation."

"I didn't say that he didn't suffer from it. I said that there are no signs of it in his writing. Anyway, I've only seen the man once."

"Well, you'll be seeing him again now."

"Yes." I didn't propose to continue discussing my patient with him, so I changed the subject. "My encounter with this man Rosier seemed to amuse Commissaire Gillon. Did it amuse you, Commandant?"

"A little." He gave me the beguiling smile.

"May I be allowed to share the joke?"

"Oh, there's no joke. It's just that, though it was expected, the contact was made a little early."

"It was expected that he would offer me a bribe to bribe Villegas?"

He shrugged. "These multi-national corporations are always out to buy political leverage if they think it may be for sale. You can't blame them. It usually *is* for sale."

"And in this case?"

"You could easily check. Why not try relaying the offer to Villegas and seeing how he takes it? He'll know whom it comes from I can assure you."

"How?"

"The use of Rosier as agent and the size of the bid. It's up two million on the last one, you see, and that was made so tactlessly that it could only be rejected."

"But bid for what?"

"Favor, naturally. If all goes well there will very soon

be a rewriting of contracts. Renegotiation of the percent-
ages assigned to the various members of the consortium will
have to take place in order to accommodate the new government's membership. There'll be haggling. Villegas will
have the casting vote, if it is needed."

"But this man Rosier—who does he represent?"

"Several of the multi-nationals own insurance companies.
If you're really curious why don't you find out which of
them owns ATP-Globe? The Chamber of Commerce reference library probably has the information. There's nothing secret about that."

"Are you telling me, Commandant, that Rosier really is
an insurance assessor?"

"Good heavens, no. He's a professional agent, a very experienced man. We wouldn't use him of course—he doubles
too easily and too often, works for both sides I mean—but
he is most able. His supposition that you had at last become
a fully integrated part of the package may have been a
little reckless, but see how quickly he moved in on you."

"Package?" He had used the English word.

"I'm sorry to have to employ these Anglo-Americanisms
but there seems to be no precise French equivalent."

"The package being Plan Polymer?"

"Oh, he mentioned that, did he?" He grinned. "The
secret codeword."

"He didn't seem to think it very secret. He spoke as if it
were common knowledge."

"I've no doubt it is, in some circles. Conspiracy breeds
codewords. They multiply like flies on a manure heap."

"He described this one as inappropriate. He preferred
Fait Accompli."

He sipped his drink. "There I agree with him. Do you
know what a polymer is?"

"Yes, I looked it up. Polymerization is a kind of chemical
event, not a reaction but a change of state, a molecular re-
arrangement. Raw rubber becomes vulcanized rubber, say,

the same substance but with different properties. The second is a polymer of the first."

"The point being, I gather, that this change of state—note that pregnant phrase—is usually brought about by the participation of a catalyst. You see? A childish play on words. Change of state, indeed! Still, if it amuses them. . . ."

"Them?"

"Rosier's employers and their business colleagues."

"Whom I could find out about at the Chamber of Commerce?"

"If you were sufficiently interested I dare say I could save you even that trouble."

"And S-dec is the catalyst."

The smile again. "If they want to think of us in that way we have no objection. What interests us is the Polymer planners' continued ignorance of your role in the plan."

"I have no role."

"We know that, but, naturally, they, with their knowledge of men, must find it difficult to believe."

"I dare say they'll get used to the idea in time."

"Or, as you get to know your patient better, you'll get used to the other one."

I put my glass down. "Is that the object of the exercise, Commandant? That, given a professional responsibility, I get drawn into making a political commitment?"

"It's probably Villegas' object." He shrugged. "Nobody's going to force you to make a commitment. Nobody can. Naturally, we would like to see Villegas given every possible assistance. Your support, your name could be valuable to his, your father's Party's, cause. You don't believe that, or anyway you say you don't. Nevertheless, it is a fact. I will be frank with you, Doctor. Our view is that you should have been approached much earlier and dealt with in a more straightforward way. That is what we advised. Well, our advice was not taken. We now know why. Paco Segura gave contrary advice and managed to sidetrack the issue. He's overplayed his hand now, of course, but his delaying tactics seem to have worked. Wouldn't you say they had?"

His manner was completely casual. He might have been discussing a film he had found rather boring. I had an overwhelming desire to get out of the room. Mumbling something about my appointment with Elizabeth, I stood up.

He made no attempt to continue the conversation or to detain me. My state of confusion must have been obvious. As far as he was concerned that last five minutes had been well spent.

He said that we would doubtless be seeing quite a lot of one another during the coming week.

Evening

It was a relief to see Elizabeth. At least for a time it was a relief.

Her femme-de-ménage cooked a light meal and we spent a restful hour going through the new batch of contact prints and choosing those for which we would order color enlargements. She said nothing at first about her meeting with Delvert and I made no attempt to ask her about it. In the past she has made it more than clear that her marriage is not a subject that I may raise for discussion.

So, when we had finished with the photographs, I told her about Rosier's approach. After all, it was she who had warned me against him. But she didn't seem much interested. In fact her response was not unlike Gillon's.

"You should have taken the money," she said. "I am sure that this insurance would pay at least the consultancy fee.

That would have been arranged with them certainly."

"I did assume that that was just his cover story, of course."

"His *apparent* cover story, oh yes. Naturally, you were supposed to see through that and divine shrewdly that his actual employer is an American member of the consortium."

"Well it's feasible, isn't it?"

She looked at me pityingly. "Not if he made it that obvious. Ernesto dear, these people, the professionals I mean, *never* let you know who they're working for. Or who *you'll* be working for if you take their money. They have layers and layers of cover, always. He could be working for anyone—the Russians, the British, the Venezuelans, the Arabs, the Israelis, the Chinese—anyone. It's no good your laughing. He could even be working for the people who are supposed to be on the losing side in this beautiful coup he talked about. Or he could be doubling, working for two of them at the same time."

"Commandant Delvert says that with this particular man that would be quite likely."

I had touched a nerve.

"Delvert! That man is himself unspeakably corrupt."

When I said nothing she got up and began pacing about the studio.

"I told you that he came as an emissary from my husband."

"You did."

"That turned out to be only partly true."

"Then it can't have been such a bad evening after all."

"He spent most of the time talking about you."

"I'm sorry."

"Don't you want to hear what he said?"

"Not unless you want to tell me. About the emissary part I take it that there was nothing new."

"Only that my husband's mistress has just given birth to

twin boys." She pointed at me accusingly. "You don't consider that new?"

It was the best news I had had for a long time, but I answered carefully. "It has a certain novelty, yes."

"Novelty! It is an affront!"

"Well. . . ."

"A deliberate affront!"

"Come now, Elizabeth. It could hardly be deliberate."

"Deliberate! The woman has been taking a fertility drug."

I managed to look medically interested. "You know that for a fact?"

"It was inferred."

"Then your husband was lucky. She could have had triplets."

Elizabeth gave me a hard stare. "Are you laughing at me, Ernesto?"

"Certainly not. Though I don't see why you should feel affronted. Your husband's mistress wanted a child by him. She now has two. These things happen."

"And this happening pleases you. You think, like Delvert, that the existence of these two bastards will induce in me a softening of the brain, eh?"

"A softening of the brain? Definitely not."

"But a change of heart, perhaps. Is that it?"

It was and she knew it. I could only shrug.

"So let us see what sort of a change of heart Delvert has in mind for *you*." She can never resist the temptation to repay instantly even a fancied slight.

"I know what he has in mind for me."

"I doubt it, Ernesto. I doubt it very much."

"Then I'll tell you."

I gave her edited versions of the two private conversations I had had with Delvert.

She didn't interrupt and after a while she stopped pacing about.

"Those are the blandishments," I said finally. "You, I take it, were invited to help guide me towards a right view of them."

She sighed. "I said he was corrupt. I didn't say he was an idiot. He asked, from my knowledge of you, for advice."

"Advice? What kind of advice?"

"Apparently it is important for them to know soon whether you can be used at all in this affair or should be discarded at once."

It was her turn to touch nerves. I think I spluttered slightly. "Discarded! And in what capacity are they proposing to discard me, may I ask? As physician, as tame spy or as hereditary cult-figure?"

She smiled, pleased with herself. "He was well aware of the fact that I would dicuss the matter with you, of course. He used the word 'discard' several times. Obviously he expected it to be passed on to you and to have exactly the effect it has had—to make you angry."

"Well, naturally. . . ."

"No, not naturally at all, Ernesto. Whether or not you are yet prepared to admit it to yourself you are hovering on the brink of a commitment. He said he wanted my advice on how best to give you the necessary push."

"And may I know what you told him? Or is that a state secret?"

"No clumsy sarcasm, please, my dear. I told him that you could not be pushed, and that unless he could find a way of engaging your sympathies for this clap-trap, CIA-permitted, S-dec conspiracy other than those already employed —cheap appeals to your father's memory and shoddy attempts to play upon other faded loyalties—you should be discarded forthwith."

"Oh, so that was your advice." A stupid comment, but I was suddenly feeling stupid.

"Yes."

"And what was his reaction?"

"He didn't accept a word of it. In fact he seemed highly amused. He said. . . . Do you want to know what he said?"

"Yes please."

"You won't like it. He said that the person I was talking about was Doctor Frigo not Doctor *Castillo*, and that Frigo was nothing more than a drab suit of protective clothing so full of holes by now that it had become pathetic."

"Charming. Do you think he's right?"

She looked at me consideringly. "I hope he isn't."

"Anything else?"

"About you, no. He knows now that he'll get no help from me. I did ask him why they'd picked on a colorless figurehead like Villegas."

"And I'm sure you were convincingly answered. Villegas is the only democratic Party leader in or outside the country with any sort of reputation or following. He'll be politically acceptable to a majority in the Organization of American States, left of center but not too far left. He's the right age for a modern head of state, not to young but vigorous and personable. He's been a university professor teaching a branch of engineering technology learned in the United States. He's an astute, politically experienced technocrat, the kind of man who ought to be in government in this part of the world. I wish there were more like him. As for his being colorless I don't know what you mean. That he won't use oil royalties to build pink marble palaces? Good. Less color and more effective land reform is exactly what the country needs."

"You're forgetting water and sewage projects and rural agricultural schools."

"What are you talking about?"

"Delvert mentioned those things as well as land reform. But he didn't pretend not to know what I meant by colorless. Do I have to tell you about your own countrymen, Ernesto? Villegas may be all you say, though I doubt it, but supposing he is. What do your people care for technocracy and sweet reason? Technocracy means machines that take away men's jobs and sweet reason is another term for cowardice. What they expect from revolution is blood on the walls and in the streets, generals' blood, policemen's blood with a landowner's corpse for good measure."

"Nonsense." I was getting quite angry with her.

"If it's nonsense why doesn't El Lobo, the wolf, call himself El Moderador the good, and if it's nonsense why does the son of Castillo the Martyr seem such a desirable acquisition to this technocratic movement? Because your people are superstitious primitives, that's why."

"Then the sooner they're re-educated the better."

"The Castro way? Shame on you, Ernesto."

"I'm not talking about the Castro way. Nor am I talking about going back to the Batistas, the Somozas, the Trujillos or the coalitions of generals. You, I take it, prefer the status quo, this committee of fat-assed landowners with their coffee fincas, their cattle ranches, their sugar centrales and their good, Communist-fearing supporters in the United States Congress."

"Don Ernesto is eloquent."

"Merde!" I had by then completely lost my temper.

She laughed. "So Delvert *was* right. The protective clothing *is* full of holes. Frigo-Castillo *is* tempted."

"Oh for God's sake, Elizabeth!"

"Why do agnostics so often invoke the Deity? I prefer *merde.*"

"All right. Merde."

She ran her fingers through her hair. It is a gesture I know well. It means that she is consulting the Hapsburg oracle and assembling precedents.

"When the Archduke Max was offered an Imperial Crown in Mexico," she said, "he was told a lot that was untrue and much that was foolish. Gutierrez d'Estrada, the Mexican who did most to persuade him that his countrymen were crying out for a Hapsburg prince to come and rule them, had not been near Mexico, much less in it, for over twenty years."

"I don't think I'm being offered an Imperial Crown, Elizabeth."

"You are being offered respect and affection. At least, those things are being dangled as bait, just as they were dangled in front of Maximilian and Charlotte. They believed what they were told. Result—he went to his death, shot by peasants in ragged uniforms, and she to madness, grovelling before the Pope and being dragged away finally by doctors disguised as priests."

"I've always understood that they believed the stories they were told because they wanted to believe them." I felt myself getting angry with her again. "My dear, I am not a romantic Hapsburg archduke, a second son with imperial ambitions. And I'm not a wishful-thinking idiot listening to émigré politicians."

She waved the objection aside. "Napoleon the Third and his ridiculous Eugénie wanted a French colony in Central America with a puppet emperor. It was a financial adventure from which they and other parvenus like them—that vulgar Duc de Morny was one—hoped to profit. What happened? As soon as Napoleon found that there was neither profit nor glory to be had after all, he withdrew the French army from Mexico—with deep regret and many crocodile tears—and left the Emperor Max to his fate. What is the difference here? S-dec and an oil consortium are in this for what they hope to make out of it—glory for S-dec, oil for the free world, profit for the consortium. Oh, I know what you will say!"

"All right, what will I say? I'd like to know."

"This time, you will say, there are only subsidies involved. This time there are no French troops, no General Bazaine, no President Juarez with an army in the provinces. This time the Americans do not invoke the Monroe Doctrine, but give the project their surreptitious blessing because they are in need of more Caribbean oil too, and don't mind letting someone else do the political dirty-work for a change. But—" she sliced the air with the edge of her hand —"it is still a financial adventure and there are still puppets to be installed. *Puppets*, Ernesto!"

"I heard you the first time, Elizabeth. In fact, I wasn't going to say any of those things. In fact, I was going to say that Delvert isn't Napoleon the Third and I am neither the Emperor Max nor poor, mad Charlotte about to grovel before the Pope."

She pretended not to have heard me, but she was getting angry herself now. "Of course," she said loudly, "if you wanted to find out who murdered your father, that would be one way."

"What on earth are you talking about?"

"You could pretend to become, a polichinelle, a puppet, pretend to make this noble political commitment." She swept across the room to the brandy bottle and twisted the cork out as if it was a Bonaparte neck she was wringing.

"Pretend to join them heart and soul, Ernesto. Gain their confidence. Learn their secrets and then betray them." She splashed rather a lot of the brandy into a beer glass. "Your mother's ghost would be delighted I'm sure."

"Possibly. But Commandant Delvert wouldn't."

"Delvert! He impresses you, doesn't he?"

"Somewhat, yes."

"Let me tell you something." She swallowed half the brandy at a gulp. "Let me tell you. Delvert will believe anything you choose to tell him that he wants to hear."

"I doubt if he would believe in a suddenly committed Doctor Frigo."

"Then why is he trying to persuade you to commit? That monster of conceit will believe anything that flatters his vanity. Why, he even believed me when I told him something he was hoping to hear."

"What was that?"

"That I would think again about divorcing Raoul, of course. I'm quite sure he believed me. He was obviously pleased with himself and his delicate tact."

"Why bother to lie?"

"It made for a more agreeable evening. Why else should I bother?"

She went back to the brandy.

I went home earlier than usual.

Sunday 18 May

Day duty at hospital.

Had phone message asking me to call Rosier at my earliest convenience—urgent. Ignored it.

This evening Elizabeth was casually apologetic about last night. Blamed all on Delvert and S-dec, but, to my relief, refrained from pursuing the vendetta.

No political discussion of any sort. Bed wholly delightful. Did I imagine last night?

No, I didn't. Still a little sore mentally. I have become used to "Doctor Frigo." The idea of his being replaced by "Doctor Polichinelle" does not appeal to me.

Monday 19 May Morning

Villegas arrived at the hospital only fifteen minutes late for his appointment. Fortunately Doña Julia did not accompany him.

Dr. Brissac was on hand to pay his respects, which my patient received politely but without noticeable pleasure.

I stayed with him while they did the X-rays. When that was over I took him downstairs and ran an electrocardiogram. He was co-operative but plainly bored. By the time I had spoken about the need to reduce his blood-pressure and gone over the test results with him—none of them was of significant interest—the X-rays were ready for me to see.

The diverticula showed up clearly, as the radiologist was quick to point out. It was then necessary for me to go through the farce of explaining what they were and how they should be dealt with and for the patient to pretend that he was hearing it all for the first time.

The only interest for me at that point was in seeing how good an actor he was. Very good, I finally concluded. The initial surprise and concern were not overdone, he asked the natural questions and was appropriately reassured by the answers. He complimented the radiologist on his skill. I mentioned the three proprietary names by which the broad-spectrum antibiotic ampicillin is usually known and asked him if he was allergic to any of them. He said he didn't know. A well-judged performance.

I had other, more pertinent, questions to ask him now. A nod and a word of thanks to the radiologist secured his withdrawal.

For a moment or two Villegas and I stared at one another across the desk, then he thanked me somewhat effusively for my help. A remark of Delvert's about charades of gratitude inspiring mutual trust came to mind, but I put it aside. S-dec had already slightly distorted my thinking on personal matters; I wasn't going to allow it to interfere with my professional judgment.

I said: "To ask a patient how he is feeling when he has had no breakfast and a barium enema may sound like a stupid question, Don Manuel."

He smiled, a little warily I thought. "So you are not going to ask it?"

"I'd like to know how you feel generally, Don Manuel, apart from these abdominal inconveniences which we now understand."

"You're the doctor, Ernesto." Again the wary look. "You don't object if I presume on my age to address you familiarly?"

"Not at all, Don Manuel. I take it as a compliment."

"Well then, Ernesto, you have examined me. What else can I tell you about myself?"

He was watching me quite intently now. It was the look I have come to know quite well: that of the man who is secretly worried about himself and hoping for reassurance. Seeing it on his face came as something of a shock.

"I notice, Don Manuel," I said casually, "that you sometimes have a slight speech difficulty. Does that bother you often?"

"Ah, so you did notice it. When?"

"Last week when I examined you it became quite noticeable. It is less so this morning."

"That's probably because this morning you and others have been doing most of the talking."

I smiled. "I expect we have. But would you mind explaining that a little? When I saw you at the villa I had the impression that you experienced a difficulty with some words, that you were aware of it and that you could with a small effort overcome it."

"I sometimes can."

"I see. But after a while it seemed to me that you no longer made the effort. Was I right?"

"No it's not like that."

"How is it then, Don Manuel?"

He thought for a moment. "When you were at school," he said then, "did you take part much in sports?"

"The usual things, yes."

"Did you run in races?"

"Sometimes."

"Do you remember how it felt when you were near the end of a hard race, and almost winning, when there was another runner beside you who also thought he could win?"

"I wasn't a very good runner, but I think I know what you mean."

"You had to do what you had thought you could not do—call upon yourself for a further final effort."

"And win."

"Or lose, because the other runner had also made a further final effort with better success. It was a contest not only of innate physical ability and training, but also of will."

"I understand."

"But this much was predictable. Your chest might feel like bursting and your legs feel as if they were turning to water, but you either won or you came second." He paused to choose his words. "You did not collapse before the finish, you did not suddenly cease to run."

"And that's what's happening with the final effort we are discussing?"

"Yes. I lose the ability to go on. I know clearly what I wish to say and I have the will to say it, but something happens here—" he touched his face—"to prevent my doing so. An unpleasant tic that affects the tongue."

"I see." To give myself time to think I made a note on the pad in front of me. Under it was the dossier with my glib misinterpretation of the signs and symptoms I had observed at the villa. Pompously I had told Delvert that one shouldn't make guesses based on insufficient data. Well, I had done just that. Now I had better try to retrieve the situation. It wouldn't help the patient to tell him that I was appalled by my own incompetence.

"When did this difficulty begin, Don Manuel?"

"Three, four months ago, when we were still in Mexico City. I put it down to exhaustion at the time. There had been a lot of long and critical discussions with some rather exhausting personages. Knowing what you do of our affairs you can perhaps imagine."

"Yes. But you are not exhausted now, and these attacks have continued?"

"I don't think of them any more as attacks. This affliction has continued, yes. It has also increased slightly in intensity. I may say that I have become quite skillful at concealing it."

"How, Don Manuel?"

"By choosing the right moment to stop talking. I could conceal it from you, for instance, by stopping now."

His speech was still fairly clear at that point. Some slurring of the labial consonants was noticeable but he had been speaking quickly.

"I hope you won't do that, Don Manuel."

"No. Since I am hoping that you can do something about it, that would be foolish."

"How often does this happen?"

"Invariably, if I go on talking long enough." He glanced at his watch. "Let us say that the race I am running this morning is over eight hundred meters. I am perhaps at the five hundred meter mark now. At seven hundred meters I shall, to use a Yanqui phrase, 'run out of steam.' Do you understand?"

"Please go on, Don Manuel."

"We shall be having guests at the villa later in the week. You may have heard."

"Yes."

"Doña Julia will be sending you an invitation to join us at some point. I hope that you will feel able to accept, Ernesto."

"With pleasure, Don Manuel." I hesitated. "May I take it that Don Paco has forgiven me my indiscretions and withdrawn his disapproval?"

He made an impatient gesture. "Paco behaves like a fool and has been told so. It was he who cancelled my appointment here last week. I wasn't even consulted."

"I was aware of that Don Manuel."

"These French don't miss much, do they? Of course it was that aspect of the situation that so much concerned him. From the moment we came here he was frightened. He insisted on protection."

"But frightened of what?"

"Of your association with French intelligence, naturally. He was afraid that they would leak too much to you and that you would draw wrong conclusions. He has always assumed, you see, against all the evidence, in contradiction of everything we know about you, that you were infected with what he calls the Florida virus."

"I don't think I know about that particular disease."

"I think you do, Ernesto. That nonsensical conspiracy theory of your father's death."

"Oh that."

"Yes, that."

"But if it was nonsensical, Don Manuel, what had he to fear? What was there to leak? It has been suggested to me, and quite recently, that Don Paco himself may have been involved in the plot against my father. In view of his recent behavior that's hardly surprising. If he wanted to protect himself against these idiotic allegations he chose an odd way to go about it."

He looked at me almost compassionately. "Ernesto, he hasn't been trying to protect himself. He's been trying to protect me."

For the past minute or two there had been a marked deterioration in the labials and increased salivation.

I said: "Don Manuel, who did organize the plot against my father?"

He answered without hesitation. "A Special Security Forces group headed by a Major Pastore who took his orders direct from a so-called 'action' committee of the junta. That was all we knew for certain at the time. Later we had reason to believe that a member of the committee, a Colonel Escalon, took direct charge of the operation, not replacing Pastore but supervising him."

"You say 'we knew' Don Manuel. Who was 'we'?"

He sighed. "Ah, that is where the sadness begins, Ernesto. The Party had an intelligence section then, small but very effective and very secret. They had actually succeeded in penetrating the Special Security Forces at quite a high level. For a month before your father's death it was known that the attempt against him would be made."

"Known by you, Don Manuel?"

"Known by me and a few others. Very few because it was necessary to protect our source in the SSF and because we hoped to learn more about the planning and especially the timing of it. In that unhappily we failed."

"But you knew that there was a plan."

"A few of us, yes."

"Yet none of you warned him."

"What were we to warn him against, Ernesto? Attending a function at the Nuevo Mundo and leaving by the front steps under the floodlights? We did not know enough to do that."

"And so no warning of any sort was given to him."

He sighed again. "You must understand, Ernesto. There

was a real need for secrecy. Yes, even from Don Clemente. We were never a monolithic party. Besides, there were factions and one of the strongest was the anticlerical."

"And those members of that faction who knew of the planned attempt decided that it should be allowed to proceed."

"To proceed but not to succeed." He leaned forward, his face working, tongue beginning to fibrillate. "That was the promise, Ernesto. An attempt that would fail, but in doing so bring additional support . . . sympathy to Don Clemente. So no compromise, no coalition with Church reactionaries needed in Assembly." He made a final effort. "All depended on us receiving more information . . . about junta's plan so it could be properly made fail. That I pointed out again . . . again. Had business do New York for office. Three times delayed going . . . because information from inside SSF not been received. Then I could delay no longer and. . . ."

At that moment he stopped speaking. His lower jaw moved twice, then he closed his mouth and looked at his watch. He kept his lips pressed hard together.

I also took note of the time. He had been speaking more or less continuously for seventeen minutes.

"Is that how it usually happens, Don Manuel?" I asked. "You are now experiencing this quivering of the tongue?"

He nodded.

"Is Doña Julia aware of this difficulty you're having?"

He reached across the desk for my note pad and I handed him a pen.

I think not, he wrote, *I can be uncommunicative at times, and have learned also to husband my speech resources.* He paused then wrote again. *Can something be done? Is there a drug for this?*

"Of course something can be done," I said.

I could only hope that I was not lying.

I went down with him to his car. The man Antoine was

driving. Parked behind was Monsieur Albert in his 2 cv. He raised a hand to me and I waved an acknowledgment.

To Villegas I said through the open window of his car: "We are most grateful, Don Manuel, for your patience and cooperation. I shall be getting in touch with you very shortly."

He nodded and, I think, tried to smile, but his face was now almost masklike.

"Back to the villa please," I said to Antoine.

Afternoon

I spent my lunch period in the hospital library. Then I telephoned Gillon.

"A matter of importance has arisen," I said. "It is necessary that I see you immediately."

"Where are you speaking from, Doctor?"

"The hospital."

"Are you alone?"

"Yes."

"This is a secure line. Can't you tell me the nature of this matter?"

"No, Commissaire, I can't. It requires explanation and decisions. This is urgent. It is essential that I see you. And it will be as well if Commandant Delvert is also present."

"I think I'll be the judge of that, Doctor, when I know what the matter is."

"I've told you that it is serious and urgent," I said sharply. "If you are unable to dispense with these procedural niceties it may be better if I approach Commandant Delvert direct."

There was an ominous silence. Then he said quietly:

"Three o'clock in my office, unless I telephone you back in the next fifteen minutes."

"Very well."

"And I warn you, Doctor. . . ."

I hung up. He had been going to warn me that my impertinence had better be excusable. I didn't care. There was too much on my mind and it had arrived too suddenly for me to bother about Commissaire Gillon's official dignity.

Delvert was just going into Gillon's office when I arrived. They both greeted me coldly. The Commissaire had obviously told the Commandant about my behavior on the telephone. Neither was used to being summoned peremptorily by importunate civilians. They sat side by side facing me like a couple of judges.

"It is understood," said Gillon to no one in particular, "that Doctor Castillo has an urgent and important communication to make."

I saw then that he had a small cassette tape recorder on his desk and that it was switched on. The no-one-in-particular was a microphone. It was meant to intimidate me, of course; my hanging up on him had angered Gillon even more than I had supposed. I ignored the microphone and Gillon. I looked at Delvert.

"This morning at the hospital," I said, "I made a second and more thorough examination of the patient Manuel Villegas Lopez. In particular I investigated the speech impediment mentioned in my first confidential hospital report on this patient. I understand that both Commissaire Gillon and Commandant Delvert have obtained access to this confidential medical report and read it."

Delvert smiled thinly.

Gillon said. "Go on, Doctor."

"Having discussed the impediment at some length with the patient I have come to certain conclusions. The first is that it may, I say *may*, prove to be an early symptom of a serious and disabling disease. The second is that tests of a fairly complex nature must be made before there can be any question of a definitive diagnosis. Third, I am competent neither to carry out the tests nor to make the diagnosis. It is consequently necessary that a consultant neurologist with the highest qualifications be called in to examine the patient without delay."

I stopped and waited.

"You said urgent, Doctor." This was Gillon of course.

"And I meant urgent, Commissaire. For the patient's sake, of course, it is reasonably urgent. From your point of view it may be critically so."

"Why?"

"Two reasons. First, because the services of the consultant must be obtained here. That is unless you are prepared to inconvenience and perhaps alarm the patient by sending him by air to the consultant."

"You could have telephoned to Fort de France. The man could have been on his way by now."

"Yes, there is a neurologist in Fort de France. He is a good man, but in this case he would most likely want a second opinion."

Delvert intervened. "You said, Doctor, that the situation may be critical from our point of view for two reasons. What is the other one?"

I chose my words carefully. "If what I suspect, though *only* suspect, should turn out to be true, you might well decide that quite considerable changes of plan were necessary."

Delvert sat back in his chair suddenly, then looked at Gillon and the tape-recorder.

"Commissaire, I think, if you agree, that we should switch off that thing and erase what is already on it."

Gillon hesitated, then shrugged and did as he had been told. Delvert turned to me again.

"Now then, Doctor, you spoke of a serious disabling

disease. . . ."

"I spoke of the possibility."

He closed his eyes. "All right, Doctor, the point is taken. You're not committing yourself because you're in no position to do so, but you have serious grounds for concern." He opened his eyes again. "Now, what sort of concern? What disease are you talking about?"

"Until I know much more than I know at present, none specifically."

"Then we'll get someone who does know and *can* talk," snapped Gillon.

"That's precisely what I'm asking you to do," I retorted. "As I said, he should be a top neurologist."

Delvert raised his hands in mock supplication. "But just a *little* more information, Doctor, please. You want to bring in a neurologist. Does that mean that your concern lies somewhere in the area we were discussing the other night?"

Gillon gave him a sharp look. The fact that Delvert and I had discussed Villegas outside his office was evidently news to him. He didn't like it.

"You mean Parkinsonism?"

"What else?"

"Well I wouldn't need a neurologist to diagnose a case of Parkinsonism, but yes, I suppose you could say that my concern lies somewhere in that area. Though as it's a large, and in parts a very misty, area it's not one in which I am prepared to sound what may well turn out to be false alarms."

"But you *are* sounding an alarm."

"I am saying from my limited experience with diseases of the nervous system that this is a case which ought to be seen and diagnosed by a more-than-competent consultant neurologist. I am also saying that in view of the peculiar importance, present and potential, of this particular patient the matter is one of extreme urgency."

"The nervous system, you say." This was Gillon again.

"You mean he may be going mad?"

"No, I don't mean that." I could hear myself getting shrill, so said no more.

"Very well then," said Delvert, "a consulting neurologist. Do you have any particular one in mind?"

"Several." I took the list I had brought with me from my pocket. "Bearing in mind the time factor I put the nearest at the top of the list. There's an excellent man in New Orleans."

"No," said Delvert promptly. "Not New Orleans."

"What about Philadelphia or Boston? There are good connecting flights via Antigua."

"Nobody from anywhere in the United States. Who is there in Paris? May I see that list?" He took it from me anyway and stared at it. "This Doctor Grandval. You've put him first. Any particular reason?"

"Professor Grandval it is. He taught at my own medical school. He is now director of the post-graduate institute of neurology."

"Do you know him?"

"I attended a series of lectures he gave ten years ago, along with forty or more other students. If you mean do I know him personally, no I don't. In any case the only way of getting in touch with him would be through Doctor Brissac as Medical Superintendent here."

"What would he do?"

"Make a formal request for a special consultation. Professor Grandval's current work program permitting, the patient could then be flown to Paris. It really would be simpler to pay the New Orleans man to fly down. There would be no language difficulty either since Villegas speaks English. Uncle Paco can afford it."

"No." Delvert looked at Gillon. "I think you'll agree with me, Commissaire, that the Doctor's proposal is totally unacceptable."

Gillon nodded. What they were afraid of, I could see,

was that the CIA would somehow get to hear of that urgent summons. Then there would be questions. What were the French playing at? What was going on with the key figure in Plan Polymer? Other alarm bells would start ringing.

"You could always give the patient's name as Señor Garcia," I suggested.

Delvert favored me with the smile. "Unfortunately there is an excellent photograph of Señor Garcia, with an article, in last week's *Time* magazine, and the text gives his name as Villegas. No. Professor Grandval will have to be persuaded to rearrange his work slightly and come here."

"With respect, Commandant, I don't see how you can do that."

"With equal respect, Doctor, you don't have to see how. And neither does Doctor Brissac. Have you discussed this latest development with him yet?"

"There hasn't been time. I haven't even written up my notes on the case for the dossier."

"Then keep your notes to yourself, those which relate to this particular problem anyway."

"He will certainly ask about the case. He is my superior. While I appreciate the need for confidentiality—if I didn't I wouldn't be sitting here—I am not prepared to tell lies to Doctor Brissac."

Delvert looked at Gillon. "You know Brissac."

"Yes, I'll deal with it. He'll keep his nose out."

Delvert nodded. "Good. I think that's all then for the moment."

I said: "No, it isn't. What am I to tell the patient?"

"What have you told him so far?"

"That I would do something. He'll probably be expecting me to work some magic cure, or at any rate to alleviate the symptoms. When he left today he wasn't feeling up to asking many questions. Later on he will."

"If he were an ordinary patient what would you do?"

"See him again within two days. I would then tell him,

in calm, matter-of-fact tones, that the disability he was complaining of was a little unusual and that I wanted him to see a specialist consultant. Tests made by the specialist would then tell us exactly what the trouble was and how best to deal with it. I would then make arrangements for him to see the neurologist in Fort de France."

"Who would want a second opinion."

"Who might, if the case were unusual, prefer to have one, yes. But with what you call an ordinary patient we would follow a normal route. There would be no political reasons for taking short cuts or making snap decisions, nor for keeping what we were doing secret. But what do I tell this patient?"

"What you would tell the ordinary one, except that the specialist will come to him."

"When?"

"Very soon. Probably this week."

"All right, I must leave that part of it to you. Let me know, please, what you have arranged as soon as you can. Professor Grandval, if he will agree to come, should be told that the case involves a speech disability."

I stood up.

Gillon had one more try. "Doctor, this speech disability of which your patient complains. Could you define its nature in general terms?"

"In general terms, Commissaire, let me put it this way. He complains in effect that when he sets out to run a fast eight hundred meters, he find that he can no longer manage to complete more than seven hundred."

This statement was received in stony silence; they assumed, understandably, that I was being facetious.

The silence persisting, I left.

Evening

I would have liked to tell Elizabeth what had happened today; but there was almost nothing I could properly have told her, except that she had been wrong about Uncle Paco, and even then I couldn't have told her why. Nor could I have explained why I now found myself feeling slightly sorry for the poor, silly old man.

His obsessional efforts to protect Villegas from my presumed infection with the "Florida virus" had been incredibly clumsy.

Who contrived the death of Jesus of Galilee? The Romans or the Jews? Pilate or Herod or Judas? The elders, the chief priests, the scribes, the captains of the temple or some other, yet more subtle, manipulators of the mob? All or only some? Who could tell for certain?

Uncle Paco had taken no chances. As he had seen it, neither Simon the Cyrenian nor Joseph of Arimathea had been beyond suspicion. But one thing had been clear. No man could be guilty unless he had been involved in the final decision-making; no man could be guilty who had been absent and far away from Jerusalem at the time.

Villegas' own portrayal of himself as an Arimathean Joseph returning from a business trip too late to change the course to which his fellow-counselors have committed him in his absence, but prepared to claim and wrap the body, is more convincing—a little more.

Elizabeth is having another argument with the Franco-Swiss hotel company over rent increases.

We played piquet for an hour with her 18th century

pack. Find that the need to handle those valuable old cards with care inhibits thought. Believe she knows this. Lost nine francs.

Tuesday 20 May Morning

Telephoned Les Muettes and spoke to Antoine. Requested appointment to see Villegas tomorrow at villa. He promised to call back.

Rosier telephoned me at hospital. Told operator to tell him I was not available.

Antoine returned my call. Villegas will see me at eleven tomorrow morning.

Wrote up notes for hospital dossier with omissions suggested—no, *ordered*—by Delvert. Feeling of guilt unexpectedly strong. This *is* unprofessional conduct.

To avoid meeting Dr. Brissac, and possibly having to dissemble verbally as well as on paper, went home to lunch.

Letter from Doña Julia in my postbox. It had been delivered by hand.

Dear Dr. Castillo,

I know how busy you are at the hospital and the difficult hours you are obliged to keep, but I do hope that I can prevail upon you to accept for once a social invitation.

Three of our compatriots are expected to arrive later this week and will spend a few days here with us. The present state of our unhappy land will doubtless be discussed with Don Manuel, but not, I trust, to the exclusion of more agreeable topics. And our visitors will certainly wish to meet you! If you can join us for

dinner on Monday evening please try to do so. We
keep traditional hours here, but please, if you can,
come early, as soon after nine o'clock as possible.

Last night Don Manuel was singing your praises.
We are all confident now that, with your wise help,
the fatigue and other discomforts which he has been
experiencing lately will soon be things of the past.

She signed herself, sincerely, Julia Heras de Villegas.

The first paragraph amuses me. Anyone reading it who
didn't know better would assume that I have been refusing
her social invitations steadily for weeks.

The last paragraph does not amuse me at all.

Afternoon

Encountered Dr. Brissac in corridor Ward C. Unusually
affable but said nothing at all about Villegas. Affability had
element of unease. Gillon must already have told him to
"keep his nose out."

Dr. B. may be better with the dead than with living patients but he is a kindly man and has always treated me well.
He is also a good administrator. I resent his being humiliated in this way.

About five Delvert telephoned to ask what time I would
be returning home as he proposed to call on me there
briefly. Told him six.

Evening

He arrived at six-thirty and refused a drink. Very brisk and businesslike.

Professor Grandval will arrive on Thursday by the lunchtime plane and leave the same night to return to Paris by the plane from Cayenne. Allowing for flight delays his services should be available from 16:00 hrs. My tennis partner at the army communication center must have been busy.

My initial incredulity did not displease Delvert, I think, but he concealed his pleasure with a show of impatience.

"You asked for Grandval, you will have him for a clear four hours. Isn't that enough?"

"More than enough."

"What will he have to do?"

"Make an examination, ask questions, take tissue samples, I imagine. But that will be for him to decide."

"What will he need?"

"An examination room at the hospital."

"Any hospital personnel?"

"No. I can assist and interpret. But Doctor Brissac will have to be informed. You can't have a man like Grandval in the hospital without informing him."

"Why not?"

"It would be discourteous to both of them."

"Professor Grandval will be in no mood for courtesies, you will find. Doctor Brissac's cooperation has already been secured. You will have authority to call upon his office for any facilities you need. What have you done about the patient?"

"I'm seeing him tomorrow. Of course, *his* cooperation will be needed too. He might decide that Thursday was not convenient to him."

"Then you'll have to change his mind, won't you?"

"He has guests arriving."

"Not until Friday or Saturday."

"Who are they?"

"Curious, eh Doctor?" He looked pleased again.

I showed him Doña Julia's letter. He glanced at it.

"Shall I translate, Commandant?"

"I can read. A lawyer, a gangster and a priest. You should find it interesting."

"A gangster you say?"

"I dare say he thinks of himself as a revolutionary, but a gangster is what he is. So is the priest in a way. As I say, you should find it interesting. It must be a long time since you spoke to any of your countrymen who actually live there." He glanced at the letter again. "Monday. I suppose she anticipates that her guests may be a bit tired after their tortuous journey from the capital. She may be right."

"You're advising me to go."

"When you show this to Commissaire Gillon I'm sure he will order you to go. Besides, as Doña Julia says, the visitors will want to meet you. You mustn't disappoint them." He gave me the letter back. "Meanwhile you have to make your preparations for Thursday. The army will be handling the liaison work in connection with Professor Grandval. They will deliver him to you, bathed and fed, at the hospital and take him back to the airport when you have finished with him."

"Or he has finished with me."

The smile. "Don't worry, Doctor. He will be treated as circumspectly as if he were the Minister himself, and perhaps with rather more respect."

He left.

Took Elizabeth to Chez Lafcadio. Half-expected to see

Rosier and was prepared to snub him firmly. He wasn't there.

Wednesday 21 May Morning

Went to Les Muettes to keep eleven o'clock appointment with Villegas. No sign of Uncle Paco or Doña Julia. Was shown by Antoine straight up to the patient's room.

He greeted me cheerfully and removed his glasses which he placed on the thick volume of typescript lying open on his desk. He made a disparaging gesture towards the typescript.

"Look at it, Ernesto! Do you know how many constitutions we have had in our Americas since Spain left us to our own devices?"

"Since eighteen twenty-one? I've no idea, Don Manuel."

"My count is forty-six to date. I may have missed out some ephemera, but forty-six is about right. That one there is number forty-seven."

"I hope it will be the most enduring."

"If anyone apart from lawyers seeking loopholes ever reads it, that is always possible."

"How are you feeling today, Don Manuel?"

"Better, distinctly better."

What he really meant, of course, was that, having delegated responsibility for his physical wellbeing, he was now thinking about it less. His speech difficulty was well under control.

"That's good. I'd like to check your blood-pressure if I may."

He immediately rolled up his right sleeve. "I have a

strong feeling that it is down."

It wasn't down—17.5 over 9.9.

"Still a bit higher than I would like, Don Manuel. However, we can do something about that."

"Medication?"

"Nothing drastic and there's no immediate hurry. What I would like to go into a bit further is the speech difficulty."

"It's quite all right today, you see."

"Yes. But it's this running out of steam you told me about. I'd like to get at the precise cause of that before deciding what ought to be done about it."

"Well, I've told you all I can. You had a demonstration. You don't want another I hope."

"Oh no. But there are people, neurologists, who specialize in this sort of difficulty, and can identify the basic problem much more quickly and positively than I could. They have their own special testing techniques for taking tissue samples that we just can't do here in the ordinary way."

He didn't like this. "You want me to go and see a specialist? Where?"

"Well you wouldn't have to go farther than the hospital here. I said we're not equipped to do these tests in the ordinary way. That's true, in the ordinary way. Luckily there's a very distinguished French neurologist, one of the most distinguished in fact, who happens to be available to us at the moment. He has agreed to stop in St. Paul for a few hours on his way back to Paris tomorrow in order to see you."

He looked at me shrewdly. "You arranged this, Ernesto?"

"I did, Don Manuel." I met his eyes. "Yes, I had some official help in doing so, but it was entirely my idea that you should see a consultant."

"A consultant from Paris?" His stare was unblinking.

"There is a good man in Fort de France whom you could

also have seen. But why bother with the good when the best is available?"

He tapped his face. "You can't deal with this trouble yourself?"

"I could try, Don Manuel, but why should I submit you to a process of trial and error, when what is needed, and easily obtainable, is expert advice?"

"Very well. I am in your hands."

He made no further difficulties. He even agreed, without demur, to my request that he be at the hospital no later than four o'clock. Professor Grandval, I explained, would have a plane connection to make later.

"Ah," he said a trifle slyly, "we can't have him missing that. He must be a most accommodating and amiable man, this Professor."

I hope he is, but doubt if his amiability will extend to St. Paul-les-Alizés.

When I got back to the hospital I made the necessary arrangements with Dr. Brissac's administrative assistant for tomorrow.

I then wrote a letter to Doña Julia accepting her invitation for Monday evening. The writing of it felt strangely like an act of superstition, as if I were crossing my fingers to ward off the evil eye. Perhaps I was.

Evening

Saw Elizabeth but said nothing to her about any of this. Most of it I can't tell her anyway. Could have mentioned Doña Julia's invitation, but had no wish to be harangued again about the Emperor Maximilian.

Thursday 22 May Afternoon

At 15:30 hrs, a telephone call from some official person at the airport to warn me that Professor Grandval was on his way to the hospital. Went down and awaited his arrival at the staff entrance. He came in the garrison commander's car driven by a military chauffeur.

He is a slim, imposing old man, very well preserved. Does not seem to have aged visibly since I last saw him. He looked tired though and wore a sullen look. Understandable. He also proved to be in a vile temper.

I introduced myself, told him my official position in the hospital and offered to carry the instrument bag he had with him.

He ignored the offer. "Who is the person in charge of this place?" he demanded.

"The Medical Superintendent, Doctor Brissac, is in charge, Professor. I was told that you would not wish to see him."

"Told by whom?" He went on without waiting for an answer. "If he is the person responsible for this banditry, for sending secret police agents to browbeat me, to utter ill-concealed threats on the subject of research funds, to make fatuous appeals to my patriotism and talk mysterious rubbish about the national interest, I certainly wish to see him."

"Nobody in this hospital, Professor, is responsible for any of those things, I can assure you."

"Oh you can, can you? Excellent! Let me tell you, young man, I have been taken away, virtually kidnapped away, from work of considerable importance, for what I must conclude, on the basis of the non-information given to me, is a mere routine consultation. Let me also tell you that if the General had been alive still this would not have happened. I would have complained of this blackmail directly to him. It would not have been permitted to succeed."

The man on the staff entrance desk was listening fascinated. It was essential that we moved on.

"This is far from being a routine case, Professor. If we could go upstairs I will attempt to explain why."

He stared at me. "Is it your case, Doctor?"

"Yes."

"Very well," he said grimly. "We shall see."

The crack of doom would have sounded more reassuring. Going up in the elevator I made efforts to stop moistening my lips repeatedly and to pull myself together. I saw him noting both efforts with bleak satisfaction.

In the examination room he sat down, ran his eye over the equipment there and said: "Well?"

I told him briefly who Villegas was and that our proposal to send the patient to him had been vetoed by higher authority. I made no attempt to explain which higher authority or why.

"And what do you think is the matter with the man?"

I told him of the tentative diagnosis I had made.

He snorted. "What do you know about that? Ever seen a known case of it before?"

"No, Professor. What I know about it I learned from listening to you lecture on the subject."

"Where? When?"

I told him. "You mentioned the case of a Protestant pastor," I added. "I remember you said that it had interfered with his preaching."

"And this politician has trouble preaching too?"

"He has the same kind of difficulty, I think, yes."

"What's your name again, Doctor? I'm bad at names."

"Castillo."

He thought for a moment. "Ah yes. I have it. The Latin American student. Your name got into the newspapers. Where is this patient of yours?"

I glanced at my watch. "He should be here any minute now, Professor. I have his dossier here and some other notes of mine if you wish to see them."

He did wish. He read it all carefully. While he was re-reading the notes the main entrance receptionist called up to say that Villegas had arrived. I told the Professor.

He nodded. "All right. Let them bring him up. One question. When he stopped speaking what happened exactly? Did he stammer first or just slow down and stop."

"Speech became jerky, then stopped. He described it as running out of steam. There seemed to be pronounced fibrillation of the tongue. He calls it an unpleasant tic."

"Any other muscles affected?"

"He seemed to have trouble with the lower jaw."

"Very well."

"Would you prefer to see him alone, Professor?"

"Does he speak French well?"

"Not well, no."

"Then you'd better stay and interpret. You can assist, too, if I need assistance."

The extraordinary thing was that the moment Villegas entered the room, Professor Grandval became a totally different man—smiling, soft-spoken, gentle and infinitely courteous. And Villegas responded. Except that neither could speak the other's language very well, they were within minutes behaving like two old friends. To establish that sort of relationship with a patient, I reflected, Doctor Frigo would need hours, or days—or an eternity. Except when I was called upon to interpret, they ignored me.

The questioning began almost imperceptibly, a smooth continuation, or so it seemed, of the initial politenesses; but it was very thorough. How often did the difficulty occur? When mostly? What time of day? How long to recover?

How long could it be deferred by husbanding of energy? What other feelings accompanied it? Was there any numbness? Twitching? Any other particular sensation? How about arms and legs? The hands? Any trouble anywhere else?

After about half and hour I could see that Villegas was just beginning to tire. Of course, he hadn't been speaking continuously because my interpreting had given him respites, but the consonants were becoming slurred. I thought at one point that Grandval might be intending to take him as far as he could go; but then the questions suddenly ceased and the physical examination began.

Again, very thorough. Finally Professor Grandval said to the patient: "I want to take some very small sections of muscle from your face, shoulders, arms and legs for examination. Tiny pieces. It won't hurt because I will give you novocaine injections like your dentist does. But there will be no drilling. You will feel nothing. A slight soreness tomorrow perhaps, because I will close these small incisions by sealing them electrically."

Another forty minutes and it was over. I had done nothing but hold the special specimen containers and, as each was sealed, write what I was told to write on the label.

"That is all," said Professor Grandval finally.

Villegas sat up. "What do you think, Professor?" The facial injections had made it even more difficult for him to articulate clearly, but Grandval understood.

"There are several possibilities, Monsieur," he said blandly. "As soon as I have been able to form an opinion I will let Doctor Castillo know. It may take several days."

"I feel like a pincushion. You couldn't make your tests here?"

"I prefer to do my own laboratory work in Paris. It is better that way. A pleasure to have met you, Monsieur Villegas."

I showed the patient down to his car and noticed that

in the SDT escort car behind it there were two men. As Monsieur Albert predicted, the security watch on the Villegas entourage has been doubled.

When I got back to Professor Grandval he was closing and locking his instrument bag.

I did not ask him what preliminary conclusion he had come to. If he wanted to tell me anything he would do so without my asking.

"I told him several days," he remarked, "so that he does not press you too much for news." He paused staring into vacancy, then added: "An interesting case. It usually starts in the hands and forearms. That pastor I mentioned in my lecture was unusual in that respect too. Difficult to spot in the very early stages. You did well."

Going down in the elevator he spoke again. "No, it wasn't your name in the papers, was it, Doctor? It was your father's. He had some sort of accident."

"He was assassinated."

"Well, with politicos I suppose that is a sort of accident. You'll hear from me by Saturday I hope."

The garrison commander's car was waiting at the staff entrance. Professor Grandval gave me a smile as he was driven away.

He said that I had done well. It is no consolation. He has now made it plain what he thinks. I would sooner have done badly.

Friday 23 May

No word from Grandval yet. Delvert called to ask when we may expect it. Told him I didn't know but would advise him when it arrived. He said that would be unnecessary. All communications from Professor Grandval to me would be carried by the army communications center.

Presumably the Professor knows. He must have had another encounter with the "secret police" at the airport before his departure last night. Can only hope it didn't spoil his dinner.

Saturday 24 May Evening

Had just arrived home when a military jeep drove up. A corporal asked to see my identity card and then delivered a sealed envelope for which I had to sign.

Inside was a message from Professor Grandval. It consisted of seven words: —

AMYOTROPHIC LATERAL SCLEROSIS
WRITTEN REPORT FOLLOWS GRANDVAL

I went and poured myself a very heavy drink. The bottle was still in my hand when the phone rang.

"You have the message?" Delvert asked.

"Yes."

"What does it mean?"

"I'm not telling you over the telephone, Commandant. I'm having a drink."

A pause. "I'll come over."

He got here in five minutes. I had a drink waiting for him. He would, I thought, need it. "Well, what does this gibberish mean, Doctor? Serious or not serious?"

"For my patient, very serious. For you, that's up to you to decide. I can tell you, though, that Villegas will not continue for very long to be of any use to you or to anyone else."

He sat down and took the drink I was offering him.

"All of it, please, Doctor," he said.

"The disease is also known as progressive muscular atrophy and that pretty well describes it. It is a disease of the central nervous system. The cause is unknown. Some theories have been advanced, including syphilis and lead poisoning, but they are only theories, and as far as we are concerned of no practical value."

"But you can cure it." It was a statement.

"No, you can't cure it. You can give what we call supportive therapy to ease the patient's worst discomforts, but that's about it. Death can take place in a few months or it may take place in two or three years, but it certainly takes place. From the patient's point of view, you might say, the sooner the better."

"Was this the serious thing you suspected?"

"No. What I had in mind was some lesser evil."

"What?"

"Muscular dystrophy. In an adult that usually involves only the face and neck muscles. It is serious but not fatally so. It is to some extent treatable and controllable."

"How?"

"Massage chiefly and keeping the patient active. Glycine has been used as a medication."

"But this atrophy, which he has, is neither treatable nor controllable?"

"Neither. Naturally, you won't take my word alone for that statement, but you're unlikely to find any doctor who disagrees with it."

"Could Professor Grandval be wrong in his diagnosis?"

"He could, but I don't think he is. You can get a second opinion of course. Perhaps you should. I've no doubt the patient will want one."

"That can be discussed later. Assuming that Professor

Grandval is right, what is the course of this disease? What happens? The speech difficulty gets worse I suppose."

"Oh yes, though I couldn't say how rapidly. This case is a bit unusual in that it was possible to make the diagnosis early because the disease drew attention to itself in this way. Usually the onset is more insidious, affecting the muscles first of the hands and forearms, then the shoulders. The leg muscles later become weak and spastic. All the muscles tend to shrink and fibrillate, that is they quiver and twitch. When the disease spreads to the brain, chewing, swallowing and speaking become very difficult indeed. The tongue fibrillates too. By that time the lips remain parted and the patient drools. Any attempt to control facial movements results in a violent contortion of the entire face."

He sighed heavily. "Delightful. Anything else?"

"Nothing pleasant, I am afraid. The patient is subject to frequent fits of laughing or crying, for no apparent or particular reason. More and more rest becomes necessary. Eventually the patient has to be fed through a nasal tube."

He stood up abruptly and took more than a sip of his drink. Then he nodded. "Thank you, Doctor. You're not by any chance exaggerating?"

"I'm sorry, Commandant. It *is* a horrible disease."

"And nothing can be done."

"I'm afraid not."

"How long?"

"I've already told you. I don't know. The speech problem will increase, but how rapidly I can't say. I used the analogy of a man running a race the other day. It was not my own, but the patient's. He will gradually stop running sooner and sooner. *How* gradually remains to be seen. And, of course, other things will happen."

"Could he last a month, more or less as he is?"

"Possibly. Possibly two months. But the rate of deterioration in these early stages is really quite unpredictable."

"I see. What are you going to tell your patient?"

"The truth, of course, sooner or later. When, I don't know. I hadn't got as far as that yet. As you have read the message to me from Professor Grandval, you will know that he is sending a written report. I shall probably wait for that. Commissaire Gillon will have to be told of course."

"Why?"

"I am at least partially responsible to him."

"That message you received a short while ago, Doctor, is an official signal and highly secret. I'll have it back please."

I handed it over.

"Commissaire Gillon," he went on, "will be told all he needs to know—that the disease is serious. And he will be told by me. Muscular dystrophy, I think you said, was the disease you suspected."

"Yes."

"Then, unless you are instructed otherwise, that's what it is."

"Are you asking me to lie to my patient, too, Commandant?"

"It might be a compassionate thing to do in this case, don't you think? After all, you have nothing to offer him except compassion, have you? But I leave that decision to you, Doctor."

He left.

After a while I walked across to see Elizabeth.

Later, I told her some of what had happened. I know that doctors are not supposed to talk about their patients—Frigo was disapproving vigorously—but I had to unburden myself a little. Besides I had already talked to Delvert.

Elizabeth, too, was brutally practical.

"I suppose a month or so would be sufficient," she said thoughtfully. "There would be the television appearances, of course, and the radio speeches, but I dare say they could be taped in ten minute sections and spliced together afterwards."

"I suppose they could."

"The live news conferences would be more difficult to manage. Still, with a little ingenuity and careful preparation it should be possible. The first two weeks will be the important ones."

"But then what? How do you manage a formal speech to the Organization of American States, for example, or an address to a new elected Assembly?"

She brooded for a time and then began running her fingers through her hair. "You make other arrangements," she said finally.

"What other arrangements?"

She gave me a somber look. "What happened to the Emperor Ferdinand?" she demanded.

I didn't know, and, since I didn't much care just then what had happened to him, I didn't ask.

I came home, and, having written the above, have taken a sleeping tablet.

Later

The tablet hasn't worked so I have taken a second.

While waiting for that to take effect I have consulted my Hapsburg reference books.

The Emperor Ferdinand, it seems, was an imbecile who suffered from rickets and epilepsy. "I am the Emperor and I want noodles," he is said to have bawled at his chamberlain during a state banquet.

Metternich succeeded in having Ferdinand replaced after a few weeks—the so-called "pre-March interregnum"—by the Archduke Louis.

The Archduke, apparently, was only stupid.

Part Three

The Treatment

Monday 26 May Evening

In her invitation Doña Julia had said that at Les Muettes
they keep traditional hours. Knew that that meant dinner
at 10:30 or even later, so made myself an omelette here
before leaving. As I was wearing my dark suit and a tie, decided not to go by moto. Took a taxi instead, knowing Antoine would telephone for another when I wanted to leave.

A mistake. I would have done better to have taken my
moto and risked being rained upon.

The two SDT men on the gate were those who had escorted Villegas when he had gone to the hospital for the
consultation with Professor Grandval, so they knew me by
sight and their check on my identity card was perfunctory.
The taxi driver was less fortunate. He and his vehicle were
both searched. He complained bitterly, though to me, not
the SDT men.

There was an extra car parked in the courtyard with a
local self-drive hire service decal on the rear window, and
I wondered if Delvert had also been invited. It couldn't be
Gillon, I thought, because he would have had his own car.

It was neither of them. Delvert had said that I would find
there a lawyer, a priest and a gangster. The last person I
had expected to find as well in that house was Rosier.

I didn't see him immediately. Everyone seemed to be
out on the terrace, but as Antoine started to lead me towards it Doña Julia hurried in and told him that some of
the guests' drinks needed replenishing.

"So glad that you were able to come, Doctor." She sounded a trifle breathless.

"A pleasure, Doña Julia."

She took me by the arm and steered me towards the hi-fi alcove. "But before I introduced you to our visitors I did want a private word with you."

I started to mumble something but she was already having her private word.

"I am worried about Don Manuel, Doctor. Extremely worried." Her eyes challenged me as if I had been about to deny the statement.

"For any particular reason?" I asked. It wasn't a casual inquiry. Four days had elapsed since I had last seen him and for a man with his condition there could be unexpected changes.

"Because he is worried about himself," she said. She threw her hands up dramatically. "Ever since he saw that Professor he has been more and more anxious as each day passes. I asked him to telephone you, but he said no. When you had the report you would tell him."

"Well, that's quite right, Doña Julia. Professor Grandval has had laboratory work to do and the report to write. Yesterday was a Sunday. I doubt if he was able to airmail the report from Paris until this morning. Perhaps by Wednesday . . ."

"But did this Professor say nothing at all to you at the time? Give no opinion at all?"

"These eminent consultants are very jealous of their reputations, Doña Julia. They do not make guesses or deliver hasty judgments, especially when they are dealing with members of provincial hospital staffs. They make certain of their facts before they speak. That is, after all, what they are paid for."

"Ah, and that is another thing. Who *is* paying this eminent gentleman?"

The truthful answer to that would have been that I

didn't know, and hadn't thought to ask Delvert. Presumably his people were. I said: "His services were requested by the hospital, Doña Julia. I have no doubt that the Ministry of Public Health will be dealing with that matter."

"It is all extremely worrying."

"Uncertainty always is. The moment I receive Professor Grandval's written report I will let Don Manuel know."

"You can see for yourself, Doctor, that there is nothing the matter with him but fatigue through overwork and anxiety for our country's future. I wish that this upsetting consultation had never taken place."

So did I. Fortunately she decided that it was time for her to resume her duties as hostess.

"But, as you say, Doctor, we can only wait and think of pleasanter things. You and our guests must meet one another."

She took me out on to the terrace.

At first sight the seating arrangement there in the candlelight looked somewhat formal like that of a council of war —which I suppose it was in a way—with Villegas presiding. But as I approached with Doña Julia, that first impression of formality evaporated. The three tables which had been lined up in a row for the occasion had hexagonal tops inlaid with pop-art tiles, and the chairs in which the councilors sat were of decorative wrought-iron, painted white, with scarlet cushions. Dishes of half-consumed canapés, full ashtrays and a couple of ice buckets with opened champagne bottles in them lent the occasion a festive air. The only man in the group not wearing a sports shirt was the priest who had on a sweat-stained white soutane with the skirt hitched up over his knees. It was more like the convivial session of a local tennis-club committee, after hearing good news from the treasurer about the state of the club's accounts, than a solemn council of war.

Both Villegas and Uncle Paco stood up to greet me. First, Don Manuel put his arm round my shoulders, beamed at the company and presented me formally to them as Doctor Ernesto Castillo Reye. With that he sat down and left Uncle Paco to perform the individual introductions. It was at that moment that I saw Rosier smiling demurely at me from the other side of the tables.

I stood there like an idiot for a moment, then Paco grasped my elbow and led me past Villegas to the man seated on his left.

He was a handsome, virile-looking criollo with lean aristocratic features that seemed familiar. About fifty I thought. The hand that shook mine was dry and firm, the welcoming smile unforced and pleasant.

"Don Tomás Santos Andino," intoned Uncle Paco; "our faithful ally and adviser on matters of constitutional law."

Delvert had told me there would be a lawyer, but hadn't seen fit to mention that the lawyer was also the current Minister of Education under the Oligarchy. He has held the post for the past four years and been responsible for the only progressive social enterprise of the period, the rural school system. Paco had referred to him as an ally rather than a comrade because, until the Oligarchy had decreed the abolition of party structures, Santos had been a Christian Socialist. Technically anyway; he is the sort of man who, while holding some strong convictions, can never be wholly at ease in any one party. In many ways an apolitical man; some might say that his presence there made him a traitor to the government he already serves.

"Don Tomás also has considerable influence with the university and senior high school students of the capital," Uncle Paco added.

"What he means, Doctor," explained Don Tomás impassively, "is that I can bring them out on the streets if that should be a useful thing to do, in the same way that Father Bartolomé can command his shanty town mobs."

"It is true, Ernesto." This was Villegas. "The governments of many other countries have discovered this already.

The defense and interior ministries are no longer the only ones with organized forces at their disposal. Those may be armed, but that doesn't necessarily mean that they can dominate all situations. Ask your French friends. No. Today, ministries of education have become power bases also."

"Though not all," said Uncle Paco, "have post-graduate groups as lively and effective as those of Don Edgardo Canales Barrios." He permitted himself a coy chuckle as he moved me on. "I think, Ernesto, that you will know Don Edgardo better as El Lobo."

El Lobo—the wolf—took no notice whatever of Uncle Paco or his little joke. He was weighing me up and he took his time about it.

El Lobo is, I believe, twenty-eight. He looks younger. The body is plump, the head round, the cheeks sallow and puffy; but the forehead is almost unlined. He looks like an overgrown, bloated and dissolute child.

The skin of the lower jaw is slightly paler than the rest, possibly because of the recent removal of a beard; but even with it he would never have appeared wolf-like. Most of these clandestine sobriquets are chosen, of course, for their inappropriateness in order to mislead, though whether they often succeed in doing so I doubt. There can be few security policemen who do not by now suspect that a man named El Flaco, the slim one, may well be extremely fat. Still, there is nothing in the least lamb-like about El Lobo. His small contemplative eyes are those of an extremely dangerous fish. Is the prey immediately edible or must there be a quick kill first?

He did not offer to shake hands. He may be one of those persons who dislike casual physical contacts; but I think it more likely that he had sensed my instant antipathy. He could be used to such reactions, and may even enjoy them.

To break the silence I said, as if in reply to Uncle Paco: "Everyone has heard of El Lobo."

The fish eyes still examined me. Was I worth eating or

might there be defensive organs, sharp spines perhaps, to contend with?

"Your trouble, Doctor, is," he said slowly, "that you have too soft a heart. I have thought so for some time."

"Oh?"

"Those swindlers in Florida. You should have had the skin off their backs."

He has a flat, expressionless way of speaking which makes it difficult to decide when he uses what might be a figure of speech whether or not to take it literally.

I skirted the difficulty. "Our Cuban friends told me the same thing. I explained to them that we would prefer to have the money."

Uncle Paco laughed. "See how equivocal our Doctor Ernesto can be?" he crowed to the others. "It might be his father talking."

El Lobo joined in the murmur of amusement, but he gave me a barely perceptible wink. I hadn't fooled *him*.

"Señor Roberto Rosier, I think you already know," Paco was saying now.

"In another context, yes."

Rosier grinned. "The Doctor and I met in Madame Martens' picture gallery. We had a most constructive discussion, didn't we, Doctor?"

"Constructive you thought? Wide-ranging I would have said."

"And what, pray, was the subject of your discussion?" This was lawyer Santos, leaning forward with a somewhat steely smile for us. "May we know? Don Roberto is an expert on many things, but I had not thought that art would be one of them."

"Oh not art, Don Tomás." Rosier waved a hand airily. "Life and death, wasn't it Doctor?"

"Among other things." I looked at Santos. "But mostly in terms of their values, Don Tomás, or rather their market prices in dollars and cents."

I had spoken acidly and I saw Villegas give Santos an I-told-you-so look which could have meant anything—"you see, pompous *and* tiresome," if it referred to me, or, "he's going to need watching," if the subject was Rosier. I didn't much care which it was. I just wished Uncle Paco would speed things up a bit.

"Don Roberto," he was droning on relentlessly, "as our principal liaison officer with the Consortium is also a valued economic adviser. Prices, changing values and modes of access to markets, especially those controlled by foreign government agencies, are his business. He deals with facts, figures, the fiscal realities of our struggle. Father Bartolomé on the other hand"—I was being steered now towards the priest—"deals in souls and certain other, perhaps less spiritual, realities. He, too, is a man of power, but of a different, more immediate kind. A power complementary to that of El Lobo, would you say, Father?"

"Only God deals in souls," said Father Bartolomé indistinctly.

In that flat, predominantly-Indian mestizo face the pipe he was sucking looked quite incongruous. It was one of those complicated European ones with an aluminum tube containing a nicotine filter in the stem and a perforated lid over the bowl.

I already knew a bit about Father Bartolomé. He is a so-called "worker priest" whose huge popular following in the slums of the capital has been alleged, by some members of the Church hierarchy, to have been secured more by his munificence in the brothels and bars than to his pious socialism and rabble-rousing skills. His funds are said to be derived from a share in a protection racket operated at the expense of the small shop-owners in his "parish."

"Only God," he repeated dogmatically.

"Quite so, Father." Uncle Paco managed to look like a bishop conceding a minor theological point. "But you deal with men made in the image of God."

"Not men," said Father Bartolomé; "merely animals with names."

"The phrase, Ernesto," Villegas put in hastily, "is actually your father's. He first used it in the Assembly. Animals with names. It caused a sensation then, and much anger. Now, those to whom it referred, the underprivileged, use it proudly about themselves. Am I not right, Father?"

"Yes." Father Bartolomé reached for his glass, drank deep and breathed heavily.

From a little over a meter away the smell was unmistakable. Father Bartolomé's wineglass contained island rum, undiluted, and he was very drunk.

"Father Bartolomé is still tired from his journey," Paco explained calmly.

The priest made an effort to get to his feet, failed, leered at me and mumbled a benediction. Out of a corner of my eye I could see El Lobo watching as if a snack-sized gobbet of raw flesh had just drifted down trailing blood.

"Coffee for Father Bartolomé," Doña Julia ordered loudly.

She was surveying her drunken guest with an obvious loathing which surprised me. Her husband was, after all, planning a coup. It would have been sensible to treat the man, however odious he might be, who could put a screaming mob of thousands on the streets armed with gasoline bombs, with a measure of tact. A quiet word to Antoine would have done. Father Bartolomé could then have been assisted to his room and left to finish the bottle in private. Uncle Paco had said she would make enemies. She had made one now. Father Bartolomé took umbrage.

"Coffee is poison!" he blared.

Paco scooped me away from the confrontation and returned me to Villegas.

"Yes, Ernesto," my patient said amiably, "it *is* rather a lot to absorb all at once. Why not take your jacket and tie off? We are all friends here and so can be quite informal.

Sit anywhere you please and have some wine."

I was glad to take off my jacket and tie but uncertain where to sit. El Lobo promptly pulled in a chair that placed me between him and Santos. The latter immediately began to cross-examine me about the French medical services in rural areas of the islands. Unfortunately he proved to be less interested in the system of dispensaries and mobile clinics, about which I know a good deal, than in the statistical basis and financial structuring of the service, about which I know little. I was relieved when Doña Julia announced that, as it had been decided by Don Manuel that we would dine al fresco, some re-arrangement of the tables would be necessary.

Serving trolleys were wheeled in by the servants and all of us, except Father Bartolomé, stood up while more of the small hexagonal tables were set in an oval. I found myself reseated, at a table set for two, with El Lobo. Even Father Bartolomé would have been preferable. But El Lobo seemed pleased with the arrangement.

"An old bore," he said, referring to Santos, "but able and useful. Didn't you think so? Asked awkward questions."

"Only awkward for me. The hospital secretary would have had all the answers. But he's an accountant, not a doctor."

"Go on, Doctor, say it."

"Say what?"

"What you were thinking—that an ability to ask awkward questions is not necessarily an indication of usefulness."

"What I was thinking was that it was strange to find him in this company."

"We need a little respectability, Doctor." He was having fun now.

"You don't find Don Manuel sufficiently respectable?"

"Oh yes. For the bourgeois leader of a center party in exile he has done remarkably well. If one did not know better one might almost be led to believe that the party actually exists."

I did not quite know what to say to that. He smiled.

"You have the same perplexed expression on your face now, my friend, as you had when you were listening to that little homily on the subject of student power. So authoritative wasn't it? Does he not know that you were in Paris during May of sixty-eight? I thought you showed remarkable restraint."

"How did *you* know?" I asked.

"Oh we know almost everything about you, Doctor. You would be surprised."

"Were you there yourself? In Paris I mean."

"As an interested observer only."

"Well I wasn't an interested observer," I said. "I was in a casualty clearing station for most of the time helping to deal with fractured skulls and ruptured internal organs. Not all of them belonged to students, by the way. In fact, of the worst, remarkably few."

"The students took care of their own."

"Nonsense! You only observed what you wanted to see, Señor Lobo."

"Have it your own way, Doctor Frigo."

"I see you've been listening to Rosier."

"Not at all. I told you we knew all about you, Doctor. After all, you *are* the Crown Prince."

I looked at him for a moment. "You're overweight and flabby for your age," I said finally. "I recommend swimming. If we weren't guests in this house I'd be tempted to start the treatment now by throwing you in that pool." I smiled. "And hope that it was empty."

He laughed. It was a peculiar implosive sound like that of a breaking vacuum flask. "That's better, Doctor. I was sure that we could arrive eventually at what Mister Rosier likes to call a meeting of the minds."

"You think we have?"

"I'm sure of it." The fish eyes made another survey. "You interest me, Doctor. Such determined innocence. There must be so many things you don't know about those of us who live in your native land."

Delvert had said much the same thing.

"I expect there are."

"Then I'll make you an offer." He paused. "My intelligence service is excellent. If it hadn't been, what Segura calls our post-graduate group would have been dead and buried long ago. We have survived by knowing, and knowing a lot. Anything you want to know, about anyone here or anyone there, don't waste time asking Paco. Even if he should happen to know he'll lie. Ask me. I never lie, it's against my nature. And don't worry. It won't cost you a thing."

Except another "meeting of the minds," I thought, some form of quid-pro-quo in the shape of a tacit alliance; but I never got around to expressing the thought because at that moment Father Bartolomé upset an entire bowlful of gazpacho. It fell in his lap.

There were too few present for the incident to be wholly ignored. Conversation became general and disjointed for a while. El Lobo did make one sotto voce comment which interested me.

"I'm afraid that sooner or later, when his usefulness is ended, someone will decide that the good Father has to be killed off," he reflected. "I wonder who it will be."

My impression was that he was considering the advisability of doing the job himself, though I dare say that at that moment Doña Julia would have been a ready volunteer.

Once the Father's soutane had been more or less cleaned up the service of dinner proceeded smoothly. Finally, when the coffee had been served, Paco tapped his glass with a spoon for silence.

"Don Manuel," he said.

My patient smiled round at us all, then glanced at his

watch. About to deliver a speech, he was timing himself to
make certain that he didn't run out of steam.

"My friends," he began, "I want to talk to you a little
about the subject of this conference here. That is, I want
to talk to you about success."

There was a murmur of approval which he promptly
quelled. "No, my friends, I am not referring to the immediate tactical success, but to that which must be made to
follow, the programed success of the future."

There was respectful silence.

"It has been said," he continued, "that no Central American government has ever succeeded in opposing the activities of the big North American corporations within its
borders, and afterwards survived. I think that this is true.
I believe that, much as we may as socialists deplore the fact,
it will remain true. Unless, of course, we choose, as our
friends in Cuba have done, to accept the Russian embrace
instead. Unlikely, you will agree. Yet, there is in our situation now a new element which changes it profoundly. We
have no need even to wish to oppose these big corporations,
whether they be North American, French, German, British
or Dutch, because we now have more to offer them than
coffee and fruit, or cotton and hardwood. In this we are,
so far at any rate, unique. So, for us, the choice lies no
longer between policies of opposition and those of subser-
vience. We can behave as men of dignity and social conscience free from economic pressures induced by the va-
garies of commodity markets and the squalid antics of
foreign speculators. We can behave as men of sense."

Another glance at his watch.

"But how are we to use this opportunity? And I say
opportunity because that is *all* it is, not the arrival of a
millennium. In eighteen months or two years time the first
wells will have come on stream. From that moment the
value of this resource, this now precious asset, will begin
to diminish. And I am not simply speaking of quantities.

Economists' and technologists' estimates vary, but we may reasonably assume that within fifteen years oil as an energy source will have much less importance than it has at present. Its importance as the base commodity in the manufacture of other things may increase—all sorts of possibilities already exist in those fields—but it is on its value as an energy source that its present price is based. So our opportunity rests upon the realization over a limited period of years of the sale of a capital asset. And when it has been realized, what then? Do we sink back into agrarian mediocrity, will we have used our time and money to buy the toys we now associate with affluence, or will we have used them to effect a transformation?"

Another glance at the watch and he went on to describe the transformation he envisaged—roads, housing, schools, agricultural colleges, rural cooperatives, water and sewage projects, petrochemical plants, hydroelectric schemes, light industry, fertilizer plants, cement, tourism, land reform, a civil guard on the Costa Rican model and social justice. I felt as if I had heard it all before. From my father, or from Elizabeth in a bad mood?

"Yes," he concluded and he was just beginning to have difficulty with the consonants, "you have all had this development dream before—the banquet which the paternalistic generosity of the wealthy nations is always promising, but which somehow never gets served, never gets beyond the printed menu and the cup of thin soup. But this is no dream. This time we will have the means for once to purchase the ingredients ourselves, to see that none is stolen or wasted and to make sure that all the dishes are prepared with due regard to our own national tastes. And take note, my friends. This is to be a banquet which all our people will attend. I thank you for your attention."

He sat back in his chair, very tired.

Beside me, El Lobo stood up and applauded as enthusiastically as the rest of us. It was only as we sat down again that I realized that he was asking me something under his breath. I didn't catch it immediately. He repeated the question.

"Is there that much bicarbonate of soda in the world, Doctor?"

I stared.

"For a nation of two million, all with severe indigestion?" he continued in his expressionless way. "Of course, much will depend on who will have been doing the cooking. Indigestion might be the least of it. There could be dysentery as well after that banquet, if not during it."

Nobody was paying any attention to us. Santos was elaborating on what Villegas had said, and the others—even Father Bartolomé, slightly less drunk now with food in his stomach—were listening to him.

"You found it ideologically unsound?" I asked.

"Fairy tales have always bored me, even as a child. I preferred to know."

"Who kept the sleeping princess under deep sedation? That sort of thing?"

He gave me his fish look. "Not as simple as you like to make out, are you? What is it you would like to know, Doctor?"

I didn't bother to look surprised. "Did your information-gathering organization ever hear of a former Special Security Forces officer named Pastore? Twelve years ago he was a major. That would be before your time as a power in the land of course."

"Dead. Accident while cleaning his pistol. Most surprising thing to happen to such an experienced officer. But there it was. Very sad, especially just after he'd served the junta so well."

"There was also a Colonel Escalón."

He gave me a quick look. "Who told you about him?"

"Our host."

"You surprise me. Very bold of him, but tactically sound.

The best lies are always well wrapped up in truth. Escalón was luckier. Promoted to general and given a coffee finca in the north. Not a big one, mind, but big enough. Earnings substantially more than a senior man's normal pension. Would you like him?"

"What?"

"I asked if you would like him. You can have him if you want. Ask him a few questions. Kill him if you felt like it when you had the answers." The eyes were watching with something almost like amusement my attempts to camouflage my confusion or find a convenient rock to hide behind.

"It's all right, Doctor," he went on kindly. "No need to decide now. Anyway I think I know what you'd do with him in fact."

"What?"

"Take his temperature and give him a couple of aspirins probably. Yes? Well, as I say, no need to decide now."

"I've told you how I knew. What was your source?"

"His old friends, of course, the richer ones. Who else? You'd be amazed how these big shots talk when they're scared. Mostly you don't even have to show them the electrodes, much less use them. You just switch on a black box with a few dials on the outside and a high-pitched buzzer inside, and that's it. They start talking. Anything you want to know. Naturally, they've been prepared, disoriented, softened up, but it still amazes me. I expect there's a medical explanation. You may know it. My guess is that when a man has been rich and secure for a long time he begins to think that he's a lord of creation. Then, when he suddenly finds himself alone in the darkness for a couple of days with just a bucket to shit and piss into, the whole world falls to pieces for him. No more dignity, very little identity. Same with the women, though you have to have only other women dealing with them to make it work. One thing you can be certain of. If it's been rich long enough it'll talk, and the stronger it starts out the weaker it'll end up. You don't like the idea I can see, but you asked and I've told you." He paused. "There's just one more thing."

"Yes?"

"Not very many people know about the involvement of our host or its extent. While I would agree that information is for use, not decoration, I think that some pieces have to be used with care and discrimination. Or not used at all unless the place and time is right. Do you see what I mean?"

"Yes, I see." I stood up. "It's been a pleasure meeting you El Lobo."

The eyes held mine briefly. "I thought we had agreed, Doctor, that lies are best wrapped in truth. A pleasure did you say? How could it be?"

"How indeed? Let's say interesting. Good night."

I picked up my jacket and tie and, going over to Doña Julia, thanked her for her hospitality.

"I am afraid I have to be on duty early in the morning," I added. "May I ask Antoine to telephone for a taxi?"

"No need, Doctor," said Rosier, who was beside her; "I'm going to have to leave myself. I have a car. I'll drive you into town."

"I couldn't put you to that trouble," I said.

"No trouble, Doctor. I was just telling Doña Julia that I had to be back at the hotel for some overseas calls. Besides a taxi would never get past those guards on the gate."

There was nothing more to be said. Everyone else there was staying in the house. Rosier and I paid our farewell respects together. They were more or less informal. Father Bartolomé was haranguing Santos noisily on the subject of the capital's slums. From the little that I heard I gathered that, for reasons he was having difficulty explaining, he does not want their present occupants rehoused.

In the car, once we had been cleared by the guards, Rosier resumed, as I had feared he would, the discussion begun in Chez Lafcadio.

"Well, Doctor, I told you I'd be seeing you again, and here we are."

"Yes."

"After a most stimulating evening."

"I'm glad you found it so."

"Well didn't you? Very thick with El Lobo you were, I noticed. I said you'd find him interesting. Remember? You'll just have to learn to trust me, Doctor."

"Why?"

"Why? What sort of a question's that? We're working together, aren't we?"

"That might be easier to answer if I knew who you were working for, Señor Rosier. And don't start telling me about the Actuarial Division of ATP-Globe again, please."

"Why should I?" he answered reasonably. "I've already told you about that. Know your trouble, Doc? You're old-fashioned. A man *can* serve two masters, believe it or not. Oh yes, I know what the Good Book says, but that only applies where there's a conflict of interest. There's nothing of that sort here."

"I wasn't thinking of the New Testament but of the fact that you've been described to me as a double agent."

"That would be Delvert. Typical of the man."

"In what way typical? His tendency to understate a situation? At the moment, Señor Rosier, you seem to me to be wearing not just two hats, but three, or even four."

He chuckled. "And how many are you wearing, Doctor? Want me to count? Family physician, political confidant, DST sub-agent. I could go on, but that's three. Right?"

It was not a question I felt like answering. We were on the outskirts of the town. I said: "Perhaps you'll drop me at the corner by the Préfecture. I can walk from there."

He seemed not to hear me. "And there's another one in the mail," he said. "You should get it in the morning."

"Another what?"

"We're talking about hats, aren't we? There'll be a

check from ATP-Globe and their standard form of consultancy contract. You just sign and return it. Okay?"

"I'll certainly return it, with the check."

"That's up to you, Doctor. I was only trying to be helpful."

He turned into the rue Racine and then suddenly pulled up outside the bakery.

"This isn't where I live," I said.

"I know but it's a parking zone. Outside your apartment isn't, and we have to talk."

"Not me. I'm going to bed."

"I'll make it short then. What's the matter with him? And don't ask me who I mean. I mean your patient, our leader."

"Goodnight, Señor Rosier." I started groping for the opener of the car door.

"I know a lot already. You'd be interested in how much."

"I don't think so."

"Want to bet?" He leaned across me and pointed to a catch. "Just pull that thing to get out. You know, even without the rest of it, that little scene of yours tonight with Doña Julia would have had me thinking."

"What scene? What are you talking about?"

"Family doctor arrives to meet honored guests. Patient's wife, instead of graciously receiving, rushes out to intercept doctor and drag him off into a corner. Lot of arm-waving. Wife obviously very upset. Why? Because Father B.'s falling-down drunk? Not a chance. It was because she wanted to know the score on the patient."

"Or because the doctor, asked for nine o'clock, was unpardonably late owing to a little trouble with the guards on the gate." I started to open the door.

"Not good enough, Doctor. Sorry. It just might have been, if I hadn't happened to know why the lady was so anxious."

I stopped opening the door. "All right, why was she?"

"See? I said you'd be interested. Natural wifely concern. She wants the specialist's report."

"What specialist?"

He sighed. "I know you're trying to defend your virginity from the wicked seducer, but just don't keep crossing your legs like that, please. What specialist? Have a heart. Do you think you can keep secrets in a place this size? Well, you may do, but let me show you how wrong you can be."

I waited while he lit a cigarette.

"It's like this," he went on. "You're in a situation where some of the activities of certain key persons may be of interest, especially when they involve out-of-the-usual contacts. Notice I say *some* and *may be*. No question of surveillance. Even if you had the manpower, in this situation it's pointless. Small town, intelligent and well-educated people plus low wage scales. All it needs is fifty francs here and fifty francs there in the right places."

"To buy spies you mean?"

"Spies! You know you're getting paranoid, Frigo. What's wrong with a few sharp-eyed, sharp-eared kids giving occasional tip-offs to a nice, friendly newspaperman? He gets his stories, they get the price of a trendy new shirt or the down-payment on new Jap motor-bike. With the older, married ones it's maybe a refrigerator. But what's wrong with it?"

"Nothing, except that you are not a nice, friendly newspaperman, Señor Rosier."

He grinned. "Who said not? I could be."

"Another hat? Or just another set of papers?"

"You're crossing your legs again, Doctor. Have you any idea how much air stewardesses talk among themselves? No, I don't suppose you have. Well, when they've had an elderly male passenger in first-class who's been shoved aboard the plane at the last minute in Orly, spends the first hour of the flight muttering nasty things about the secret police and is met on the tarmac here by an army car which takes him away without his even clearing customs, they talk. And the airline minibus driver, who takes them to their hotel, listens. Got a nose for news that boy. Mystery man, thinks he."

"I see." I began to look forward to telling Delvert this.

"He also gets the name, Grandval. At the hospital so far there's nothing much, of course, except that Doctor Castillo is not working the normal routine. Interesting, but only mildly so, until later in the afternoon up drives an army car with an elderly man in a very bad temper who talks of secret police persecution and kidnapping. Are you with me?"

I nodded. The staff-entrance desk porter hadn't missed a word.

Nor, it seemed, had he missed the subsequent arrival of Villegas—Antoine was known to him as the major-domo of Les Muettes—escorted by the two pig-types in a second car. The ceremonial departure later had not been missed either, though he had failed to get Grandval's name. That had been picked up again at the airport, though, by a man on the departure desk who handled the passenger lists.

"So then," Rosier concluded, "it was just a question of checking out Professor Grandval and wondering why our friend urgently needed the services of a famous neurologist."

"Just a precautionary measure."

He gave me a disbelieving stare. "Pretty elaborate one wasn't it?"

"Over-elaborate in my opinion, but then I didn't make the arrangements."

"Which in the event proved unnecessary, of course. No adverse findings. You've already had word, eh?"

I opened the door. "Señor Rosier, I really am going to bed now. If you want to know more you'd better lay out another fifty francs to the staff-entrance porter at the hospital." I got out. "If he noses around long enough you may find out that I shall be prescribing a course of massage for Don Manuel."

He leaned across the seat I'd just left. "Then why haven't you yet told Doña Julia the good news, eh Doctor?"

"Who said I hadn't?" I retorted, and slammed the door in his face.

As I walked on down the street, I half-expected him to come after me with more questions; but he didn't. He just drove away.

He may feel that he now has all the answers he needs. I hope so, though I doubt it. Feel tonight as if I have been put through a mincing machine—Rosier one blade, El Lobo the other.

Tuesday 27 May Morning

Must try to set down this day's developments calmly and in order. Must *not* get emotional, as will do no good either to my patient or myself. Essential that facts be recorded without embellishment to speak for themselves.

On arrival at the hospital found three letters in my box. One of them was from Paris. Naturally, I opened that first.

It was from Professor Grandval. With his laboratory findings and their precise analysis was a covering letter.

Having confirmed, from a subsequent assessment, that the cabled diagnosis had been correct, he went on:

> *An interesting case, if only because of early diag-*

nosis, though of what help that can be to the attending physician is questionable.

You will be all too well aware of the prognosis. The book injunction to "keep up the patient's good spirits" you will doubtless weigh, if you are allowed by those in authority to do so, against this man's evident good sense.

Supportive therapy will not in my judgment allow you to postpone the evil day for long in this case. Doubtless you will already have realized that.

I would welcome monthly progress reports, as detailed as possible, if the so-called authorities permit. There is so much about which we know so little in these cases.

I put both letter and report in my pocket.

The second envelope had a Montreal postmark. Inside was a check for five thousand dollars drawn on the Nassau branch of a Canadian bank. Above the indecipherable signature were the words *Actuarial Division, Special A/C No. 2.* The check was attached to a four-page printed contract which I did not trouble to read, and an addressed envelope for its return. Across both check and contract I wrote SENT IN ERROR—RETURNED TO SENDER adding my signature and the date.

I was enclosing them in the return envelope when it occurred to me that I ought to have some evidence that the check had been returned. There was a photo-copier in the Secretary's outer office, so I went up there and asked if I could use it.

I took two copies of both check and contract. One set of copies I had intended to give to Gillon for his files, the other I shall attach to this account. It was as I was leaving that the day's nastiness really began.

When I thanked the girl there for letting me use the copier she said: "Enjoy your vacation, Doctor."

She is an attractive girl. I smiled, but didn't pay much attention to what she had said. Some staff members have been known to manufacture excuses for lingering in her office. I assumed that the remark was some sort of private joke between them, something I didn't know about. So, I smiled.

When I got back to my desk I enclosed the check and contract in the Montreal return envelope and sealed it. Only then did I open the third envelope. I hadn't bothered with it before because it was an unstamped internal hospital memorandum. It could have been anything from a request for economy on laundry to another warning about staff parking in the places reserved for ambulances.

It was neither. It was from the Secretary's Office to me personally and said that, on the instructions of the Medical Superintendent, my request for two months' paid leave of absence, commencing June First, had been granted. The necessary reallocation of case responsibilities would be notified by the Medical Superintendent's office prior to May 31.

That was all—that and a scrawl which, for those familiar with it, was the Secretary's signature.

I telephoned Dr. Brissac's office immediately. His secretary had evidently been expecting my call. Dr. Brissac could see me at eleven o'clock, no sooner.

I managed to do some work until then, but if the purpose of the delay had been to give me time to cool down, it failed. When I entered Dr. Brissac's office I was even angrier than I had been at first.

He was wearing the mulish look which, with him, means that he is embarrassed. I suppose that should have mollified me somewhat, but it didn't. When he motioned me to sit down I just placed the memorandum on his desk and remained standing.

"As you must know, Doctor," I said, "I have made no request whatsoever for leave of absence, paid or otherwise."

He glanced at the memorandum. "There appears to have

been a misunderstanding on the part of the Secretary's Office, Doctor," he said. "They must have presumed that it was at your request. An understandable error, as you have, in fact, an accumulated entitlement to annual leave. I will, of course, see that the mistake is rectified."

"That *both* mistakes are rectified I hope, Doctor."

He looked at me unhappily. "I assure you, Doctor, that this is none of my doing."

"I didn't suppose that it was. Indeed, I should imagine that, with the normal annual leave roster in operation, my absence now would cause some inconvenience."

"Yes, it will."

"*Would*, Doctor, if it were to occur. I ask that it doesn't. I ask that you countermand this instruction to the Secretary and advise him that I have neither requested leave of absence nor wish to accept it. In fact I *won't* accept it."

The mulish look returned. "The matter is out of my hands."

"As a subordinate of yours in a hospital for which you are officially responsible, Doctor, am I entitled to no consideration, no protection?"

He stiffened up. "You have always been given the utmost consideration here, Doctor. In my reports I have always described you as a most valued member of my staff. You have had my highest recommendations and I have twice secured, at your own request, official acceptance of your refusals to accept promotion elsewhere. I do not expect, and am not asking for, gratitude. The consideration given you has been well-earned and thoroughly deserved. But do not accuse me, please, of withholding it."

"I am asking for your protection, Doctor."

He thumped his desk with a fist. "Protection, fiddlesticks! You shouldn't have got yourself mixed up in politics."

The effrontery of this was too much. "May I remind you, Doctor, that it was upon *your* recommendation that I became 'mixed up' as you call it with those people down at the Préfecture?"

It was a little unfair of course; he had only allowed me to suppose that he had been instrumental in securing for me the Villegas "appointment"; but I was too angry to care.

He shrugged helplessly. "I'm sorry, Doctor. I am not attempting to blame you, believe me. It is just that my responsibility is limited. If a policeman were to come into this hospital and attempt to give me orders about the running of it, he would quickly be sent about his business. This is different. In this case. . . ." He shrugged again.

"I see, Doctor. I take it that you would have no objection then if in this case I take matters into my own hands."

"That's where they are, I am afraid, Doctor. If you think you can change their minds down there, by all means try. Meanwhile I will see that the impression in the Secretary's Office that this leave of absence takes place at your request is corrected. It will not, in any case, count against your annual leave entitlement."

It was obviously the best he could do. So I thanked him, apologized for some of what I had said and left.

From an empty examination room on the first floor I telephoned the Préfecture and got through to Gillon's secretary. She, too, had had her instructions. In my mind's eye I could see those gold teeth flashing imperiously as she informed me of the impossibility of my being able to speak to the Commissaire at any time that day or at any other time in the near future. Her answers became curter as I persisted. Finally she said that if it were useful or necessary for the Commissaire to speak with me he would doubtless do so.

I telephoned Delvert.

He at least was willing to speak to me. In fact he was waiting to do so.

"I had hoped that you would get in touch earlier," he said a touch reproachfully. "We have several matters to discuss."

"You may have several, Commandant, I have only one."

"Well, we shall see when we meet. But first, I think you received a communication from Professor Grandval this morning."

"I did."

"He was not authorized to send it to you directly. In fact, he was specifically instructed not to do so. If, as I suppose, it consists of a report on his consultation here, I am afraid that I shall have to ask you to let me take care of that for the moment. You had better bring it with you."

"I had intended to do so."

"Good."

"You will need it for the information of my successor."

"Your what?"

"My successor as court physician to the occupants of the villa Les Muettes. As of now, I am resigning the appointment."

"You are? I am sorry to hear that, Doctor."

"After the treatment to which I have been subjected this morning you can scarcely be surprised."

"What treatment was that?"

I told him. He made clucking noises.

"Your annoyance is quite understandable. It was tactless of the Commissaire, and premature. The matter of your leave of absence was one of the things I was hoping to discuss with you today, after we had had a word or two about last night's meeting."

"Well there's nothing to discuss now. You had better think about a replacement. Meanwhile, if you are going to be remaining in the hotel for the next hour or so I can drop the report by during my lunch period."

"No, I don't think that will do, Doctor. I have a better idea. At what time will you be leaving the hospital today?"

"At about six."

"Then supposing we meet about then."

"Very well. Where?"

"Not here. And not at your apartment either, I think. With Monsieur Rosier distributing down payments on Japanese motorcycles so generously we can't be too careful. Who knows? Even your femme-de-ménage may by now have been suborned with the promise of a trendy shirt."

"All right. Where?"

"At Madame Duplessis' house I suggest."

"I don't see her agreeing to that."

"But I do, Doctor. She is sitting opposite me at this very moment, nodding her head."

"Oh."

"At six then."

The fact that it wasn't until some time after he had hung up that I even began to wonder how he could have overheard that conversation last night in Rosier's car, shows the state of mind I was in. There is nothing more muddling, apart from anger itself, than the dull aftermath of it.

Evening

Elizabeth received me with the resigned air of a well-insured householder who has decided to accept as calmly as possible an invasion of armed robbers.

"Your friend's upstairs," she said.

That meant the studio. I found Delvert sitting there in the most comfortable chair. He was nursing a glass of white wine.

He nodded to me cheerfully. "Madame Duplessis informs me," he announced, "that she intends to see fair play."

"What I actually said was," Elizabeth began in a loud

voice, but he didn't allow her to finish.

"Or words to that effect. Quite so." He raised a hand to indicate that the point was taken. "Is that the Grandval report you have in that envelope, Doctor?"

"Amongst other things, yes."

"What other things?"

I produced photocopies of the check and ATP-Globe contract and handed them to him.

He examined them idly. "And what am I supposed to do with these, Doctor?"

"Anything you like, Commandant. I have other copies. You will notice that I wrote on the check before returning it so that it can be seen not to have been cashed by me. I don't wish to be accused at some later date of receiving bribes or other unprofessional behavior."

"Oh I don't think anyone is likely to accuse you of that. Or, indeed, of anything else as far as I know."

"Except perhaps stupidity," said Elizabeth.

It was by now apparent that she was in an ugly mood. We were in for a rough time.

Delvert gave her an irritated look. "My dear Elizabeth, I am, as I said I would be, delighted by your presence at this little friendly discussion, but that sort of remark is not helpful."

"It helps me."

"Possibly, but you are not the one who needs help just at present. Those who are in need are the Doctor and myself. Supposing you give him a glass of wine."

"You'd sooner have beer, wouldn't you Ernesto?"

"Yes."

If Delvert was by then regretting his choice of a meeting place he managed to conceal the fact reasonably well. "As long as it isn't a cup of hemlock, we can perhaps get on with our business. You said, I think, that you have Grandval's report with you, Doctor?"

"Yes." I took it out.

"You've made no copies of this I hope."

"No." I detached Professor Grandval's covering letter before handing over the report.

"What is that?" he asked.

"A private letter from Professor Grandval to me. It came with the report."

"May I see it?"

"You may, Commandant. Bearing in mind that you might decide to confiscate that, too, I took the precaution of replying to it this afternoon. In my letter to the Professor I thanked him both for his report and for his courtesy in disregarding the highly improper instructions he received from your people about sending his report. And, by the way, my letter has already been mailed."

He gave me the smile. "For a man who has, in order to express his profound dissatisfaction with an unsatisfactory state of affairs, tendered his resignation, you seem singularly bellicose. I thought that these grand gestures were supposed to have a cathartic effect."

"It wasn't a gesture."

"That is something I am hoping we can discuss."

Elizabeth was handing me a glass of beer. "Be careful, Ernesto," she said.

This time he didn't object to her intervention. "Good advice," he remarked. "We must both be very careful." He read Grandval's letter and then looked up.

"For a layman like me, of course, this is a good deal more informative than a technical report."

I said nothing. He read it again, then tapped it with a forefinger.

"This evil day to which he refers. I take it that means the day the patient dies."

"No, it doesn't. It means the day on which you have to tell the patient that he's going to die."

"Ah. Presumably there is a standard ritual for breaking the news in these cases."

"Far from it. Why do you think he calls it the evil day? There must be almost as many rituals for 'breaking the news,' as you call it, as there are doctors in practice."

"Oh come now!" he protested. "I realize that it can't be a pleasant duty, but surely it's not that complicated?"

"You think not, Commandant? When I was a student, there was a surgeon at the hospital who used to try to make it uncomplicated. It was something of a joke. When a patient with, say, a terminal cancer had had time to recover from the surgery which confirmed it, this man would order screens put around the bed. Then he would march in, stand at the end of the bed, say 'I regret to inform you that you have a terminal cancer,' and then immediately march out again."

"Well at least it was frank and forthright."

"It wasn't in the least frank or forthright. I told you. He left *immediately*. That was the point. He never gave the patient time to collect himself sufficiently to ask the essential question, 'How long have I got, Doctor?' He didn't have the guts to stay and wait for that, because then he would have had the embarrassment of explaining that he didn't know and so couldn't tell. That was how uncomplicated he was."

"I see."

"I doubt if you do, Commandant. Among the students there used to be another joke on the subject, a story about a patient who dies and goes to heaven. When he gets there, though, he's a bit puzzled and uncertain of where he is. Then he sees a nurse standing beside him, so he asks her: 'Nurse, am I dead?' And she replies: 'I'm afraid you'll have to ask your doctor about that.'"

Delvert laughed.

"I don't think that's funny," Elizabeth said.

"Oh I don't think it's meant to be, is it Doctor, except as a reductio ad absurdum? A doctor has failed to do his duty by his patient, but the nurse is sticking strictly to the rules. Am I right?"

"About the absurdity of supposing that there can be any fixed rules, yes. In fact, a great many nurses often do the doctors' job for them without being aware that they're doing so. Nurses' attitudes towards patients they know to be dying vary a good deal, but quite often they give the game away, either to the patient, who may be observant, or, more often, to the visiting relatives. The thing is that someone in the family has to be told. There may be legal or financial reasons why that's necessary. There are always moral ones, or, if you don't like the word 'moral,' reasons of humanity."

"And sometimes, I am afraid, Doctor, there must be political reasons, or reasons of state, for postponing the evil day." Delvert was looking at Grandval's letter again. "What is meant by 'supportive therapy'? Is that equally complicated?"

"That depends on the case. In this one it is merely a euphemism for deceit."

"That sounds like Doctor Frigo speaking."

"I don't care how it sounds, but deceit is what it amounts to, medical deceit that is. It could take various forms, of course. Prescribing massage and giving him useless injections would be one. Telling the patient he's feeling better and persuading him to believe you would be another. Or if that won't work you tell him he must be patient and give his medication a chance. You can explain what a unique clinical picture he represents and talk vaguely about a new drug that's being developed which is going to make a lot of difference to conditions involving the central nervous system. Naturally you dose him with sedatives and antidepressants as required. And when he starts to go down hill fast, as you have always known he will, you give him a perplexed look and say, 'We're not looking as well as we should today—we must do something about that.' So then you give him something to make him think he feels better for a few hours. That is supportive therapy for Monsieur Villegas."

"Monstrous!" said Elizabeth angrily. "Are all doctors as bad as this?"

I bridled. "Well I could always march in, stand at the end of his bed and say, 'Sorry, my friend, you have amyotrophic lateral sclerosis and it's incurable, so just lie back and suffer.' "

"So instead," said Delvert, "you propose to march in, stand at the end of the bed and tell him you resign."

Elizabeth rounded on him like a tigress. "That is grossly unfair and you know it."

"Children, please!" He held up his hands in mock surrender.

But she was in no mood for games. She used an obscenity new to me.

It didn't seem to be new to Delvert. He raised his eyebrows. "I have always understood," he said, "that the Hapsburg court was invariably polite to foreign envoys, even when they represented régimes of which it disapproved."

"The Imperial court was always entirely correct," she retorted; "but its loyal subjects were not always so forbearing."

"Well then, while I am waiting to be torn to pieces by the mob, perhaps I may have a little more of this excellent wine."

It is only rum that he sips, apparently. Wine he actually drinks. As soon as Elizabeth had taken his glass he turned to me again.

"You haven't yet told me, Doctor, how things went at the villa last night."

"From our conversation on the telephone I gathered that you already knew," I said sourly.

"Ah, you picked up that allusion to Rosier, I see. I hoped you would. Naturally, we have listening devices covering most of his activities."

"But not at Les Muettes?"

"There too. Unfortunately Paco Segura seems aware of their limitations. Apart from your brief word with Doña Julia all conversations took place on the terrace I think."

"Yes, they did. What difference does that make?"

"A lot, I'm afraid. These directional microphones have no discrimination. It's the noise of the crickets out there, you see. One receives only snatches of conversation. Increase the sensitivity and you just get more crickets. I thought you handled Rosier very well, if I may say so, but what was the subject of that cordial chat of yours with El Lobo which he mentioned in the car?"

"It may have looked cordial to Rosier. At one point I mentioned the possibility of throwing him into the swimming pool."

"I wish you had. How did he annoy you?"

"He seems to think I have political ambitions."

"Which might conflict with his own no doubt. He'll have to go of course. That sort of creature has its uses, but our Anglo friends aren't going to put up with the Marxist-Leninist following. Far too dangerous."

"As a matter of fact El Lobo said much the same thing about Father Bartolomé—that he'd have to go."

"Well perhaps some sort of mutual elimination can be arranged. What else did El Lobo say?"

"He boasted of his intelligence service."

"With justification. It's very good. Did he offer you any samples of its work?"

I had no intention of answering that truthfully. "He described some of his methods," I said. "That was more than enough for me. No doubt I'm squeamish."

"No doubt he guessed you were. El Lobo would enjoy making your flesh creep. Your patient made some sort of speech. Did he have any trouble?"

"No. He timed himself carefully."

"Was it a good speech?"

"It was—" I hesitated—"virtuous, I suppose."

Elizabeth had come back and been listening. "Have you ever heard a politician's speech that wasn't virtuous?" she inquired.

He smiled at her. "You ask that of a politician's son? By virtuous he means portentously banal."

He put his wine down. "I'm sorry about this morning," he said slowly. "Extremely sorry."

"This, Ernesto, is where you have to be careful." Elizabeth sat down facing us.

Delvert gave her a long look. "Elizabeth, my dear, I had been hoping for a private meeting with Doctor Castillo, not a tripartite conference."

She made no move to go. He turned to me again with a shrug.

"You were being extremely sorry about this morning," I reminded him.

"Yes." He paused. "You must have realized, Doctor, that my powers here are strictly limited."

"By the DST people?"

He looked surprised. "Oh dear me no. By persons of considerably greater importance. I mean my own superiors. You know my rank. I am a commandant. Do you think that in an affair of this importance involving a multi-national energy consortium, a mere commandant would be allowed in any way to determine or modify policy? I can only implement my masters' decisions."

"I have always understood that the powers of some staff officers far exceeded those that would be normally associated with the ranks they hold."

"Well, I dare say there have been such cases, but I can assure you that I am not one of them. I may have a certain latitude as to the means of carrying out my orders, but I can only advise if I believe that a modification might be useful. That does *not* mean, however, that my advice will always be accepted."

"And in my case, I take it, your advice wasn't accepted. Hence your sorrow."

"Look at it, please, from my superiors' point of view. This Villegas is a person of essential, if transient, importance to a carefully conceived plan, the executive responsibility for which is theirs. In the delicate set of circumstances surrounding the project, you, whether you like it or not, are not only this man's medical adviser but also in your own person a political factor of actual or potential significance. An unexpected complication, in the shape of an illness, is introduced into the calculations. Your continued presence can minimize its immediate effect, your absence perhaps increase it. What, they ask in Paris, should be required of this young doctor? Simply that he take a long paid vacation, be given a free trip to the land of his birth and, because he is who he is, receive a certain amount of respectful attention from his compatriots. His medical duties to his important patient would call for only nominal efforts on his part. Is that too much to ask of a government servant? Certainly it isn't. Let the necessary leave of absence therefore be arranged. And forthwith, please."

"Very nicely put," said Elizabeth.

Delvert ignored her. "As I said, Doctor, I am permitted to advise. I did so. I said that there were some aspects of your relationship with your patient that had led me to believe that it might be better to request your cooperation than to require it. I suggested that if you felt that you were being ordered to do this and were being given no choice in the matter, your reaction might well be to take umbrage and resign. Their response was not, I am afraid, sympathetic."

"He means that they weren't taking any nonsense from a pipsqueak foreign doctor and told him to threaten you with dire penalties." Elizabeth again.

Again he tried to ignore her. "There's no need for us to go into that. The point is, Doctor . . ."

I interrupted him. "But I would like to go into it, Commandant. What exactly am I to be threatened with?"

"By me, Doctor, with nothing. I am merely explaining the circumstances."

"But I have resigned."

"I'm hoping you will reconsider that decision."

"And if I don't, what will they do?"

He sighed. "Revoke your permits to reside and practice medicine on French territory for a start."

"But only for a start?" I think I spoke calmly but it was quite an effort to do so. I could only hope that my intestinal reaction was not audible.

"I explained," he went on apologetically, "that a Spanish-speaking doctor with your qualifications would have no difficulty at all in moving to Mexico or South America to practice. They said that, since they could and would arrange to have your present passport made invalid at the earliest possible moment, that might not be as easy as I thought. They know, of course, that you could probably buy a passport which would be valid in Colombia or Ecuador, but the fact of your being a deportee would make it expensive. I can't, of course, place myself in the position of criticizing my superior officers, but I must admit that they can on occasion be quite ruthless."

Elizabeth gave a short laugh. "That trick of uttering threats while pretending to disapprove of them," she said, "is known as the Delvert technique. You play the threats down in order to give them maximum force."

Delvert went white and for a moment I thought he was going to do something violent; but he managed to control himself and took a sip of wine before he answered her.

"Would you please leave us, Elizabeth?"

"No."

"Then perhaps the Doctor and I should leave you." He felt for his briefcase,

I said: "Personally I find Elizabeth's comments quite helpful."

He hesitated then sat back again. "As you please. We will be silly little gentlemen in the great lady's salon."

Elizabeth refilled his glass. "Knowing how to accept defeat gracefully, Armand, was never one of your accomplishments. Always the lapse into heavy-footed sarcasm."

His ignoring of her now required an obvious effort. "Very well," he said to me briskly, "we must try to pick up the pieces. The situation we are now faced with is that Doctor Frigo, in a fit of pique, has decided to abandon his patient."

I wasn't having that. "Oh no, Commandant. The situation is that Doctor Castillo has declined to be used as a political pawn and that the patient is being removed, or is removing himself, from the place where Doctor Castillo can have access to him."

"You were appointed his physician. You accepted the post and its responsibilities."

"I was given no choice. Commissaire Gillon instructed me to accept. As for the responsibilities, there was no thought then that he might actually be in need of a doctor. I was put in there as a part-time spy by Gillon and because you and the patient thought that I might turn out to be of some political use."

"We won't quibble over words, Doctor."

"Nor distort the facts, please."

"All right." His patience was being sorely tried. "Doctor Castillo, in a fit of wholly understandable pique, has decided to abandon his patient. Is that more to your taste?"

"I am not *abandoning* the patient."

"Oh but you are. I have conceded that neither your professional nor your personal sensibilities have been given the consideration they deserve. There should have been more delicacy, more tact. You were entitled to your moment of annoyance. But why inflict it on your patient?"

"I am not inflicting anything on him."

"No? Let me ask you this. Have you thought about a possible successor?"

We were getting on to ground that I suddenly realized was slippery. "Any competent Spanish- or English-speaking man will do. Finding him is your business."

"And, of course, you would give him the facts of the case."

"The medical facts, of course. Where the political aspects of it are concerned, those explanations will be for you to give, or withhold, as you see fit."

"And you would then just retire from the fray."

"From the case, yes."

He shook his head wonderingly. "Do you really believe what you are saying, Doctor? I find it hard to credit."

"That patients sometimes change their doctors?"

"No. That a doctor with a patient who is mortally ill, but doesn't yet know it, can calmly wash his hands of the case and walk away."

"Commandant, you talk as if my staying with him could save his life. If Grandval's diagnosis is correct—and I don't think anyone's going to get a second opinion which says it isn't—nothing can. It is simply a question of how long the disease takes to kill him."

"And to what extent his sufferings can be relieved?"

"Yes."

"You spoke earlier of supportive therapy. You described it as being, in this case, no more than a kind of medical deceit. Who, do you think, would be better qualified to practice that deceit effectively in the early stages of the disease? A doctor whom the patient knows, likes and trusts, or a complete stranger?"

"That question is unfair!" Elizabeth said sharply. She was drinking quite a lot of wine I noticed.

"What's unfair about it?" He was answering her, but he

kept his eyes on me. "If he prefers not to answer let him say so."

"Oh, I don't mind answering," I said. "The patient knows me, yes. But whether or not he likes and trusts me is debatable. I'm my father's son so it is obviously politic for him to *seem* to like me and appear to trust me. When he knows the extent of his illness, he may well prefer a stranger."

"Then tell me this. Do you believe that it's truly kinder and more humane to postpone your evil day at this stage than to be brutally frank?"

"Yes."

"And medically acceptable to do so?"

"Yes."

"Then what would be wrong with telling him in two months' time that you, his doctor, are dissatisfied with his progress and want a second opinion?"

"Nothing. It would be one way of preparing him for the bad news. You should propose it to his new doctor."

He shook his head slowly. "There is going to be no new doctor. There is no need for one."

"I disagree."

"There is no need for one, because I am not prepared to accept your arbitrary decision to abandon your patient simply because you don't like the way Gillon and I are obliged to do our duty."

"I'm afraid you're going to have to accept it."

"No. There is only one condition upon which I would be prepared to do that." He paused. "If you were to give me a positive, categorical assurance that you believed, for good and sufficient reasons, that this man Villegas played a decisive part in bringing about your father's assassination."

"Infamous!" said Elizabeth. She was refilling her own glass again.

"Infamous? I disagree." Delvert had found his smile

again. "I don't think that any man, even a doctor, should be asked to give aid and comfort on a permanent basis to his father's murderer." He picked up his briefcase again and began to pat it gently as if it were a small pet animal. "Of course," he went on, "it is possible that Villegas may have some residual sense of unease, a feeling that he may not have done enough to *prevent* the assassination from taking place, but that surely couldn't amount to a presumption of guilt, could it Doctor?"

He was still patting the briefcase and his eyes looked into mine. I knew at that moment that my conversation with Rosier had not been the only one monitored. There had been a "listening device" in the examination room when I had seen Villegas. He knew exactly what had been said by the patient, and, if I wanted to argue further, he had a transcript of the interview there in his trusty briefcase.

I suppose I could have flown into another rage, denounced him and the entire French government and again resigned. I didn't because I was tired and because I felt suddenly that in all this Villegas is as much a victim as I am.

I still have that feeling.

"No, Commandant," I said, "it couldn't amount to a presumption of guilt."

"Well then . . ."

"Ernesto, stop!" Elizabeth had risen to her feet and was waving an empty bottle at me. "You are submitting to trickery!"

"Trickery?" Delvert managed to look utterly astounded at the idea. "If the Doctor decides, as a reasonable and honest man, that he should follow the dictates of his professional conscience as he sees them, where is the trickery in that? What *can* you be talking about?"

She pointed the bottle at him like a fat accusing finger. "About Doctor Basch," she said.

We both stared. This seemed to incense her.

"Don't pretend you don't know," she snapped. "Everyone knows. Doctor Basch was sent by the Imperial court at Vienna as physician to the Emperor in Mexico. Not that there was anything physically wrong with Maximilian. It was thought proper that all persons of exalted rank should have their personal physicians. I admit that this Basch, a German, was a fool and that he allowed himself to be used disgracefully by those intriguing against his patient, but not even poor Maxl's worst enemies, not even Schmerling or those vile Bonapartes, would have refused Doctor Basch his proper compensation, his modest fee."

Delvert started to say something. He got no farther than, "My dear Elizabeth, I really don't see . . ."

"Filthy, penny-pinching blackmailers!" She was brandishing the bottle like a club now. "With one hand they offer the most infamous threats, with the other they offer what? A free charter-flight trip with a dying man to the country of his birth—a horrible place at the best of times—and the possibility of an official welcome of machine gun bullets!"

"I don't think the Doctor will have to worry about bullets," Delvert said mildly.

"Because he will be too busy dodging the hand grenades and mortar shells or because they are such bad marksmen there? That wasn't his father's experience. It is a disgraceful proposal. This is an exemplary service he is being asked to perform. Do you deny that?"

"In a way it is exemplary, yes. But . . ."

"Then it should be rewarded in an exemplary fashion. A million francs would not be excessive compensation in the circumstances."

"My dear Elizabeth . . ."

"Oh yes, I know! You are not empowered to authorize expenditures of that order. It would have to be referred to Paris for a decision."

"Yes, but . . ."

"Exactly! But—" she pointed the bottle again and glared

at him over the top of it through narrowed eyes—"you *are* empowered to dispense certain sums on your own authority. Up to one hundred thousand I believe. Don't dare to deny it because I know the way the Department works in these matters."

"You know something about the way it used to work, I regret to say, yes." He did not seem unduly concerned.

"Ah, then it's more than a hundred thousand now, eh?"

He glanced at me. "Would you consider fifty thousand an adequate fee, Doctor?"

"I hadn't thought about it."

"But now that Elizabeth has thought for you . . . ?"

"Penny-pinching and niggardly!" She had put the bottle down and was reaching into the cupboard for yet another. "Fifty thousand is absurd."

He stood up. "Doctor, may I take it that you will visit Les Muettes tomorrow?"

I shrugged. "Rather than be deported, yes."

"And that you will accompany your patient next week?"

"If he wishes me to."

He turned and bowed. "Thank you for your hospitality, Elizabeth."

She took no notice. She was opening the new bottle of wine. I went down to see him out. At the door he paused.

"I hope you will forgive a grave impertinence, Doctor, but it seems possible that you may at times have seriously considered the possibility of marriage with Elizabeth."

"Unfortunately she is already married."

"This morning she signed the papers necessary for her to obtain a divorce. That was why she was at the hotel when you telephoned. The legal process should not take long. I thought you might like to know."

"Yes. Thank you."

"A further presumption. May I suggest that marriage into the Hapsburg family, even a remote branch of it, can never be a simple undertaking?"

"I am well aware of that."

"I thought you would be." He opened the door. "Other men in your position might feel that, all things considered, it would make sense to leave things as they are."

With a nod he was gone. He had been grossly impertinent. I just hadn't been quick enough to tell him so.

I went back upstairs. Elizabeth had made a start with a larger glass on the new bottle of wine.

Only once before have I had to put her to bed. That was on the night her mother left after a two-week stay.

Tonight was the second time.

Wednesday 28 May Morning

Word has got around that I am to take a leave of absence. Had to put up with some ill-natured remarks from some colleagues, especially the married ones. The leave roster has been re-arranged forcing postponement of two family vacation trips to France. The official explanation for my absence—urgent personal and family business—is plainly absurd; staff-room murmuring, only half-jocular, about my sinister influence over Dr. Brissac tempted me at one point to tell them the truth.

Temptation resisted, but I was almost glad, on telephoning Les Muettes, to receive not only an appointment with Don Manuel for noon but also an invitation to stay on for lunch.

There was still a double guard on the gate. My friend Monsieur Albert was one of them, however, so I was able to ask, without seeming improperly inquisitive, about the guests.

"All gone, Doctor," he said. "Taken away last night in an army truck I'm told. Glad I wasn't on duty. That priest, I hear, was so drunk they had to carry him."

Had to run the gauntlet of Doña Julia and Uncle Paco before I saw my patient. Both were looking tired but calm; after four days of Father Bartolomé their ability to tolerate the more conventional anxieties must have increased considerably.

I am not a skillful liar, but when the person you are lying to wishes to believe, not much skill is necessary. The robust, matter-of-fact approach which I had decided upon worked well with Doña Julia.

"Then it is as I told you, Doctor. From what you say this nervous trouble can only be the result of fatigue and overwork."

"Not *only* that, Doña Julia. With these nervous conditions involving the muscles the actual causes are obscure. Naturally, the public hears more about those which affect children and young adults, and progress is being made, but about causes there is still uncertainty."

"But the condition *can* be treated?"

I avoided a direct answer. "Rest, massage and massive injections of certain vitamins are indicated at present. But the greatest need is for patience. These things which arrive slowly are often slow to go away. The most important thing is that he should rest."

That last statement at least was no lie. It was a pity that, in the circumstances, it had to sound foolish.

"But how, at this time, is he to rest?" she demanded. "Knowing what is to be required of him, how can you ask such a thing?"

"I realize the difficulties, Doña Julia. But at least we can all see that as far as possible he conserves his energies."

"Is that why you have agreed to come with us?" asked Paco suddenly.

Doña Julia stared. "What is this, Paco? The Doctor is

to come with us? If this is true why wasn't I told?"

"I only heard myself a short while ago," he said. "I was with Don Manuel when Delvert telephoned. The Doctor, at his own request, is to be given leave."

"But this is splendid!" She gave me a brilliant smile. "So Don Manuel changed your mind after all."

I did not have to look at Paco to be aware of the malicious twinkle in his eyes; I could sense it. He might not know exactly who or what had "changed my mind" but he would certainly know that it hadn't been Don Manuel.

"The hospital owes me leave, Doña Julia. This seemed a good time to take it."

"Then you will be able to see that he does not overtire himself and that the régime is continued."

"I hope so."

"You must be very firm," she said. "Don Manuel is too casual about himself. He allows others to tire him. There must be strict discipline."

"Which I will need your help to enforce, Doña Julia. And now I think I had better start laying down the law to the patient himself."

"Yes, of course. But you will be staying for lunch. Now we shall be able to make it a celebration." She went towards the servants' quarters calling loudly for Antoine.

This time Paco climbed the stairs with me. We went very slowly and halfway up he stopped.

"What is it called, this trouble of his?" he asked.

I had hoped to avoid using the direct lie, but now there seemed no way out of it.

"It's a form of muscular dystrophy. There are several. With middle-aged men this one is not uncommon."

"I should be interested to read the consultant's report, Ernesto."

"I doubt that, Uncle Paco. It's a highly technical document."

"Technical jargon always interests me."

"Well, I'm afraid I haven't got it with me. These things go into the hospital dossier normally, and are confidential. I wasn't proposing to trouble Don Manuel with it."

He didn't press the matter, but I have been warned. As far as Uncle Paco is concerned, my sudden conversion to the Democratic Socialist cause is suspect.

My patient seemed to have no such doubts. He came towards me with arms outstretched and a broad smile on his face.

"Ah, my dear Ernesto, what an excellent day it has turned out to be!" He embraced me and then took both my hands in his. "And how does it feel to be an adventurer at last?"

"Is that what we are Don Manuel? Adventurers?"

"Some more than others, but all of us a little." His laugh was euphoric. "I feel well today, let me tell you, so you do not need to ask."

"I can see that. All the same. . . ."

"Yes, of course. You have had the report. Sit down, Ernesto, and tell me about it. I liked that Grandval of yours, a warm man. He has been able to explain, I hope, how we can stop this tongue and face of mine continuing to misbehave themselves."

"He has identified the reason for their misbehavior, yes. Correcting it, Don Manuel, you may find a laborious process."

"But it can be corrected, eh?"

"I propose that we make a start today, if you agree."

"I am in your hands, Ernesto. Whatever you say should be done shall be."

I gave him the same explanation I had given his wife and then went into more detail. I had arranged for a masseuse to visit him daily, and would visit him myself on alternate days to give him the vitamin and other injections at present indicated. His contribution to the treatment must be to limit his consumption of wine to one glass per meal, to take no other alcohol and to take the maximum amount of rest possible. I stressed the importance of rest several times. It was the only piece of honest advice I *could* give him.

By then his normal shrewdness had reasserted itself.

"A laborious process, you said, Ernesto. Does that mean a long one?"

"Yes, Don Manuel, it does. You must not expect immediate results. I noticed that you timed yourself when you were speaking the other night. You should continue to do so. It may be weeks before we can look for any change." Also possibly true.

"You realize that we shall be leaving in ten days?"

"That will obviously be a time of great strain for you. I intend to see that the strain is minimized."

"You will become a martinet, Ernesto?"

"Without hesitation, if necessary."

"Have you sedatives in mind? I shall need a clear head."

"When you need a clear head, Don Manuel, you shall have it, I promise you. The massage should, of course, be continued. I will get someone from the hospital there. It need arouse no comment."

The last remark was, I think, the only mistake I made. What I had had in mind was the problem of explaining to another, and doubtless curious, doctor the precise purpose of the massage. Any suggestion that the new head of government was suffering from a chronic illness such as muscular dystrophy would be most inadvisable.

He pounced immediately. "No comment? What comment *could* it arouse, Ernesto?"

I managed a smile and an evasion. "I'm afraid that I am already beginning to think of the need for safeguarding Presidential dignity, Don Manuel. An attractive masseuse arriving here every evening to treat you will arouse no comment. In the Presidential Palace, with newsmen watching every move, it may be wiser to choose a masseur."

"My wife will no doubt agree with you."

The evasion worked, but it had been an awkward moment. Must be more careful what I say in future. Took his blood pressure—slightly down—then busied myself with the injections.

Lunch was on the terrace. Champage. Reminded the patient that he must limit himself to one glass.

He grinned at Doña Julia. "You see? I am no longer my own master."

Conversation was about the television and radio recording crews who are to arrive tomorrow morning. Villegas is to make four short speeches announcing the fall and flight of the Oligarchy, and its replacement by a Democratic Socialist government under his leadership as President. Elections for a new Assembly are to be held as soon as an electoral register of all adult citizens can be compiled. Militia to be abolished and replaced by a civil guard which will incorporate country's defense forces.

Two of these recordings will be for domestic consumption and will end with appeals for patriotic unity and civic calm. The others will be for the foreign radio and TV media and will invite recognition of a stable and moderate democratic government with a program of reform and peaceful economic development.

I learned that my adherence to the cause was not the only item of news supplied by Delvert this morning. It seems that the United States Ambassador has thoughtfully arranged to be absent from the capital during the coup. He will be attending a meeting of the Organization of American States in Bogotá where, on hearing that the coup has succeeded, he will make an impromptu off-the-record speech anticipating early recognition by Washington of the Villegas government and recommending early action along the same lines by other member states.

Uncle Paco thinks that only Guatemala and Nicaragua will be slow to respond.

Told patient to spend this afternoon resting in bed and

arranged with Doña Julia to see that Antoine and the guards were warned to expect the masseuse. Paco tried to bring up the subject of the report again as he showed me out. I said firmly that Don Manuel knew all about it now and that the less it was discussed the better.

Evening

Elizabeth still has a bad hangover. How bad I did not realize until I thanked her for bullying Delvert into paying me a fee.

"What fee?" she asked dully.

I explained.

She closed her eyes. "Oh yes, I remember saying something about that. How much did he promise you?"

"Fifty thousand."

"He didn't give you anything in writing did he?"

"No."

"You'll be lucky if you get ten."

I gave her some soluble aspirin and left.

There is, though, one consolation in all this. For Elizabeth I am no longer that pathetic dupe, that ambitious, deluded Archduke Maximilian who once believed that he could become, in fact as well as name, Emperor of Mexico. I have been demoted. From being The Great Polichinelle, an inflated puppet dancing for French speculators, I have become an insignificant Imperial cypher, the court-appointed physician Dr. Basch.

I prefer the new role.

Thursday 29 May Morning

Began handing over case-load to colleagues. Ill-feeling somewhat abated but still painfully jocular. Sample: "Obviously someone has died and left you a fortune. Think of us poor devils when you're counting it."

Evening

Took Elizabeth to dinner at Chez Lafcadio.

Later, in bed with her, wondered briefly if I should ask whether or not Delvert's statement about her divorce is true.

Decided against. When she wants to tell me, if ever she does, she will.

Friday 30 May Afternoon

Saw patient while he was taking his post-lunch bed rest. Television and radio sessions of yesterday tired him.

Crews, he said, were French-speaking but man in charge was Mexican. The television speeches were delivered by him sitting behind his desk. The Mexican—clearly a Delvert agent in the know—assured him that they will look as if they had been done with him sitting at a desk in the Presidential Palace. Lighting and other technical problems, including blown house-wiring fuses, caused delays which enabled him to conserve strength and maintain muscular control. Complained of "twitching" in upper right arm though!!

Massage a success. Has convinced himself that he already notices an improvement as a result of it. Gave him injections and left him to sleep until masseuse arrives.

Intercepted on way out by Uncle Paco with a sealed envelope for me which I recognized as having come from the Préfecture.

"We've all had one," he said. "They were delivered by the guard this morning."

The letter inside was brief and signed by the sous-Préfet. It informed me that the special arrangements made for those traveling with the party of Monsieur P. Segura on Sunday 8 June had been completed. Members of the party should present themselves not later than 18:30 hours on that day at the Villa Les Muettes. Baggage should consist of not more than one valise of normal size and a single piece of hand baggage of the type accepted for air travel. No cameras would be permitted. The sous-Préfet assured me of his most distinguished sentiments.

"I hope they don't use one of those army trucks to collect us," remarked Uncle Paco; "and one valise each is ridiculous. I shall protest about that."

Evening

A photographic session with Elizabeth—six paintings. For a while I almost succeeded in convincing myself that nothing much has changed since the last one.

Saturday 31 May Evening

Last full day at the hospital for eight weeks.

At least, I suppose it will be eight weeks. If Elizabeth's vision of machine gun bullets, grenades and mortar shells turns out to have been prophetic, I could be back sooner— or not at all.

Am meeting her at seven.

Have decided to terminate this deposition for the present. If Delvert or Gillon knew of its existence they would certainly be displeased and might well decide to confiscate it. Obtained a shallow carton and some adhesive tape from the dispensary before leaving today. Shall make a parcel of all this paper, seal it up and deposit for safe-keeping in the bank on Monday afternoon.

Have bought a two-franc notebook about passport size which I can carry in my pocket. Even when the need for written evidence of a legal nature is ended—as it now seems to be—I will have to keep some private notes. For one thing, I have promised Professor Grandval that I will send him detailed reports on the patient's progress. Any case book on that subject will have to be very private.

I depose that all the above is correct to the best of my knowledge and belief.

Signed, 31 May at St. Paul-les-Alizés.

CASTILLO

Tuesday 3 June

Patient V. again complains twitching right deltoid. Some weakness evident. Not yet palpably spastic.

Thursday 5 June

Patient V. again complains twitching right deltoid. Some questions its usefulness. In spite of my initial orders to contrary seems masseuse has become talkative to extent of answering his questions. No doubt they were persuasively put, but will again warn her. Reminded V. that he was promised patience.

Saturday 7 June

Dinner with Elizabeth.

Our last evening together for some time. And our last meeting, too. Although I will not be leaving until the evening, she refuses to see me tomorrow.

She dislikes all leave-takings, I know; and this one she specially dislikes. To use her own words: "I refuse to stand waving a handkerchief and weeping like a fool while my brave little soldier-boy goes marching off to war."

I pointed out that I wasn't her brave little soldier-boy, that I wasn't going to war and that I proposed to take a taxi anyway; but she remained firm. I didn't pursue it. Had no wish to spoil the evening with a row.

Glad later, because the evening became wonderful. No goodbyes. But as I was leaving she gave me a wrapped present. "Something for the journey," she said.

Have now opened the wrapping. The present is a book, as I had known by the feel of it, but of an unexpected kind. It is the first volume of an old four-volume edition of the correspondence, personal and diplomatic, of the Empress Maria Theresa published in Vienna.

It puzzled me at first because the title is in German, which, as Elizabeth knows, I cannot read. Then I opened it and saw that Maria Theresa's personal letters had been written mostly in French sprinkled with Italian, and that they had been reproduced in the original by the publishers.

As I leafed through the book I found a page marker. A three line passage had been underlined.

*Je vous embrasse de tout mon coeur; ménagez-vous
bien, adieu caro viso.
Je suis la vôtre sponsia delectissima.*

I felt myself deeply moved. Dear, sweet Elizabeth. How
tender of her, and how thoughtful, to send me off on this
wretched journey, not only with a declaration of her love
and concern for me, but also with a promise!

For that is what it undoubtedly is. The letter of Maria
Theresa's to which those words were added as a postscript
was written to her betrothed on the eve of their wedding.
She had adored him for years and, now that all those horrible obstacles to their marriage had been overcome, she
was reaffirming her devotion. This was the prospective wife
to her husband-to-be, opening her arms in joyous anticipation of the union she had for so long craved. Delightful!

And then I began to wonder about that lucky bride-
groom, Francis Stephen, Duke of Lorraine, into whose
shoes I was, metaphorically speaking anyway, now being
invited to step. What manner of man had he been?

I have just looked him up, and wish now that I hadn't.

He was not without some merits it seems. He was gay,
handsome and spirited, a great huntsman and possessed of
a peculiar ability to deal effectively with financial matters.
In most other respects, however, he was a nincompoop.

He fancied himself as a statesman, but allowed himself
to be blackmailed and browbeaten into giving his own
duchy of Lorraine to the French. He was told and believed,
that unless he did so, Maria Theresa could not become Empress. As a sop to his pride they promised that he should
one day inherit Tuscany.

He fancied himself as a soldier and leader of men, and
went off vaingloriously brandishing his sword to smite the
Turks. When the Turks promptly and thoroughly defeated
him he went scurrying back to Vienna complaining that he
was ill and blaming his staff for the disaster.

The Viennese despised him because they thought he was
a Frenchified coward. The French despised him because
they had successfully cheated him of an ancient inheritance
and because he had submitted to Viennese bullying.

He was almost illiterate and, unless scrutinizing a set of
accounts or flying hawks in the hunting field, generally
foolish and incompetent. Throughout their married life,
both before and after she became Empress, he was continu-
ally unfaithful to Maria Theresa.

She saw through him completely, gave him court appointments in which he could do no harm, and continued
to adore him. When he died, almost thirty years after she
wrote that postscript, she was shattered by her grief.

I have just read it again.

Dear Elizabeth. It was a wonderful thought and I am
deeply grateful to her, but I don't think that I shall take the
book with me. It is, after all, a single volume of a set which
I'm sure is rare. I dare not risk losing it. Besides, I am no
good at all in dealing with financial matters and have never
been able to understand accounts. I must remember to tell
her.

Sunday 8 June

Listened to morning radio news from Fort de France.

The coup seems to have begun. Reports of serious clashes
last night in capital between students and militia. Some fire-
bombing and looting by shanty-town mobs.

Father B. is on the march.

Midday news gave further details. "Left-wing elements"
in army reportedly siding with student demonstrators. Mi-

litia protecting central areas of city, port installations, airport, power station and "other key points." Some street-fighting. President absent at OAS meeting in Bogotá but government claims "firm control." Capital radio station still on the air but broadcasting only music. Cable reports coming out describe situation as "confused."

Does not sound promising. Telephoned Les Muettes and asked Uncle Paco what was going on.

My concern amused him. "My dear Ernesto, there's nothing to worry about. It is not the situation that is confused but the radio news room at Fort de France. Have you packed?"

"Yes."

"Good. Don't be late."

That was all I could get out of him. Lunched at Chez Lafcadio. Some Frenchman—Talleyrand was it?—once said that he always arranged to dine well during a coup d'état, as it helped pass the time agreeably. My motive for doing so probably cruder. As I am going to be traveling by air that may have been the only chance I will have of eating decently today.

En route from Guadeloupe

Nearly midnight. First chance I have had to note our progress—if that is what we are making.

Arrived early at Les Muettes by taxi. Paco's fears about army truck unfounded. A minibus came. Curtained windows and Commissaire Gillon sitting beside the driver.

Our party—Don Manuel, Doña Julia, Uncle Paco and me —left at 18:45 hrs, and was driven to the airport; not to the normal departure building though, but round by a side road along the perimeter to a gate in the fence on the far side. There was a small twin-engined plane waiting plus an army scout car and a guard of soldiers in camouflage uniform with automatic rifles.

Paco's protest about the baggage allowance had failed, and no wonder. There were only eight passenger places in the cabin. Gillon got in with us. Our baggage was stacked by the three unfilled seats behind.

I sat next to Paco. Just after we took off he gave me a wad of tattered banknotes. "That's two thousand," he said; "at the present rate equal to a hundred dollars U.S. I don't suppose you'll be needing it, but you may as well have it with you."

The flight to Guadeloupe took ninety minutes. When we landed we taxied to an area normally reserved for the French air force.

That long runway at Raizet, the airport outside Pointe-à-Pitre, is peculiar in that one end of it is only a few meters from a main road. It was busy with Sunday-night traffic when we arrived, a fact which made the presence of the armed troops which surrounded the plane as soon as we stopped somehow incongruous. What were they supposed to be protecting us from? Reporters or Sunday drivers?

Off the runway there was a line-up of big air force transports and one civilian DC8. It was towards the latter that we were shepherded by Gillon and a man in police uniform who was there to meet him. I couldn't see the name of the airline to which the DC8 belongs. Definitely not Air France—some Caribbean charter company. Our transfer from the small plane took less than three minutes. Two soldiers handled the baggage which was again placed in the cabin with us. Gillon came aboard, but not to stay. He had a brief conversation at the door with Uncle Paco, shook Don Manuel's hand, kissed Doña Julia's and, with a nod to me, left. Through a window I saw him join the policeman in an airport police radio truck.

We are in what is normally, I suppose, the first class section. Seat arms have been removed so that we can lie down if we wish, and possibly sleep. No air hostesses—just the flight crew and a mestizo steward, Spanish-speaking, who looks like an ex-policeman discharged, and still resenting the injustice, for excessive brutality.

Uncle Paco, when he had settled himself, spoke to me across the aisle. "All well," he said, "and more or less according to plan. There's been a little trouble with air-traffic control at the other end and they don't want us to take off until that's settled, but it shouldn't be more than half an hour."

"What's our flying time?" I asked.

"We can't take the direct route. Don't want to get clearances to fly through any foreign air space. About five hours they say. Why?"

"I'd like Don Manuel to get some sleep. I've got tablets for him."

"Well, better wait a bit. He won't take them until we're airborne."

We waited on the ground for two hours.

After the first hour Paco got out and went off to find the reason for the delay. He returned after a while looking amused.

"We'll have to wait a bit longer," he said to Don Manuel.

"Air-traffic control still?"

Paco grinned. "That was just a fairy-tale. It seems that there are rather more candidates for the flight out the other end than had been anticipated. They've had to find an extra plane."

"Where have they chosen to go?"

"Jamaica has agreed to accept them for twenty-four hours as transit passengers. They'll pick their individual destinations there."

"Can't we have something to eat and drink while we wait?"

The steward was prevailed upon to hand out the boxes of food provided for the journey. Each contained two stale ham sandwiches, a banana and a bottle of gassy lemonade.

Just after 23:00 hrs the steps up to the plane were taken away and the door shut. Five minutes later we took off.

Gave Don Manuel two 100 mg. capsules sodium seco-barbital. Gave Doña Julia and Paco one each. Took one myself. There is no drinking water on board as, according to the steward, the guard refused to let the airport service truck approach us. Have had to make do with more of the lemonade.

Hotel Nuevo Mundo
Room 202

Monday 9 June

It has been a disturbing 24 hrs. Don't know why I should find this remarkable. Coups d'état are intended to disturb. What I really mean perhaps is that seeing my own country again for the first time in over 12 years would have disturbed me, even without the coup.

Still dark when we approached the coast. Don Manuel and Doña Julia had slept on the flight. Paco and I had dozed. The hitches began while we were still in the air. We had started preparing ourselves for the ceremonial arrival—Doña Julia in one of the toilets and Don Manuel shaving himself with a rechargeable electric razor—when the pilot sent back word to say that we were being refused permission to land and threatened with A.A. gunfire if we tried to do so.

Paco lumbered forward to discover why. It turned out that on the ground they were asking for proof of our identity. We had to fly out to sea again and circle for twenty minutes while the jumpy A.A. gunners were given new orders and the equally jumpy control-tower personnel persuaded to stop talking nonsense and switch on the landing lights.

Our pilot, presumably unnerved by the threat of gunfire, made a bad landing, bouncing the plane down on the runway with sufficient violence to burst open two of the galley lockers. The reverse thrust that followed produced a cascade of plastic cups and plates from the open lockers and a volley of oaths from the steward. Doña Julia, shaken at first, now lost her temper. It was outrageous, she cried, that a head of state should have to suffer these indignities upon entering his country, and showed an utter contempt for protocol.

Don Manuel told her quite sharply to be quiet and pull herself together. At least, he said, we were safely on the ground and if it was protocol she was worried about we would all, soon enough, be up to our eyes in it.

We were. The area in front of the airport building was now ablaze with floodlights and as the plane swung into it I saw a battery of cameras and a podium with microphones. Steps were quickly wheeled to the door and the steward, abandoning his attempts to dispose of the galley debris by kicking it under the seats, opened up.

First to come aboard was Santos wearing a dark suit and tie and looking, despite the wall of damp heat now moving in from outside, both cool and calm. Behind him was a man in the uniform of an army colonel. He was looking less calm. Santos introduced him as the officer commanding the troops who had so efficiently seized the airport on Saturday night.

Clearing his throat first, the colonel explained that he was there, as senior officer on the spot, to assure His Excellency, the new President, of the loyalty and devotion to his person of the entire army, and that all there was secure and under control.

Don Manuel gave him a pleasant smile. "Have the representatives of the foreign press arrived, Colonel?"

"Yes, Excellency. One planeload direct from Miami and another which came via Antigua early today."

"Were *they* threatened with gunfire before being allowed to land?"

"No, Excellency." Sweat poured off him. "That error of judgment in the case of your plane arose from excessive zeal on the part of the gunnery officer and the change in the plane's expected time of arrival. The original orders were too rigidly adhered to. There was also a lack of coordination. The officers concerned have been severely reprimanded."

"Good."

From then on he completely ignored the colonel. It was left to Santos to report a rather more serious instance of excessive zeal on the army's part.

This concerned the Presidential Palace.

While most members of the militia had quietly disposed of their uniforms, left their weapons in the barracks armory and proceeded to make themselves as inconspicuous as possible, the militia unit stationed at the Presidential Palace had decide to defend it to the death. As the commander of this particular unit had known that he was on Father Bartolomé's personal list of those to be strung up publicly as soon as captured, the decision had not been entirely heroic. He had probably counted on being captured by the army after putting up a token resistance. Unfortunately, the militiamen under his command had taken his last-stand order seriously and had fought with determination. An army assault team had been called in. In their winkling-out of

the defenders they had used considerable force and made
rather a mess of the Palace. In particular, two stone pillars
supporting the main balcony, on which new presidents had
always stood to be proclaimed and then acclaimed by the
populace, had been damaged by high explosive. The main
interior staircase and state apartments had also suffered.
Scaffolding was being erected even now to make the balcony safe, but it would be some days before the Palace
could be considered habitable. Meanwhile, the second floor
of the Hotel Nuevo Mundo had been commandeered to
accommodate the Presidential suite.

"I refuse," said Don Manuel promptly, "to go to the
Nuevo Mundo. I am surprised, Don Tomás, that you should
have even considered the possibility. I am not here as a
foreign businessman seeking a contract."

"The second floor has a balcony, Don Manuel. You
must show yourself to the people."

"Then I will show myself from the balcony of the Palace
of Justice. That, at least, can be given a symbolic significance."

"For the Castillo devotees, Don Manuel, the balcony
overlooking the steps of the Nuevo Mundo would not be
without significance."

He looked at me. Don Manuel pointedly ignored the
look.

"We have no interest in factions," he declared, "nor in
their devotions. We are here to make a new start for *all*
our countrymen, not to evoke ghoulish memories of the
past. I will be proclaimed at the Palace of Justice."

At Les Muettes, Santos had been treated with the utmost
deference and respect. Now he was being addressed as an
underling. He seemed neither surprised nor offended.

He said patiently: "Accommodation there is limited, Don
Manuel. Apart from the building staff quarters there is only
the Procurator-General's apartment."

"Then he must be requested to accept, until the Presi-

dential Palace is habitable again, our hospitality at the
Nuevo Mundo. Where are the foreign press staying?"

"At the Hotel Alianza as arranged. There have already
been numerous complaints and several attempts to bribe the
manager of the Nuevo Mundo. He has his instructions, of
course. The Yanqui news agencies, plus the New York
Times and Washington Post, to be allowed rooms, but only
on the upper floors."

"Good. Then that is settled. Ourselves at the Palace of
Justice, our suite on the second floor of the Nuevo Mundo.
Now let us get out of here."

His manner, his whole disposition, seemed quite suddenly
to have changed. Is this a form of reaction? Years of deference to alien authority can leave their marks on the exile.
Or is this how the immediate prospect of autocratic presidential power normally affects a politician?

As he walked down the steps from the plane you would
have thought he had been enjoying that power for years.

The colonel had paraded a substantial guard of honor,
and when Don Manuel appeared the members of it, led by
officers and N.C.O.'s who had obviously been well-primed,
cheered wildly and waved their rifles in the air. Militarily
speaking, I suppose, this was deplorable, but Don Manuel
seemed to like it. Half way down the steps he paused to
raise both hands in acknowledgment of the welcome. There
was a ripple of flashes as the still photographers recorded
the moment. Then he continued the descent, courteously
turning to assist Doña Julia down the final steps and so
providing another pictorial opportunity for the cameramen.

Santos and Paco tried then to steer him towards the
podium, but he strode on past it to the lined-up reception
committee. Santos quickly overtook him and began the
presentations. I followed Doña Julia and Paco and so heard
few of the names.

We went from left to right. Those on the list were
mostly civil functionaries and provincial mayors who had

long been secret Democratic Socialist supporters, or who now said they had, and senior police officers who had had disagreements with the militia. I shook hands with any of them who offered to shake hands with me. Most didn't, because as Don Manuel moved along the line there was a general breaking of ranks and a flocking after him. Discipline was restored somewhat when the cameramen began complaining loudly that it was the new President they were there to photograph, not the backsides of a herd of cattle. The senior policemen reacted instantly and, having pushed forward themselves, now faced about and pushed back, ordering everyone in stern tones to "show respect."

The foreign dignitaries were on the right of the line, and it was as the crowd thinned that I saw Delvert standing there and heard him being introduced as Counsellor of the French Embassy representing His Excellency the French Ambassador temporarily absent through illness. Quite a lot of the other foreign ambassadors were also represented by deputies. A striking exception was His Eminence the Papal Nuncio, a resplendent figure with what at a distance looked like an acolyte in attendance on him.

By then I had become used to shaking hands without having been introduced and had for some time ceased attempting to give my name. So many people were chattering at once that, back where I was, one would have had to bawl in order to be heard. I was disconcerted, then, when as I bowed over the Nuncio's hand I heard him say quite distinctly in my ear: "I am delighted to meet you, Doctor Castillo. May I introduce you to Monsignor Montanaro?"

Montanaro, the "acolyte," who now moved forward to shake my hand, was a very small old man with rimless glasses, smiling eyes and an air of great distinction.

"A pleasure, Doctor Castillo." He held on to my hand with surprising firmness. "I have been so looking forward to meeting you that I prevailed upon His Eminence to allow me to accompany him. Your first visit for many years.

A memorable occasion. I must not detain you, but I am most anxious to know when you intend visiting your father's grave."

I was about to say that I hadn't even thought of visiting it, but didn't. My hesitation elicited a helpful word from the Nuncio.

"We are aware, of course, that you are here as Don Manuel's physician, but he is unlikely to be needing your services until this evening. The Monsignor, I know, is most anxious to join you in prayer at a memorial that you have never yet been permitted to see."

"Would this afternoon be too late, Doctor?" asked Montanaro anxiously. "At four could we say?"

"Well. . . ."

"A car will pick you up the Nuevo Mundo. You can be back there by five."

Before I could think of an adequate way of refusing, they had passed me on with infinite courtesy to the Dutch consul-general.

A minute or so later I was shaking hands with Delvert as if I had never seen him before in my life and hearing Rosier described as the Central American respresentative of the Latin-American Chamber of Commerce.

The sun had just risen. When I looked again at Rosier he was already wearing dark glasses.

The airport is twelve kilometers from the capital. It seemed longer. I was hungry and thirsty—the lemonade had left behind it a taste of metal. Between St. Paul and here there is a one-hour time difference. No one had thought of providing even coffee at the airport because it was only six-thirty. Breakfast was awaiting us at the Nuevo Mundo.

Don Manuel had had to agree to a stop there anyway. The Procurator-General was an important official who administered the day-to-day workings of the courts. His eviction, even though temporary, could not be unceremonious; and his agreement to it had to be obtained. The task had been delegated to Uncle Paco.

It was not an easy one; I was in the same car with them and the officer in charge of security when the cavalcade set out, so I know. The old man was a lawyer and a tough one. Appeals to his sense of patriotic duty he disposed of with the retort that he had a duty to the administration of justice. Was it believed that, under the new régime, the judicial business at present conducted by him from his apartment would no longer need to be done?

"I am aware," he went on nastily, "that the most effective way of destroying a government by coup is from within, but my understanding has always been that sensible interlopers did not destroy those useful parts of it which worked for the public good. Unless, of course, the intention is anarchy. That may be the intention of Father Bartolomé. I had assumed that it was not Don Manuel's. Perhaps I was wrong."

Paco extricated himself from that by pretending, with a stertorous chuckle, to treat the proposition as a joke and then uttering a vague threat. Energy and flexibility of outlook would be the criteria by which public servants in future would be judged. Then he returned to cajolery. Surely the Procurator's wife would not object to enjoying the hospitality of the Nuevo Mundo for a few days? It would be a little holiday for her. And there was the problem of security.

The security officer picked up his cue briskly. How true that was! All the arrangements would now have to be revised for a second time. Since all government installations, and the Nuevo Mundo, were now under heavy guard, additional official cars would now be needed to operate the shuttle service.

My murmured reminder, intended to be helpful, that the Palace of Justice was within easy walking distance of the Hotel was immediately slapped down. *No* one, even if he carried one of the official passes to be issued immediately, would be permitted to enter the Presidential residence on foot—no, not even the new President's doctor.

After that I shut up and looked out of the window.

The road from the airport has not improved since I last saw it; canefields on one side, jungle on the other, pot-holes galore and, at every point along it where there has been a fatal accident, at every bend that is, a concrete block on the verge with the rusting wreck of an overturned car perched there as a warning. I had forgotten those skeletal cars. They must have been replaced many times over the years. In this climate rust eats quickly; and besides, the door-panels of a smashed car can be used to patch the leaking roof of a house.

There were other things that I had forgotten: the stink of the barrios on the outskirts of the city, the squalor of the shacks in which their people lived, the stray pig rooting in the mud around them. I had forgotten the women breast-feeding infants with a fifty-fifty chance of surviving long enough to be weaned, and those who had survived staring at you large-eyed from the filth with their fingers in their mouths. I had forgotten the open drains. Men not much in evidence. Those who had work to do had already gone to it when we passed by.

And then the city itself, oddly picturesque in places with bright flowering trees and allamanda bushes, but mostly ugly and decrepit. Even the few modern buildings like the Hotel Alianza (named for The Alliance for Progress) look decayed, the concrete streaked with rust from window frames and balconies. Jungle weeds sprout through the asphalt of the car parks and run riot over the uncleared building rubbish in the adjoining wastelands. Only the much older stone buildings seem to have retained any dignity. If, though, they seem less imposing now than when I knew them as an adolescent, that is to be expected; I have become unused to them. The palm trees *do* look the same though—like tired, untidy women.

Few people on the streets, but, at every crossroad, troops. More nearer the center of the city—how seedy it is!—with tanks and troop carriers in the side streets. Two whole blocks in the central shopping district almost completely gutted by fire, with ancient fire trucks still there and their crews poking about in the ruins.

The Procurator snorted derisively at the sight. "Not many pickings left for them," he remarked; "Father Bartolomé's army of the faithful will have seen to that. Still, Don Manuel mustn't complain. His audience will have been much increased."

I looked at him. He smiled slyly.

"You surely don't think that they burned the shops until they'd looted them, do you Doctor? They brought trucks with them. Television sets had first priority, of course, before refrigerators and air-conditioners. But furniture and clothing, even such trifles as radios and jewelry, were not neglected." He glanced at Paco. "Democratic Socialism in action, eh my friend?"

Paco pursed his lips. The Procurator-General's annoyance is understandable, but it occurs to me that if he goes on expressing it in those terms he may lose his apartment permanently, and his job with it.

On arrival at the Nuevo Mundo we found chaos; possibly due to Don Manuel's change of plan, but I doubt it. There would have been chaos anyway, with army and police trucks blocking the driveway so that not even our escort could get in. A lot of shouting, gesturing and running to and fro ensued, in which our security officer immediately joined.

While we were waiting I told the Procurator that I would be wanting to get in touch with the medical director in charge of the General Hospital. Did he happen to know the man's name?

"Doctor Torres," he said; "a very good man I am told. He qualified in the United States. But you may have difficulty in reaching him at present."

"Have there been large numbers of casualties?"

"Over a hundred, officially, though that may be a low estimate. Many more are certainly being treated privately and will remain unreported. However—" again the sly look—"an excessive work load was not what I had in mind when I spoke of difficulty where Torres is concerned."

"What then?"

"His family is quite wealthy you know. His parents were among those who left yesterday on the first plane out. Torres senior is one of the so-called oligarchs. It is possible that Torres junior later thought it prudent to follow his parents' example."

"In that case who would be left in charge?"

"There are other doctors there. I presume that the most senior would take over."

"Why do you want to know?" asked Paco.

"I want to borrow a physiotherapist for Don Manuel."

"Wouldn't a private one do?"

"If I knew of a properly qualified one, yes. But there will be a security problem with anyone having direct access to the Palace."

The security officer was climbing into the car again as the cavalcade once more began to move.

"What security problem is this, Doctor?"

I explained.

"Well, you had better go with this person from the hospital to vouch for him at first. It looks as if I shall have to work from the Palace of Justice now. You had better see me there about. . . ." He broke off. "Look at those fools. You would think they had had no orders."

We had arrived.

The Nuevo Mundo is an old hotel built in the grand manner. It was modeled originally, I have been told, on the Ritz in Madrid. However, the need in this city to build so as to avoid both the termites and flood waters from the inadequate storm drains led to modifications. One of these was the raising of the ground floor. This, in turn, led to the construction of a broad flight of stone steps up to the entrance—the steps on which my father died.

I managed to walk past the spot, seen so often in the photographs, without appearing to pay it any attention.

After we had all been installed in our rooms, and the policemen still searching for spies and saboteurs in the wardrobes had been withdrawn, breakfast was served in a private salon.

It was well served and did everyone good. Even the Procurator's temper had improved—he had learned that he was to move from his apartment into the Presidential Suite. Don Manuel was looking tired but cheerful. He had also for the moment dropped the presidential We.

"I needed that," he said as he finished his second cup of coffee. "And what do you intend to do with your day, Ernesto?"

"That depends on you, Don Manuel. Sleep perhaps. I couldn't prevail upon you to rest, I suppose."

"There is too much to be done. The Proclamation will be at the Palace of Justice at seven-thirty tonight. I would like you to be present for that."

"Then I had better come at six, Don Manuel. I hope to bring a masseur with me. It will also be time for your injections."

Santos looked startled. "Injections?"

"Vitamins, Don Tomás."

"Ah."

I thought for a moment of mentioning my date with Monsignor Montanaro but had no opportunity of doing so. By then they were discussing protocol and the arrangements for film and television coverage of the Proclamation ceremony.

As soon as they had left for the Palace of Justice, I came here to my room, undressed, had a shower and set about telephoning the General Hospital.

The Procurator's suspicion that Doctor Torres had fled the country with his parents proved unfounded, but I still had difficulty in reaching him. Everyone here is security mad. The usual switchboard operator has been replaced by an army man with orders to log all calls in and out. He is also unfamiliar with the board. When, eventually, I did get the hospital the operator there was also obstructive. Doctor Torres was too busy to receive calls. I could leave a message. Tempers everywhere very edgy. I now lost mine and commanded operator in the name of President Villegas to put me through. Ridiculous, but she did as I asked.

Doctor Torres in a temper too.

"Torres. What do you want?"

I began to explain who I was but he cut me short. "I've heard all that, otherwise I would not be speaking to you. What do you want?"

I told him.

"What is the condition to be treated?"

"Fibromyositis involving neck and shoulders. Daily massage and rest have been giving relief. But I need a good man and preferably a discreet one. I don't want stupid rumors being started about this patient's health."

"No rumors will be started from here, Doctor. I will send you the best therapist we have. Daily, you say?"

"Yes. I can't determine a regular time yet, you understand, Doctor."

"I understand. This man's a black, by the way. Will that be acceptable to the patient?"

"Perfectly."

"The man's name is Paz Piñeda. Where is he to go?"

"The Palace of Justice this evening. But, as security precautions are strict, I think I had better take him along myself. A pass can be arranged for subsequent visits. If you agree I will pick him up by car at the hospital."

"At what time?"

"Five-thirty, if that is convenient, Doctor."

"He will be waiting for you at the main entrance."

End of conversation. I got into bed and slept for three hours.

Contretemps at 23:00 hrs. The two-franc notebook now full. No hotel stationery in room. Tried telephoning night duty operator. Got toilet paper. Searched room and was considering using shelf-lining when found in a shirt drawer leather folder full of writing paper. Obviously belonged to last occupant of room who forgot it when obliged to leave in a hurry. The paper is of excellent quality, as it should be—it belongs to the Honduras representatives of the Chase Manhattan Bank. Trust they will forgive my commandeering it. Coups and commandeering seem to go together.

After lunch made effort to buy flowers for visit to cemetery, but failed. None available as growers of everything including vegetables have been forbidden to bring goods to market during "emergency." Went back to bed until roused by telephone. Monsignor Montanaro waiting below.

Had half-expected that he would be unable to get through security ring. Reason for his success soon apparent. He had borrowed the Papal Nuncio's personal car which has CD plates. Driver a young priest.

As we drove off I explained why I had no flowers. He smiled graciously. Having anticipated that difficulty he had had a wreath made for me by the Sisters of the Sacred Heart. It would be awaiting us at the cemetery.

It was, along with a crowd of about a hundred persons, mostly women in black, and a posse of cameramen.

My father's tomb is not the most ornate in the cemetery; where tombs are concerned my countymen's tastes tend to the extravagant. Still, it is far from modest. I remember the design for it being discussed in Florida, and my mother's fury when the junta censored the inscription she had composed. "Martyred for his people's sake by evil men," had been among the phrases disallowed. In the end she had had to settle for his name, plus hers, and the dates of his birth and death.

As soon as I saw the crowd I wished I hadn't come, but it was too late to back out. The wreath turned out to be an enormous confection of red and white flowers. The tomb had been decorated, too, with many photographs of my father, all in elaborate frames with quotations from his speeches on them. Presumably these were products of the back-room Castillo cult industry about which Delvert told me in St. Paul.

The diminutive Monsignor managed the affair with remarkable dignity and some ventriloquial skill. Throughout the ceremony I received from him sotto voce stage directions. His slightly parted lips scarcely moved at all.

As the crowd parted respectfully to make way for us there was some genuflecting. He ignored it. "We approach and stand with bowed heads, Doctor," he was murmuring, "you beside me on my left. When the wreath is brought to you, you acknowledge it gravely but in silence. Then, turning slowly, you step forward and place it so as not to obscure the inscription. Pause, bow again and step back beside me. We kneel then together in silent prayer. When I stand for the blessing remain kneeling. I will tell you when to rise. We will turn away together and return slowly to the car. Some of the people will attempt to touch you. Take no notice. This is for you a private communion with the departed."

I did as he told me. There was nothing else I could do. It was about as private as a football match. The photographers scurried about crouching and bobbing busily. Although it was broad daylight the sky was overcast and most of them were using flash. The young priest who had driven us seemed to be the only person there inclined to restrain them. One who tried to climb on top of the tomb for a high angle shot was quite sharply reprimanded and then hissed by members of the crowd, but the Monsignor took no notice of this at all. A light tap on my shoulder told me when he had completed the blessing. I got up then and we began our solemn progress back to the car.

It was as well that he had warned me about the touching. I found it horrible and it was hard to take no notice. One old woman threw herself on the ground in front of me and I had to step over her. By the time we reached the car again my feelings towards Monsignor Montanaro were murderous.

He evidently sensed the fact. As we drove off he said: "Thank you for your patience, Doctor. I think you may be feeling tricked and humiliated. I beg you to delay judgment. You do not yet realize, my son, how much good you have done today."

"Good for whom, Monsignor?"

He smiled sadly as if it had been a foolish question, but I noticed that he made no attempt to answer it.

"Have you heard Don Manuel's radio speech?" he asked after a bit.

"No."

"It has been broadcast at intervals all day. After so much martial music it is refreshingly sensible. Tonight we are promised television of both the speech and the official proclamation. That will be live. There will be little time for the commercials. What a pity the Bishop is absent abroad at such a time."

I turned to look at him. He was smiling coyly as if inviting me to share a joke. I had no difficulty in refusing the invitation.

At the hotel he seemed disposed to come inside with me. I was glad to be able to tell him that I was due at the Palace of Justice. I was given another smile as he left.

Obviously a shuttle car that would take me to the hospital before going to the Palace involved an argument with Security; but I am getting used (too rapidly?) to issuing ultimata in the name of President Villegas in order to browbeat the unwilling. Still, I was ten minutes late at the hospital.

Paz Piñeda received my apologies with surprise. He had expected me to be an hour late. Doctors always were, he said.

He is a young man, thirtyish, with a slow smile and a big mop of hair. Brown rather than black, with a beaky nose and prominent cheekbones. A lot of Arawak blood there, I would say.

He had two bags with him, one quite large. I asked him about it.

"Fibromyositis I was told, Doctor," he said. "Nothing was said about heat but I brought a portable just in case it was needed."

"That was thoughtful, Señor Piñeda, but for this patient gentle massage is all that is required."

"I see. By the way, Doctor, most people call me Paz. It's shorter."

The Palace of Justice is an imposing affair—not florid like the Presidential Palace, a baroque monster with churrigueresco embellishments—but 19th-century Graeco-Roman with a massive portico. The balcony above was still being draped with flags when we arrived and two television vans with a generator truck beside them were parked in the forecourt. Batteries of floodlights had been installed on the high railings and on the roof parapets of the office buildings opposite. There were electric cables everywhere.

Luckily the security officer was there discussing crowd-control with a subordinate, so I didn't have to search for him. Paz's identity papers were produced. When I had explained what his medical duties entailed he was issued with a pass. All this took time though, and it was nearly six before we got to Don Manuel.

The Procurator-General's apartment was spacious and comfortable with tall windows giving on to the balcony— no wonder he had been reluctant to move. Now, it was jammed with people, mostly men but a great many had brought their wives for the great occasion, even though, according to Doña Julia, they had not been invited. The atmosphere was that of an overcrowded cocktail party. Santos, Paco and the provincial mayors were there, of course, as well as El Lobo in a paramilitary bush shirt and Father Bartolomé. El Lobo gave me a grin—he is growing his beard again I noticed—but I was not surprised that Father B., clean and sober for once, failed to recognize me. Don Manuel, I saw immediately, was both excited and very tired. I took Doña Julia aside, introduced her to Paz and insisted that we took charge of her husband immediately.

She protested at first. "All these people are here to pay their respects, Ernesto, and there is his television interview being broadcast at seven. The proclamation ceremony follows. You cannot expect. . . ."

"Yes I can, Doña Julia. It is an hour before he needs to see his own face on television, if he feels he has to, and a further half hour before he needs to go before the cameras outside. Unless you wish him to make news by collapsing during the ceremony he must rest immediately on a bed. I shall give him something to maintain his strength and the massage will ease the tensions. You promised to help me. I must insist that you do as I ask and at once."

She hesitated, then showed us to a bedroom. After a few minutes Don Manuel came in looking irritable. I introduced Paz who then tactfully withdrew. As the door closed my patient rounded on me.

"You are being absurdly high-handed."

"Not absurdly. Take off your top clothes, lie down on the bed and don't talk. If you want to get through this ceremony without running out of steam you had better do as I say."

We stared at one another for a moment, then he began to undress.

"You are behaving irresponsibly," I went on. "No, don't answer. You know it's true. This proclamation is a mere formality. Tomorrow would have done as well. Now lie still please."

I gave him the injections and then, orally, a large combination dose of dextroamphetamine and amobarbital.

"The masseur will take twenty minutes, but don't get up when he leaves. I'll come and tell you when it's nearly seven o'clock. Then you may get up. You should be feeling better by then, but don't imagine you are. Keep as quiet as you can and drink water."

I left him and told Paz to go ahead.

In the drawing room Santos tried to draw me into conversation with Rosier and the group around him. But I excused myself and had a drink instead. There were television sets in each corner of the room, all showing scenes of our arrival this morning. As nobody else was watching I assumed that the station was just repeating what had been shown earlier. I caught sight of myself being greeted by the Nuncio. My smile was strained. In my dark suit and carrying my medical bag I looked, I thought, like a traveling salesman—one with some commodity to sell which he knows from bitter experience nobody wants.

I had kept me eye on the time and the door. When I saw Paz reappear I went with him downstairs again. He had the two bags to carry and I wanted to make sure he got a shuttle car.

He seemed strangely silent. Then, while we were waiting for the car, he suddenly spoke.

"What did you say was the diagnosis, Doctor?"

"Fibromyositis. Why?"

"I just wanted to be certain that I had it right."

"I'll telephone you at the hospital, Paz, to confirm tomorrow's appointment."

"Very well, Doctor. Goodnight."

It was ten to seven when I got back upstairs. I went in and told Don Manuel that he could get up.

"How was the massage?" I asked.

"Excellent. An interesting man that."

I left him to dress. Shortly afterwards he returned to the drawing room. At seven there was a hush as his television appearance was announced.

It went off reasonably well. The crew at Les Muettes had done their work well. The fact that he spoke as if from the Presidential Palace passed unnoticed. Either he had not actually used the word "presidential" or some technician had managed to cut it out. There was applause at the end. By this time the floodlights outside had been switched on and the television screens began to show pictures of the outside of the Palace of Justice and the assembling crowd. This, El Lobo informed me with a knowing leer, was almost entirely composed of university and high-school students brought in by buses from a special assembly area. "Santos power, you see Doctor? It is exactly as he promised you. Youth comes running when Don Tomás calls." He leaned forward and whispered in my ear. "Some of it anyway. I shall soon be introducing you to a few of *my* friends. Much more interesting, I promise you."

He moved away before I could answer. I went in search of Doña Julia to tell her I was leaving. Paco intercepted me. It was only then that I learned that I was expected to stay for the ceremony and stand on the balcony where I could be seen by the cameras.

I tried to object but he wouldn't listen.

"It is a sacrifice your natural modesty must make for the cause," he said fatuously. "Public relations, Ernesto. We must all have an air of respectability tonight and your solemn countenance is indispensable. Between Father Bartolomé and the representative of the Port Authority would be a good place for you I think."

I didn't agree, but there was no sense in arguing. For an unhealthy man of his age, Paco had done well to stay on his feet after the strains of the past 24 hours. He had probably rested during the afternoon, but now he was having to resort to the brandy bottle in order to keep going. When the move out on to the balcony began I kept well away from him and Father Bartolomé. From trying to photograph Molinet's lumps of stone for Elizabeth I know something about the importance of key lights. I thought that if I could mingle with the provincial mayors there was a very good chance of my not being seen at all by the cameras except as one vague grey blob among others.

It was El Lobo who put paid to that idea. His hand gripped my elbow and his voice said, "No modesty please, Doctor. This is your place." The next moment I found myself standing beside him right up against the balustrade.

I couldn't see anything beyond because the lights were blinding, but there was sudden cheering from a section below. Evidently he knew it was for him because he acknowledged it by raising his left hand in a clenched fist salute. His right still gripped my arm, but the pressure relaxed.

"You see, Doctor?" he murmured. "Nothing like a majority, of course, nor even a substantial minority, but the ones who matter. Santos has the sheep. I have the militant goats. What did you give our revered new President back there? A pep pill?"

I tried to move away but the grip tightened again. "No, you'd better stay. They're all watching now. It wouldn't do to look as if you were afraid to let the people see you."

By then I probably couldn't have moved anyway. Those at the back were elbowing their way forward, some almost fighting to get into the lights.

Then Santos called loudly for silence and announced Don Manuel. A great cheer went up as he came forward to the microphones. On the balcony some cheered, some clapped and some did both. El Lobo was among the latter.

The Presidential oath, I seem to remember, has in the past been administered by the reigning Minister of Justice. As he was among those who had gone—abdicated is the word perhaps—the Procurator-General was given the job. He looked less than delighted by the honor and the elderly woman just behind him—his wife presumably—looked quite sour. She was probably brooding over the mess of spilled drinks and smoldering cigar butts behind her in their apartment.

Don Manuel—or should I call him El Presidente now?—took the oath in a loud clear voice. I couldn't help wondering though *which* Constitution he swore to uphold, the existing one or number forty-seven, the one he was browsing through at Les Muettes? Perhaps it doesn't matter.

He made a short acceptance speech. This was only the beginning of a new era in the country's long history. There was much work to be done, but for a truly united people it would be an era of unprecedented peace and prosperity. Not peace for a few, not prosperity for a few, but, through firm policies of social justice, peace and prosperity for all. He asked for their trust, hoped to earn their affection.

Modest.

After the rest of us had cleared off the balcony he made three appearances with only Santos beside him, and one with Doña Julia.

Arranged with Paco that massage tomorrow will be at six unless contrary instructions are received. Saw Doña Julia for a moment. She will get patient to go to bed as soon as she can. She didn't deny that she, too, was exhausted. Nothing more I could do. Security had arranged that a few shuttle cars to Nuevo Mundo would operate from rear entrance of Palace through streets closed to crowd.

Back soon after nine. Security men in foyer watching television. Crowd not moving from Palace. Still much excitement. Expected that El Presidente will make another balcony appearance. Rumor, originating in Bogotá, that United States has already pledged recognition of new régime. Most unlikely. Probable distortion of U.S. Ambassador's semi-official statement at OAS meeting.

Still, if Delvert is watching, and he almost certainly is, he will be pleased.

Tuesday 10 June

I am in political disgrace.

I had been hoping to sleep late this morning—God knows I was tired enough—but those two naps I had yesterday plus the hour time difference defeated me. I was wide awake at seven, so ordered breakfast.

I had eaten the fruit and was just pouring coffee when someone started hammering on my door. This didn't surprise me. With the breakfast I had also ordered the newspapers. The waiter had said that he would have them sent up from downstairs. Naturally I assumed that the person hammering was a bell-boy with the papers but no pass key, so I called to him to push them under the door. There was more hammering and then I heard Paco's voice shouting for the floor waiter.

A moment later a pass key turned in the lock, the door flew open and Paco charged in like a maniac. He was followed by Rosier. Both were in pyjamas and both were clutching newspapers.

Paco stood over me brandishing papers in my face. "What the hell do you think you're doing?" he screamed and then began to splutter incoherently.

Beyond him I caught a glimpse of the terrified waiter,

key in hand, before Rosier slammed the door in his face.

I put the coffee pot down and said good morning. There didn't seem anything else to be done until Paco calmed down. He was shaking with anger and purple in the face.

Rosier was more coherent. "You haven't seen them?" he asked.

"Seen what?"

"The newspapers."

"I've just sent for them."

"Take mine and prepare yourself for a shock." He dropped them on my tray. "At least I hope it'll be a shock."

There are only three daily newspapers published in the capital—*El Día* and *La Hora*, which constitute the popular press, and *El Nacional* which is read mainly for its business news and legal notices. *El Nacional* rarely prints news pictures on its front page.

This morning it had four. Two were of Don Manuel: one of him on the steps of the arriving plane, the other of him taking the presidential oath. A third showed the line-up on the Palace balcony, with me standing woodenly beside El Lobo as he gave his clenched-fist salute. The fourth was of me kneeling before my father's tomb with Monsignor Montanaro standing over me.

El Nacional's pictures were comparatively small. Those in the other two papers covered whole spreads. *La Hora*, always mildly anticlerical, favored Don Manuel. *El Día* gave the Monsignor and me a whole page to ourselves under a single word—REUNITED! There was I, looking like a penitent crow, being blessed by a wizened cherub. There was I, in fact trying to ward off one of the touchers, but being made, by the Monsignor's delicate gesture of remonstrance, to look as if I were appealing to her for aid and comfort. They also had a blow-up of El Lobo and me looking as if we had been the only ones on the balcony— the caption was COMRADES OF THE FUTURE? The news that the newly sworn-in President had entrusted the task of forming an all-party cabinet to Don Tomás Santos was enclosed in a small box.

I screwed the papers up, threw them on the floor and rang the bell.

"What's that supposed to mean?" asked Rosier.

"My coffee's cold. I want a fresh pot."

Uncle Paco had begun to recover. "You must be insane," he snarled.

"I think so too. I should have stayed in St. Paul."

"May we save the jokes for later, Doctor?" Rosier was getting flushed now. "Obviously you didn't stage this production yourself. Who did?"

"His Eminence the Papal Nuncio."

"I said no jokes, Doctor."

I was now beginning to get angry myself. "And who the hell are you to say anything, Mister Rosier?"

"Señor Rosier has diplomatic status," snapped Paco.

"And you're the new Foreign Minister," I retorted. "So if you want to reprimand somebody summon the Papal Nuncio." The waiter came in answer to the bell. "More coffee please."

"For three señor?"

"For one."

As soon as the door closed Paco exploded again.

"You're lying!"

"Don't say that Uncle Paco, or I shall have to throw you out instead of asking you to leave, and you're too old for violence. At the airport yesterday morning the Papal Nuncio suggested that I visit my father's grave in company with Monsignor Montanaro."

"You should have refused!"

"To put flowers on my father's grave? I would have performed that duty anyway I hope."

"With Montanaro? Do you realize who he is?"

"A high dignitary of the Church here I assumed. Who else would be with the Nuncio?"

"He is the man who has been demanding the excommunication of Father Bartolomé."

"I'm sorry. I didn't know that."

"Ah, you are beginning to see sense."

"I'm beginning to wish that I had been politer to the Monsignor. Excommunicating Father Bartolomé is an excellent idea. I hope the Vatican agrees."

"He *is* insane," said Rosier and added what sounded to me like the English equivalent of *merde*.

I glowered at him. "Then you will have something to report to the Latin-American Chamber of Commerce at their next meeting."

"But why did you not consult?" Paco demanded. "Don Manuel asked you at breakfast what you were going to do. I heard him myself. Why were you so secretive?"

"I wasn't being secretive. It wasn't unnatural that I should visit my father's grave, was it? If you think I enjoyed the display that was made of the occasion—and I had nothing at all to do with that—or that I like my face being plastered all over these stupid newspapers you are very much mistaken."

He sighed heavily. "Well you can save your explanations and apologies for Don Manuel. He will receive you at eleven this morning."

"What's the matter with him?"

"He is extremely angry."

"Possibly, but I asked whether there was anything the matter with him. Has he been vomiting, has he a temperature? Because unless there is some medical reason why I, as his doctor, should go to see him this morning, I don't propose to do so."

"You forget yourself, Ernesto. He is now your President."

"And I am his doctor. My next appointment with him is tomorrow at six. If he wants me at the Palace in any other capacity he'll have to order my arrest and have me taken there by force."

The waiter bringing my fresh coffee prevented him from answering immediately.

"Is that the reply you wish me to give him?" he said at last.

"Not if you think it will anger him still further. That would be bad for his blood-pressure. Give him any reply you think suitable. Last night you were telling me about the importance of public relations and of the value of my solemn countenance. Perhaps something along those lines will do. If he doesn't like the way this public relations job was handled and wants apologies, let him get them from the Nuncio or Monsignor Montanaro. He won't get them from me."

"An act of flagrant insubordination!"

"With respect, you're a silly old fool."

"You'll regret this, Ernesto."

"I already deeply regret it, but for personal reasons, not because it has upset Father Bartolomé or Don Manuel."

There was a polite tap at the door. It was the boy from downstairs with my copies of the newspapers.

Paco and Rosier left without another word. I drank my coffee. It tasted horrible. In countries where they grow the stuff it frequently does.

For something to do I sat down and wrote letters to my sisters apologizing in advance for the newspaper photographs that they will undoubtedly see before very long. I also told them that I was the new President's doctor. That I knew would please them.

Showered and shaved. At ten o'clock there was a telephone call from Santos' office at the Ministry of Education. Don Tomás wished to speak with me if it would be convenient. If not, perhaps I would return his call.

I braced myself for another dressing-down from higher

authority and said that it would be convenient to speak now.

To my surprise Don Tomás did not even refer to the newspapers except to say that, as I had doubtless read in the press, he had been entrusted by the President with the task of forming a new cabinet. Naturally, this was a heavy responsibility and would take time as there were many posts to be filled. He would value my advice in certain areas. Could he prevail upon me to call on him at the Ministry tomorrow? At ten-thirty in the morning say? That would be convenient? It would not interfere with any commitment I had to Don Manuel? Good. Until tomorrow then.

I was still puzzling over this when the telephone rang again. This time it was Dr. Torres speaking from the General Hospital. He didn't sound as if he had had time to read, or even glance at, newspapers.

"Doctor Castillo, I regret to trouble you, but a matter concerning your patient has arisen which we should discuss some time today. With your agreement I propose to change the physiotherapist assigned to your patient."

"I'm sorry to hear that. Piñeda apparently got on well with the patient. May I know the reason for this change?"

"Not over the telephone. Could you come here to the hospital?"

"When?"

"As you may have heard, we are overwhelmed with work here. Would five this afternoon be inconvenient? You could then instruct the new therapist and provide him with the pass which I understand is necessary. The name is José Bandon Valles."

"Very well. At five, Doctor."

As I wrote down the name of the new physiotherapist I knew that I would have to give a false explanation for the change to Doña Julia and the security people before I got the true one from Dr. Torres. Judging from his caution on the telephone it is likely to have a political basis. If this is later discovered by the security people, and I can be accused of having lied, the consequences may be serious.

So, Delvert will have to be told of the situation and be prepared to deal with it. Let him do some worrying. As far as I am concerned he is the person responsible. I telephoned the French Embassy.

Counsellor Delvert was not available. I left a message for him to call me back and then got on to the Palace security man. He was inclined to be coyly chatty about my press coverage—"your face, Doctor, must be as familiar to the public today as Don Manuel's"—but I pretended not to have seen the newspapers. I told him, enunciating the words rather indistinctly, that the President's masseur was suspected of having a streptococcal throat infection, and that for the President's own safety the man had been replaced. My idea was that, if later challenged, I could claim that I had been misheard, and that what I had really said was that the masseur had been suspected of political disaffection. I asked that a pass be made out for the replacement and delivered to me by shuttle. I would see that it reached him at the hospital. Meanwhile he should advise Doña Julia of the change.

He agreed immediately. Was there anything else he could do for me? There wasn't, but his readiness to help interested me. I had already noticed that my telephone calls were now being dealt with efficiently. Newspaper publicity has its uses. For the moment I am a personage. I know that it won't last, but while it does. . . .

At midday a man telephoned from the French Embassy to say that Counsellor Delvert was still in a conference with His Excellency the Ambassador, now happily recovered from his indisposition, but that he would be pleased to see me at seven o'clock this evening. His Excellency was giving a small cocktail party at which I would be most welcome. A formal invitation would be sent to me by hand.

Could it be assumed that I would accept? It could.

Had lunch and wrote up the above notes. Wonder if I have been too frank in places—e.g. the attempt to deceive security man. Wouldn't like him to read that. Still, can't be bothered to rewrite, and, as my father used to say, "never make alterations which can be seen unless you have a creditable and convincing explanation for them." I wouldn't have. However, in this security-happy place you can't be too careful. There is a shallow tray at the bottom of my medical bag. Shall hide all these pages under that. The bag has a combination lock intended to foil drug thieves.

Tuesday 10 June
Nearly midnight

Have been sitting here for an hour trying to order my thoughts. No use. The only order that will hold good for more than a few minutes is that of events. Think I must be in what the psychiatrists call a state of "fugue." Have never quite understood what they mean by it. A fugue is very far from being confused. They may not like it, but if there has to be an analogue to describe this state I would choose that of the recurring decimal—a longish one like the value of the constant π, exact only at infinity.

Just the events then.

Went to the hospital at five in the afternoon to see Dr. Torres.

About five years older than I am. Hair already beginning to grey slightly though. Long-nosed *peninsulare* features.

No mestizo blood in *that* family. Grey eyes. A very handsome man and an utterly exhausted one. When I walked
into his office the effort he had to make to get up out of
his chair to shake hands was obvious, though he tried hard
to conceal it. But if his body was exhausted his mind was
functioning well enough.

He waved my apologies aside. "I didn't suppose, Doctor
Castillo, that you were calling upon our services to save
yourself trouble or for your own convenience. As it happens our physiotherapists are among the least burdened of
the staff here at the moment. Until yesterday we were using them as nursing auxiliaries."

"You had over a hundred casualties I hear."

"Is that what they told you? We have at least double
that number and more coming in all the time—those who
went into hiding and are now too far gone to stay there.
I suppose I shouldn't be telling you that." He rubbed his
unshaven chin as if it itched.

"My function here is purely professional."

"Is it? Well, I suppose one shouldn't believe newspapers,
even when they print pictures." He caught the stiffening
of my face and managed to smile. "They're in there," he
said and pointed down to the waste-basket by his desk.

"I'm afraid I'm wasting your time, Doctor."

"Yes, but I'm letting you waste it. Frankly, I haven't sat
down for so long that, now that I *am* sitting, I'm taking
any excuse I can find to stay in this chair. I'll try not to
waste *your* time though. The problem with Paz is what
interests you."

"Yes."

"By easy stages then. Paz is somewhat older than he
looks. He is also a highly qualified man. After preliminary
training in Mexico City he spent a year at the University
of California medical school at San Diego. He could have
remained there. He chose to return. He likes his own people. I told you that he was the best I have. He is."

"But?"

"He was told that your patient is suffering from fibromyositis. Having seen and treated the patient, he does not agree."

I could feel the blood moving into my face. "I asked for a physiotherapist, Doctor, not a diagnostician."

He pulled out a bundle of cigarillos from his desk drawer. "I made a small bet with myself that you would say that, Doctor. In your place I would have said it myself." He held out the cigarillos. "I don't suppose you use these things."

"No."

"Your loss." He extracted one from the bundle and lit it. "You received your medical education in Paris I think."

"Yes."

"I wanted to go to London. My father decided otherwise. He is one of those men who remain permanently convinced that the more a thing costs the better it must be. No use explaining that it is as possible to get inferior medical training in the United States as anywhere else. If the student's cost of living is higher, then so is the standard of his tuition. I was cunning though. I showed him on a map how near Baltimore was to Washington D.C. and that clinched it. I went to Johns Hopkins."

"Congratulations."

"My point is, Doctor, that, barring certain minor differences between us in medical mores, and the fact that you are primarily what in the United States is called an internist while I am primarily a surgeon, our professional outlooks have much in common."

"I suppose they have."

"Particularly, I imagine, on the subject of primitive medicine as practiced by the devotees of voodoo, vodun, santeria, orisha, obeah and suchlike beliefs."

"Witchcraft, you mean."

"Or old religion. The name is unimportant. Naturally, I

am aware, as you must be, that many of our colleagues, especially those in the psychosomatic field, have studied those things very seriously and perhaps usefully. As practical men working with patients most of whom need to be weaned from superstition rather than encouraged in it, *we* have to be more hard-headed."

"Yes."

"That said, I must tell you that Paz's father, grandfather and great-grandfather were all, when they were alive, renowned here as witch-doctors."

"Oh. Arawaks?"

"Arawaks or their mixed descendants and I am obliged to you for not laughing aloud. The Church called what they practiced 'brujeria.' I don't know what the Indian word was. Paz is shy about it, as you would expect a technician to be, and dislikes discussing the subject. Nevertheless, he seems to have inherited, or in some other way acquired, powers which I can only describe as insights of a special kind. You may laugh now if you wish."

"I'm not laughing, Doctor. I've heard of similar cases among the Caribs. Does he claim healing powers?"

"He doesn't claim anything. That's the whole point. I used the word 'insights' and that's what I meant. I have nine carefully documented cases of this. He has treated hundreds of patients since he came to us, always conscientiously, carefully and strictly according to the book. Just once in a while he has approached the man in charge of the case with questions. There is no challenge, no lip-chewing. You have met him. He is a gentle, polite man. And in these cases I have referred to he has politely posed questions. Not necessarily about the wisdom of the treatment he has been instructed to give, but about the true nature of the patient's illness."

"Does he offer to diagnose?"

"Only in a vague way. It is something to do with his physical contact with the patient. In effect, he says, and most apologetically, 'I will do as I am told, but I don't think the patient will receive any benefit.' With some members of my staff he is not, as you may imagine, very popular. He has so often been right."

"I can imagine. I gather that he doesn't think that Don Manuel would benefit from his ministrations."

"No, Doctor, he doesn't." He crushed out his cigarillo. "And neither do I."

"Paz's insight?"

"Paz thinks he's going to die soon and is distressed at the prospect. Distressed he can become fanciful. But he is also a trained technician. He said that when he treated your patient both deltoid muscles were fibrillating. No insight or fancy required to observe that. I thought it as well, in view of the circumstances, to give you another therapist."

"I see."

"I hope you do, Doctor. This is your country too, I know, but your formative years as an adult have been spent in exile." He forced himself up out of the chair, then sat down again abruptly, took his shoes off and began to massage his feet.

"I belong here though," he said after a while; "and to a family with heavy debts to pay to our people. I saw and heard your patient speak last night. Platitudes but with light behind them. The future beckons. We have won a prize in an international lottery, we have struck oil. Nothing is too good for us. The United States, or those acting for them, may even allow us a government of liberal tendencies as long as we behave ourselves. I know all this. But we have been cursed in the past with too much sickness, Doctor, most of it mental."

He stood up again and flexed his toes. "I make no apology for speaking to you in this way. At a guess I would say that you didn't really *like* your father—I don't say love, that's for children—that you didn't really *like* him as a man any more than I like mine. I may be wrong, but I will say it. This country has a chance of a kind, a hope, perhaps the last. But we cannot allow ourselves any more to be led by half-men, by senile reactionaries or by anachronisms such as my father. Nor can we afford many of the ready alternatives—opportunists of your father's stripe or brash bullyboys from the far Left. Above all we cannot afford sick men, sick in mind or sick in body. At all costs we must have stability and with it continuity." He perched himself on the corner of his desk. "It isn't fibromyositis at all, is it?"

"No."

"You've had a consultant to see him?"

"Professor Grandval of Paris."

He hobbled over to a bookcase and found the reference book he wanted. After a minute or so he shut it with a snap. He had his clue—a neurologist.

"Muscular dystrophy?"

"That was a possibility, yes."

"We don't see much of it in this part of the world. Paz wouldn't know what to make of it." And then he realized what I had said. "*Was* a possibility, eh? The consultant finally rejected it?"

"Yes." I would hate to be cross-questioned by Dr. Torres when he wasn't tired.

After a moment he eased himself back into his chair. "I presume you know what sort of game you're playing, Doctor?"

"I regret to have to tell you that I do."

"You'll find your new therapist downstairs."

I was dismissed, but I stood my ground a little longer.

"Does Paz gossip? Is he indiscreet?"

"No. But he is completely honest, and also extremely tenacious when puzzled and searching for the truth. Of course he lacks certain of our skills. He cannot reassure our patients with falsehoods. That, in some cases, can be highly dangerous. I'm sure you agree."

"I asked because the excuse I gave the Palace of Justice

for the change was that Paz has a strep throat. If I had known what you have just told me, of course. . . ."

"You would have invented a different excuse. Don't worry, Doctor. I'll remember if I'm asked. I'll remember everything."

His contempt for me was now complete.

I found the new therapist and the shuttle car I had arranged for him, gave him the pass that would admit him to the patient and told him what to do. When he had gone I went searching for my own car and driver.

The General Hospital is a rambling place, some of it quite old, most built in the twenties. More recent additions have encroached on the original interior courtyard. The result is that there is no one clear parking place but four or five, none of which can be seen until you get to it.

They picked me up at the second.

It was still light but the sun was low and the courtyard shadowy. There was a brief rustle of footsteps and then they were walking so that I was between them.

"Slow down, Doctor, no hurry." It was the one on the left. "Our car's just beyond the corner there."

The one on the right showed me the pistol she was holding flat against her stomach. "We sent your driver off," she said.

They were both young, the man with a short, neatly-trimmed beard, the girl with long straight hair. The bush shirts they wore were of a familiar pattern.

"El Lobo?" I asked.

"Of course." The man again.

"Why kidnap me?"

"Kidnap Saint Frigo? You must be joking. He just wants comradely consultation in a friendly atmosphere of solidarity."

"I'm due at the French Embassay shortly."

"Of course you are. That's where we told your driver to pick you up. Only a cocktail party though, isn't it?

Won't matter if you're a bit late."

Their car was old but the engine ran as if it were new. I was placed in the back with the girl. As we started off she smiled at me.

"If this were a kidnapping, Comrade Doctor, you'd be on the floor with a sack over your head and an injection to keep you quiet. As it is, you just enjoy the ride."

"What sort of injection?"

"I don't know what stuff we use. Why?" I noticed that she kept the gun pressed against her stomach. Habit perhaps.

"Just medical curiosity."

At first we seemed to be heading for the docks, then we swung left towards the almost deserted delta area. Few of the channels there are navigable for any distance. The early summer rains which fall on the mountains bring down so much silt that, apart from the main channel which affects the port, most remain undredged. They are left to the mangroves and the mussel fishermen. Still, nearer the sea there are a few small boatyards and a yacht anchorage. In the days when big money still lived in the city there was even a yacht club, and some expensive weekend houses were built nearby. It was to one of these that I was taken.

Built on concrete piers with a landing stage below and a cantilevered terrace jutting out, it had obviously been planned at a time when it was believed that hitherto uninhabitable sites in the area could be made habitable by the magic of DDT. It had long been abandoned by its owners and, too far out for squatters, it had remained so. Recently someone had cleared the old track to it with machetes, but by car it was still only just approachable.

By now the sun had gone and the place was in darkness, but as we approached a flashlight beam showed on the terrace and then was deflected downwards on to some stone steps.

"There's El Lobo signaling for you," said the driver.

"Just go on up. We'll take you to the French Embassy later."

By the time I got to the top of the steps the mosquitos had found me. El Lobo chuckled. He was wearing a gauze contraption like a beekeeper's hat over his head. "Don't worry, Doctor," he said, "we're all screened inside."

They were not only screened but also completely blacked-out. It was extremely hot in the barrack-room. I call it that, because that's what it looked like: a long bare space with eight camp beds in it, four a side, and a trestle table in the middle with eight chairs. On the trestle table stood two pressure lamps. He motioned to me to sit down and took off his gauze hat.

"If you wanted to talk," I said, "wasn't there an easier way of doing it than with this cloak-and-dagger nonsense?"

"Oh yes. If it had been just talk I could have come to the hotel, but I wanted to show you something as well." He looked at me thoughtfully for a moment. "Did you intend to screw Father Bartholomé's balls off, or did it just happen?"

"As far as I was concerned it just happened."

"I thought so. Montanaro's a clever little bugger. You'll have to watch yourself now, though, won't you? The knives will be out. You're seeing Santos tomorrow morning I hear."

"You hear a lot."

"Didn't I tell you at St. Paul? There's not much we don't know. But just at the moment there's one important piece of the picture missing, and *you* know what it looks like." When I said nothing he went on. "Rosier knows something, not much but something and he's worried. Delvert probably knows more but isn't saying, and there's no way of making him. But you must know it all. What's really the matter, medically I mean, with our self-proclaimed President?"

"Fibromyositis. Muscular pain in the neck and shoulders."

"I know that's what you're saying at the moment, and I know that just a few days ago you were saying something else. Some sort of dystrophy. Now I could *make* you tell me, but I don't want our relationship to move on to that kind of footing. I'd prefer to do a deal with you." He waited again. "No comment?"

"None whatever."

"All right then, I'll go on. Supposing we were to do a deal. What would you say if I told you that I could deliver my side of it here and now?"

"Ask what on earth you were talking about."

"General, formerly Colonel, Escalón, that's what I'm talking about. The man who had your father killed. Don't you remember? When we were in St. Paul I asked you if you'd like to question him. You couldn't decide, or didn't want to. Maybe you thought I was just talking. I don't know. But I wasn't just talking. He's in a room upstairs, and we have everything he's said down on tape. We've even transcribed it. All you've ever wanted to know—on a platter."

The heat in the place was suddenly insufferable. I slipped off my jacket and undid my tie. He watched me calmly.

"Naturally," he went on, "I could just have run the tape for you and produced the transcript. But in your place that would have made me suspicious. Anyone can make a tape and transcribe it. That doesn't mean that it has the provenance claimed for it. Better, I thought, for you to see the General in person, alive and disposed to be cooperative. Then you could be quite sure. So we've cleaned him up a bit, given him a deci of brandy and told him to expect a visitor. Well?"

"If you could fake a tape, you could fake a General. How do I know who he is?"

"I was wondering if you'd ask that." He fished in his

pocket, brought out a thin bundle of papers and began passing them across the table to me. "That's an old cutting from *La Hora*. Colonel Escalón congratulating a winning polo team. He's in the center of the picture. Taken fifteen years ago. Doesn't look much different now. Worn quite well. Here's another picture. Taken ten years ago. General Escalón attending a reception for the U.S. Vice-President. That's him third from the left. And here's his current civilian identity card, though he's still using his military title as you would expect. Sixty-six now, but he's led a healthy life. Some loose flesh around the neck and under the eyes, but no great change."

I examined the pictures carefully. Lobo was quite right. The same face looked out at me from each one—the same alert eyes, the same straight nose, the same firm, soldierly chin with its characteristic tilt upwards, the same prominent thyroid cartilages.

I nodded. "All right. These are photographs of General Escalón."

"Then let me introduce you to the man himself."

I followed him upstairs. There were four doorways along the passage there. A bush-shirted young man stood in front of one of them. At a nod from El Lobo he unlocked the door.

Inside was what had once been a main bedroom. Now, all it contained by way of furniture was a card table, with a portable tape-recorder and a bottle of brandy on it, and four rattan chairs. An oil lamp hung from a hook in the ceiling. As we entered, another of El Lobo's paramilitary girls rose from a chair by the table and stood respectfully at attention. The old man sitting on the other side of the room didn't move.

As Lobo had said, he had been cleaned up. He was wearing a white shirt, freshly pressed slacks and sandals. They hadn't been able to do much about the mosquito bites though. Several of those on his arms and bald head he had scratched and they were bleeding. The face I had seen in the photographs downstairs had a grey stubble on the jowls and upper lip. The once-alert eyes now stared at us dully. He had an empty glass in his hand.

"General," El Lobo said, "may I present Doctor Ernesto Castillo?"

The General looked me up and down, then raised his empty glass in a kind of mock salutation.

El Lobo gave the girl a sharp look. "I said one deci only."

"That's all I gave him."

The General spoke. "Quite right. Less than a glass. Contrary to popular belief one's toleration of alcohol tends to diminish with age." He pointed the glass at me. "He's a doctor. Ask him. The same thing happens with other drugs."

"We're not here to discuss medicine, General." El Lobo pulled up a chair. "We're here to talk about your part in the murder twelve years ago of the Doctor's father, Clemente Castillo."

"I've told you all about that. I've told you everything I know, about that and a lot of other things."

"Then you can tell it again. In particular we would like to hear again about Manuel Villegas' involvement in the assassination plot."

The General yawned. "I've told you all of it."

El Lobo got up and went to the tape-recorder. "Sit down please, Doctor, and listen. You've heard the General's voice now. You'll know it again when you hear it on tape. It'll sound slightly different because he was under stress then, but not much." He looked at the girl. "You've got the right reel on? And fresh batteries?"

She nodded and he switched on. The General's voice came out of the machine with a note of hysteria in it.

> *But I've told you. I've told you ten times. Of course he was a double agent.*

Who was a double agent? El Lobo's voice.

Villegas. That's who we're talking about isn't it? Villegas was our man only, our man only . . . at first. It was through him we penetrated the Democratic Socialists. But he got scared . . . they always do. So we allowed him to pretend that he'd penetrated the SSF and feed them back odd bits of information. What we didn't know then was that he'd really penetrated us! It was that fool Pastore's fault. Villegas knew everything, including when to get out. All that careful planning ruined, and Pastore was responsible.

"Oh switch it off!" The General was on his feet and waving the glass from side to side. "I'd sooner hear my own voice than that thing squawking."

El Lobo switched it off. "Sit down, General, and, if you don't want to be put back in your old room, you'll keep calm. Are you ready now to answer our questions?"

The General sat down again immediately and stared at his glass. "Yes."

"Then we'll go back to the beginning. Why was it decided to kill Señor Castillo?"

"Because he had become a nuisance, dangerous. He was about to form a Coalition that would have led in the end to only one thing, civil war. That was the Action Committee's unanimous opinion. He had to go. A plan was made."

"And how did Villegas come into the plan?"

The General sighed as if bored by having to explain the obvious. "Any fool can plan and carry out a political assassination if he has the means at his disposal. The intelligent planner looks beyond the act itself and the desirability of it. What other benefits, he asks, can be made to accrue? In other words, who can most advantageously be blamed for the act? In that case the answer was simple. The Democratic Socialists themselves should be blamed and their Party split. So we decided to use Villegas. Instead, thanks to Pastore's bungling, he used us, or tried to. He wanted Castillo dead, because he planned to take his place. But he didn't want any split, so he sabotaged our cover arrangements."

"What cover arrangements?"

"We had organized a direct connection between the arms used in the killing, Czech Model 58 assault rifles with folding stocks, and their purchase a month earlier by one of Castillo's own lieutenants."

"Which one?"

"Paco Segura."

"Did he in fact purchase them?"

"Of course not. But we had all the evidence to prove that he had. Until Villegas got at it through Pastore, that is."

"So Villegas let you assassinate Castillo, knowing exactly how and when it was to be done, but left you with no one in his Party to blame."

"That idiot Pastore was double-crossed completely."

"And Clemente Castillo too, wouldn't you say, General?"

"That's all you expect of politicians, isn't it? Naturally they double-cross one another. If we hadn't moved quickly and proscribed their Party, we'd have had a Coalition led by Villegas at our throats."

"And Pastore took the blame."

"He'd earned the blame. A stupid incompetent! What would you expect us to do? Pin a medal on him?" His eyes wandered. "I'd like some more of that brandy. That's if you want me to go on talking."

"Let's ask your victim's son. What about it, Doctor?"

"Give him the whole bottle," I said and got to my feet.

"You don't want to question him yourself?"

"No, thank you."

I opened the door and went out into the passage. The young guard stood back to let me pass.

"Is there a toilet here?" I asked.

He pointed to another door. I didn't have time to close it behind me. El Lobo and the guard stood outside and watched me while I vomited. When my stomach was empty I straightened up and the found that the flush didn't work.

"I'm sorry," I said.

"That's all right. No proper drains here for years. I've heard that the Nuevo Mundo's food has been getting worse lately. They need new kitchens."

"That's very tactful of you, Lobo, but it wasn't the hotel food."

"Shall we go downstairs again, Doctor? A little whisky might help I think."

I followed him down. He got a bottle of whisky and two glasses and then sat facing me across the table. I sipped the whisky he poured and closed my eyes for a moment. I heard him get up and go back to the cupboard. When he returned he had a long envelope in his hands. He was holding it by the edges and dropped it on the table in front of me.

"Feeling better?"

I nodded. He sat down again.

"I'm afraid the General was a little fuddled tonight," he said. "On the tapes he is much clearer and more specific both about Villegas' double role and about the attempt to implicate Segura which was frustrated—the gun-purchase trick which misfired I mean. He probably told Paco about that part of it, how he saved his life and so on. That would account for the old man's loyalty to him don't you think?"

"Yes."

He pushed the envelope towards me with a fingernail. "Those are copies of the relevant parts of the transcription in case you want to use them. No incriminating fingerprints until you put yours on the envelope."

"Thank you." My jacket was on the chair next to me. I took the envelope and put it in an inside pocket.

"And now what do you intend to do about Villegas?"

I took another sip of whisky. "Nothing."

"Nothing?" He grinned. "Well, I could have guessed that you weren't going to give him an injection that would kill him. That would be a bit risky even for you. But I'm sure that your friend the Monsignor would be glad to arrange publication of those transcripts if you asked him."

I drank some more whisky. "You asked me what was the matter with him. I don't mind telling you now. He has a disease of the central nervous system that's going to kill him anyway. Nothing can be done about it."

"What disease?"

I told him, in detail.

"How long?"

I sighed. "The same old question. I don't know. I can tell you this. Within a matter of months he will almost certainly be incapable of transacting business publicly. There'll be no hiding it."

"How many months?"

"Two, three, I can't say for sure."

For a moment he was silent. Then he said: "Who else knows, apart from this man in Paris?"

"Delvert."

"Who doesn't want the boat rocked until his mission's accomplished. I see. Now, this disease. Does it affect the mind, change the personality, weaken the power to reason?"

"Eventually it reaches the brain. If you are asking me if he is in any way gaga now, the answer's definitely no."

"Then we haven't much time." He glanced at his watch. "And neither have you. It's past seven. You'll be late for your cocktail party. What about the General? What would you like us to do with him? You've kept your part of our bargain so it's your decision. Kill him or send him home? Which is it to be?"

"Has he any children?"

"None by his wife. Three illegitimate by a woman who

works on his finca. The eldest is eight."

"Does he support them?"

"Dotes on them. Proof of the old shit's potency, see?"

"What would you do?"

"Send him home. He's served his turn. But then he didn't kill my father."

"Send him home."

I put on my jacket and stuffed my tie in a pocket. He resumed his beekeeper's hat as he showed me out.

On the way back to the car I was bitten again. The two in the car had kept the windows shut and it was like an oven inside. By the time we got to the French Embassy I was a mess. If I hadn't had my invitation card I don't think they'd have let me in.

I asked for a bathroom and was very promptly shown to a lavatory adjoining the cloakroom. I was still trying to rinse the tastes of vomit and whisky out of my mouth when Delvert strolled in. I took no notice of him. He watched me for a moment before he said anything.

"One would think," he remarked then, "that a man of El Lobo's intelligence would have more sense than to locate even one of his safe-houses in a mosquito swamp. And such mosquitos! I still itch at the thought of them."

"You've been there?"

"Not as recently as you. Both His Excellency and Madame are most eager to meet you, but you would probably prefer to cool off in my office first. It's air-conditioned."

He led me to it up some back stairs, the cocktail party noise fading as we went. It was a very small office, obviously not that of the real Counsellor, but, as he had said, air-conditioned. I wasted no time in coming to the point.

"In St. Paul," I said, "you stated that if I were to believe, for good and sufficient reasons, that Villegas played a decisive part in bringing about my father's assassination, you would accept my resignation from the post you gave me as the man's doctor."

He nodded.

I took El Lobo's envelope from my pocket. "Here are transcriptions of tape-recordings made of an interrogation of General Escalón. They are quite authentic. I have met the General myself and he confirmed that."

"Under duress?"

"He had had a little too much brandy, but he wasn't wearing thumbscrews and he spoke freely."

He took the envelope, read the contents, looked impassive.

"Extremely interesting. Don Manuel is far more complex than he appears. He suprises even me. That's if General Escalón is telling the truth."

"I believe he is."

"And so you want to resign. Understandable. But haven't you made that course a little difficult now?" He lifted a copy of this morning's *El Día* and held it in front of me. "How are you going to explain such a sudden, and apparently irrational, decision?"

"I don't have to give an explanation."

"You? A person of such consequence?"

"Very well then, I won't resign. I'll do what you yourself suggested the other day. I'll say that I am dissatisfied with the patient's progress, call in Doctor Torres from the hospital and ask him to arrange for a consultant neurologist who will give a second opinion. I then bow out and leave it all to Doctor Torres. I should tell you, though, that he is a Johns Hopkins graduate and would certainly get someone from Baltimore for a patient of this importance."

"Let's leave the manner of your withdrawal from the President's household for the moment. You have an appointment with Don Tomás tomorrow morning I think."

"Yes."

"He will offer you the portfolio of Minister of Education in the new government."

"Absurd!"

"I dare say. Politically it would look well though. In practice, Don Tomás himself, who created that highly successful department, would guide your footsteps and correct the errors of your inexperience."

"Naturally, I shall refuse immediately."

"Why? You won't be asked to accept immediately. You will be given twenty-four hours to consider the proposal."

"I shall still refuse."

"But for what reason?"

"I don't have to give any reason. I can just get on a plane and leave."

"That sounds more like Doctor Frigo than Doctor Castillo. Besides, I don't think you would find it as easy as that."

"You mean you'll see that I'm denied an exit permit?"

He slapped a hand down on his desk. "No, I don't mean anything of the sort, Doctor. I realize that you've just had an upsetting experience, but I am not General Escalón. I'd be obliged if you didn't address me as if I were."

"My apologies, Commandant."

"When I said that you wouldn't find it easy I meant that you will be under considerable moral pressure to accept. In St. Paul you didn't believe me when I spoke of the Castillo cult. You know better now. And this hasn't exactly helped play it down, has it?" He flicked the newspapers with the back of his hand.

"That was an accident. A priest offered to take me to my father's grave. I accepted. Why not? After all those years I wasn't at all sure that I could even find it by myself."

"Well it's done now anyway. But that's not all. Don Tomás can be persuasive. You, of course, can also be obstinate. But consider. You talk of bowing out from your post with Don Manuel in favor of this Doctor Torres."

"Who already knows what the trouble is."

"You told him!"

"Of course I didn't tell him. But he happens to have an

exceptional physiotherapist as well as being an able man himself. On the available evidence, he guessed. You can't keep these things as secret as you seem to think."

"But you still have to bow out. How do you do that gracefully? Confront Don Manuel with Escalón's confession?"

"The man's mortally ill already. I'd rather not see or touch him again if I could avoid doing so, I admit. He's detestable and I no longer feel obliged to do anything for him except hand his case over to a competent successor. Confront him? What would be the point?"

The smile. I had almost forgotten it. "That's sensible of you. Judging from this transcript, I would say that, unless he has very much changed over the years, if there were a confrontation, you would instantly become a very bad security risk indeed. I wouldn't give much for your chances of avoiding elimination. Father Bartolomé would jump at the chance of obliging him where you're concerned just at the moment." He brushed the ugly thought away. "On the other hand, if it looked as though you were about to accept a portfolio in the provisional government, your new duties would provide a completely credible excuse for giving him a new doctor."

"That still doesn't get me to the plane."

"Not immediately no, but within a few days, and if you are still of the same mind, there should be no difficulty at all."

"What about all these moral pressures you spoke of? Are they just going to evaporate?"

"No, but they can be neutralized. You've not read your country's Constitution, I take it."

"Which one?"

"It doesn't matter which one. They are all unanimous on one point. In the current version it's Clause twenty, Section eleven. No person who has ever sworn allegiance to, or adopted the nationality of, any other country can hold Ministerial office."

"What of it?"

"In here—" he tapped his desk drawer—"I have a French passport which shows that you became a naturalized French citizen two years ago."

"But I didn't."

"I'm sorry, but this passport says you did. And when, deeply distressed, you feel obliged to reveal this sad fact to Don Tomás and your other colleagues, your resignation will be in your pocket, ready. It cannot be refused. A statement will have to be issued. You may even have to give a news conference in which you reaffirm your respect for the Constitution and the wisdom it embodies."

"Is this true?"

"Perfectly. As for your public supporters here, including Monsignor Montanaro, they may regret and even deplore the fact that, in a weak, unguarded moment, you allowed yourself to be seduced from your true allegiance by the perfidious French, but there will be nothing they can do about it. You were after all a lonely exile. They can only bow to the rule of law and try to forgive themselves for sending you away."

I stared at him, suspiciously I'm afraid. "May I see this passport?"

"Of course." He took it from the drawer and handed it over.

It was as he had said.

"May I keep it?"

"May I keep this?" He held up the transcript.

"I haven't read it."

"Do you really want to?"

I shrugged. "I've heard the General."

"Then keep the passport, Doctor. There's just one thing about it that you should know, however."

"It's invalid. I see."

"Not at all invalid. Perfectly genuine in all respects in-

cluding the naturalization. All we ask is that you do not
use it immediately, for a week at least let us say, until you
would have had time to read the Constitution or . . ."

"Until the boat's tied up and it doesn't matter if someone
starts to rock it."

"I see you understand. The passport is perfectly valid
unless we say it isn't. So, Doctor, don't do anything hastily
that can be done calmly. Above all, no fireworks. Are we
agreed?"

"All right. Agreed."

"Then let us go and meet His Excellency."

I don't really remember much about His Excellency but
Madame his wife was most attractive, an intelligent jolie
laide of the kind who can always beguile me.

Her fine eyes ran a quick survey before she decided how
best to cope with me. Then she put out her hand.

"You should beware of press photographers, Doctor.
Never again let them pose you. You look so much better relaxed, less severe."

"That's due to mosquito bites, Madame."

"Oh dear, are you very susceptible?"

"And to delayed shock," said Delvert. "Don Ernesto has
just learned that he is to be invited to join the new government."

"Then we shall see much more of you. Good. You know
Elizabeth Duplessis, I believe. I do hope that you can per-
suade her to visit us. She could stay here, couldn't she,
Armand?"

Delvert smiled and nudged me on. The audience was
over.

The police driver, slightly bewildered still, but reassured
by the presence of so many other official cars, brought me
back to the hotel.

There was an unpleasant little incident outside.

As I started to go up the steps I became aware of a group
of kneeling figures with candles lit before a large square

object. I paused and then saw that the object was a framed oleograph of my father. I went on up and called the manager.

He wrung his hands but said that he could do nothing. "They say that the blood still comes out of the stones," he explained; "your father's blood, Doctor. We know that this is absurd and impossible. Well—" he hesitated—"at least I know. I was assistant manager here at the time of your father's martyrdom."

"My father's death you mean. Well?"

"The blood soaked into the stone of the steps and could not completely be removed by—" he looked abjectly apologetic—"by washing."

"By scrubbing and detergents you mean. So?"

"Those stones were replaced by new ones. It was at the request of the police, you understand."

"Don't those people know that?"

"They have been told. It makes no difference."

"Even though it's absurd and impossible?"

He spread out his hands helplessly.

"Can't anyone tell them, send them away?"

"Doctor, it has been tried. They always come back. Perhaps if *you* told them. . . ."

It was the last straw. I didn't even bother to answer him. I got my key, ordered some sandwiches sent to the room and then sat down with my recurring decimal.

I feel a little better for having put all this down. It will now go into the bottom of my bag, along with the (possibly invalid) passport.

Three sleeping tablets. Am becoming addicted.

Wednesday 11 June Morning

Received by Don Tomás promptly at ten-thirty. Very affable.

"Let me begin by giving you some good news," he said. "Repair work on the Presidential Palace has gone forward quicker than expected, at least in those portions of it which most concern Don Manuel."

"Very good news, Don Tomás."

"There is still scaffolding on the main portico, of course. But the architects' first reports on the staircase and state apartments have fortunately proved to be on the pessimistic side. Don Manuel will formally take possession tomorrow morning at eleven. As this will be a ceremonial occasion, the senior Cabinet members and his personal suite will accompany him there from the Palace of Justice. You will be there as a member of his suite of course. We assemble at ten-thirty."

"I understand."

"Personally, I regret it, Don Ernesto." His eyes twinkled at my questioning look. "Personally, I would prefer to see you there as a member of the Cabinet."

"It is good of you to say so, Don Tomás, but a person with my total lack of administrative experience could scarcely aspire to such an honor."

"By a person of education and high intelligence such experience can be quickly acquired. Although I cannot yet offer you one of the five senior posts, it would make me very happy indeed if you would accept an appointment of the second rank. I refer to the Ministry of Education."

I think I showed appropriate amazement. "But, Don Tomás, that is *this* Ministry, yours!"

"And I have taken great pride in it, Don Ernesto. But as First Minister I must relinquish it. I shall have in addition, for a while anyway, responsibility for Economic Affairs and Mineral Resources. In our negotiations with the Condominium this will impose a heavy burden. It would be a comfort for me to know that my work here, which as you know has not been unsuccessful, will be continued responsibly along the existing guide-lines."

Delvert was right. The new Minister of Education is going to have his hand held firmly, whether he likes it or not. I managed to look suitably overcome.

"A great honor, Don Tomás. I hardly know what to say. May I have time to think?"

"Of course. That is the normal courtesy in these matters. Refusal in writing within twenty-four hours or acceptance is assumed."

"My request for time, Don Tomás, arose only from my consciousness of having other responsibilities."

"As Don Manuel's physician you mean? Surely you could combine the two."

"If I were entirely happy about Don Manuel's health that would present no difficulty."

"I know you give him these vitamin injections, but surely there's nothing serious to concern you."

"He has been subject to considerable nervous strain. He has certainly been overtaxing his strength. It had been my intention to call in Doctor Torres to get a second opinion."

"Well, that will be for Don Manuel to decide. Torres, eh? You know his background I hope."

"Yes, Don Tomás. I also know that he is strongly in favor of your new government and totally opposes the thinking of men like his father. The fact that he stayed at his post when he could have gone to the United States, where he is qualified to practice, should not be forgotten I think."

"He impressed you, Doctor."

"To the extent that I think he would make an excellent Minister of Health. Such an appointment would also broaden the political base of the administration."

"That point had already occurred to me," he said drily.

"I beg your pardon, Don Tomás."

"No need to do so, Ernesto. You were correct to say it. The more liberal in our thinking we can show ourselves to be the better. The right men in the right jobs irrespective of their backgrounds. Have you any other similar thoughts?"

"El Lobo."

"Ah there we *are* in a difficulty, I am afraid. A Marxist-Leninist gangster? A terrorist? Our more important allies would certainly look down their noses at an appointment of that kind."

"And yet it was he as well as your student activists who helped force the Oligarchy into accepting the fact that their position had become untenable. A Marxist-Leninist? But also a pragmatist I think. And would our allies prefer to see him under Cuban protection heading a Government of National Liberation in exile? Hardly a threat to our stability, I agree, but surely a permanent nuisance. He is an able man. Would it not be better, having made sure that he had no power base, to utilize his ability?"

He thought for a moment. "Social Security under the Minister of Finance, was that the sort of thing you had in mind?"

"Or Posts and Telecommunications under the Minister for Industrial Development."

He smiled. "I can see that I'm going to have to watch you, Don Ernesto. You're a politician already."

And on that happy note I left, to make way for the next

prospective officeholder. Borrowed a copy of the Constitution from the Ministry library on the way out. Am sure Delvert is right, but no harm in checking.

Afternoon

Saw Dr. Torres by appointment. Not an easy interview. My claim that I had been impressed by what he had said yesterday about healthy leadership was treated with polite skepticism. He still dislikes me. Can't blame him. But at least he agreed to see Don Manuel, *if ordered to do so officially*, and also to organize a second opinion *if the patient requests it.*

Now, all I have to do is face Don Manuel without betraying myself. Must just hope that I can.

Evening

When I arrived at the Palace of Justice the masseur was still with the President, but Doña Julia was lying in wait for me.

"I was hoping you'd come early Ernesto." She took me into a small sitting-room. "I am deeply worried about Don Manuel."

With coaxing I got the facts out of her.

Yesterday had been a terrible day for Don Manuel, ter-

rible. To begin with there had been that bestial Father
Bartolomé, only half-drunk true, but absolutely vile.
With some reason to be annoyed perhaps—I got a reproach-
ful look—but nevertheless intolerable in his behavior. He
had had to be forcibly removed by the security guards. A
shattering experience. And then meetings, meetings—with
Don Paco, Don Tomás, Don this, Don that. Nothing had
been spared him. He had even been obliged to give an audience to the United States Ambassador, just returned from
Bogotá. Then, more meetings about the move tomorrow to
the Presidential Palace. She had tried to make him rest, but
it had been impossible. He had not liked the new masseur.
He had even complained about me. He was the President.
I should see him every day, not every other day when it
suited me. He had gone on and on about this.

And then something horrible had happened. They had
been alone, thank God, after dinner. She had just begged
him again to go to bed and he was promising her that he
would, when suddenly his whole face had changed. His
mouth had opened and then he had grimaced at her like a
wild beast and a curious noise had come from his throat.
He had been like that for about half a minute and then he
had seemed to collapse, bursting into tears.

She had got him to bed somehow without anybody seeing. He had gone to sleep then, dressed as he was. Three
hours later he had woken up and seemed all right again. But
what was this terrible thing?

"He's been overtaxing himself, Doña Julia. I have warned
him."

"Then now you must *order* him, Ernesto."

"Presidents don't like orders, Doña Julia. I hope to bring
in Doctor Torres from the General Hospital to help. You
will like him. He was trained in Baltimore."

She heard the masseur coming out then, so I didn't have
to say any more to her. I wonder if she knows what kind
of a man her husband really is. I find it hard to believe. No,

not hard, impossible.

Don Manuel was still lying on his bed. He greeted me sullenly.

"So, Ernesto, you have decided to desert me."

"I don't think so, Don Manuel."

"Oh don't try any tricks with me. You saw Don Tomás this morning. Do you think he hasn't reported?"

"I didn't think that if I were to serve you as a Minister that would count as desertion."

"Nicely put, Ernesto, but still crap. You'll never make a Minister. Except in your profession you're a total idiot, and don't let anyone persuade you otherwise. Look how you let Montanaro take you for a ride! And look at the trouble it's caused me. Just to put flowers on a tomb according to Paco. You're an idiot!"

"Then you should instruct Don Tomás to withdraw the offer."

"And what would you do then? Go back to St. Paul?"

"Of course. You shouldn't be treated by an idiot. Now stop talking and keep still. I'm going to examine you."

I did so, and thoroughly, forcing myself to touch him. Blood-pressure was quite high. Even in the arms there wasn't yet much discernible muscular change though. A slight shrinkage, possibly, but I couldn't have sworn to it.

"Well?" he said when I had finished.

"I am not satisfied. I propose to ask Doctor Torres to arrange for a second consultant opinion."

"What was wrong with Professor Grandval's?"

"Nothing probably, but I want to make certain."

"Who is this Torres?"

I told him.

"That family! He'll cut my throat."

"Not unless it needs cutting. Hold still please."

I gave him his injeictons and repacked my bag. He started to get out of bed.

"No, stay there for an hour please. You have a busy day

tomorrow. I'll arrange for Doctor Torres to see you with me after the move into the Presidential Palace."

He looked at me steadily. "You're very sure of yourself today, aren't you Ernesto?"

"Doña Julia asked me to be firm. I'm merely carrying out her wishes."

"Doctor's orders, eh?" He paused. "Ever heard of a man named Escalón? General Escalón?"

It was quite a jolt. I managed to busy myself refastening my bag. "General who?"

"Escalón. He's been reported missing from his home in the north."

"I imagine quite a lot of people in the north are missing from their homes, Don Manuel. Planeloads of them."

"But he doesn't interest you?"

"Why should he?"

"He's the man who killed your father."

"I've put flowers on my father's grave. The men who shot my father are long dead."

"As far as you are concerned the matter is closed?"

"I've said so."

"Then don't think of changing your mind. That's a Presidential order. It's like a doctor's order in a way. The person who disobeys it has only himself to blame if the consequences prove unpleasant. You understand?"

"You're talking too much."

"I asked if you understood."

"I understand that all lawful and sensible orders should be obeyed."

"Good. Now I'll give you another one. Stay away from El Lobo. He has become a security risk."

"I see."

"I doubt if you do, but it doesn't matter. Just stay away from him. I may be obliged to lose my doctor. I don't want to lose my new Minister of Education too. I'll see you in the morning, Ernesto. It will be a formal occasion remember. Wear a jacket and tie please."

"Goodnight, Don Manuel."

Doña Julia was waiting for my report. I told her that I intend to request Dr. Torres' presence at the Presidential Palace for a consultation on Friday, that is the day after tomorrow. I asked her for a note on presidential paper formally requesting Dr. Torres' attendance.

"Has Don Manuel agreed?"

"Under protest, yes."

"Very well." She gave me the note.

When I got back here I found that I was shaking. The sooner I can rid myself of this patient the better. My hatred of the man is just tolerable because it is qualified by pity for the body. That he should be able to arouse fear in me as well is something I hadn't expected.

I should have done so. After all, Delvert did warn me. General Escalón's disappearance alone has made Lobo suspect. I, too, am now in danger of becoming a "security risk."

Feel I should warn Lobo. But how? Get an official car and drive out to the delta? Absurd, even if I knew the way. Besides Delvert had said that it was only *one* of his "safe-houses."

El Lobo will have to look after himself.

Thursday 12 June

El Lobo *has* looked after himself.

At least, I suppose that is one way of looking at the events of this ghastly day.

As instructed, I reported at ten-thirty at the Palace of

Justice. Don Tomás, Paco, Finance, Interior, Defense and Economic Development were already there, plus a contingent of the Civil Guard. These were mostly police with some army, but they all wore the "new" Civil Guard uniform—actually some old army-ceremonial whites which had been dyed dark-green for the occasion.

There were no speeches. Don Manuel was clearly saving himself for the television appearance on the real Presidential balcony later in the day. The security officer passed out copies of a list showing the order of the procession and who was to go in which of the cars already parked in the forecourt outside.

The Civil Guard contingent went out first and formed two lines down the steps in guard-of-honor fashion. They didn't do it well, because the police among them weren't used to army words of command and the officer-in-charge was ex-army. Still they managed it eventually. A rather muddled procession then formed up in the rotunda.

The idea was that the lesser lights should go first and get into their cars, so that when the President and Doña Julia went down and got into theirs the procession could immediately move off. I was among the least of the lesser lights and so was among the first out, along with the Procurator and his wife and another senior official. We were supposed to be in the same car.

Unfortunately, the security officer who had prepared the procession list had failed to number, or distinguish in any other way, the cars to which it referred. The result was that when Don Manuel and Doña Julia began their descent of the steps, the rest of us, including the senior Ministers, were still milling about at the bottom trying to find out which car was which from the drivers.

The shots when they came didn't sound like shots at all. There was just a loud grating noise, as if one of the drivers, maddened by being asked for the tenth time the number of his car, had suddenly decided to destroy his gearbox.

But at the same moment Doña Julia screamed.

The shots hit Don Manuel in the chest and he fell backwards at first. Then, his left arm reaching the steps before his right turned him sideways. As I ran up towards him he began slowly to roll down. I stopped and held him on his left side.

Amid the pandemonium, it was the Procurator who kept his head. He knew where the telephones were.

All the same it was seven minutes before an ambulance arrived. All I could do meanwhile was to try to stanch the bleeding, and stop people from picking him up like a sack and carrying him to a car.

He died in the ambulance and without speaking.

Dr. Torres had come down and was waiting when we got to the hospital.

"An autopsy?" he asked when he had examined the body.

"As quickly as it can be done please, and as thoroughly."

"Do you propose to assist me?"

"Not necessarily. But I shall have to be present. The Cabinet will expect me to report."

"Then you had better assist."

His work was not as dashing as Dr. Brissac's but immaculate nevertheless. I had summoned a police ballistics man and when the five bullets, some fragmented, had been removed, these were handed to him in a marked container. He took them away. Torres then proceeded to do exactly what Professor Grandval had done in St. Paul—take sections of muscle for examination. After a while he paused in his work.

"If you want to write a preliminary report on the immediate cause of death," he said, "I am prepared to sign it. A fuller report can follow."

"I doubt if it will help to find the person who fired the shots. Still. . . ."

I did the report.

I also had to send to the hotel for some fresh clothes.

Those I had been wearing could only be thrown away. It was late afternoon before I could report in person to Don Tomás. There was not much I could tell him. He knew more.

"According to the police the bullets were probably fired from an M-16 automatic rifle. That is a type used by the United States army."

"Probably? Don't the police *know?*"

"They have not recovered the actual rifle, but it was certainly fired from the roof parapet of the office building opposite, a distance of about a hundred and thirty-five meters. The parapet was rendered accessible from outside the building by a temporary ladder leading to floodlight supports. The television people had not had time to dismantle them yesterday. As to the perpetrator of this outrage, the police have reports from eight eye-witnesses. All say that immediately prior to the shooting they saw a priest in a white soutane on the parapet. He was holding some object which none saw properly. One of the witnesses thought it was a motion picture camera of some sort. Obviously he was mistaken."

"Yes."

"Father Bartolomé has also been found, dead." He paused. "The police are at work on that too. The body was discovered about three hours ago by workmen laying a power cable near the bulk-carrier dock extension. There was a pistol beside him. An apparent suicide."

"Has his house been searched, Don Tomás?"

"Yes. No rifle there either. The investigation is continuing. I have called for a full meeting of ministers, which naturally you will attend in a dual capacity, for eight tonight at the Presidential Palace. We hope to know more by then."

"And Doña Julia?"

"She is remaining for the moment in the Procurator's apartment and is under sedation. In view of your pressing official duties it seemed advisable to call in another doctor."

"Presumably you will wish me to make special arrangements at the hospital about the body."

"For a lying-in-state? Yes. I take it the face is . . . er. . . . ?"

"Unmarked? Yes. The chest wounds, though extensive, will not be visible. The Cathedral I assume."

"Doña Julia will have to be consulted. I will announce the decision at the meeting tonight."

I have just come back from that meeting.

As I had never attended a ministerial meeting of any sort before, let alone one following the assassination of a President, I was prepared to be impressed. And to begin with I was. The dreadful thing was that before long I began to be afflicted with a strong desire to laugh. Delayed shock no doubt. There was little to laugh about.

I didn't see El Lobo there at first or perhaps the affliction would have developed sooner.

The meeting began, inevitably, with a solemn statement by Don Tomás of the fact, which everyone knew, that President Villegas was dead. There would be a lying-in-state at the Cathedral.

Then Uncle Paco rose. He had been in touch with the United States and those other foreign governments who had already expressed their intention of recognizing the new régime. As a result of his representations the form of recognition would be modified. The Presidency of Manuel Villegas no longer existing, recognition would be given to the Provisional Government headed by Don Tomás.

Murmurs of relief. The chief of police was then summoned to make his report. It added little to what I had been told by Don Tomás earlier. Father Bartolomé's movements that day had not so far been traced. The previous night, however, he had been drinking heavily and had seemed "depressed."

I was called upon formally to confirm the hospital report

that death had been caused by gun-shot wounds and by
nothing else. Death had taken place while I was present in
the ambulance. Murmurs of sympathy.

It was the security officer's turn next. I did not envy him
the cross-examination to which he was subjected. Why had
the ladder to the parapet not been removed? Because the
television people, whose ladder it was, had been too busy
installing equipment for the arrival at the Presidential Palace. Then why had no security personnel been assigned to
the parapet? No answer. Pressed, he claimed that he, too,
had been short of men.

Now, about this quarrel between Don Manuel and Father
Bartolomé of yesterday morning—what had that been
about? He did not know exactly but Father B. had been
heard to utter threats against the President. At Doña Julia's
request security guards had been ordered to remove him.
Had Father B. been drunk? Perhaps, but difficult to say.
What had been the nature of the threats he had heard uttered? Father B. had threatened Don Manuel with eternal
damnation.

Ordered to make a written report, he was allowed to go.

It was at that point that my affliction began to bother
me. Perhaps it was stimulated by the security officer's skid-
ding wildly on the marble floor in his haste to leave us.

In the grim silence that followed, El Lobo rose to his
feet.

For a moment I didn't recognize him and I don't think
many others did either. He was dressed like a highly respectable young business man.

"Minister," he began politely, "may I be permitted to
offer some comments on the evidence we have just heard?"

"Certainly." Don Tomás turned to the rest of us. "Don
Edgardo Canales is present here as prospective junior Minister for Social Security Affairs." There was a rustle of
incredulity which he quelled with a glance. "I think that in
such a matter as this we would all be interested to hear any

observations that El—" he caught himself just in time—
"that Don Edgardo would care to make."

Just one person snickered. He got indignant looks.

"Yes, Don Edgardo?"

"With the deepest respect, Minister," El Lobo said
gravely, "none of this evidence makes any sense at all. What
are we being asked to believe?"

We waited for him to tell us. He did.

"Yesterday Father Bartolomé was drunk and quarrelsome. I would be surprised if anyone here finds that in any
way unusual. He was rarely anything but drunk. Yesterday,
you may think, he had reason to be, according to his lights,
more than usually quarrelsome. As a result he uttered
threats of eternal damnation. Gentlemen, I have heard him
utter far more serious ones. I have heard him threaten a
merchant with fire bombs. The man had objected to paying
an extortionate price for the good Father's protection."

There was utter silence now. He went on.

"Father Bartolomé was a sixty-year-old alcoholic who
frequently found difficulty in standing. Have any of you
looked at the television crew's ladder to the parapet? I have.
It is nearly vertical. You are being asked then to believe
that this aging alcoholic not only climbed the ladder, but
did so carrying an automatic rifle weighing some three kilos.
You are further asked to believe that he then fired a burst
of five rounds at a range of over a hundred meters, and at
a moving target, and hit it with every shot." He looked at
me. "Doctor, what was the diameter of the wound area?"

"Hard to be precise," I said. "I understand that this type
of bullet has an explosive effect on impact. About thirty
centimeters."

"For a breathless alcoholic trying to focus on a moving
target, an amazing performance, gentlemen. I don't believe
it, but let us assume that he achieved the incredible. What
then? In his white soutane and still carrying his rifle he
then descends rapidly and disappears, to be found later four

kilometers away with his brains blown out and a revolver in his hand. How did he get away? He himself couldn't drive. Who drove him then? The same person who took his rifle and gave him instead a revolver with which to kill himself?"

He sat down abruptly.

Don Tomás waited to see if anyone else wanted to speak before he said: "Thank you, Don Edgardo, but what exactly is it that you are recommending? A Commission of Inquiry?"

El Lobo rose again slowly. For a moment the fish-eyes surveyed us all as if we were a shoal of small fry scarcely worth the trouble of swallowing.

"A Commission of Inquiry by all means, Minister. But only if its terms of reference allow it to investigate the possibility of an entire conspiracy. An investigation into how poor, sodden, foolish Bartolomé could have done all this alone would have little value."

"You speak of a conspiracy, but conspiracy by whom?"

"Naturally, Minister, I have no direct evidence to offer, only conjecture at this stage. But I think that the questioning could most profitably be directed towards the late Father Bartolomé's gangster associates."

It was a clever piece of impudence. I could feel the wave of approval which surged through the gathering. They now had the excuse they had so long needed for liquidating the Bartolomé gang. A Commission of Inquiry would soon do the trick; and Don Edgardo, the bright new boy, might well be allowed a place on it.

I was interested to see, though, that when the meeting broke up they avoided him. He would have his uses no doubt, but it was as well to be cautious. You didn't make a friend of the termite exterminator. He was standing alone when I went up to him.

"Congratulations," I said.

"On what, Doctor?"

"A fine performance. Two birds with one stone as rec-ommended by the General. And, of course, congratulations on your appointment. I tried to get you Posts and Tele-communications, but I don't suppose you care."

"Posts and Telecommunications?" He grinned. "Surely you didn't think they'd fall for that?"

"Why not? It's harmless as a power base."

"Something you can switch on and off, stop and start again, is never harmless."

"Perhaps not. There's one thing though. I warned you about it in St. Paul."

"Yes?"

"You're overweight. You should take off at least two kilos. I mean it. Going up a short ladder like that shouldn't have made you breathless, even wearing a soutane and carrying a rifle."

The fish-eyes were still. "What risks you run, Ernesto," he said softly. "Supposing I were to take you seriously?"

"No reason why you shouldn't. I just thought you'd like to know that your timing was good. Don Manuel had heard of the General's disappearance and was beginning to draw conclusions. You were first on the list. I was threatened. If I'd known how to reach you last night I'd have warned you."

He looked almost compassionate. "You'll never make a conspirator, Ernesto."

"No?"

"Who did you think I was obliging? You? The moment he had word that General Escalón had been taken we were all as good as dead, all on the list, me, you, Paco and the General. The General certainly knew the score. Told me he was going into hiding as soon as we dumped him. Say what you like about the late Don Manuel, he was no fool. His trouble was that, being a respectable new President and so much in the limelight, he'd had no chance to organize a private killer squad. That sort of set-up takes time and

great care in personnel selection. He'd have probably found
what he wanted among Bartolomé's lot in a day or two
and arranged for an intermediary to cover himself, but he
couldn't hurry the job, however much he may have wanted
to. So, until he could act, he had to bluff. That's why you
were threatened."

"I'm sure you know about these things. After all you're
our expert."

He nodded vaguely. "We'll be meeting again soon, I
expect. Here or at the funeral."

Saturday 14 June

End of lying-in-state for Villegas. Mass in the Cathedral,
Monsignor Montanaro officiating.

Doña Julia on arm of Uncle Paco. At her request I was
also of the family group. The three children were flown in
yesterday—the girl and young boy from Mexico City, the
older boy from Los Angeles. The latter attached himself
to me. If I had liked him this could have been embarrassing
—I might have found myself identifying with him. As it
was there was no temptation at all to do so. He wasn't
upset, just bored. All he wanted to do was get back to
California as soon as possible.

"Think I could leave Monday?" he asked.

"Well. . . ."

"You're in the government aren't you?"

"Minister of Education."

"Oh hell. I suppose my father told you he wanted me
to go to MIT."

"He told me you wanted to go there."

"Well I don't, apart from the fact that I'd never make it anyway. You might tell my mother that."

"All right. What *do* you want to do?"

"Agriculture. Get my hands right down into the earth."

"I thought machines did that better now."

He didn't bother to answer. "You know the one person here I really want to meet? El Lobo. I don't suppose you know him."

"Quite well. I'll introduce you."

I did.

Later, after the burial, I shared a car with Lobo back into the city.

"What did you think of young Villegas?" I asked.

He shrugged. "Maoist, but he'll get over that. He'll learn. Could be useful in a year or two."

"In Social Security?"

He emitted his implosive laugh. "My dear Ernesto, when Santos becomes President next month there are going to be changes. Paco can't last long can he? You've only got to look at all that blue lace on his cheeks. There are at least ten other doubtfuls. Shuffle and reshuffle, that's how it's going to be for quite a while."

"I hear quite a lot of people talking about stability."

"Ah, *talking* about it."

"All right then, *longing* for it."

He patted my knee. "Tell you what, Ernesto. You cling to your illusions, I'll cling to mine. Agreed?"

"If you'll promise me one thing."

The fish-eyes slid round. "What?"

"Don't ever tell your young Maoist friend that his father died a martyr to the cause."

The idea greatly amused him. He giggled all the way back to the Nuevo Mundo.

Thursday 19 June

Full Cabinet meeting. Don Tomás announced with deep regret my resignation, made necessary by the terms of the Constitution, Clause 20, Section 11. It had been the Minister of Education himself who had drawn his attention to the anomaly. The sense of public responsibility shown by Don Ernesto had been in the highest tradition, and entirely worthy of his name.

A suggestion, put forward by some eager idiot, that the Clause should be modified or ignored was dismissed by Don Tomás with words of contempt which had my whole-hearted approval. Only barbarians tamper with or ignore Constitutions.

The subsequent press conference was happily dull. Arrivals from obscurity may be news. Departures to it are a bore.

Delvert thought that it would be unwise if he were to accompany me to the airport. He was sure I would understand.

Friday 20 June

The one who did accompany me was Monsignor Montanaro. As I was persuading the cashier at the Nuevo

Mundo that the whole of my bill, not just part of it, should be charged to the Ministry of Education and/or the Presidential Office, a call came from him. Unless I had made other arrangements we could go together in his car.

It was not as comfortable as the Nuncio's and the Monsignor drove himself. He drove slowly and badly. Since I was taking a connecting flight to Antigua that had never yet managed to arrive on time, I didn't care how slowly we went.

"A pity that you feel you must go," he said as we lurched through the barrios. "We need doctors more than Ministers of Education."

"You have excellent doctors, Monsignor."

"If Doctor Torres has his way we will need many more."

"You will get them I'm sure."

"What troubles me really, Don Ernesto, is the shape of things to come."

"Of affluence, Monsignor?"

"Oh we won't have that for years, oil or no oil. I meant the prospect of immediate improvements."

"I don't think I understand."

"Let us take medical improvements then. Endemic diseases are an evil you may say."

"Yes."

He wrenched the car back from the edge of a drainage ditch to the crown of the road. I presume that God was with us. If we had met a truck traveling in the opposite direction on the next bend there would have been a major disaster.

"Yet are endemic diseases wholly evil? Rid yourself of them and, where fifty persons out of a hundred were sick before, you now have one hundred healthy. But you have also doubled your economic problem. True?"

"Yes."

"When people become well and energetic they want work or interesting leisure. If you have neither to offer them they become angry. Then they turn to the El Lobos. Oil will make no more work than coffee, just bank balances. In good years coffee has done that too."

"I have no answer, Monsignor. Have you? Christian Socialism perhaps?"

"Oh no."

"I'm sorry, but. . . ."

"I am not offering the Church as an escape hatch, Don Ernesto, any more than you, I would think, would offer Democratic Socialism, whatever that is. No government, however well-intentioned, can do things *for* people without also doing things *to* them."

"Forgive me, Monsignor, but that is part of a sociological platitude. The rest of it is that you can only do things *with* them. Comforting but meaningless."

"Not entirely I think. It was Father Bartolomé's view for a while. He did much good among his people then."

"You surprise me, Monsignor."

"Oh, of course he became corrupt and disgraced us all. It's so easy. Easy for priests, but even easier for governments."

We got to the airport soon after that. Only two near misses, and the incoming plane was a mere half-hour late.

As we said goodbye and I thanked him he clasped my hands.

"Don't believe what they are saying now about Father Bartolomé, Don Ernesto. He never climbed those steps and he didn't fire those shots. He couldn't have done. Without glasses he could scarcely see. But he would never wear them in public, or even in private unless he had to. A curious vanity that no one seems to have mentioned. Perhaps because they didn't know of it. Careless of them though. If one is going to blame a man for a great crime one ought to know everything about him. Difficult, unless one is God."

Went through into the departure lounge. Nothing left to

do but wait and think.

I am no longer Doctor Basch.

I have declined the dukedoms of Lorraine and Tuscany.

I was never Maximilian.

I was nearly an Emperor Ferdinand, someone promptly to be disposed of when he became a nuisance.

As a keeper of secrets I have been a failure, and as a man of action ineffectual. Even Colonel Apis would have thought twice before sending me to Sarajevo.

Not Gavrilo Princip then; not even Cabrinovic who threw the bomb that missed.

What will I be back in St. Paul?

Doctor Frigo again?

Only occasionally now, I think, and in a modified version.

No doubt Elizabeth will have the full answer—a fitting reincarnation based on sound precedents.

Perhaps an 18th century Hapsburg general who didn't lose *all* his battles?

There must, surely, have been one or two.

Eric Ambler

Eric Ambler was born in London in 1909. Following his graduation from London University, he served an apprenticeship in engineering and, for several years, wrote advertising copy. In the period from 1937 to 1940 Mr. Ambler won fame with five novels of intrigue which have become classics: *Background to Danger, Epitaph for a Spy, Cause for Alarm, A Coffin for Dimitrios,* and *Journey into Fear.* He joined the British Army in 1940 and was discharged a lieutenant colonel in 1946. After the war Mr. Ambler wrote and produced a number of motion pictures for the J. Arthur Rank Organization. For his screenplay of Nicholas Monsarrat's *The Cruel Sea* he was nominated for an Academy Award. In 1951, *Judgment on Deltchev,* his first novel in eleven years, was published. This was followed by *The Schirmer Inheritance* (1953), *State of Siege* (1956), *Passage of Arms* (1960), *The Light of Day* (1963), *A Kind of Anger* (1964), *Dirty Story* (1967), *The Intercom Conspiracy* (1969), and *The Levanter* (1972). Mr. Ambler is also the editor of *To Catch a Spy: An Anthology of Favorite Spy Stories* (1965).